AF324731

Campbells Came

by

Raleigh Bruce Barlowe

ISBN 0-7414-2139-9

Published by:

INFI∞ITY
PUBLISHING.COM

1094 New De Haven Street, Suite 100
West Conshohocken, PA 19428-2713
Info@buybooksontheweb.com
www.buybooksontheweb.com
Toll-free (877) BUY BOOK
Local Phone (610) 941-9999
Fax (610) 941-9959

Printed in the United States of America

Printed on Recycled Paper

Published September 2004

For My Bonnie Jean

THE SEVEN CAMPBELLS

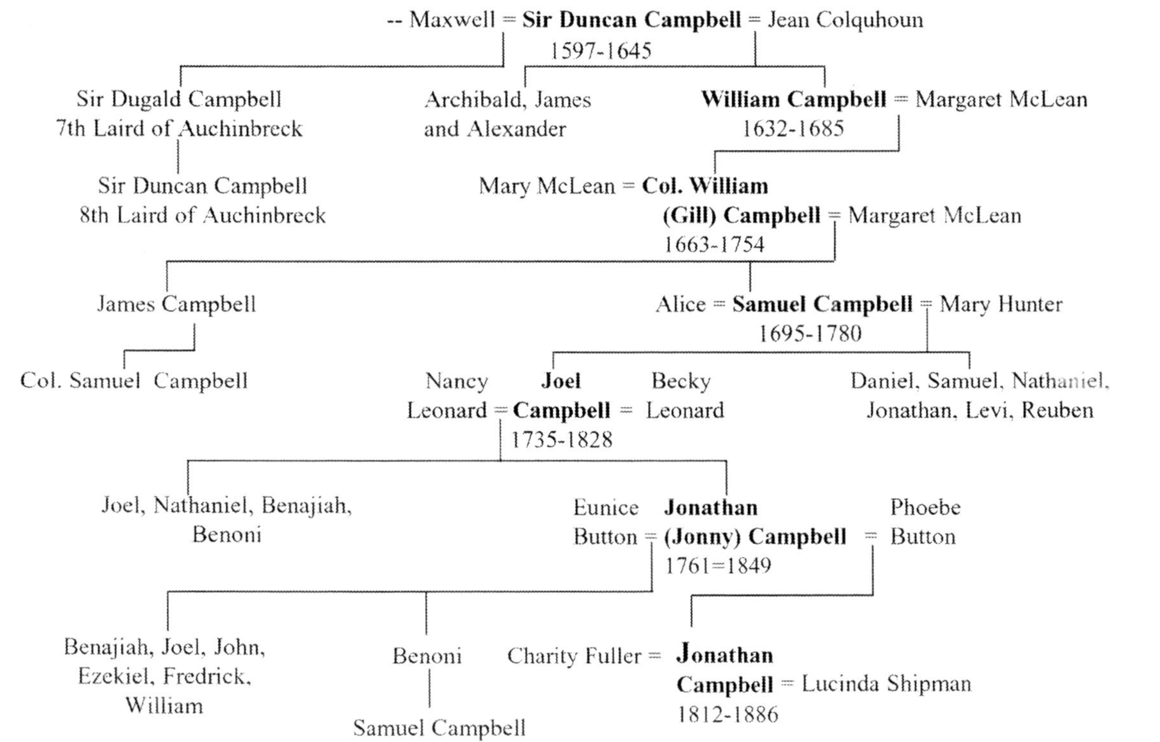

PROLOGUE

Once again it was a killing time in Scotland. Festering grudges were disrupting the uneasy peace that had calmed the long years of rivalry and intermittent warfare between the ever-restive clans. The pride most Scots had felt some 40 years earlier when England had taken Scotland's king as its monarch was fast giving way to a revival of the centuries old distrust of all things English. The royal Stuarts had seemingly forgotten their Scottish roots; they had become mostly English in their thinking and behavior. Worse still, King Charles was pushing for religious reforms that tampered with the sacred covenant of the Scottish Kirk.

Sectional rivalries pitted the interests of the more prosperous residents of the southern Lowlands against those of the hardy, more barbarous Highlanders. But a bigger problem was that of interclan rivalry. Individual clans, each headed by a noble laird who commanded the allegiance of its members, were still conniving and fighting against each other to avenge past wrongs and secure new benefits. Loyalty to a clan's chief took precedence over loyalty to the king.

Of all the rivalries, that between clan MacDermaid, known for almost 500 years as the Campbells, and its neighbors was most notable. The Campbells lived in and near the highlands of western Scotland. They were divided into numerous branches or cadets, all of which looked to their chief, the Marquis of Argyll, for leadership. Argyll was a figure of national importance, if for no other reason than because he could marshal an armed force of over 5,000 followers to back his demands. Their willingness to use their might to smite enemies both near and far made them the most dreaded and hated of the clans.

On the national front, recent decades had seen a steady widening between the political interests of the Scots and their King. James VI, who had ascended the English throne as King James I in 1603, had chosen to keep the administration of his two kingdoms separate. With England, he had recognized the need to accept policies that had the support of the English Parliament, the members of the House of Commons of which were elected by his subjects. With Scotland, he had a freer hand because he was always able to stack the membership of the Scott's Parliament in his favor.

The system of dual administration had worked throughout James' reign because he was attuned to Scottish concerns. He was acquainted with the Scots leaders, understood their complaints and demands, and had the good sense to back away from actions that might lead to major discord. His son Charles, who though born in Scotland, was a Scot in name only when he ascended the throne in 1625. He had been educated and raised at England's Anglicized court where he accepted the Episcopacy doctrine of the Church of England as the true religion.

Haughty, arrogant and opinionated by nature, he believed he ruled by divine right and pleasure. He saw his Scots subjects as boorish and deluded when they resisted his plan to bring religious reform to their land.

Charles' concept of needed reform clashed head on with the accepted covenant of the Scottish Kirk. It ignored the fact that most Scots had accepted the brand of Protestantism John Knox had brought to the land some 80 years earlier and that the Scottish Parliament had accepted Presbyterianism as the Established Church of Scotland.

People had objected some years earlier when King James tried to extend royal control over the Kirk by asserting his right to appoint bishops who would follow the Episcopalian model in administering church courts and controlling the choice of ministers. While some loyalists had accepted this innovation as not inconsistent with Presbyterian doctrine, it was totally rejected by others who saw it as creeping Episcopalianism, as an effort to make the church a tool of the state and perhaps even a step toward a return to Catholicism.

Only a few years into his reign, Charles chose to push reforms far beyond those sponsored by his father. His order for compliance with the Five Articles of Perth, which included a requirement for kneeling to receive communion, was met with widespread opposition. Further resistance was stirred by his effort to exalt the status of his appointed bishops, his insistence on a right to dictate clerical attire, his questioning of the Kirk's belief in predestination, and his rejection of the popular belief that the Scots were a chosen people. Peace continued as long as little effort was made to enforce the royal reforms. Near riots erupted and angry denunciations were heard when efforts were made to enforce the king's will.

A breaking point in Charles' campaign for religious reform came 1636 when he ordered the Kirks to accept the English Book of Prayer with its prescription of liturgy and rituals. Arrogant and stubborn with a conviction that he could do no wrong, Charles took little counsel from his Scots advisors as he proceeded to dictate what his Scots subjects should believe and do. His demands met with widespread rejection by ministers of the Kirk and their laymen.

This opposition, which might have been softened, had Charles shown an inclination to compromise, steadily stiffened. After months of parleying to little avail, the defenders of the covenant defied royal authority by holding an assembly at Glasgow in 1638. The Assembly denounced Episcopacy and demanded a return of the governing of church affairs to the Kirk's presbyteries, synods, and general assemblies.

The Campbells played a passive role in their support of the Kirk during the early rise of the Covenanter movement. Archibald Campbell, the Lord Lorne who headed the clan in the absence of his father the seventh Earl of Argyll who lived in self-exile with a Catholic wife in southern England, chose to take no action. Following his father's death in 1638, however, he attended the Glasglow Assembly and cast his support to the Covenanters, a decision that brought him to the forefront as a leader of the Covenanter cause.

Military and political ferment in Scotland bubbled up and down during the five years that followed the Glasgow

Assembly. The Covenanter leaders were often divided on what they should do. Charles too was constrained by lack of English support for his Scottish policy, by the quarrel he was having with the English Parliament, and by the civil strife that had broken out between his cavalier supporters and the opposition roundheads.

A Scots army faced down threatened English invasions during the Bishops War of 1638-39 and a second Bishops War in 1640. Irish renegades invaded Kintyre in 1641 and were repulsed by the Campbells. Rebellion broke out in Ireland that same year and a Scottish army of 11,000 men was sent there, with promise of English recompense, to restore peace.

Continued opposition to Charles' rule led to an outbreak of civil war in England. The king's opponents in the English Parliament sought Scottish support and negotiated an agreement with the Covenanters known as the Solemn League which pledged England's abandonment of Episcopacy as its state religion in exchange for Scots support for Parliament's war against the king.

An army of 21,000 Scots invaded northern England in 1644 and seized Newcastle and then York. Meanwhile, the quarrel between the Covenanters and the king continued with few signs of settlement. When Charles showed limited willingness to modify his stand, the Covenanters countered by demanding larger concessions.

Argyll gained status during the 1638-43 period as a leader of the Covenanters. Tall, stern, slightly cross-eyed, and somewhat gaunt in appearance, he displayed skill as a politician but not as a military strategist. Among fellow politicians, he was ever able to hold his own. As a military commander, however, he was often overly cautious and more than once stirred up criticism for using the forces at his command to settle personal scores against rival clans.

Argyll's Covenanters never enjoyed the full support of their Scottish neighbors. From the beginning on, they were opposed by groups of royalists who clung to their traditional loyalty to the crown. Sir James Gordon, the Marquis of Montrose, emerged in 1644 as the recognized champion of this faction. He had started as a Covenanter and had signed the National Covenant in 1638. Disillusioned later by the confused policies of Covenanter leaders and prompted by a dislike of Argyll, he shifted sides and offered his support to Charles.

Unlike Argyll, Montrose possessed a handsome commanding figure well blessed with personal charisma. Once he took to the field, he also displayed strokes of military genius. With a small army of well-trained warriors, he captured Dumfrees in 1644, took Morpeth, defeated Lord Elcho at Tibbermore, and routed the Covenanters under Lord Balfour at Aberdeen. Montrose's strength was augmented in June 1644 when the Irish Earl of Antrim sent three regiments to his aid. Alastair Macdonald, a dauntless warrior who hated the Campbells with a passion, led this force, part of which had been beaten off by the Campbells in an earlier raid on the Western Isles.

The Irish reinforcement provided Montrose with a well-trained cadre of seasoned fighters that soon showed ability to outfight the green and frequently poorly trained draftees that filled the Covenanter ranks. That the Irish were little more than brigands was demonstrated at Aberdeen in September, where after putting a Covenanter army to flight, they joined with their Highlander allies in occupying the burgh and engaging in a three day orgy of plunder, rape, and killing against a citizenry which until then had supported the royalist cause.

Argyll led a Covenanter force that reached Aberdeen two days after Montrose's army left. During the weeks that followed he came close to catching Montrose and his army near Fyvee Castle and might have defeated them as he had the larger army. Unaware of his strategic opportunity, he allowed the royal force to escape. With chagrin over this failure gnawing at his self-esteem he resigned his overall command of the Scots army in 1644 and returned to his estates in Argyll where he still commanded the Scots force in the West Highlands and Isles.

As the year reached its end, the Covenanters had five armies in the field. They had a large army under

General Leslie opposing the king's royalists in northern England. A smaller mercenary force was still in Ireland refusing to leave until England paid for its service. General Baillie headed a military presence in the Lowlands. The Earl of Seaforth commanded 5,000 men at Inverness, and Argyll had a segment of the Scots army with him in the west. Opposed to them was Montrose's mobile and elusive force which seemed able to strike anywhere without notice.

Montrose faced the prospect of spending the winter in the Highlands where he could have gone into winter camp. His position was complicated by a chronic need for supplies. Booty and pillage from the Lowlands were needed if his men were to see the winter through. More than that, his army was composed mostly of Irish ruffians and a motley mix of Highlanders from the Macdonald, MacLean, Stewart, Lamont, and McGregor clans all of whom had deep-seated grievances against the Campbells.

With his army's need for booty and craving for revenge, Montrose led a quick foray into Argyll's domain in mid December. Avoiding the accepted routes that the Campbells watched, he led his men in the dead of winter across a supposedly impassable mountain by way of Loch Tay, through Criandarich to Glen Orchy and Loch Awe from whence he struck at the heart of the earl's domain. Totally unexpected, the raid caught the Campbells completely unprepared. Husbands and sons were slaughtered; their homes pillaged and burned, their livestock and stocks of grain looted. The raiders swept on almost to Argyll's castle at Inveraray before turning tail and racing back to the safety of their Highland refuge.

Campbells Came

Part One

Sir Duncan

1645

Dawn comes late in January in Scotland. Today it seemed to come later than ever. A dense fog blanketed the vale, a fog so chill, dank and thick that one could slice it with a knife. The weather outside was hardly fit for man or beast. Inside the great house of Auchinbreck, the Laird of Auchinbreck, his grandsons and servants were scurrying about with obvious anticipation. Word had come from Inveraray the night before that Sir Duncan Campbell, the laird's eldest son, was back from the Irish war. Everyone knew that duty required that he report first to the great Marquis of Argyll and that his lordship would probably ask him to spend the night at Inveraray castle. Today though, he would surely ride on to Auchinbreck for a long awaited homecoming with his father and his extensive family.

Sir Dugald Campbell, 6th Laird and 1st Baron of Auchinbreck, tall and square shouldered with a scraggly gray beard, a mane of white hair, and a pair of bristling black brows was still a striking figure as he moved about the commodious quarters of his large house giving instructions to the servants who were preparing for his son's return. Sir Dugald was the sixth of his line to head the Campbell cadet of Auchinbreck. He had fought in many a skirmish for the Campbells during his lifetime and had played a key role in pushing the Macdonalds out of Kintyre, the peninsula that stretches south of Auchinbreck into the Western Sea. Somewhat crippled by past exploits and afflicted with the aches and pains expected by men and women who had reached the age of 70, he had for some years been retired from military service.

After checking to assure himself that his instructions were being carried out, the old laird sat before the roaring blaze in his great room and called for his breakfast. Meg brought him a healthy portion of oatmeal porridge with milk, some buttered bread and cheese, and a cup of grog. As he sat slowly eating before the fire, his thoughts went back to the days of his early youth. As a lad of four or five or maybe it was six he had sat in this very room with another Sir Dugald Campbell, his great grandfather and had heard him tell of Campbell lore.

Sir Dugald had boasted of their descent from the great Colin Campbell and his son Neil, both of whom had fought to place Robert the Bruce, another of their ancestors, on the Scottish throne. He had also told him that it was his great grandfather, the lad's fourth great grandfather Duncan an Adn Campbell, whose exploits had made it possible for his eldest son to become the first Earl of Argyll while the first son of his second wife became the first Laird of Auchinbreck.

Sir Dugald was proud of his family heritage but prouder still of his own family. He and his wife, who had died some seven years earlier, had had two children, a son Duncan who was now Sir Duncan and a daughter who had married a young lord who was now the laird of another clan. Duncan had stayed on with him in the family's great house and would in due time succeed him as Baron of Auchinbreck. He had won distinction among his peers as a military commander and was the most respected of all the Campbell officers. At any rate, it was he whom Argyll had sent as Lieutenant Colonel to command the Campbell contingent of the army the Scots government had sent two years ago to contain the uprising in Ireland.

Sir Dugal basked in his son's reputation as a soldier. He was prouder still of Duncan's seven stalwart sons. Duncan had married three times. His first wife had died from the plague without giving him an heir. His second wife had two children: Dugald and a daughter who had died young. Jean Colquhoun, his third wife was the mother of four sons: Archibald who was now 18; James, 17; William, 12; and Alexander, 10. Sir Duncan also had two natural sons: Donald, 25, and Duncan, 24, born to servant girls who had warmed his bed in the months following the death of his first wife.

The two older sons, Donald and Duncan, were now stationed with the army Argyll had quartered some miles to the north at Inverlochy. Dugald at 20 was being trained to someday take over as Laird of Auchinbreck. He was living at Argyll's castle at Inveraray where he and Argyll's son, Lord Lorne, were close companions. The marquis had already secured a knighthood for Dugald and had made him his military aide. The four younger boys lived at Auchinbreck with their mother and grandfather and where Archibald and James were members of the laird's military guard.

As he thought of his family, Sir Dugald beamed with pride. He was indeed a lucky man. He had not just one but a full seven strong and healthy grandsons who could and would contribute to the future welfare of the clan. Auchinbreck had been spared from the ravage of Montrose's December raid, but he knew the Campbells must guard against another attack. Only a year ago his men had joined their neighbors in rolling back the Irish invaders who had tried to retake Kintrye. They would be back, of that he was certain; but next time the Campbells would catch and punish them for their crimes.

Sir Dugald was unhappy about the quarrel that separated the Covenanters from King Charles but fully supported Argyll's insistence that the Campbells must stand for the holy covenant even if this meant opposing the designs of a far off king who had forsaken the Presbyterian creed of his native land for the Episcopacy of his English court.

Sir Dugald was a born and bred supporter of the Covenant preached by John Knox and embraced by the Scottish Kirk. He had hated it when the old earl had left the Kirk to marry a Catholic and agreed that it was best that he had chosen to live in exile abroad. With the new earl, who was now Marquis of Argyll, championing the cause of the Covenant, all was on its way to being right again with Scotland and its Kirk.

The old laird was just finishing his porridge when William and Alex came running into the room.

"Is da coming yet?" Alex asked.

"I told him it is still too early," William answered and then turned to his grandfather for verification.

"It will be some hours yet," the old man told them. "Your father is probably having his breakfast with the marquis at his castle at this very moment. They have business to talk about and it would be foolish for him to take to the road before the fog lifts. Once it does, it will take nigh half a day for him to get here so you can best study your lessons and find other things to do until this afternoon."

"Will he bring Dugald and Donald or Duncan with him", William asked.

"Let's hope that he can. Whether Dugald comes will depend on what the marquis wants. If Donald and Duncan are at Inveraray, I'm sure they will try to come."

"I want them to come," Alex echoed. "We hardly ever see them any more. Most of all, I want to see da. He's been gone so long I hardly know what he looks like."

"You will remember him when he gets here my boy. We all will."

* * * * *

It was early evening when Sir Duncan arrived at the great house with his sons Sir Dugald and Duncan. Donald had been aboard a ship carrying supplies to Argyll's garrison at Inverlochy when his father came to Inveraray and thus had missed his father's homecoming. The travelers were tired after their long ride but the three riders joined heartily in the festive fun as Sir Duncan was greeted with hugs and showered with questions raised by his wife, his father and six of his seven sons.

Everyone had questions about what Sir Duncan had done during the last two years in Ireland. There were also anxious questions about why Argyll had recalled him from his regiment in Ireland. What was it that the marquis wanted him to do?

With the first onslaught of questions, he brushed bravado aside and answered quite modestly that he had done nothing more in Ireland than march his army back and forth to maintain peace and order. There had been little fighting of consequence and certainly no victories that gave him a claim to glory. About the future, the only thing he could say for certain was that Argyll had called him back from his Irish command to take charge of the army at Inverlochy.

"We have some way to go yet in making our plans," he told them, "but you can be sure the marquis wants us to defend our land from future raids and that we will devise a strategy for meeting and destroying Montrose and his brigands."

"Every Campbell is praying for your success in avenging that affront to our honor," Sir Dugald assured him as their discussion was ended by a call that they seat themselves at the banquet table to enjoy a festive homecoming meal.

Much to the disappointment of Jean and his younger sons, Sir Duncan cut his homecoming visit at Auchinbreck short on the second day to ride back to Inveraray. "The marquis insisted on my early return", he explained, "and the situation is such that we have no time to waste."

The younger Sir Dugald and his half brother Duncan were both on military leave and were slated to return to Argyll's headquarters with their father. When the four younger boys heard of the decision to leave, all of them shouted demands that they go too. Sir Duncan was pleased with their response but quickly insisted that they remain at the great house to protect their mother.

Continuing, he said: "I love you all and would be proud to have you in my command, but there are responsibilities we cannot ignore. I suppose I could take Arch or Jamie with me. Both of you have had military training and are old enough to live with the other soldiers. Arch, it is best though that you stay here with grandda to supervise the defense of Auchinbreck in case we have another raid. Jamie can come with me if he chooses but I would rather that he stay here. As for Will and Alex, I know you would tear the hearts out of Montrose's rabble. But you are still too young to serve in a Scots army. You must stay here, study your lessons and take your training until you are older."

"That's not fair," William protested. "The war will be over before I can help."

"Hold your horses, son," his father assured him. "This war will probably wobble on until all of us are sick and tired of it. Enjoy your years as a lad, Will. You will have plenty of time and opportunity later to show your mettle."

* * * * *

Evening had come with a black starless sky before Sir Duncan and three of his sons, Sir Dugald, James and Duncan, reined their horses in at the gates of Argyll's castle at Inveraray. Once they had passed through the gates to the bailey, Dugald took leave from them to go to his quarters while his father directed Duncan to take James with him to the guard house barracks.

"Show him around and find him a bed," he instructed. "This is a big change of life style for you, Jamie, but you might as well get used to it. If all goes well, I will take you to see the marquis tomorrow."

With his sons cared for, Sir Duncan strode on to the marquis' quarters in the castle keep and asked if Argyll wished to see him. A guardsman, who informed him that Lord Archibald had suffered an accident the previous afternoon when his horse had slipped on some ice and thrown the earl to the ground, met him at the doorway. Argyll had wrenched his shoulder in the fall. The injury was not life threatening; no bones were broken; but he had several miserable days ahead and would be carrying his arm in a sling for at least another week.

"I am sure he will want to see you in the morning," the guard answered in response to Sir Duncan question about Argyll's well being. "As for now though, the surgeon has given him something to dull his pain and ordered him to get some sleep."

Sir Duncan was about to leave when another of the marquis' aides informed him that Sir Colin Colquhoun had ridden to the castle from Glasgow that afternoon and had left a message that he would enjoy supping with Sir Duncan if his schedule permitted.

"Colin Colquhoun! Why, of course, I would like to visit with him. He is my wife's youngest brother and I have not seen him for months."

An hour later the two men were seated before a roaring fire in the great room of the Red Thistle Inn. The owner had brought them an ample sampling of the house's best whiskey along with two bowls of barley broth soup, the beginning of a larger meal to come. Their talk at first dealt with family chitchat, with details about their daily lives and about their families.

By the time they were ready for their slices of beef and bread, they were ready to speak of more weighty matters.

"Bring me up to date about this standoff between the Covenanters and King Charles," Sir Duncan asked.

"There is no real progress to report," Colquhoun answered. "I am sure you know what the situation is. The Covenanters threw out their challenge and drew a line supporting the position of the Kirk against the king's Episcopalian reforms in '38. King Charles fussed and fumed and ordered them to accept his will but their answer was a resounding "No". Charles sent armies against us twice and both times, our men held him for no gain. There have been some signs of late that he is beginning to see the light, particularly since his English Parliament does not support his policy on Scotland and is feuding with him on other matters. But every time he offers to give a little, our Covenanter leaders ask for more.

"I am a loyal supporter of the Kirk and the Covenant, Dunc, but as you know I'm not much of a churchman. There are lots of things about this standoff I probably will never understand. To begin with, why should we be warring with the king about details in religious belief? We all believe in God. We are Christians, and believe in a hereafter. What we are fighting about involves mere details in how our churchmen interpret the scriptures."

"What do you mean by details?" Sir Duncan asked.

"One of the biggest hurdles as I see it is that Charles and his Anglican bishops insist that we must kneel when we take communion while our ministers reject the practice of kneeling as heresy. You know as I do that priests and parsons can find scriptural support for almost any stand. My objection is that I just do not think their differences in interpretation are important enough to justify warring against others.

"Another matter that divides us is the question of church government. We Scots like to pick our own ministers and have the Kirk rule itself. We oppose Episcopacy because it follows the Catholic pattern of letting the king appoint archbishops and bishops who in turn select the priests and ministers who deal with the people. Charles has a good reason for favoring their Prelacy. It gives him the power to control the church, what it teaches, who teaches it, and to name the bishops and churchmen who sit in our Parliaments.

"I am all in favor of the Covenanter argument that our Scots Kirk should be free from royal control. I have mixed feelings though about the argument that we should get the English Parliament to adopt Presbyterianism as the official national religion of England. It sounds good to our ministers. But its makes little sense for the simple reason that there are hardly any Presbyterians in England. Yet the English Parliament might agree to do just that if adoption will secure Scottish support for their fight against Charles and his rule.

"The Puritans in England insist on purifying their church and don't mind embarrassing the king and his bishops. At the same time, England has a growing number of religious Independents who want no governmental controls on religion. Neither group has any real interest in our Kirk or its Covenant. They may go along with a half-hearted adoption of the Covenant if they see that as a way to gain their short run interests but they will end up turning their backs on us."

"You have been around the country and even down to London, Colin. How do you see this stalemate between the royal forces and our Covenanters turning out?"

"My guess is that it will go on for several more months. No one is willing to compromise. The roundheads who oppose Charles and his royal cavaliers are going to give the king's party a real run for its money. Charles could regain full control by changing his policies and accepting some of the advice Parliament wants to give him. The question is: will he? If he clings stubbornly to his past position, he runs the risk of losing everything. As for Scotland, I am not at all sure which side we should look to for support. We have been backing Charles's critics but could very well end up on the wrong side."

"I know the marquis is much involved in defending the Covenant and is working with the Scots government; but where does he fit in the picture?"

"For some months now Argyll has been the real power behind the Scots government. Since they put him on the Committee of Estates that runs affairs for Parliament, it has been him more than anyone else who is running the show."

"What is he trying to do?"

"As I see it, he has a two-fold policy. He is a defender of the Covenant and wants the king to leave Presbyterians alone in Scotland. He favors abolishing Prelacy in England but would leave that decision to the English Parliament. So far as government is concerned, he is loyal to Charles but wants him to cooperate with the Scots and English Parliaments."

"That sounds reasonable. Why is he having trouble?"

"He has the support of most Covenanters but not of Charles on the church issue. His big problem is on public policy. Superroyalists like Huntley, Hamilton and Montrose, are willing to let the king rule without regard to Parliament. At the other extreme, there is a strong group of churchmen who would rather do without the king if he does not accept their religious beliefs. With popular support swinging back and forth between the two sides, the marquis is having a rough time holding a steady course. What he can do depends very much on the king who wants no sharing of control with any independent voices in either the Scots or the English Parliament.

"If our Covenanter leaders can get their act together, if they can show some singularity of purpose and quit interfering with the decisions of our military commanders, we might bring all of Scotland under the peaceful control of the Covenanters. But what happens here will depend on the success you and our other Scots commanders have in putting Montrose in his place."

"And that brings us to the question of Montrose and what I am supposed to do to stop him. You can appreciate my position, Colin. I am here with Argyll and am surrounded with advisors who have nothing favorable to say of Montrose. It would be easy to believe all they tell me but that would be foolhardy. What I really need is impartial information so that I might understand what I am up against without underrating him.

"I knew him at Edinburgh slightly some years back. At the time he impressed me as being a cocky and confident young Covenanter who was just itching to lead our cause against the king. How has he changed?"

"I would say you had him pegged about right. The big change, of course, is that he switched sides. He is still the cocky confident leader of men you remember. There are differences of opinion as to why he changed. His supporters say he saw the light and returned to his loyalty to the crown after chafing under the confused and often-contradictory leadership provided by the early Covenanter leaders. Others say he shifted because he felt that the Covenanters were more inclined to look to Argyll, whom he hates, than to him for leadership and that Charles bought him off with a promise of rank and power should he return to the royal camp. In any case he returned and was soon honored with promotion to the rank of marquis."

"What of the man himself? How is he regarded by the average Scot?"

"One cannot speak of an average Scot. Those who lean to the Covenanters see him as a turncoat and renegade. The royalists in our midst, and there a good many of them, see him as the king's white knight. He is the modern Saint George who will slay the Covenanter dragon. Those people who are trying to maintain a sense of neutrality between the two causes have a generally favorable view of him. Montrose the man, his handsome features and personal charm enamor them. He is a leader who makes friends easily and radiates confidence.

"On top of that, he has a superb record as a military commander. He is sly and quick to seize on his enemies' weaknesses. From what I know of his victories over Covenanter commanders last summer and fall, I would rate him as a military genius. He had his own way until Argyll scared him out of Aberdeen. Argyll might have beat him if he could have caught him after that, but Montrose was always able to slip away from danger."

"That brings us to Argyll," Sir Duncan interrupted, "what do these unbiased Scots say of our chief?"

"What I have to say on that point is just between you and me, Dunc. I do not want to be run out of Argyll on a cold winter night like this. The simple truth is, our leader is not popular in Edinburgh or anywhere else outside of

Argyllshire. He has two strikes against him. First he is a Campbell and you know, as do most of the people in this land, that the Campbells are the most hated of the clans. It is like my da used to say: All it takes is the sound of bagpipes and people crying 'The Campbells are coming' to put joy in your heart if they are coming to help yee or the fear of death in yee if they aren't.

"The Campbells are always good company to have if you need help and that is why the Covenanters will always look to them for support. Over time though, the Campbells have used their power to beat down most of their neighbors. With our marquis as their head, they are still doing it. And this record means that they are the brunt of thousands of grudges that won't easily be forgotten."

"What is that second strike against him?"

"That is Archibald himself. He just does not compare with Montrose in personal appearance or charisma. Overall, I would rate him as a good statesman. He has shown ability and talent in his political dealings and he has displayed more commonsense with most of his decisions than his fellow Covenanter leaders have. But he has become an easy target for criticism. People don't like his cold stern mannerisms and call him "old squint eye", blame him for the caution he showed as a military commander, and criticize him for some mistakes he has made along the way as when he took his troops north to settle his quarrel with Lord Huntley when he should have been marching on England."

"What are they saying about the raid Montrose led on Argyllshire last month?"

"That raid is an excellent example of what I mean when I say the marquis has become the target of lies and misinterpretations that demean his character. His enemies blame the success of the raid on his short sightedness and stupidity. They accuse him of cowardice in fleeing from here and of doing nothing to defend his people. It is true that the raiders caught the Campbells completely by surprise by crossing that impossible mountain, but it is not fair to argue that Argyll should have anticipated an attack that not one person in a thousand would have expected. As for the charge of cowardice, his critics never mention that he left here to rally the troops whose approach caused Montrose's raiders to turn tail and race back into the highlands."

* * * * *

It was bitter cold in the Highland glen where Montrose and his men had sought shelter against the winter. A foot of new snow covered the mountain meadow and an icy breeze made the chill seem degrees colder than it was. Icicles hung from the entrances of the several dozen cave like huts the men had built, almost burrowed into the mountainside. Wisps of smoke worked their way upward through tiny openings in the turf-covered roofs of the huts as the men inside huddled in their blankets around smoldering fires.

"Tis not what I call civilized," growled a young giant who was wrapped in a tartan blanket of the Macdonald clan.

"What more could you ask for, my lord?" gibed his companion. "It was your idea that we should spend the winter here on this glacier rather than in the comfort of Castle Lichton. We could be there now enjoying the good life. We could be snuggled in a warm bed or mayhap sitting at your father's table with your women folk serving us steaming slabs of meat to be washed down with flagons of honeyed mead."

"Lay off, lay off, James. If you do not like it here you know you can leave. Of course, you would likely freeze to death before you got out of this vale, but you are not bound to stay."

"Hold on, who said anything about me leaving. I'm in this as deep as you are, Malcolm Macdonald. What's a little cold when we are fighting for our gracious king."

"Gracious king? The James Pfister I know doesn't give a hoot for King Charles or his family."

"If not for him, what else am I fighting for? I am sure not wearing blisters on my bottom for the way he treats his Scots. And I'm not here because he is running a holy war against the Covenanters who are preaching all that tripe about saving the Kirk and the Covenant."

"I say that we are here James because God has made it our sacred duty to give our loyal support to Charles as our king and sovereign."

"Big words, my lord. But tell me this: would you be here fighting with this rabble if old Squint Eye was not leading the Covenanters?"

"You raise the damnedest questions, James. If Argyll were to switch to the king's side, I would have to join up with the Covenanters. My family has suffered too much from the overbearing arrogance of the Campbells for me to ever want to share a command or even a part of Scotland with them. I hate them with a passion and would like nothing more than to drive them into the western sea. You are more than a little right when you say the real reason we two are here is because we like Montrose and think he can use our help in putting the Campbells in their place."

The relative stillness that surrounded their hut was broken by the sound of a gun discharged in an adjacent hut followed by angry shouts and a string of curses. Two men burst out through the overlapping cowhides that had covered the opening to the rude abode, the first of them trying to escape a brutish giant who was swinging a cudgel near his head.

"Spirit of Jesus", he yelled. "Yee ain't gonna blow me brains out without me looking."

The first man took a vicious blow to his ribs as he turned and made a headlong dive that tipped his assailant into the snow. Both came to their feet somewhat sobered by the morning cold. The soldier with the club was still in a belligerent mood but was stopped from taking further action by two other men who came out of their huts and held the two fighters apart.

"Meant no harm to ya Clancy. Twas an accident," the first man claimed. Somewhat appeased, Clancy accepted the apology but only after denouncing his companion's ancestry and threatening to brain him proper if it ever happened again.

"What was all that ruckus about?" James asked as Malcolm, who had invited mayhem by sticking his head out of their hut, returned to the darkness near their fire.

"Our Irish neighbors are at it again," he sneered. "They aren't content to live like pigs. They quarrel among themselves like a pack of starving curs. God, how I hate them. Scum of the earth, they are. They are nothing but a gang of uncivilized lawless cutthroats. They live for plunder, raping our women, and just brawling. I can barely wait until Montrose can send the thieving papal bastards back across the water. Next to the Campbells, there is no one I detest more."

Calm yourself friend." James cautioned, "I want to stay off their hit list. Still they are handy to have around in times like this. Montrose can count on them both because they are seasoned fighters and because unlike his Highlanders they cannot slip out of camp and go home to mama when things don't go their way."

"Speaking of our great leader, what do you think the marquis was planning when he ordered his officers to meet with him later this morning?"

"Haven't the foggiest idea," James replied. "We will know soon enough. As for me, I hope he has some plan for enforcing discipline. Every day we are getting busted heads with more brawling and feuding among the men. It is getting so far out of hand that the men no longer pay attention to their officers' orders. It takes no military genius to see that this cannot go on. We must tighten up somehow. One cannot blame the men for being restless if all they do is sit here in the cold."

Two hours later Sir James and Sir Malcolm joined 30 other officers in the crowded main room of the only real house Montrose had found in this Highland vale. It was the largest room available at the marquis' headquarters and would have been crowded with only half that number in attendance.

Montrose moved about in the jostling crowd, greeting several by their given names, smiling, shaking hands, and patting many on their arms or shoulders. Like his men, he was wearing dirty clothes and the beginning of a scraggly beard half hid his handsome face. The room soon became overly warm, a situation that fueled resentment among many of the officers, several of whom were already in a surly mood, a mood the marquis countered with a display of charm and confidence.

Recognizing their growing impatience, Montrose made his way to the long end of the room where he stood next to Alastair Macdonald, his chief lieutenant and leader of the Irish brigade. Realizing that many in the crowd could not see him, he mounted a bench and said: "Gentlemen, I have called you here because the time has come for action. All of you have heard enough complaints to last you a lifetime. The men do not like their food or drink. They complain that we have no women in camp. Except for the Highlanders who have learned how to live through this atrocious weather, they claim and I agree that our winter has not been fit for man or beast.

"If this were the regular army we could have half of our men whipped for lack of discipline, for violating and ignoring your orders. Yet we can hardly blame them. Our big problem is that this army is bored by inaction. They need work and excitement to bring them back to fighting order.

"You understand our situation. We are secreted here in the Highlands where we are safe from attack but where we will soon be short of supplies. Most of the Lowlanders think we are living high on the cattle and grain and other booty we boasted we took from the Campbells. What they do not know is that we arrived here with not over a twentieth of the supplies we claimed we took.

"Our situation is precarious. Seaforth has 5,000 men in winter quarters less than 50 miles from here at Inverness. Baillie has a large Coventanter army quartered in the Lowlands, and Argyll has maybe 2,500 at Inverlochy. None of them are a threat to us because they all prefer staying by their fires to fighting in the cold of winter. Come spring though, they will put a squeeze on us. We can sit here and take our chances in a fight against heavy odds or we can go on the offensive and pick off one or two of them when they least expect it. I say let's go to war. Let's take Inverlochy."

With this announcement, several of the officers cheered. The room was soon a scene of confusion as everyone tried to speak at once. All feelings of physical discomfort were forgotten as everyone thought of the responsibilities and adventure that lay ahead. It took several minutes for the din to die down, When he could again make himself heard, Montrose called for order and asked if there were any questions.

Lord James was quick to ask: "How can we get there without being spotted? The fort at Inverlochy lies on Loch Eil at the base of the mountain fastness of Ben Nevis. There is only one coastal road in to the interior and there are enough Campbells along it to give all sorts of notice of our coming."

"You can put that worry out of your mind, my lord, Montrose responded. "It may be the fastest and easiest route but we will not be marching along the Loch Lochy road. I am not taking you along any route where we can be wiped out in an ambush. We'll be moving through rough country and you will have to do some climbing; but our scouts assure me that they can get us to Ben Nevis with only a few wild animals knowing that we are in the area."

"How can we be sure they are not expecting us?" several men asked.

"No one can give us a guarantee that they aren't," the marquis replied. "After the surprise we gave them last month, they should be leery and more watchful than usual. Still with a foot of snow on the ground, a mountain separating them from where they think we are, and their scouts watching a road we will not be using, there is a better than even chance they will be asleep in their beds at the hour we attack."

With the questions answered, Montrose said: "I take it we are agreed so let's do it. Get your men ready for action. We will leave at daybreak the day after tomorrow. Inverlochy may be only 20 some odd miles away, but going the way we will be going, it will take two days for us to get there. We can have fires the first day out but none after that so have your men dress for the cold and have them carry enough cooked food to fill their bellies."

* * * * *

Argyll's ketch sailed down Loch Fyne from Inveraray to the Kilbrannon Sound with the midnight tide. On board were the marquis, Sir Duncan, four of Duncan's sons-Sir

Dugald, his heir apparent, James, Donald and Duncan-, four other men from the castle, and the ship's normal crew.

"Were it a warmer time of year and were it not for this blasted shoulder, we would ride to Inverlochy," the marquis told them. "I always enjoyed riding along the mountain trail past the crags and through the vales. There are few more beautiful places on earth when the sun is out and the spring flowers are in bloom. But it is no place to ride during the last week of January. It is too easy for even the most sure-footed horse to slip or stumble and one sprained shoulder is enough. Next time it could be my neck."

With a clear sky and favorable wind, the ketch glided quietly and silently through the coastal waters of the lake and sound. Once they reached the North Channel that separates Scotland from Northern Ireland, they turned north, passed the Mull of Kintyre and set a course for the Sound of Jura. With favorable winds and ideal sailing conditions, the ship might have shot through the sound, threaded its way past some islands to the Firth of Lorne and then sailed on the late evening tide up Loch Linnhe and Loch Eli to Inverlochy.

Such was not the case today. Contrary winds stirred up the coastal waters and threatened to wash their ship westward into the Atlantic. After much tacking back and forth, they reached the protection afforded by the isles of Islay and Jura. Nightfall found them sheltered in a cove near the northern end of the Sound of Jura. Conditions were better the next morning and the weather several degrees warmer as they worked their way on to the Firth of Lorne and waited for the late morning tide to carry them to their destination.

Word spread through the armed camp while the ketch was being docked that Argyll had come and that the new commander of the army was with him. A crowd quickly gathered to cheer the marquis and his party as they stepped ashore from the ketch. The cheers gave way to disappointment when Argyll announced that he was planning to leave with the ship on the midnight tide. There was cheering again, however, when he proclaimed the day a holiday.

"I want you all to celebrate the installation of Sir Duncan as your commander. Tell the cooks to give us the best banquet they can provide on such short notice. And you will get a double issue of grog. I'm asking Captain Angus to take charge of the entertainment. Give him whatever help he asks for because every man here is to go to bed with joy in his heart."

Sir Duncan asked Donald to serve as his orderly and take responsibility for getting his gear transferred to his new quarters. He then instructed Duncan to take James with him to find their quarters in the camp. Dugald, who attended Argyll as his aide, stayed with the marquis as they moved about the camp.

The houses in the small settlement at Inverlochy showed definite signs of age. People had lived there for hundreds of years, many of them gaining a livelihood from the traffic that came through the geologic split that almost divided northern Scotland into two lands. Inland a few miles was Loch Lochy. Beyond was Loch Ness and the burgh of Inverness which fronted on the North Sea. Except for the narrow ribbon of water provided by Loch Eil that gave it navigable access to the western sea, the village was nestled between two rugged mountains. A high mountain fastness faced it across Loch Eu and the village itself was located at the base of Scotland's highest mountain, Ben Nevis, which towered some 4,400 feet above the seaside village.

The decaying ruins of an old motte and bailey fortress stood on a hill dominating Inverlochy. The old fort had been abandoned some 200 years before. Construction had been started on a newer and larger fortress but long sections of its curtain had never been completed. Ever since the Campbells had established their dominion over the area, no pressing need had been felt for a fortress with 40-foot walls that could withstand a siege. Structures had been built, however, to provide living quarters for a governor and large staff of guards and workers.

Inverlochy had in recent decades become a favored meeting place for clan conclaves. Large groups from the various Campbell cadets assembled here every year during times of peace to renew their ties of family friendship and to participate in intraclan games and ceremonies. A large assembly hall with attached kitchens had been built to accommodate these groups and give them a place where they could meet and find shelter during periods of inclement weather. Living quarters adequate to accommodate several hundred visitors had also been provided at the edge of the village. These were the quarters now occupied by Argyll's 1,500 Campbells and the 1,100 soldiers loaned from Baillie's army.

While the marquis went to the governor's house to rest, Sir Duncan made a personal inspection of the camp. With Donald at his side, he walked from one end of the encampment to the other. Along the way he met and stopped to talk with several friends and lairds from other cadets. He looked into a dozen or more of the rooms occupied by soldiers and noted that most of them were designed for summer not winter use. He inspected the gun and powder rooms, the stables that accommodated the small contingent of cavalry he had at his disposal, the large assembly hall, the kitchens, and the storerooms where food was kept.

His inspection left him far from satisfied. With his regiment in Ireland, he had been accustomed to the command of soldiers who dressed neatly, who kept their quarters and gear in good order, and who were quick to obey orders. The armed force he inspected today did not measure up to his expectations by any of these standards. Many of them wore dirty ragged attire, some of their barracks were dens of disorder, as often as not their fighting gear was not stacked in readily accessible places, and only a few of the men snapped to attention at his approach.

More than once, he told Donald of his distaste. "Our work is cut out for us," he said. "Beginning tomorrow things are going to change around here. They will have to if I am to convert this rabble into a real army." His annoyance reached a peak when they visited a storeroom next to the kitchens where the whiskey was stored. Several casks of the fiery brew were stacked near the entrance. Behind them was a pile of rubbish and debris. Looking at the pile of discarded junk, he turned to Donald and ordered: "Your first job tomorrow, son, will be to get someone to move this trash out and burn it."

His inspection tour completed, Sir Duncan went to the room where Argyll was resting. He was frank in reporting his appraisal of the situation and telling the marquis his plan for instilling greater discipline and order. Argyll nodded his approval and said: "You have my full backing Colonel. That is the job I brought you here for. I'm looking to you to make this a fighting force the Campbells can be proud of."

"If it is all right with you, my lord, I would like to start this afternoon by calling our troops to order and have them practice a few defensive maneuvers."

"You can do that tomorrow but not today," the marquis observed. "I promised the men a holiday and that is what they will get."

"To insure our safety, sir, I am ordering a doubling of the number of scouts we have watching the road from Loch Lochy. We should place some at strategic places downstream to watch for invaders and it would be wise to post a few along the mountain trails that go up Ben Nevis."

"I said not today, Dunc," the marquis answered with a chuckle. "You forget that I am the commander-in-chief today and that I declared this a holiday. After I leave tonight you can do what you think best, but today I will have my celebration. Anyway, what are you so worried about? This must be the most secure spot in all Scotland. We have scouts who can warn us of any threat to our security. We command both sides of the canyon that leads to Loch Lochy. The land to the south is Campbell country and no one is going to come at us from that direction. Any attack from the highlands behind Loch Eil would call for boats to cross the lake and there are no boats to be seen. That leaves Ben Nevis behind us and even an army of mountain goats would have trouble attacking us from there. "We are as safe here as you would be in your great room back in Auchinbreck so get yourself a drink and settle down for an afternoon and evening of celebration."

Sir Duncan was not really satisfied with the marquis' decision but knew him well enough to let his decision stand. He returned to his quarters where he found Donald visiting with his brothers Duncan, Dugald and James. The four young men were chuckling about past escapades and were more than happy to have family time with their father. James was excited about his new role as a soldier, Donald about his new duties as aide to his father, and Dugald a bit envious of the others because he had to return with Argyll to Inveraray.

For Sir Duncan, this was a moment to cherish. While in Ireland, he had missed the company of his boys. Here he was in a military camp, with four of his sons all borne of different mothers. Yet they were good friends, all looked alike, and all seemed headed for productive lives. What he saw and felt made him a proud father.

Late in the afternoon, Sir Duncan and Sir Dugald were called to a short impromptu gathering with the several lairds who were in attendance at the camp. All told there were 16 lairds present together with several sons and brothers who might some day succeed them. Every cadet from the far-flung cluster of Campbell subclans was represented. Argyll thanked them for their support and said: "You all know we have had some setbacks of late. Beginning now, that situation is going to change. With Sir Duncan of Auchinbreck here to lead you and you giving him your full support, we'll soon turn this situation around. And with that said, my lords, I say let the celebration begin."

The celebration began with the sound of bagpipes as two bands of pipers; one at each end of the encampment proceeded to lead the troops, both those from the Highland clans and the non-Campbell soldiers from the Lowlands, to the assembly hall. The hastily arranged tables that had been set up there were loaded with heaping platters of fish, roast beef and lamb, cheese, bread and butter, and the few vegetables that were available at this time of year. Cakes, tarts and sweet meats were stacked on a side table while mugs for ale and whiskey were provided for every soldier as he entered the room.

Good cheer abounded as the men ate and drank. There were jokes, some rowdy horseplay, and much laughter; but with their officers monitoring their behavior, there were no arguments and no fights. Once the men finished eating, the tables were cleared away and space was provided for dancing and games. Some of the men showed their skills at arm turning and other feats of strength. A few challenged others to wrestle. With pipers present though, most of the men chose to sing and dance.

As the evening wore on, Argyll had several elder members of the clan tell their younger colleagues about past exploits of the Campbells. At this point most of the troops General Baillie had loaned to the marquis quietly slipped away and returned to their quarters. This did not embarrass the Campbells because they knew they were soon to enjoy the high point of the evening, a recital of the past glories of the clan, a program feature that over the years had become almost a ritual to be repeated at clan gatherings.

One of the clan senachies, a man who had been trained to memorize and tell the oral history of the clan, was greeted with cheers as he walked to the center of the hall. His narration, told in rhymes, recounted the 800-year history of the family. He told of how they had once been known as the clan MacDuibhn, of their descent from royalty, of how they received the Campbell name when Archibald, also known as Gillespick, MacDuibhn had gone to Normandy and come back with the name of Campus Bellus. He recited the glorious exploits of past leaders of the clan fighting for the king and how Sir Colin the Great and his son Sir Neil Campbell had helped place Robert the Bruce on the throne. How their descendant Sir Duncan an Adn Campbell, the 13th Campbell, 5th McCailen More, and 15th Knight of Lochow had married the granddaughter of Robert III and paved the way for his son to become the first Earl of Argyll.

The party broke up well before midnight with many men stumbling half drunk to their quarters. There were still a substantial number though who joined Sir Duncan and Donald as they accompanied Argyll to his ketch. Once the earl and his party were on board, the ship cast off much cheered by those who remained behind. With a clear moonlit sky, a light supporting breeze, and the out flowing tide, the ship was soon a distant shadow.

As Sir Duncan returned with Donald to their quarters, he said: "Best we get some sleep, son. Tomorrow we are going to make this summer campground over into a real army post."

* * * * *

Montrose's army started its march south from its Highland hideaway to Inverlochy on January 31, the same day that Argyll sailed with Sir Duncan's party from Inveraray to Inverlochy. The weather was milder than it had been; the skies were clear and the temperature was now above freezing. There was complaining in the ranks as the men slogged along through the still deep snow. Most agreed that the warmer temperature was better than the freezing cold of last week. Many, however, cursed the warmth that changed the crisp dry snow to a slick wet surface that made for a more hazardous marching while also soaking the shoes and boots of the marchers.

The army made good time as it marched for awhile along a road that paralleled Loch Ness. Then leaving the easy route, the marquis' guides led them up into a mountain fastness. They were now out of sight of any possible Campbell scouts or sympathizers. Up into the mountains they went, through narrow canyons, up steep inclines, past crags and walls of sheer granite, along twisted trails where a slip could mean a fall of several hundred feet. Their route would have been difficult to follow in midsummer. In January with snow on the ground and an ever-present threat of avalanches, it seemed sheer madness.

As Montrose had correctly assumed, the army moved at a far slower rate the first afternoon than it had in the morning. By nightfall, it had marched only slightly more than half of the way to Inverlochy; but it had reached a sheltered glen behind a mountain ridge where it was safe to camp and it had moved this far without anyone suffering bodily injuries.

The men ate their cold rations and huddled together for warmth at night. Fires were something to be wished for. It was unlikely anyone could have seen them or their smoke but no one was taking any chances of detection.

The second day of march was one of pain and misery. Most of the men had stiff and aching muscles. While the weather conditions were good, the marching conditions were atrocious. The route selected by the guides was as challenging and foreboding as it had been on the first day. All through the day men marched and led their pack horses up and down mountain trails, through impassable passes and past points where their entire force could have been wiped out had an opposing army been stationed there to ambush them.

In late afternoon with the sun already setting, they reached a ridge on the down side of Ben Nevis. Below them, the guides told them, was the village of Inverlochy with Argyll's military encampment. Montrose and Macdonald walked to the edge of the ridge that shielded their presence to appraise their situation. The sound of bagpipes and occasional cheering could be heard from the camp. The marquis ordered his men to make themselves as comfortable as they could for the night. No one was to show himself to possible observers from the camp. Their presence was to be a closely guarded secret until the first light tomorrow when they would charge into the camp and destroy it.

As the evening progressed sounds of singing and mirth told the royalist force that Argyll's men were celebrating. Some were tempted to join with them, arguing that the enemy was half drunk and would be easy pickings. Disappointment was expressed when the cheers at midnight alerted them to Argyll's departure by ship from the camp. Alastair Macdonald counseled the possibilities of a midnight raid, but the marquis held steadfastly to his original plan. There would be no assault until dawn.

As light began to show in the morning sky of February 2, Montrose's men were roused from their fitful sleep. Stiff muscles were massaged and the men were advised to eat some of their dwindling rations. When all seemed ready, Montrose ordered them to move quietly over the ridge and down the mountainside. Macdonald and his Irish brigade were awarded the privilege of charging into the Campbell barracks. Montrose would lead a charge against the center where the assembly hall was located while Lord James was assigned command of several squads with orders to raid the quarters occupied by the Lowlanders and inform them that this was a strike against the Campbells and that they were free to leave if they would be gone within the half hour.

The attack proceeded as planned. Most of the royal forces were down from the mountain and at the edge of the encampment before their presence was discovered. A chance incident kept the attack from being a complete surprise. A lone soldier whose full bladder prompted an early visit to a camp latrine saw their threatening shadows and raised a cry of alarm in the brief moment before he was slain.

With the shouted warning sounded, men started to emerge from barracks to see what was happening only to find themselves met by the swords and dirks of Macdonald's bloodthirsty Irish brigands. No shots were fired at first as the raiders chose to do what slashing and stabbing they could before the whole camp would be brought to it feet by the sound of gunfire. Minutes after the rest of the royal force launched their attack, Lord James had his men fire their guns to get the attention of the Lowlanders to whom he gave his ultimatum. The sound of their gunfire together with the mounting volume of cursing, shouts, and death cries from dying Campbells soon had the entire camp in a turbulent uproar of confusion. Some lairds tried with little success to organize a defense. Their efforts to make order out of the chaos were fruitless as men stumbled about in near panic.

No one asked for mercy and no mercy was shown as the royal force pursued its savage advantage. Caught unprepared without notice, most of the Campbell men were bewildered; some were still half asleep or suffering from hangover headaches; many were totally disoriented; and hundreds were stumbling about without weapons for their defense. On every side, they were being slashed down, skewered, and in some cases shot. Those that remained on their feet were milling about much like agitated flocks of sheep while hordes of voracious wolves were intent on their slaughter.

Sir Duncan woke with a start when he heard the first shout of warning. By the time he heard a second muffled cry of distress, he knew his camp was under siege. Swearing under his breath, he realized he should have foreseen this emergency. He quickly ordered Donald to dress, arm himself, set off a general alarm, and rally as many men as possible to join with him in establishing a defense line outside the assembly hall.

With the first dozen men that joined him, he set up a defensive position behind a half built wall that afforded some protection as they fired their guns at the raiders. Others were able to join them, but it was soon apparent that less than a hundred men would succeed in getting to him. A lad from the Campbell barracks insisted that all was lost in that quarter; and two soldiers who came from the Lowlander sector complained that their fellow Lowlanders were spineless cowards who had been quick to grab their gear and depart from the area.

Sir Duncan wondered what had happened to his sons, Duncan and James, but had to put their fate out of mind as he had no way of getting a message to them. As Montrose turned his fury against their defensive redoubt, Sir Duncan realized the hopelessness of his situation. Thoughts of surrender were unacceptable. He was determined to fight on with his men until the last man died.

As he contemplated the end in sight, he suddenly decided that that was not the end he wanted for Donald. Calling him to his side, he said: "Our position here is hopeless, son. With some luck we can hold them off for maybe another ten minutes. They will overpower us and they have a single objective, to kill every last one of us and then steal everything of value in the camp."

"I'll be here fighting with you until the end."

"No, I do not want that. You are already wounded," declared his father, "We must do something to make sure you will continue to live. I want you to leave here and hide in a safe place until they get their bellies full and leave."

"Desert you and hide, only a coward would do that, and I am no coward."

"I know full well that you are as brave as any man here. I am not ordering you to save your skin just because you are my first-born. It is important that you be saved because once the royalists win they will make up a story about how they won a smashing victory under the most trying of circumstances. It will be filled with lies and half truths designed to demean the honor and valor of Argyll and the Campbells. You must survive so that we will have an eye witness who can tell what really happened."

"But there is no place to hide. Should I try to leave you, they would mow me down before I could get ten feet away."

"There is no activity back by the storerooms. We can cover you while you slip over there. Go to the room with those casks of brew and hide yourself under that pile of rubbish in the back. Once they find the whiskey, they will forget all about searching for escaped soldiers."

Donald was making ready to leave when Sir Duncan pulled him into a manly embrace. "God save you, son. Tell your brothers of my love for them and the Campbell cause. And one other detail, if your way is clear when you pass the gunpowder room, set a fuse to it. Those bastards don't deserve our powder. Anyway we need some excitement to see us off."

With Sir Duncan's men firing their last volley at the royalists who would have been watching had their heads not been protected behind the barrier wall, Donald ran to the storeroom. He knew he should hurry to his expected hiding place. But seeing no one in the immediate area, he stopped, turned and went instead to the powder room where the camp stored its gunpowder. He fixed a long fuse to one of the barrels, lit it, paused to make certain it was burning, and rushed as fast as he dared to the whiskey storeroom. He had no more than slipped behind the racks of casks when the building shook and he heard the roar of the powder blast.

The explosion gutted some of the common buildings near the assembly hall but had no effect as far as Donald knew on the fighting. He was far enough away from the blast to escape unhurt and pleased when he found that it had twisted the doorway and caused several casks to break free from their racks and roll to where they blocked entry to the room.

The room was dark and it was some moments before his eyes adjusted to the diminished light and he was able to find a hiding place amid the stack of rubbish. Then there came the long hours of waiting. He heard no firing of guns after the explosion and for some time only an occasional scream or the bark of a command. A gnawing in his stomach reminded him that he had had no breakfast. Yet he knew he would have to ignore his hunger pains for at least another day.

He thought of speeding the passing of time by sleeping but decided it best that he stay awake as long as possible. He fixed his hiding spot so that he would not be able to sleep on his back should he became too tired to remain awake. For the first time in his life, he admitted that his tendency to snore could cost him his life.

After what seemed an eternity, someone tried to open the door and found it jammed shut. Two men came with an axe and hacked their way into the storeroom. When they saw the casks, they lost all interest in searching for anything else. A royalist officer came by minutes later and asked if they had found anyone. "No need for looking," one of the finders answered. "The door was locked and no one could possibly have hidden here."

Throughout what Donald assumed was the early afternoon several men visited the room. He heard what sounded like the opening of one of the casks. Soon men were making merry. After an hour, the merriment gave way to an argument, an outburst of mutual cursing, and then to brawling. Quiet was restored when an officer came to the room, saw the casks, and ordered the placing of a guard at the entrance of the room to prevent further sampling of the content of the casks.

Later in the afternoon men came to take three of the casks away for what Donald assumed was consumption with the evening meal. As complete darkness enveloped the room, Donald overheard two guards discussing their victory. He ignored their boasting but listened carefully when one expressed the wish that Montrose would keep his army here for awhile. "If we hauled them stiffs out of their barracks, we could stay here more comfortably than back in our mountains."

"Don't wish for it," the other responded. "If we stayed here we would have to bury the critters and no Macdonald is going to waste his good time burying a Campbell. Anyway, the chief has decided that we will load the horses with all they can carry tomorrow and take the cattle and head up the high road to Loch Ness."

The all night presence of two watchful guards at the entrance did as much as anything to keep Donald from yielding to the demands of his empty stomach that he find his way to the kitchen for a scrap of food. The night seemed to go on forever. Morning brought a burst of activity as men again came to remove eight of the casks from the room. An officer then decreed that the remaining casks should be drained. While his men complained of the loss, he assured them: "If we can't take them with us, it sure ain't proper that we leave any for Campbells to enjoy."

Donald waited for what he thought was an hour after he heard Montrose's army leave before he crept from his hiding place. No one was in sight, so he went to the kitchen. Pots and pans were strewn about and most of the camp's store of food was gone. With some searching, he was able to find some leftovers from the meals of the past two days. With his hunger appeased, he started his dreaded tour of the grounds.

Waste and destruction greeted him on every side. The scene of butchered bodies, some stripped of their clothing, many mutilated by hateful hands, sickened him and made him fear he would lose the food he had so recently craved. His found his father's body and those of the men who had fought bravely by his side. All were dead and most had been stabbed a second time to ensure that no life remained. His father's head had been severed from his body and was found some distance away, dropped apparently by someone who thought of it as a souvenir worth carrying away.

Dead bodies, many with their throats cut, some ripped open, were strewn about all of the area occupied by the Campbell barracks. Donald dodged about trying to avoid stepping on any bodies as he made his way to the place where he had last seen Duncan and James. Duncan's body lay on the ground skewered by a sword or lance outside the door to his barracks while poor James had been caught inside and had had his head half severed before he ever had a chance to fire a gun or raise his sword.

He was sick at heart when he left his brothers' death scene and wandered back toward what was left of the assembly hall. His first impulse was to leave this terrible place. But how could he leave? All of the horses from the stables were gone; it was a long walk to Inveraray even in the summer, and without a knowledgeable guide he could never find the way. He knew someone should inform Argyll of the massacre and arrange for burying the dead. But who could do it? Of the 1,500 Campbells who were at the camp, he was the lone survivor, and he was not in fit condition to handle the burials by himself.

It was with surprise and relief that he saw an old woman kneeling by a body as he walked to the other end of the camp. She shrunk away in fear from him when he called but calmed down when he assured her that he was a survivor of the massacre. She told him that the raiders had not been content with killing the soldiers in the camp. They had also murdered all of the men and boys who lived in the village. All of the women and girls who were over seven had been raped, some of them repeatedly. Every house had been pillaged and some of them burned. And now the survivors in the village faced starvation unless help could be found.

Donald suddenly realized that the women of the village faced a more threatening problem than he did. He said what he could to console the poor woman, and lied when he assured her that Argyll's ship would be back within a few days to bring supplies for the camp.

His lie suddenly became his fervent hope, the only logical solution to his problem. He took the woman with him to the kitchens where they worked together salvaging what food supplies they could. It was there that she told him that he had been lucky because some of the raiders had boasted that they would burn every building in the camp to the ground before they left.

A return to subfreezing weather conditions made life tolerable in the midst of the killing field during the next two days. Donald dug a grave for this father and his two brothers but did not feel he had the strength to make it large enough for others. Time passed fast as he handled numerous small tasks. All the time though, he prayed and hoped against hope that the marquis' ship would indeed come as he had promised.

His prayers were answered on the morning of the third day when Argyll's ketch again swept to the village dock on the morning tide. The crew learned of the massacre with alarm and decided to leave with the outgoing tide within an hour to carry the news to Argyll and to solicit the help needed for burying the dead and for restoring viable life in the village.

Donald reached Inveraray the next day where he reported directly to Argyll and then begged a horse so that he might ride on to Auchinbreck. It was a heartbroken father, wife, and three sons who listened to his account when he told of Sir Duncan's death. Sir Dugald, who had known more than a little sorrow in his lifetime, consoled Jean and her boys. "Such is life," he told them. "We must be grateful to God for the good memories we have of him and of Duncan and James. It is up to us to carry on their work; it is for us to restore and preserve their honor."

Young William was less willing to accept the tragedy that took his father and two of his brothers from him.

"They can not do that to us Campbells," he cried. "Just you wait, I'll show them; I'll make them pay for killing my da."

Campbells Came

Part Two

William

1647-63

Birds were singing in the trees. A light mist veiled the morning sun in an otherwise clear sky. The greenish amber oats were almost ready for harvest, the grass in the meadow lush with verdant fullness. Flowers too were in bloom- yellow daisies with their brown eyes and red blossoms of thistle starting to take form.

A bonny fair-haired lass of eleven with blue eyes and a smattering of freckles on her nose left the house with a pail in her hand and walked to the cattle enclosure. It was milking time and with no brothers to handle the chore, she hummed a nursery tune as she started to do what she knew had to be done.

It was while she was milking Purdy, the red cow with the white spots and fierce upward pointing horns that she heard it. It was a sound not common to the barnyard, like the gentle purring of her cat, only louder. As soon as she finished milking, she put her half filled pail aside and went looking for the source of the strange sound.

The noise came from the other side of a haymow. A man she had never seen before laid there sound asleep and gently snoring. Without speaking, she grabbed her pail and hurried to the safety of her mother's kitchen where she shrieked:

"Mama, mama, there's a strange man out there. He is sleeping on our hay."

The girl's mother grabbed a knife. With her husband off to war and she and her Meg living here alone, she had good reason to suspect any strange male visitors to her house. Together they stole out of the house and went to the haymow. Looking down, she said: "Why he is only as boy, Meg. I think he means no harm."

"Should I waken him?"

"Aye, but let's do it the gentle way. Tickle his nose with this oat straw."

Meg grasped the straw with obvious pleasure, knelt down beside the sleeping lad and tickled his nose with the straw. Without stopping his snoring, the boy's arm shot up and swatted at the straw as though it were an offending fly. When Meg laughed, his eyes opened; he looked at her in wonder and then sitting up demanded: "Who are you?"

"You should be answering that question, not us," the mother responded. "I am Jean MacLean and this is Meg, my Margaret. Now tell us who you are. What are you doing here?"

"I am Will," he replied. "This is where I stopped to sleep when I got lost on the road last night."

"Will who?" the mother queried. When Will hesitated without answering, Jean added: "Oh, I can see by your kilt that you are a Campbell. Campbells are not popular here, but you are safe with us. My mother was a Campbell."

In response to her prodding, Will admitted that he was William Campbell, that he was 15, that he had been in a skirmish yesterday with some Macdonald men, and that his brother Archy had ordered him to go home. He had started for home but had become lost on the way.

When she learned that he had not eaten since the previous morning, she insisted: "You must be starving. Come to the house. We will find you a scrap of food and you can be on your way."

As he started to rise, she saw him wince with pain and saw that there was dried blood on his leg. She reached out, lifted one side of his kilt and saw a bloody gash on his thigh.

"Oh, you are wounded. Help me get him to the house Meg. Get some fresh water from the well. And now Master Will I am going to wash out that wound and put a hot poultice on it to draw out the poison before it does you harm."

"But I must get on my way to Auchinbreck."

"Your brother sent you home because you were wounded and could not keep up with the others, didn't he? Well you are not going home today, not tomorrow either, not until I see that you can walk without pain. Your mother would rather miss you for a few days than have you dead."

It was easy to yield to her instructions. He was content for awhile to lie on the cot where she placed him. As the afternoon wore on, he became restless, went outside, and found a scythe and tried to cut some tall grass. The activity triggered a pang of throbbing pain that sent him back to his cot. After resting awhile, he rose again and asked Jean if she had any weapons at the house.

"Nothing except a few knives," she told him. "My Hector took his gun and sword with him when he went off to fight. I remember though that he had a bow he used before he got his gun."

Will searched among the absent owner's scant supply of tools and found the bow together with a half dozen arrows. He sharpened the arrows, restrung the bow, and tried using it to shoot at a target. The exercise tired him so he again returned to his rest.

On the second afternoon, he went again to the field of ripening oats to see if he could make himself useful. He had walked behind a tree to relieve himself when he saw two men approach the house. He heard one of them demand food and drink, but did not hear Jean's reply. He then heard the second man gloat: "We can get food later. Let's take them now, Barney. You can ride the old dame while I fancy the young one."

With that outburst, the first speaker grabbed at Jean. She held her own and slapped his face while Meg turned and started to run. In his rage, the first man raised his arm to smite the mother while his friend started to chase after Meg. Neither threat to their virtue and safety was completed. Two arrows, shot in fast succession, reached their mark. The first stopped Meg's pursuer dead in his tracks when it sliced through his neck. The second killed her mother's assailant when it penetrated his rib cage before he could deliver the blow that was meant to bring her to her knees.

Once they caught their breath, Jean and Meg were exuberant in their show of gratitude. While appreciating their attention, Will cautioned: "Later, later maybe. Right now I need your help. Help me clean the arrows and dig a grave. They might have friends nearby and we cannot have them come here and find either bodies or blood."

No other stragglers came to the small farm. Two days later, Will felt himself enough repaired to take his leave for the long day's hike back to Auchinbreck. As he took the food they packed for him, he thanked them for their care and looking at Meg's smiling face joked: "God willing, me thinks I will be back after the fighting is done."

* * * * *

The massacre at Inverlochy had come as a staggering blow to Argyll. Sixteen lairds and the cream of his army were lost. His power was broken for now. But he was far from prostate; his predicament was temporary. Cream has a way of rising to the top. All of his lost lairds had sons or brothers who were able, willing, and eager to take their places in the clans' hierarchy. All he needed was time to bring his reservoir of power back to its usual level. Young William Campbell of Auchinbreck was typical of the young men and boys who moved to fill the void.

During the year that followed his success at Inverlochy, Montrose enjoyed more victories over the armies the Covenanters sent against him. His Irish adherents invaded Kintyre and spent the winter of 1646 there. But the Campbells were not idle. They fought back and in 1647 ousted Macdonald from his hold on Campbell land.

Though only 12 when his father died, William grew up fast. As a boy passing into puberty, he labored and fought alongside much older men in upholding the Campbell honor. At 13 and 14, he fought alongside his brother Archibald under the direction of his grandfather Sir Dugald and at 15 he and Archy did the work of grown men in the final skirmishes that sent Macdonald's Irish renegades back to Erin.

It was during a clean up operation in the summer of 1647 that Will was wounded. With the gash on his leg, Archy had insisted that he go home. It was on his way that he met Jean and Meg MacLean. A day after he left them, he was back at Auchinbreck where he was greeted with loving attention.

Sir Dugald, the old Laird of Auchinbreck, was away on a visit to Inveraray when Will returned and did not get back until the next day. As usual he wanted an account of Will's activities. "First though," he said, "I have a message for you. Lord Lorne is looking for men for a new cavalry corps. The marquis usually insists that a lad be at least 16 before he goes into service. He knows though that you have already been fighting for two years so he will waive that rule for you. Your brother Dugald has reserved a place in the corps for you if you want it. The choice of whether or not you go is up to you."

"Want it? Of course, I want it. When do I go?"

* * * * *

Although already hardened by months of military service William Campbell still had much to learn when he joined Lorne's cavalry corps. As its youngest recruit, he found himself a mere youngster competing with older men. He needed time both for his body to mature and for acquiring new skills.

Fortunately for him, the corps was formed during a lull in the military strife that had swirled about the holdings of the Campbell clan. The civil war in England, which had started in 1642, ended in '46 after Parliament's armies won several victories over the royalist followers of the king. Montrose, who had gone on from Inverlochy to win a major victory for the royalists at Kilsyth, then suffered a smashing defeat at Selkirk after which he fled to Norway. Alastair Macdonald, whose Irish invaders had made life miserable for the Campbells at Kintyre and on Ismay Island, had finally been ousted and was back in Ireland where he was killed in '47.

Will's tour of duty at Inveraray was saddened by the death of his grandfather in '48 and of his mother a year later. Meanwhile, important events affecting the Scots were occurring in England. Hoping that the Scots would provide him with security and support, King Charles turned himself over to a Scots army that was still stationed in northern England in '47. His hopes were misfounded as the Scots in turn relinquished him to an English army when Parliament paid the arrearage owed for its use of the Scots mercenaries in Ireland.

The reformers in the English Parliament abolished Prelacy (Episcopacy) as England's National Church in 1647 thus opening the way for the spread of Presbyterianism and self-government of religious congregations. About this same time, Charles escaped from his English captors and while free met with some representatives of a royalist wing of the Covenanters and agreed to an arrangement known as the Engagement under which he made several concessions including recognition of Presbyterianism as the state religion in Scotland.

Charles acceptance of the Engagement prompted a rise of royalist fervor among the Covenanters. Argyll saw it as an inadequate solution. Far from accepting it, he stood aside in '48 when the Engagers recruited a royalist army, led by the Duke of Hamilton, who invaded England with the intent of freeing the king who had again been captured.

Hamilton's army was soundly defeated at Preston in August by Oliver Cromwell who then marched north and captured Edinburgh. At Cromwell's insistence, the Scots Parliament passed its Act of Classes, which excluded the royalists from further participation in Scotland's government.

Meanwhile, Charles was recaptured in England and placed on trial for treason. News of his execution in January 1649 brought outbursts of grief throughout Scotland. Argyll, who headed the Committee of Estates, was blamed for not trying to intervene though there had been virtually nothing he could have done.

While these events were taking place, William was stationed with his corps in Argyllshire. With his fellow dragoons, he honed his skills as a warrior who fought on horseback, participated in corps maneuvers, and provided various services for the marquis. This situation suddenly changed in 1650 when word reached Inveraray that Montrose had landed on the northern shore of Scotland with a small army of Danish and German mercenaries.

Argyll quickly called his son Archibald who was Lord Lorne, Captain James Campbell, the commander of his cavalry corps, and William, who now bore the rank of lieutenant, to his presence. "It is time for action," he told them. "We have no word about Montrose's strength but know he is a viper who threatens our very existence.

"General Leslie has an army in the Lowlands that is marching north even now to meet him. As yet they have no need for additional foot soldiers, but they can and probably do need cavalry. I have decided to send 40 of our best men to Inverness as soon as possible. Lorne will stay here with me, but I want you, James, and you, William, to get your men furbished. Be ready to leave tomorrow morning. With spring here, the roads to the north are passable so you should ride to Inverlochy and then up the road past Loch Lochy and Loch Ness to Inverness.

"While you are at it, William, stop at your father's grave at Inverlochy. You and every man in your corps should say a prayer there because that is where every one of you lost a father or brother or both. God willing, you can go on from there to avenge their death."

The northward march went as planned. On the second day, the troop reached Inverlochy where they stood at solemn attention to show their respect for their fallen brothers. Two days later, they passed the far end of Loch Ness and trotted into Inverness. They were told there that General Leslie was hurrying north with his army and that he had sent orders for Colonel Archibald Strachan to move ahead and block Montrose's advance to the south from Dunbeath in the far north where he had taken Sir John Sinclair's castle after a short siege.

The Campbells rode on directly to rendezvous with Strachan's force at Tain. With their arrival, Strachan had 220 horse and 36 musketeers to support his foot soldiers. The next day on April 27, Strachan's force marched to Wester Fearn on the southern shore of a long inlet known as the Kyle of Sutherland. Strachan was familiar with the terrain and knew, when his scouts informed him that Montrose was encamped under the lee of a steep hill known as Craigcaoinichean, that it would be inviting suicide to attack him there with its easily defended mountain pass.

Strategy was needed to draw Montrose's force down to more level ground where Strachan's cavalry could be used to advantage. The main body of Covenanter cavalry was ordered to move forward out of sight behind a hill that hugged the coastal road while his foot soldiers advanced along the road behind a vanguard of 20 horsemen commanded by Lieutenant William Campbell. Montrose's scouts saw the advancing army and concluded that it represented the strength of Strachan's force.

The ruse worked. Montrose and his lieutenants misread the situation. Spurred by the report that the small detachment of cavalry was flying Campbell colors, orders were quickly given for the army to leave its mountainside camp and march through the pass to a more level plain where Montrose's cavalry could wreck havoc on the enemy.

* * * * *

Sir James Pfister smiled as he rode out of the narrow glen. It was mid afternoon. The news he carried was not to his liking and he had been riding hard since early morning, but the view before him was one to bring him cheer. Ahead were Bonar Bridge and the blue waters of the Kyle, which stretched out to Dornach Firth with the blue green silhouette of the mountain fastness of Craigcaoinichean beyond. It had been three full days since he had left Montrose's camp and he was more than a little pleased to find it still there.

He was pleased by the promise of security offered by the campsite. Located as it was on rough ground between the steep incline of the mountain and the waters of the Kyle, it could have been assaulted only by an army coming from the east through a narrow easily defended mountain pass. It was a secure defensive site, one that reflected Montrose's genius as a commander. Of course, it was not an appropriate site for marshalling one's army against an enemy. More level ground was needed for sound military maneuvers. But this site had been chosen because its position made it a secure haven for an expanding army, not as a place for battle.

James trotted into the camp and went directly to Lord Montrose's tent. The marquis greeted him with a quick salute and immediately demanded: "How did it go? When are the Mackenzies coming?"

"I cannot say they are coming at all, my lord. Old Brian hemmed and hawed, talked about waiting until his men could plant their fields, said they probably would come later, but refused to dispatch any men to us now."

"Damn these Highlanders with their suspicious loyalties. The Rosses and Munroes were with us along with the Mackenzies before and should be today. Don't they realize we are the ones who have their best interests at heart?"

"Has any help come from the Rosses or the Munroes?"

41

"No, they are stalling too. They have promised help; but our scouts say about 300 of them are serving with Strachon."

"How firmly are they committed?"

"That is something I can't say. With their past history, I would rate them as half hearted allies of the Covenanters. If we can give Strachan or Leslie one good drubbing they will likely desert en masse and join our side."

"Then we must plan for that drubbing. What information do we have about Leslie and Strachan?"

"From the little word we have, it seems that Leslie's army is coming north but has not yet reached Inverness. Strachan has moved north with the force he had at Brahan and has set up camp at Tain. Strachan will be a nuisance but his handful of men is nothing to worry about. Our big concern is getting and training enough men to face Leslie."

Sir James' conversation with the marquis was interrupted when an excited guard burst into the tent with a report that a troop of Covenanter horse had been seen on the Western Fearn road. Turning to Sir James, Montrose said: "This could be the opportunity we need. Get yourself something to eat while I check out the reports."

Twenty minutes later James returned to the tent to find that it had become a hive of sudden activity. The marquis explained: "Two other scouts have verified the report that there is a troop of 20 horse out there flying Campbell colors. They are just lolling along and seem to be in no hurry to get to the pass. Major Lisle has gone out to reconnoiter and should be back with us in a few minutes.

The major returned as expected. He had seen the troop of horse and a small army of maybe 400 men now coming in sight. When the marquis asked if this might be a ruse, a local nobleman who had accompanied Lisle answered: "It is just as the major said, my lord. Their force is small and the horses they have are the only ones aside from those we have in the entire shire."

"This is our opportunity", Montrose announced. "A quick victory here will sway the support we need from the Highlanders to our side. We know they won't try to force their way through the pass; and anyway we need a bigger victory than we could claim by just defending the pass.

"This is what we will do. We have three times as many footmen as they have and more than twice as many horses. Major Lisle will stay here on this side of the pass out of their view with our cavalry while I lead our army through the pass. We will take up a fighting position on that flat plain next to that little lake at Carbisdale. Once we are in position, Lisle will bring our cavalry through the pass and lead a charge that will remind the Campbells of the lesson we taught them five years ago."

The royalist officers moved quickly to call their men into formation and started their march to the appointed battleground. Strachan's smaller force saw them coming but made no attempt to engage the oncoming army in battle. From all appearances, they were more interested in organizing a defense than in fighting. The situation suddenly changed when Lisle's cavalry started to come in view. At that point, a trumpet sounded, the 400 soldiers surged forward and the 200 dragoons Strachan had hidden behind the hill that fringed the coastal road swept over its brow and down onto the killing field.

The battle was over in less than a half-hour. Major Lisle's cavalry advance was met and quickly overpowered by Strachan's dragoons. When they were driven back on their own foot, the scene changed to a maelstrom of confused disarray. Strachan's musketeers and footmen went into action along with the cavalry and Montrose's 1200 mercenaries and raw recruits broke and ran.

Montrose tried to stem the tide and rally his men. His efforts were thwarted by the fury of the onslaught. Men on both sides of him were being stricken down. At one point, a tall young dragoon who wore a Campbell tartan engaged him in hand-to-hand combat. He was distracted for a moment when his flag bearer was shot and killed while fighting by his side. The dragoon shouted, "This is for Inverlochy" as he delivered a blow that knocked Montrose from his horse and would have killed him were he not protected by body armor.

Montrose was able to get to his feet and remount his horse. With abysmal defeat and possible death facing him, he ordered his men to group about him as they fled back to the security of their Craigcaoinichean camp. Only a small segment of his force made their way to what they hoped was safety. All but a few of his cavalrymen were dead as were most of the Scottish recruits he had attracted to his cause. His mercenaries were the only ones who retreated with a semblance of order and like his raw recruits most of them were slaughtered on the battlefield or drowned in the waters of the Kyle.

Wounded and attended by a few of his remaining officers, Montrose tried to organize a defense on the hillside below the site of his camp. Too few men got through to do the necessary work. Strachan's cavalry stormed through the pass in hot pursuit of the routed army and his footmen were not far behind. The defending royalists were soon overwhelmed. With the end in sight, Montrose joined a handful of his officers in mounting their horses and fleeing from the scene.

All through the night the marquis rode with little said to his few companions. They had no food; most of them were wounded; with no hamlets or cottages on their route, there was no place for them to stay. There were no recriminations. The men rode on in silence. Each had painful questions of "What if?"

Montrose examined his own conscience. Why was he still alive when so many of his followers had been killed? Why had he been so misguided, so stupid as to assume that it was Strachan and not him who was marching into a trap? Who was that young Campbell who struck him from his horse while reminding him of Inverlochy?

Inverlochy. How this day's events paralleled that occasion. The battle of Carbisdale was the antithesis of that at Inverlochy. Both battles were decisive with almost every man in the losing army slaughtered, but the victors were of different sides. In both cases the victors won because of their successful use of the element of complete surprise. In both cases, the losers lost because they had stupidly failed to seek basic information they should have had about the presence of enemy forces.

"Yes, if that young dragoon was seeking revenge for damage done him at Inverlochy, he picked the right day and place for it. It was my unquestioned decision to destroy that

Campbell troop that sucked me out of my secure camp. With trickery, the Campbells turned the tables on me."

* * * * *

In the aftermath of the battle, William was far from sure how he felt. It had been a great victory. He should feel elated now that the Campbells were avenged. But he had found no joy in killing. The sight of several hundred fellow Scots lying on the ground around him, their bodies mangled and lifeless, revolted him. True, some of them had deserved to die, but many were the innocent sons of farmers or fishermen from the Orkneys or from Sutherland or Caithness who had fought only because their lairds had told them to.

He marveled too at the extent of the destruction. Montrose had lost his entire army, more than 1,200 foot and most of his forty horsemen. They had been smashed by Strachan's force of 220 horse and only 400 foot. The three to one advantage Montrose had had in foot soldiers had counted for naught. It was those 200 extra cavalry that had brought chaos to his cause and carried the day when they charged down from that grubby hilltop. He shuddered when he thought of the fate that would have awaited him had the extra cavalry come late or not at all.

The morning after the battle was a time for reevaluation. A large pit was dug for the common burial of the dead. William visited the site where he had struck Montrose down to see if by chance his body might still be there. The bodies of some dead lords were identified. Montrose was not among them. With no evidence of his presence, Colonel Strachan concluded that he must have been one of the few horsemen who had slipped away from the field when it became evident that the royalists faced annihilation.

Strachan sent several dragoons, William among them, along the trails that led north and west from Bonar Bridge to find traces of Montrose or the route he had taken. They all came back empty-handed. The marquis' trail was cold so Strachan retired with his force to Tain where they waited for the arrival of General Leslie.

Montrose's flight soon became a tale of misfortune and misery. He had first intended to see his way north to

Thurso from whence he might have caught passage to the Orkneys. Not knowing the way, his party became lost amid the woods of the rough mountain country. At one place he was able to change his clothing to the common garb of a Highlander. He and his friends then wandered for two days without food in a mountain wilderness. On the third day, now separated from his companions, he begged some bread and milk from a herder and hid beneath a trough when a pursing search party came asking if he had been seen. Finally on the fourth day, he reached the house of the Laird of Assynth whom he remembered had royalist sympathies.

Assynth set aside Montrose's offer of gold to see him to safety. Instead, he confined his guest to the cellar of his castle while he bargained with General Leslie for larger gain. An agreement reached, Leslie's officers arrived a few days later at Assynth's castle and Montrose started a long journey to Scots justice at Edinburgh.

William was one of the party of cavalry that accompanied the royalist prisoner as he was taken south. The party stopped at several castles along the route, at most of which the unfortunate prisoner was mocked and reviled. At Kinnaird, Montrose was allowed to see and take leave from his two youngest sons. The next night was spent at a fortified house a few miles from Dundee. While there, the mistress of the house plied the Covenanter guards with strong ale and brandy before opening the doors for Montrose' escape.

William commanded the outer guards and it was he who apprehended the unknown man in the dark cloak who was leaving the grounds in the middle of the night. Positive identification of the prisoner was not possible in the dark of night. Refusing the offer of an award and taking no chances, William ordered that the man of mystery be held until he could be plainly seen. His suspicion that all was not well at the house was soon verified. The marquis was returned to his prisoner status and from then on more securely guarded.

Once the escort party reached Edinburgh, Montrose was turned over to the Covenanter authorities who promptly confined him to prison. William was pleased to find Argyll and Lorne in Edinburgh. Both were anxious to hear his report about the victory at Carbisdale and Montrose's capture, after which Lorne said: "You have earned some time off. You can relax and enjoy life here in Edinburgh this next month until after Montrose's trial."

"No," William replied, "if I have time off and a choice, I will ride back to Auchinbreck. There are things there I need to do".

Lorne chuckled as he agreed: "I had forgotten that you have had time to get homesick. Give your brother Dugald my regards and report back here in a month. Now go and have a good time."

The sight of familiar mountains, lakes and glens, heartened William as he approached Inveraray. Beyond he knew it would take only part of a day to ride to Auchinbreck, but a visit to the house of his childhood was not his first objective. Several times in recent weeks he had wondered what had happened to Meg and Jean MacLean. It had been more than three years since he had left them, three years during which he had only occasionally remembered his short stay with them. So it was out of curiosity as much as anything that he pointed his horse west for a ride to the farm of Hector MacLean.

He was not completely certain of the location of the farm. As he approached it to ask for directions, Meg saw him and ran to her mother. "He's come, he's come," she shouted.

"Who has come, dear?"

"Will, William Campbell, the boy I found under a haycock."

"You must be mistaken. Your eyes are playing tricks on you."

"No they aren't. He said he would come and he has. Just you look."

Jean looked. William Campbell was taller, broader and more mature now than he had been. He was a grown young man; still beardless and decidedly handsome in his uniform as a dragoon wearing the Campbell tartan. He was older but she recognized him in a flash and rushed to greet him.

William was somewhat dismayed by the fervor of his reception. Meg and Jean were both gloating over him and tripping over each other as they tried to tell him of all the things that had affected them in the last three years. It was obvious the family had prospered; obvious too to William's discerning eye that Meg was blossoming into a beautiful young lassie. They insisted that he meet Meg's father who would be back at nightfall and that he spend the night with them. In the late afternoon while Jean worked with her pots and kettles, Meg took him by the hand and gave him a tour of the family property.

He was agreeably surprised when Hector returned to the house, was introduced to him, and said: "So you are the lad Meg found under a haycock. William, you are most welcome here. I owe you much and thank you now for saving the lives and virtue of my two girls. You may not know it, but you are a hero here. We've heard more than one report from Inveraray about your deeds with the marquis' cavalry, your promotion to a lieutenancy, and your leadership of the troop Argyll sent to Inverness."

William was flabbergasted but had the presence of mind to acknowledge Hector's greeting, thank him, and then ask: "Have you heard about our victory over Montrose?"

"No, I haven't, though the fact that you are here hale and hearty tells me that. What happened?"

William told him about the battle and about Montrose's journey to Edinburgh and added that he was back here to check on some matters at Auchinbreck. Hector asked many questions as their conversation continued through supper and afterward until the fire burned low and they concluded that it was time they go to their beds. All through the discussion the two women said little but looked on their hero with pride as they gave rapt attention to his every word.

William indicated his intention of going on to Auchinbreck as they were breaking their bread the next morning. Meg objected that he should stay another day and Hector assured him that he was welcome to stay. When he insisted that he must go, they reluctantly accepted his decision. "We have hardly had a chance to know you," Meg complained. To which, he answered: "After all the talking I did last night, you know more about me than I know myself."

As he was preparing to leave, Hector took him out of listening range of the two women and said: "Come again, son. You are good company and we have much to talk about. You may not know it, but when I saw you yesterday, I wondered at first if you had come to ask for my daughter."

"Not on this visit, sir," William answered with a smile. "I am still too young to think seriously of marriage and so is Meg. We must know each other far better before we make a decision that serious. Anyway I must get my land and decide on my career before I seek a wife."

"Good thinking son. On your first point, I say plan to come back soon. Jean and I will stay out of the way so you can become better acquainted with Meg. On that land business, let me make a suggestion. Your brother is the new Laird of Auchinbreck. That means you will be pushed out, but you rate high enough with the marquis and with Lorne to ask them for a piece of good farmland. Argyll has a lot of good land in Kintyre that he took from the Macdonalds. Set your eye on getting some of it."

After thanking them for their kind reception and promising to come again, William mounted his horse and started to ride away. He had not gone a hundred yards when he stopped, ran back and gave the smiling Meg a hug that lifted her off her feet and a kiss on her lips. Without a word, he then mounted his horse again and quickly rode away. A half day later, he announced his presence at the great house of the Laird of Auchinbreck.

Sir Dugald, the new laird since the death of his grandfather two years earlier, was William's elder half-brother. Though sons of different mothers and a dozen years apart in age, the two men shared a strong bond of respect and affection. They had spent much of the preceding five years apart as Dugald had served first for some months as Argyll's aide and then after Sir Duncan's death at Inverlochy as his father's replacement as the Lieutenant Colonel who commanded the Argyll segment of Munro's Scottish army in Northern Ireland. He had been relieved from that post the year before when he followed Argyll's lead in refusing to support the Engagers ill-fated invasion of England.

Dugald was happy to greet him and anxious to hear of the role William and the Campbell cavalry troop had played in the defeat and capture of Montrose. They had not talked long, however, before they turned to discussion of the topic on which William sought clarification. "Will," his brother blurted, "you know I have been slow to act on this property matter since grandda died. But I will be getting married in another few weeks and then I will be living here full time with my wife. You and your brothers have been free to live here and you will always be welcome to come and visit and even stay awhile once I am married.

"But you know what our rules on inheritance are. The barony of Auchinbreck and all the property that goes with it are mine. I have talked to the marquis about it and together we have agreed that you and your brothers will each receive other estates. I have already arranged for Archibald to get land at Kaoackimillie. No decision has been made yet on the land that will go to you or to Alex."

"That is what I wanted to hear Dug. As long as I am with the cavalry, I will be living in the barracks and will have little need for a separate estate. Someday though, I want to marry too and I will need a good farm or an estate where I can take my wife. I've heard there are good holdings on Kintyre, on those lands we took from the Macdonald's. With your help, I hope to get some of it."

Sir Dugald readily agreed to William's request. A future landowner on Kintyre he would be. With that promise secured, he asked if he could spend a few days at his childhood home before going back to Inveraray and then on to Edinburgh. Dugald laughed while shaking his head: "You had no need to ask, brother. Of course, you can stay and welcome too. There is one thing I want you to tell me though. You are fresh from the army and from Edinburgh. What do the people there say about our chief, the marquis?"

"They talk and they say plenty. Some like him and some don't; and those who don't are careful what they say to me lest their words invite a bloody nose."

"Surely you have learned to hold your temper."

"I do better than a lot of Campbells. One good thing about life in the cavalry is that it teaches you to think before you act. On that matter of what people think of Argyll, what people around Edinburgh say was news to me. I knew Argyll was important but until I talked to them I hardly realized how important. He is the most important magnate in all Scotland.

Being chairman of the Committee of Estates makes him the real ruler of Scotland. Most people are happy with him. But there is plenty of criticism too. Some say he is a dictator and call him King Campbell."

"What are his plans for you when you get back to Edinburgh?"

"All I know is that your friend Lorne insisted that I return within a month."

"They will put you to good use, Will. All I can say is: Give them good service and keep on agreeable terms with both of them. Our future depends on it."

* * * * *

William enjoyed the changing vista as he rode eastward and south from the rocky crags and mountains around Inveraray to the rolling hills and flatter plains about Edinburgh. It was early summer, the days were clear and long, and crops in the cultivated fields were following their annual cycle of sprouting from seed, rising from the soil, growing skyward, producing their bounty of grain and fodder, and then dying if not harvested.

He proceeded directly to Lord Lorne's quarters on his arrival in the capital city. Lorne thanked him for returning before he was expected, asked if there was news from Inveraray, and instructed a groom to take his horse and gear to Argyll's horse guards barracks. These details handled, he turned to William and said: "We have some plans for you cousin. Father and I have discussed this matter and are agreed that you did a great job in handling Montrose and that you are our best choice for a mission we have in mind.

"Let me explain. For some time now, the marquis has been negotiating with Prince Charles to get him to come to Scotland. We have offered to crown him as king if he comes, signs the Covenant, and agrees to some other conditions. So far he has been playing games with us. He has refused our offers but hinted that he might change his mind. All along he has played Montrose and the other royalists against us. With Montrose gone, we are fairly sure he will see the light and agree to come."

51

"There is something here I do not understand, my lord. Only a month ago I was fighting against the royalists and now you are saying we will be supporting Charles as our king. Are we changing sides or what?"

"The situation is complicated, Will, and I'll admit that most people may think we are running around without any clear idea of where we are going. Our big problem is that our people have different ideas on what we want in religion and in government. With religion, most accept the Covenant but there are places where almost everyone leans toward Papacy and here and there we have Scots who favor Episcopacy. The business of governing was simpler when everyone was a Catholic. We complicated the situation when we threw out the king's Episcopalian bishops and insisted that the Kirk should rule itself."

"But why should that be a problem? Why don't we let everyone believe as he wishes?"

"That is the position Cromwell and most of the Independents in England favor. But it won't work. We have had national churches for hundreds of years. Kings like them because they give them a handle to keep their people in line. That is one reason Charles fought to keep Prelacy when we tried to throw it out. We want a national church too because we see the sacred Covenant as the true gospel every true Scot should accept.

"Religious differences are only part of the picture. We also differ in our attitudes about government. For centuries, we have honored and fought for our kings. Nowadays, we have some who argue as they do in England that we can get by without them. Maybe we could but the scriptures speak much of kings and that is the system that God ordained.

"Most of our people accept the Covenant but they do not act alike when it comes to views on government. From the very start of our opposition to King Charles, we were divided because some Covenanters were royalists at heart who supported the king regardless of his stand on religion. Others were ready to flock to his support if he would compromise on certain issues. Still others insisted that the king sign the Covenant, rid himself of his former friends and advisors, and live a life approved by our ministers.

"The Covenanters have had problems because our policies have not been consistent. They have shifted on oft occasions to reflect the stands of different groups. We Campbells fit in the middle group. My father supports the Covenant and he will not abandon his beliefs to support the royalist cause. At the same time, he is not a diehard. When we have followed the preaching's of our diehard ministers, we have usually ended on the losing side even though they have insisted that theirs was the only road to everlasting glory. For the same reason we have avoided siding with the Exchangers and ultra royalists who favored the crown every time Charles threw a few crumbs their way.

"You asked if we are switching sides by fighting Montrose one month and inviting the king to come here the next. We are not being inconsistent. We have been royalists all along. But we support the Covenant and insist that if Prince Charles comes here to be king that he supports it too."

Lorne stopped, looked intently at William to see if he had any questions, and went on: "Sorry for that long discourse, Will, but your question deserved a complete answer. Now let me explain where you fit in. If the prince accepts our offer, he will probably arrive here by ship from Holland during the next few weeks. We have asked him to leave his party of friends and advisors on the continent, but he will probably bring some of them along. Once he is installed here, we will provide him with a regiment of house guards. He will also have a horse guard and a full quota of other servants.

I will be the colonel in charge of his house guards and the Earl of Englinton will lead the horse guards. We want you to serve as Englinton's lieutenant and as the prince's personal aide. You are not there as a spy though we will expect you to remember our interests. What we really want you to do is to provide good service to the prince so he will think well of us. If you two get along and he likes you, return his affection and serve him as you would my father or me."

* * * * *

On June 23, 1650, just a month and two days after Montrose was hanged, Prince Charles anchored off the coast of Scotland in Moray Firth. His coming had been a subject of intense negotiations. The Covenanters wanted him to come as king but had insisted that he must first endorse the Covenant, that he leave most of his friends and royalist advisors on the continent, and that he accept several other stipulations. Charles had refused the conditions, sought compromises, and finally gave in when he concluded that acceptance was necessary if he was to claim his crown in Scotland.

The prince who looked out on the coast of Scotland that day was a tough-minded realist. He had just passed his twentieth birthday and had already learned the necessity of compromises if one was to survive. He had last seen his father five years earlier when Charles I sent him to the West Country for his protection. From there he had fled to the Isles of Sicily and Jersey and then to France where his Catholic mother tried to convert him to her religion.

Unlike his father, Charles was not motivated by strong religious convictions. He accepted Episcopacy because it was the religion of his father and of the country he hoped to rule. Regardless of outward appearances, he had no intention of changing. In defiance of the terms the Covenanters had given him, his travel party included several men whom the Covenanters considered as undesirables. Now he hoped they would accept him without his signing the Covenant. On this condition, they refused to yield. Their obstinacy angered him, but in the end he signed.

It was a hollow achievement for the Kirk whose leaders had demanded the king's conversion to their creed. But the news that Scotland had a Covenanted King was enough to open the gates of the nation to him. Crowds gathered to cheer his arrival. The Scots Parliament sent a delegation to welcome him. Funds were voted for his use, and plans were initiated for his coronation.

Once the king was established, the Marquis of Argyll was one of the first Scots nobles to secure a private audience with him. The marquis came attended by Lord Lorne and Will Campbell. Argyll assured Charles of his allegiance and promised his political support. He introduced

Lorne as a laird who could be of particular service to the royal cause. Turning to Will, he said: "This young man, your majesty, is my kinsman. He is an officer in your horse guards. I have arranged for him to serve as your aide both because he is young like you and because I am certain he can be of real service to you."

Lorne stood aside while Will was introduced. He found himself suddenly comparing the two young men before him. They were of about the same age; both were tall and of athletic build. But their similarity stopped there. The king wore his wavy black hair down to his shoulders. He had dark eyes, a swarthy coloring, and pockmarked pudgy facial features that made him something less than handsome. Will in contrast, was a blue-eyed blond with a fair complexion who wore his hair in the short-cropped style favored by many younger Scots.

Will remained with the king after his introduction. At first he felt somewhat embarrassed as no one paid much attention to him and he seemed to serve no function. Two hours later the king noticed him as a group of courtiers were leaving his presence. He called him and Will quickly went to him.

"So you are my especially assigned aide? I suppose that means you are here to spy on me."

"No, indeed, your majesty, the marquis gave me explicit instructions not to spy on you. I am here to give you special service and help make your stay in Scotland a happy experience."

"Do you really expect me to believe that?"

"I am a Campbell, majesty. If I knew for certain that you were conspiring against my clan or its chief, I would be tempted to turn against you. But I do not believe that will happen, so I am pledged to serve you as you wish."

"Nicely spoken, my Scots friend. The real question though is what can you do for me?"

"That will depend on your needs. There may be nothing today, but there will be times when an aide can be of use."

"Yes there are. The thing I would like you to do for me right now is find me a woman."

"A woman?" Will stared at him in disbelief.

"Yes, a woman. You know what they are for don't you?"

"I am newly here, your majesty. I wouldn't know where to start to look."

"That is what I suspected. Have you ever had a woman?"

Will looked at him with a blank expression on his face and then shook his head. Charles laughed and added: "Well, that is one difference between us. I've had women ever since I was 14. I even have a year old son back in Holland."

"Are you married?"

"What difference does that make?"

* * * * *

The surge of euphoria and renewed commitment of support for the crown that swept across Scotland after Charles' arrival was short lived. Argyll did what he could to uphold the royal standard, but his stand was weighed down by the objections and carping of diehards within the Covenanter ranks. Complaints about the landing of undesirables in the king's party forced Charles to dismiss several of his attendants. More vehement charges came from the straight-laced churchmen who decried the king's licentious style of living and condemned the fact that he had merely signed the Covenant. They would be satisfied with nothing less than his complete conversion to the Presbyterian faith.

Charles tried to placate his critics. He attended services of the Kirk and even endured a half-day of hammering away by four ministers who preached that his father, the late King Charles, was already in hell, that his mother with her acceptance of Catholicism would surely join him, and that he too must quickly repent and accept their version of the gospel if he wanted salvation.

With his general indifference to religious persuasions, the ranting of the ministers was annoying, abusive, and even insulting at times but still no more effective in changing his beliefs than rain on a thatched roof. Will, who sat through several of these sessions with the king, had a negative reaction. "They behave and talk like a bunch of idiots," he told Lorne. "If I were not already a supporter of the Covenant, I would be so put off by their abusive ranting and bigoted intolerance that I would never again want to hear a minister of the Kirk."

One of Charles' chief objectives in coming to Scotland was his hope that he could recruit an army he might use to invade England and regain the English crown. Most of the leaders in the Scots Parliament were reluctant to endorse that goal. Some extremists among them even took the stand that no military support should be provided for any move by the king against England. A majority, however, saw a need for having an army that could consolidate royal authority in Scotland. For this purpose, authorization was approved for recruiting an army of 26,000 men. Meanwhile, England's Commonwealth government viewed the reception given to Charles as a declaration of war. Cromwell, who had been campaigning against royalist insurgents in Ireland, was recalled and sent north with an army to forestall an expected invasion.

With the approach of Cromwell's army, General Leslie marshaled his force for the defense of Edinburgh. Food supplies were gathered, castles in southern Scotland were garrisoned, and formidable fortifications were provided. Charles announced his intention of joining the defenders. Under pressure from extremists, the Committee of Estates ordered that he be quarantined away from the army until he proved his devotion to the Covenanter cause.

Charles took matters into his own hands. Defying those who would restrain his exercise of the rights he felt were rightfully his, he visited the army. The common soldiers cheered his appearance. Groups of Engagers and royalists in the military camp declared themselves for him. The committee of ministers and church elders who were acting for Parliament, which was in recess, however, were infuriated by the reception he received. They insisted that Charles promptly attest to his acceptance of the Covenant, that he condemn his father's misdeeds and his mother's idolatry, that he promise his own repentance, and that he agree to accept the peace terms Charles I had rejected in 1646.

Argyll lobbied with the committee to get it to moderate its stand, to soften the wording of its demands. Led by men of rigid beliefs such as the gospel spouting Archibald Johnston of Wariston, the committee refused to budge. Most of its members firmly believed that any deviation from the letters of the Covenant would bring the damnation of their souls and arouse the wrath of an insulted God against the nation.

Argyll apologized to the king for the obstinacy of his colleagues and counseled him to give the demands temporary acceptance. "When you get to England as king you will be freer but for now you must tolerate the demands of these madmen if we are to move ahead."

Charles held out against yielding to the demands for awhile, but realizing that his success was at stake, finally agreed to sign all but the condemnation of the actions of his parents. His decision was applauded by many in the army but was firmly rejected by the diehards who insisted on complete compliance with their demands.

With more lobbying, Argyll was able to get some softening of wording that allowed the king to show the respect he felt for his parents. Charles signed the modified document with grave reluctance; it was clear the extremists had succeeded in their effort to discipline and demean him. He was humiliated by the experience and resolved in his mind that he would never forgive those who had perpetrated it. Shortly later he left the army and went to Perth.

Not content with its success in trying to dictate what the king could think and do, the committee of extremists next turned to what it regarded as a necessary reorganization of the army. The army had numerous officers who were royalists or Engagers who they insisted be ferreted out and discharged. Fulfillment of this demand stripped General Leslie of some his best officers.

The decision to rid the army of officers who were suspect because of their religious or royalist views could not have come at a worse time for the defense of Edinburgh. Until then Leslie had been able to hold Cromwell's opposing force at bay. With the purge, the morale of the army and its effectiveness as a fighting force was adversely affected. Worse than that, the leaders of the Covenanters repeated a mistake they had made several times before. They issued tactical orders to their commanding general that should better have been left to military strategists. Compliance called for moving the army away from its defenses. In the battle of Dunbar that followed Leslie lost 14,000 men and all of his artillery. Four days later Cromwell entered Edinburgh again as victor.

Charles felt crushed and demeaned by the abusive treatment he received before his capitulation and removal to Perth. With criticism and complaints heaped on him by subjects who should have been supporting him, he had little recourse but to fall back on the consolation offered by close friends. Wilmot and Buckingham did their best to cheer him; but it was his Scots aide, William Campbell, who helped most to restore his hopes for a successful reign.

Charles was suspicious of Will when the two first met at the end of June. As the summer wore on, he came to see Will more often as a trusted associate and confidant. Though very different in their backgrounds, the two men felt a genuine liking for each other; Will showed his devotion by providing faithful and useful service; and Charles found himself turning to Will both for advice and companionship. They rode together, hunted in the royal woodlands, tested their skills at falconry, and tried to outdo each other in sports.

Will was with the king when he visited Leslie's army in August. He was heartened by the reception the troops gave their king and more than a little shaken by the demands the churchmen made of him. Throughout the negotiations over his acceptance of the extremists' demands, he carried messages back and forth between the king and Argyll. More than once, he assured Charles that Argyll had not abandoned him, that he was laboring to secure the best terms possible from the churchmen who were then in the driver's seat.

Will also was at Charles' side at the time of his humiliation, when he felt himself demeaned and feared that he had forsaken honor and his prospect for salvation by signing the Covenant and dishonoring his parents. Will cheered him then with the assurance: "This dastardly act was not of your making, majesty. God, the angels in heaven, and your subjects here and in England know it was forced on you. If it is a sin and a stain on anyone's honor, it is on them, not on you."

Buckingham and Will were with the king at Perth when news reached them of Leslie's defeat at Dunbar. Charles was visibly shocked. The loss of his army put an end to his dream of a military conquest of England. He was also bitter about the contribution the extremists made to the defeat. "They were so smug, so sure their religious purge of the officers would bring them victory," he moaned. "Will they never learn that battles are won by men who fight, not by preachers threatening the enemy with damnation?"

Leslie was able to retreat with the remnant of his army to Stirling where he marshaled his men behind a line of defense that Cromwell chose not to challenge. A lull in the fighting followed during the last months of the year while Cromwell turned his attention to besieging several castles his army had bypassed in southern Scotland.

Charles reacted to the new situation by asking the Commission of the Kirk and the Committee of Estates to involve him in their military decisions and by proposing reorganization of the army, this time with inclusion of the royalists and Engagers. These proposals offered a reasonable course for the nation, but the extremist leadership rejected both out of hand. For them, the defeat at Dunbar was a sign of God's anger; anger that could only be appeased by a national fast and continued pursuance of the course led by the godly few.

Argyll found himself walking a taunt rope at this point. As leader of the moderate wing of the Covenanters, he was firmly committed to defending the Covenant while at the same time restoring the monarchy. To succeed in this venture, he saw it as essential that the Scots be united. Arrayed against him on one side was a strong following of royalists composed of Catholics and Covenanters who placed first emphasis on loyalty to the crown, the Engagers who Argyll had opposed some months before, and a sizable group who hated him simply because he was a Campbell. On the other side he had to contend with the extremists among the Covenanters who preferred no king at all to one who did not fully subscribe to their beliefs.

Four weeks of confused negotiations between the three groups followed. Argyll strived as best he could to secure unity and Charles offered to make him a duke and Knight of the Garter if he could succeed. The extremists, however, insisted on going their own way while the royalists indicated willingness to give the king their independent support.

Frustrated and discouraged by the seeming inability of the squabbling groups to agree on a common course, Charles took matters in his own hands and made plans to leave Perth and join a band of royalists and Highlanders in the north. The plan for his escape was bungled and ended as a fiasco. Only a small segment of the army he expected to find at the Glen of Clova near Aberdeen were there to meet him. Meanwhile, a body of cavalry was sent by the Committee to secure his return.

Will Campbell rode with the troop and found Charles tired and disheartened in a cabin where he had taken temporary refuge. Will met with him alone and persuaded him to return to Perth with the assurance that he could do so with no loss of honor.

Charles' foiled escape caused several leaders of the Kirk party to reconsider the counter productive nature of the policy they had pursued. More tolerance and willingness to cooperate was shown than had been the case since midsummer. There were still strong differences of opinion, recriminations, demands for punishing this group and that, and refusals by some to join in a unification effort. But by December Argyll was able to lead a majority of the Covenanters in denouncing some actions of the extremists as scandalous and injurious.

Agreement was reached to permit recruitment of royalists and Engagers for an enlarged army. Arrangements also were approved for Charles' coronation. The southern third of Scotland together with its capital were in English hands when Charles was crowned as King of the Scots on New Year's Day, 1651, in a small church at Scone. The rite was as pompous and solemn as the teachings of the Kirk permitted. Once again, Charles was required to subscribe to the Covenant. This time, however, he did so without protest and almost with relief.

* * * * *

The first months of 1651 saw accommodation of most of the conflicts that had torn at the nation's fabric the previous year. Argyll and his party were intent on retaining the king's favorable opinion. Friends of the king who had earlier been labeled as undesirables were allowed to return to his court. Decisions on military and governmental matters that had been made without his input were now made in his Privy Council. He attended and participated in the sessions of Parliament; and he was formally designed as commander-in-chief of the army.

With Charles now more occupied with the affairs of government, Will saw less of him than he had in earlier months. The king sought the pleasure of his company on frequent occasions though, sometimes to ask his opinion on various matters, occasionally to request special services, and most often to indulge in the joint enthusiasm they had for riding and manly sports.

As winter turned to spring and then summer, Will could not help but notice that Charles was coming into his own. He was happier, more content, less prone to angry outbursts than he had been. His confidence was restored and he looked to his future with optimistic anticipation. Will wondered whether the change should be attributed to the king's satisfaction with his new mistress, to the return of earlier friends to his court, or because the events taking place around him were falling into place. Whatever the reason, Will saw the change as good both for the king and for Scotland.

What could have been viewed as Argyll's triumph in securing national unity was marred by the king's insistence that ultraroyalists be admitted to the government and the military on an equal basis with the Covenanter moderates. Charles' argument for the change was logical because most of the recruits for the army now came from the traditionally loyalist regions of the northeast. Southern Scotland from whence the Covenanters had secured most of their recruits in years past was unfortunately under English control.

Admitting the royalists to control on an equal basis with the Covenanters called for Parliament's repeal of the

Act of Classes. Argyll opposed the change but had no choice but to accept it. The repeal brought an abrupt end to his years of dominance in Scots politics. He could no longer be thought of as King Campbell because the king now found himself more inclined to look to Lord Hamilton and the royalists for advice.

By midsummer Charles had relatively full control of the realm he had left above the waist of Scotland. He had an army of 18,000 men still holding their own behind earthen entrenchments near Stirling. It was then that Cromwell, who was again probing the strength of the royal defenses, shipped an invading force across the Firth of Forth, established a beachhead on the other shore, and outflanked the defenders at Stirling, defeated them at Inverkeithing, and swept on to capture Perth.

Cromwell's maneuver won the war for the Commonwealth in Scotland. Charles lost 4,000 men and hundreds more were deserting. An English army lay to the south of his men while Cromwell's principal force stood between his army and its source of supplies in the north. Charles had dreamed of a victory to be followed by an invasion of England. He had even gone so far as to instruct royalist friends in England to be ready for his return. Now with humiliating defeat facing him in Scotland, he chose to make a wild move. He decided to lead his remaining 12,000 men on an invasion of England.

The bold audacity of Charles' plan was endorsed with enthusiasm by most of the army. The nation's older and more seasoned leaders viewed it with alarm. When Will reported the nature of the plan to Argyll, the marquis responded bitterly: "It is complete idiocy. He doesn't have a chance of defeating the armies England will throw against him. This is what I feared when he started leaning on Hamilton and the other royalists for military advice. They have already lost more than one army to the English and now we will lose another."

When Will asked whether he should stay with the king, Argyll shook his head. "I am not sending my men or your cavalry unit with him. We are going back to Inveraray where we will soon be needed. The decision of whether you accompany him is up to you. It is a dangerous undertaking but I did assign you to him as his aide and that offer should be honored as long as he commands a Scots army."

Will gave little thought to his option of leaving the king's service. He was young and full of desire for adventure. Unlike the older men of his clan, he was attracted by the daring nature of the invasion plan. It was a venture that could bring him glory and honors or possibly death. Like most young men, he saw himself as immortal as he hastened to join the king in making necessary preparations for the long march south.

Charles' army started its march south the next day. The army units Cromwell had stationed south of Stirling were bypassed. With six days of fast movement, the Scottish army reached the English border north of Carlisle. It stopped there just long enough for Charles to issue a manifesto to his English subjects and for his troops to proclaim him King of England.

During the ten days that followed the army continued its march to the south. The garrisoned towns of Carlisle, Chester and Shrewsbury were bypassed. Crowds gathered in the smaller towns and hamlets to see and cheer the king. The reception given them was for the most part lukewarm with a disappointingly small number of men flocking to the royal banner. At the same time, however, they encountered little hostility and the token-armed resistance they met at one bridge was easily beaten off.

Charles and Hamilton wanted to turn the army eastward for a march on London. Others insisted that the army first stop for rest and refurbishing its supplies. Worcester was picked as a logical camping site because its fortifications could easily be repaired, the surrounding countryside offered bountiful supplies, and it was located in a region where support for the royal cause was thought to be high.

The army had hardly more than invested itself at Worcester when Cromwell approached the town from the east with an army of 28,000 men. His cavalry wrested control of the bridge that spanned the Severn river from the royal force and Charles found his army sandwiched between attacking forces from both the north and the south.

Cromwell attacked on the morning of September 3. Charles and his staff saw the beginnings of an attack on one of the town's suburbs from the top of the cathedral tower. He rode immediately to the suburb to bolster the spirits of his men. He then returned to the main body of his troops and led a charge against one wing of Cromwell's army. The charge met with initial success but the king's hope for victory turned to dire defeat when Cromwell used his three to one advantage in numbers and the superior training of his men to crush the royal assault.

Will fought side by side with the king and saw dozens of his comrades fall as they steadily gave ground before the advancing foe. Their situation was already desperate when Wilmot came from the cathedral tower with word that reinforcements had been seen coming to add weight to Cromwell's counter attack. Grabbing Will by his arm, he bellowed: "Get the king. The day is lost and we must leave while we can."

Charles and a few of his close associates were able to escape from Worcester through its last open gate. Behind them the killing continued for several hours until the royalist army was wiped out. Hamilton, Lauderdale, Cleveland, and Montgomery were taken as prisoners within the town while Derby, Leslie and Middleton were captured as they were fleeing from the battle scene. Lord Hamilton, whose leg was smashed by a cannonball, died a few days later from gangrene; Lord Derby was beheaded; and the others were cast into prison. Most of the common soldiers were killed in the fighting. Of those who survived, few reached Scotland again while many were sent as slaves to the sugar plantations in the West Indies colonies.

Buckingham was able to ride away to safety. Aside from him, Charles, Wilmot and Will were the only ones of the king's close associates who remained free. With their hurried departure from the town, they knew they would be pursued once their absence was noted. Neither Charles nor Will had a ready answer for their problem. Fortunately for them, Wilmot had some knowledge of the area and had secured valuable advice from Lord Derby, who had told him that in the event of an emergency he should ride west to

Whiteladies and seek refuge there with a Roman Catholic family named Penderell.

The Penderells received them without protest and took quick action to send their horses to a safe haven while they disguised the three refugees as farm laborers. When Will asked Tom Penderell if he thought they would be safe, Tom answered: "We are taking a chance, same as we always have. You can be sure that the authorities will be here soon to check on us. But we Catholics have been hiding our own from the authorities for a hundred years since the days of Queen Mary. We know how to do it and how to keep our mouths shut."

"But even if you succeed in hiding us, won't they be looking for the horses?"

"They will, but it is already too late for them to find them. Those fine mounts you came on are split up now and look like common plow horses."

The three men did not have long to wait before two mounted guards came to the farm asking if they had been seen. While they hid quietly in a secret compartment of the barn, they heard their host deny that they had seen any strange visitors. Two days later armed men approached them while they were walking on a road. As the men approached Charles instructed Will to say nothing as his Scottish brogue could give them away. He and Wilmot then put on a convincing act that assured the men they could not possibly be the suspects they actually were.

There were other occasions when they were hidden in a house, or were fortunately away when representatives of the Commonwealth came looking for them. Their closest encounter with their would be captors came one afternoon when the Penderells sent Charles and Will to a nearby farm to meet a neighbor who had volunteered to hide them. They had no more than arrived and were standing under a huge oak tree when an unusual birdcall was heard. "Hurry up into the tree", the neighbor implored. "Mounted guards have been sighted and I do not have time to hide you."

Up into the tree Charles and Will went. They were sitting astride branches far up in the foliage when three horsemen from Cromwell's cavalry stopped below them. They heard the men complain about their fruitless search and grouse about the order that they camp out while they scoured the area. Content with the searching they had done that day; they decided to make camp under the spreading oak. They prepared their evening meal there and later unrolled their blankets for spending the night. The miserable night Will and the king spent in the tree did not end at dawn as one of the men stayed there while the others rode away in search of food. It was mid afternoon before the tree dwellers found it safe to descend from their leafy abode and go with the neighbor to his safe house.

Ten days of dodging and hiding passed before Charles was able to ride away in the guise of a tenant farmer's son accompanying the sister of a former royalist officer who had a pass to visit a friend near Bristol. From there he was able to gain the protection of Francis Wyndham, a former royalist officer, who found the ship on which he sailed to his exile in France.

The three hunted men agreed that it was best that they part company when it was decided that Charles would go to Bristol. Shaking Will's hand, the king thanked him for his faithful service; more faithful he said than that he had received from any other Scot. "You go with my thanks," he said. "Now you can return as you should to that girl you told me about. Marry her and enjoy your life."

Tom Penderell had no qualms about Wilmot's departure. "He is well able to care for himself. But you, my friend, face a serious problem. Cromwell's men are still watching every road for Scots who are trying to return to your country. You in particular have a problem because they have a price on your head. They know you escaped with the king and they have your description."

Will was deflated by this advice but knew it was sound. When he asked what he best should do, Tom advised: "Stay with us for a month or two. We can use your help with the harvest. After that I think we can find a place for you on a ship that is headed for Dublin. From there you can work your way north and find a ship to take you safely back to your land."

* * * * *

It was a bleak morning in early February when the Glasgow bound *Irish Belle* dropped Will Campbell off on the southern shore of Argyllshire. Will paid scant heed to the dusting of snow that whitened the landscape, nor to the pale yellow pumpkin of a sun that shown in the veiled southern sky. Once ashore, he took a deep bracing breath of the brisk Scottish air and let out a whoop of joy. He was home; home again in the land of the Campbells.

He was as happy as he had ever been and propelled by anticipation as he started his trudge inland. A half hour later as he emerged from some woods and looked for what he hoped would be a road, he was still undecided on where he should go first. Duty dictated that he go to Auchinbreck and perhaps from there to Inveraray. His heart, however, demanded that he go first to Meg's home in Glenlachen where he could assure her that he had not forgotten the tender moments he had spent with her last summer. On that last visit, he had pledged his troth and promised to return before the autumn leaves fell. Instead he had sent her a note of explanation when he went off with Charles on his march into England.

Some hours later, Hector MacLean saw him as he approached the family home. "Will, William Campbell," he shouted, "You've come back like Meg said you would. And we were believing you were dead."

Will grabbed his friend into a fond embrace. After a quick exchange of greetings, he asked: "And why might you think I was dead?"

"Because no one else has come back from that battle. All of our Scots boys were killed, put in prison, or sent off to the colonies where they will die from the fevers."

"Not me. I was lucky enough to escape with the king."

"With Charles?"

"Yes. He made his way to southern England and then on to France. I left him near Bristol, had to hide out for awhile, and then was able to come back by way of Ireland."

"Whatever happened son, you are a welcome traveler here. Come to the house. Our women will be overjoyed with your return."

There was great rejoicing at the MacLean household that evening as Meg and her parents demanded a detailed explanation of what had happened to him during the last eight months. As he told of his association with the king, of the fateful battle, and of their escape, he realized he had indeed had an eventful experience.

When he asked about events in Argyllshire, there were few surprises. The farmers of the area had suffered from a poor harvest; the marquis was known to be deeply in debt; General Monck had forced almost every lord in the land except Argyll to yield to his authority; and Argyll was being pressured even now to accept English domination.

Hector gave Will a few free minutes to be alone with Meg while he fed and milked his cows. But though she wanted his undivided attention for herself, she graciously shared his company with Jean, both of whom treated him like the prince of their dreams. Hector joined them for supper. After eating the two men talked well into the night about their country's future. Neither saw viable reasons for optimism.

When they turned to personal affairs, Will said: "I must go to Auchinbreck before I can make any plans. Sir Dugald and Lord Lorne have promised me a settlement in Kintyre. If they can still give it to me, I'll give them what help I can until things settle down. Once that happens, I want to take Meg as my wife and see if I can be a successful farmer and father."

Hector loaned him a horse the next morning for his ride to Auchinbreck. Sir Dugald met him there with outstretched arms. "When no word came of you, we feared we had lost you, Will. We did not give up hope though because word got to us that they had put a price on your head."

"A price on my head here?" Will replied. "Is it safe for me to be about?"

"That is a good question," his brother replied. "You are safe enough here. It is best though that you not go to Inveraray, at least not for a while. Some visitor from Edinburgh could recognize you and that could put us all in danger. I'll go there myself tomorrow to tell Lorne and the marquis of your return. I am sure they will have plans for you. Of course, they will want to keep you out of sight. But there is no chance they will lose you among the hundred or so other William Campbells we have in these parts."

Will contented himself with two days of leisure while Dugald was away. Dugald was back on the afternoon of the second day with Lord Lorne. Lorne was bubbling with curiosity. "I had to come," he claimed. "Not only did I want to see you, Will, I also want a first hand report on what happened at Worcester. With no survivors coming this way, the only reports we have are the exaggerated tales Cromwell's crowd has chosen to tell us."

Lorne and Dugald plied him with one question after another as he told them of Charles' ill-fated invasion, the defeat at Worcester, and his escape with the king. Lorne also had news for him. Cromwell had shown that he was very much the conqueror, not the friend, of Scotland.

"One would think," William ventured, "that he should be a friend of the Scots. After all, it was our army that helped him gain an upper hand in England and he is just as much opposed to Prelacy as our Covenanters are."

"Some people may see it that way" Lorne responded, "but the Lord Protector doesn't. Far from accepting Scotland as an equal partner, he intends to dominate us; and as for religious preferences, he detests Prelacy, but also our acceptance of the Covenant. He left General Monck in charge here when he followed you to Worcester. Since then Monck has forced the submission of every Scots nobleman of note except Argyll to English rule. Monck is gone now. He is off fighting a war in Holland. He left Major General Deane here to negotiate for Argyll's surrender."

The marquis had the option of defying Deane's army. He knew, however, that that decision would only lead to his ruin along with major sanctions against the Campbell clan. The best he could hope for was some form of compromise that would allow him to retain his honor.

"Once we see our way through this, we will need your help, Will. I cannot put you back in the cavalry. If someone reported your presence there, your life could become an item in the negotiations so let's keep you out of sight. You can really help us though if you have ideas on how we can save our honor and our skin while we cave in to General Deane's demands."

William thought for a few moments before answering: "One thing for certain, we do not have enough trained men or materiel to fight them off. Maybe we should follow the advice of one of the men who helped hide the king. He said when you cannot face an enemy down with strength it is best to drown them with kindness and cooperation."

When Will asked if this might be an appropriate time for him to claim and start working on his settlement, Lorne cautioned the need for delay. "Vesting you with an estate now would call undue attention to you. After things settle down, I will go with you to Kintyre and help you get settled.

After Lorne's departure, Will took Hector's horse back to Glenlachen and during the three months that followed tried to make himself useful both at Hector's farm and at Auchinbreck. A call for more exciting action came in July when Lorne requested a meeting with him at a cross roads some distance from Inveraray.

Lorne reported that Argyll and Deane had come to an agreement. The marquis had surrendered in the face of over-powering pressure. He agreed to accept English rule, recognized that Scotland was now a part of the Common-wealth, and promised he would take no action to resist its authority. In return for his cooperation, Argyll retained his titles, property and administrative position in western Scotland; and the Commonwealth government assumed responsibility for repayment of the huge loan he had advanced to the Scots government while Charles was king. Deane had also insisted on the posting of English garrisons at five sites within Argyll's domain.

"We want to ease the burden of this occupation on our people," Lorne explained. "That means no show of hostilities. As I see it, now is the time for your policy of kindness and cooperation. The marquis wants our people to comply without any public proclamations. Right now we need to get word out to our people who live around the five posts about how they should conduct themselves. I am putting you in charge. Take whatever help and supplies you need to get our people to stay in line."

Will picked five of his cavalry colleagues and by nightfall they were on their way to visit the five post sites. At each site, Will called the local cadet leaders together and explained that the English were coming and that it was important that they receive a cordial reception. "We do not expect you to like them, but it will be best for the clan if we give them no excuse to vent any anger on us. Our objective is to make them think we are cooperating with them while we at the same time are giving them good reasons to leave as soon as they can. Now this is what I want you to do."

Will went on to explain: "They will probably follow their usual policy of drawing as much as they can on local food supplies. When they ask for your meal and cattle, promise them your help but explain that our people are living on the verge of starvation. If you drive your cattle back into the hills, hide your cheese, and have little grain around except maybe some oatmeal, they will have good reason to believe you.

"When they march in, stay off the roads. Get your men up among the rocks that border every pass. Shout greetings to them and let them know you are there. That will have them wondering if this is a safe place to be. Then once they set up their camps have groups of men, women, and children crowd into their posts when they are least expected asking for food and drink."

The Highlanders accepted their instructions with en-thusiasm. At every pass the English cavalry and foot passed through, they were met with cheers and cordial greetings from men half hidden behind the rocky crags and boulders that lined the steep sides of the mountain walls. Requisition-ing officers found scant supplies of food at any of the posts; and far from being shunned, the garrisons at four of the posts were soon surrounded by crowds of cheerful hungry well wishers.

Deane's garrisons could not complain of ill treatment or of a less than cordial reception. The post commanders, however, had good reasons to question the wisdom of staying at their posts. The weakness of their position was demonstrated in mid August when a troop of horsemen came back from one of the posts through the wilds of Argyllshire by way of the narrow mountain pass at Glen

Crow. As they proceeded single file through the pass, they were chilled by the shouts of more than a hundred Highlanders Will had stationed along both sides of the narrow mountain pass. No reprisals were ordered when this event was reported at Deane's headquarters at Dunbarton. Official action was taken shortly later with orders to evacuate the posts at Lough, Kincairn, and Tarbert and to reduce the size of the other two garrisons.

Lorne was so pleased with the outcome of Will's 'kindness and cooperation' program that he sent instructions for Will to meet him at Wester Kames, one of Lorne's properties located south of Auchinbreck and near the Island of Bute. Will was impressed on his arrival with the natural beauty of the holding. The main house was much smaller than that at Auchinbreck, but it was of adequate size and of good stone construction while the surrounding fields and woods gave the holding a look of prosperous husbandry.

The two men spent the night at Wester Kames and rode on the next morning to the ferry that took them across Loch Fine to Kintyre. As they rode south along the peninsula, Lorne reminded Will that this was land the Campbells had taken from the Macdonalds only a few years earlier. "As you can see, it looks like good farming country; but it has suffered from neglect. Much of the land now covered with brush and woods can be cleared again to make good farms. Unfortunately, nearly all the buildings are in ruins and will have to be replaced."

They spent the night at a wayside tavern and rode on the next morning to an area where Lorne and his father had several tenants, good farmers brought in from Ayr, at work reclaiming neglected fields for productive use. As they approached the top of a hill, Lorne said: "Just beyond here you will see the property I have picked for you. It has a good house with suitable out buildings together with some excellent farm land you can let out to tenants who can handle most of your farming."

Will approached the promised area with joyful antici-pation, anticipation that turned to disappointment when he saw the house. What had been an attractive house only a day before was now a smoking ruin. The outbuildings had been set afire; trees in the young orchard had been chopped down; everything of value had seemingly been destroyed.

Lorne looked at the scene aghast. What could possibly have caused this scene of destruction? He and Will rode quickly to the house where Lorne leaped from his horse and had turned to speak to Will when Will saw the dark figure of a man charge them with a pike held like a lance. "This is for you Campbell," the attacker shouted as he bore down on Lorne's undefended backside. Will had no arms at hand but by experience in Lorne's cavalry used his horse as his tool of destruction. The attacker was knocked off his feet by the stallion's unexpected charge before he could strike his deadly blow. Will was on top of the sprawled form within seconds, disarmed him, and demanded an explanation.

Examination of the smoking ruins revealed the fact that the assailant had killed the tenant who occupied the house together with his wife and two children. At first the assailant refused to speak; but rough handling by tenants from the area evoked a confession that he was a Macdonald who had once lived in the area who had returned to wreck revenge on the Campbells who now held the property.

After they had turned the prisoner over to the local authorities, Lorne surveyed the damage with anger. "We took this land from the Macdonalds by fair means. It is evil of them to kill our tenants in return. I had planned to give this property to you Will. But it is not a fit gift now."

"It is a good property, my lord. With some sweat and muscle power I am sure I can clean it up and restore it to productivity."

"No, Will. It is not a fit gift, at least not for you. I will have my tenants restore it; but you deserve a better gift. You can have Wester Kames in its place. Would you accept that as a substitute?"

"Wester Kames! Meg will love it and so will I."

* * * * *

Will spent the last months of 1652 preparing for his move to Wester Kames. He was looking forward to his twenty-first birthday early in the new year while Meg would be seventeen a month or two later. By family agreement and with the approval of the minister of the Glenlochy kirk, they would be married in April. It was a happy time for Meg and him; they were in love and wanted to be together. But it was also a time for reevaluation.

Will's employment until now had been with Lorne's cavalry. Now he was planning to become a yeoman farmer. But what did he know about farming? He had no fear of work but knew that successful farming called for more than just muscles and sweat. It called for wise decisions at the right time. With careful study he could learn the knack of successful farming; but for now it would be best to lean on the advice of Hector and of his more experienced tenants.

Will and Meg were married as planned and soon after moved to Wester Kames where they spent their honeymoon planting their fields and caring for their young animals. Will was content with his peaceful life away from military camps and felt no desire to return to them. Thus it was with genuine regret that he heard in mid July that the Earl of Glencairn and the Earl of Belcarres had raised the royal banner at Kallin and issued a call for supporters of King Charles to flock to their side.

Glencairn's uprising caused a major riff in Argyll's household. The marquis refused to repudiate his agreement with General Deane. He had sworn he would not oppose the Commonwealth and fully intended to keep his pledge. More than that, he had good reasons to distrust Glencairn and the former Engagers who followed him. Lorne, in contrast, was quick to respond to the royal call and soon found himself operating in direct opposition to his father's orders. Sir Dugald was Lorne's principal supporter among the Campbells and assumed without asking that Will would lead Argyll's troop of horse north to join the royalist rebels.

Will was a reluctant participant as he led his horsemen north to Glencairn's Highland camp. The reception they received was far from cordial. Glencairn wanted their military strength but showed no willingness to trust Lorne. Lord Kenmore showed similar enmity while Macdonald of Glengarry, a long-time enemy of the Campbells, was so incensed when he first saw him that he drew his sword and started a fight that Will and the other bystanders had to stop.

Kenmore's sour regard for Lorne was intensified when the two officers were dispatched to Kintyre with a body of horse to cope with the defiance of a group of Argyll's tenants who opposed the rebellion. Lorne and Will negotiated with the tenants and arranged for their surrender with a promise of amnesty. Kenmore was outraged with their mild terms and denounced Lorne for the favoritism he showed his tenants.

Lorne and Will returned to the Highland camp but were soon disgusted by the treatment they received and the continued bickering. Belcarres insisted that men who would swear their support to the Covenant guide the revolt. Glencairn objected; the two leaders quarreled; and, overruled, Belcarres fled to the continent. When Lorne also decided to leave, a strong mounted force was sent to force his return; but Lorne escaped with most of his cavalry. His foot soldiers stayed for a while and then walked away, a few at a time, to return to their homes.

Glencairn's uprising continued into 1654 but collapsed when General Monck returned to Scotland and routed the insurgents. With the suppression of this uprising, peace was finally restored. The union with England that Cromwell forced on the nation was not popular. People disliked domination by a mostly English corps of officials. But despite this dislike, Scotland enjoyed a happier situation during the next few years than it had for a long time. Laws were administered with even-handed justice. Religious toleration prevailed with neither the exponents of the Covenant nor those of Episcopacy being allowed to dictate to others. Trade prospered and people enjoyed an economic prosperity, which was new to them.

Will left the cavalry to live at Wester Kames where he and Meg planned for a future of successful farming. Lorne was back at Inveraray. He and the marquis remained on bad terms with each other for several months but reconciled in 1655. From then on, they worked together to restore the clan's sorry financial status.

The period of comparative calm was suddenly disrupted when Oliver Cromwell, the Lord Protector of the Commonwealth, died in September 1658. Nineteen months of political intrigue followed during which General Monck and various others conspired to seize power. Monck finally gained an upper hand, switched sides, and brought Charles II back to the throne in May 1660.

When word of Charles' return reached Inveraray, Lorne was quickly dispatched to London to offer Charles the congratulations and loyalty of the Campbells. A report of Lorne's cordial reception led Argyll to believe that he too would be welcome at the royal court. Will offered to accompany the marquis on the trip but was put off with Argyll's observation: "I am sure Charles would be pleased to see you, Will, and that his pleasure could aid our cause. We have every reason though to expect friendly treatment from him. Besides with your wife six months pregnant, it is your real duty to remain here with her."

Argyll's reception when he presented himself at Whitehall in July was not at all what he expected. Lorne went before him to the king's chambers and asked that Argyll be allowed to enter and kiss Charles' hand. The request was denied. Argyll's appeal to Lord Clarendon, Charles' chief minister, was rejected; he was arrested and conveyed to the Tower where he remained imprisoned until December.

In December Argyll was taken under guard by ship to Edinburgh where he was charged with treason. Fourteen charges were made against him. In the long trial, which stretched from January until the end of May, Argyll successfully refuted every charge. At what should have been the end of the trial, he was acquitted on every count. But fair justice was not the objective of the royalist officials, several of them former Engagers and most of them long-time haters of the Campbells. They wanted Argyll's head by fair means or foul.

An answer to their intrigues came after Argyll was acquitted but before the verdict was read when some letters written by Argyll to Monck were delivered to the court. In them Argyll had assured Monck of his cooperation at the time Monck was putting down the Glencairn uprising. This evidence, supplied by Cromwell's general who was now one of the king's henchmen, was considered proof of treason against the king.

Charles had issued an instruction that the final decision in the trial be referred to him for review. Knowing this, Argyll felt confident that Lorne, who had remained in London could get the king to modify the court's decision if it went against him. When Will offered to go to the king, Argyll advised: "Stay close at hand here, Will. I expect to be freed; but if my enemies prevail, I will need to send you post haste to the king's side to ask for my life."

Glencairn and Middleton, the two Campbell-hating royalists who ran the trial, chose to ignore the king's instruction for his review of the verdict. When the sentence of death by execution was read on May 27, 1661, they denied Argyll's request for a ten-day respite that would permit his appeal of the verdict. The date of execution was set for two days later.

Argyll gave every outward appearance of being resigned to his fate and cheerful as he accepted the verdict. Far from the hopes of his detractors who had predicted that he would break down, he walked calmly from his prison to the site of the guillotine on the day of his execution. He addressed the crowd that had come to witness his death, avowed his acceptance of the Covenant, said his final prayers, and placed his head and neck below the unique contraption known as "the Maiden" which severed his head from his body.

* * * * *

Disheartened, wondering at the cruel twist of fate that had turned Charles against the man who had crowned him as king in Scotland and convinced that the marquis had died a martyr to the Covenanter cause, Will took Lady Campbell back to Inveraray and retired from there to Wester Kames.

All he wanted now was the opportunity to enjoy the peaceful life of a gentleman farmer. Meg was the light of his life. Their two tiny daughters, Jean and Margaret, were little angels who filled their hearts with joy. He wanted nothing more than the freedom and time to be with them.

Peace and contentment were possible in Argyllshire where life could go on with little regard to what was happening in the rest of Scotland. Throughout this other Scotland, Glencairn, Middleton and the other royalists who were running the king's government were seeking revenge for every slight the ultraroyalists had suffered during the years the Covenanters had been in control.

Backed with the support of their handpicked Parliament. they rescinded the legislation that had established the primacy of the Covenant and talked seriously of rescinding every law that had been enacted in Scotland since 1633. Royal authority reestablished Episcopacy. Bishops were appointed; Presbyterian ministers were ordered to secure Episcopalian reordination; Johnson and Guthrie, the two ministers who had led the criticism of Charles during his first years as king, were executed; regulations were enforced for prohibiting attendance at Presbyterian services and for not attending services sanctioned by the bishops. Fines were levied on former Covenanters; their estates in many instances were appropriated and turned over to royalists.

Lorne was a principal target for retribution. John Middleton, a former officer among the Engagers who had been wounded at Worcester and thereafter imprisoned by his English captors, had a deep-seated grudge against Argyll that was not satisfied by his engineering of the marquis' execution. He made no secret of his desire to have both his title and his estate. He was frustrated when Lorne succeeded his father as ninth Earl of Argyll and was instrumental in keeping him from becoming a marquis.

Middleton did Lorne a major disservice when he disallowed the claim for 400,000 marks the Argylls had been assigned against the estate of Lord Huntly. The assignment had been made by the government in lieu of repayment of a loan the marquis had made to the king's government at the time of Charles' coronation.

The loss of this claim left the new Earl of Argyll with insufficient assets to cover payment of his outstanding debts. He made the mistake of complaining of the treatment he had received in a letter to a friend. The letter was purloined at the post office by his enemies and quickly used as evidence that he was inciting civil opposition. Middleton demanded that he be tried for treason. Charles agreed with some reluctance to the insistence of the Scots royalists that

Lorne be arrested and tried but this time provided that any verdict of guilt must be submitted to him for royal review.

As was the case with Lorne's father, the trial was engineered to secure the verdict Middleton wanted. Meg was again pregnant, but this time Will was in close attendance on the head of his clan. As soon as the verdict was announced, he rode as swiftly as he could to London where he presented himself four days later at Charles' court.

The king was pleased to receive him and gave careful attention to Will's assessment of Middleton's tyrannical behavior. "Will," he said, "we would like to keep you at court. We have a real need for advice from men who can think of benefits to others than themselves. We would like to keep you here too because we have shared much in our past. We know though that you must hurry back to Edinburgh with a pardon for your lord. You will have the pardon and we will send a confirmation of it to the commissioners by separate carrier. One other detail, which we would not have you bandy about to others as yet, you can tell your lord that Scotland will not have to suffer from Middleton's scourge much longer."

Back in Edinbursgh, Will delivered the royal order that brought freedom for the Earl of Argyll. Together, they rode back to Inveraray where news awaited him that Meg had delivered a boy, a son she had chosen to name William Campbell. Will was elated with the news of the birth but not with that of the name. "Another William," he growled in half disgust, "and I wanted to call him Gillespic."

* * * * *

Campbells Came

Part Three

Gill

1679 - 96

"Be careful son. Come back whole." Those were the last words young William Campbell, known to his family and friends as Gill, heard as he and his best friend Roddy MacDowel left the Campbell courtyard at Wester Kames. Gill smiled as he thought of his mother's concern for him. He remembered that she had always watched over his health and safety much as a mother hen watching over her chicks.

This excursion was something Gill and Roddy had been planning for weeks. His mother had first vetoed the idea of two lads riding off in a search for unknown adventure. His father though had given support to their plan. "After all Meg," he had explained, "the boys are 16. They have been riding with older men for most of their lives. They are old enough to be mustered into service if we had a war."

Gill appreciated the faith his father had in him. They had been close for as long as long he could remember. His father had never told him much about his own youth, but Gill knew he had served in Argyll's cavalry when he was 16 and that he had been one of King Charles closest associates back when the king lived in Scotland. Now his father was offering him independence and he was eager to show that he deserved it.

The trip the boys had planned was not a long one. At most they should be home within three weeks. They planned to ride to Inveraray and then turn north into the real highlands along a mountainous route that would take them to Inverlochy and on to Lake Ness.

They would be traveling on horseback through a wild roadless land where there were only scattered trails. Yet they would be in Campbell country where they could count on the friendship of those they met and where one look at the blue and green plaid of the tartans they wore clasped at their shoulders would be enough to assure those they met of their good intentions. They had the means for shooting an occasional rabbit or bird and carried enough biscuit and meal in their saddlebags to keep them from going hungry. Their tartans could be spread to keep them snug and warm as they slept under the open skies.

Gill was in familiar country until he passed Inverary. From there on, they found themselves in a wild enchanted land. Steep rocky hillsides and snowcapped mountains reared up ahead and around them. Here and there they rode through glens that were lush with abundant grass. Patches of wild flowers graced their path. Many hillsides were covered with the fresh green growth of thickets and heather. Clusters of azaleas and rhododendron added color to the scene while the clear skies, towering forests, blue waters of occasional lakes and sparkling spray of cascading streams showed nature in its grandeur.

They rode long stretches along tortuous paths without seeing anyone. Here and there they saw ugly specimens of highland cattle, sheep and horses and also the rough stone and timbered hovels of fellow Campbells. More than once they were hailed by voices from among rocky crags bidding them good day or asking their business. More than once they also were happy to find people who could give them directions as to where they were going.

Their ride took them to Inverlochy where Gill stopped to see the place where his grandfather and two of his uncles had been killed. Roddy also was interested because it was the place where uncles on both his father's and his mother's side were buried. From there they rode on to Loch Ness where they looked for but saw no monster of the sea.

The most moving experience of their adventure came as they were riding homeward. At the village of Dorkleith they were invited to share a meal with a local family and asked if they planned to attend the outdoor preaching service that evening. Gill had heard of these conventiclers but had never been to one. He knew they were an outgrowth of the harsh religious reforms the king's government had adopted in its effort to close the Presbyterian kirks and force the people to accept Episcopacy. Conducting outdoor services was against the law; people caught attending them could be punished with imprisonment; and ministers who preached at them could be sent to the gallows.

The invitation to attend reminded Gill that he had grown up in a quiet tension-free community. Throughout most of Scotland, the king's commissioners, most of whom cared not a whit about religion, had seen enforcement of a return to Episcopacy as a convenient way to punish the Covenanters who supported the Kirk. With the enforced acceptance of Prelacy, ministers had to be confirmed and recertified by the newly appointed Episcopalian bishops. Many ministers gave up their callings rather than accept the new order; some shifted to holding services in private homes or outdoors, practices soon branded as illegal, while many areas were left with no practicing local clergy.

This had not been the case at Wester Kames. The old minister of the local kirk was a peace loving and kindly man. Lacking the inner fire that caused many ministers to defy the bishops and the government, he had found it more practicable to accept the order for re-certification and then had continued to preach and serve the needs of the community as he had when the Covenanters ruled.

Attendance at the outdoor service made a lasting impression on the two visitors. The minister, a Mr. Johnson, had been educated at the university in Edinburgh. He had a deep resonate speaking voice, a fiery manner, and a message to deliver. Neither of the two lads had ever heard the gospel preached in so memorable a manner.

In his long sermon, Johnson assured his listeners that their fate had already been scripted, that God knew before they were born whether they would be saved or damned, but that they could expect salvation and a place in the Kingdom of Heaven because they supported the Covenant and were Scots, the true children of God. To bolster their claim for salvation, they should obey the teachings of the Bible, show respect for their parents and clan leaders, and show quality in their actions by being frugal, industrious, and charitable to others.

The two boys decided to stay over another day when they learned that Johnson would preach again the next afternoon. The next morning they explored the area near the village and found a wooded cove they thought might make a good hiding place for outlaws. While eating an oat patty at noon, they speculated on what heaven must be like. At Rod's prodding, Gill decided that heaven must be like Scotland only a bit warmer. "It will have blue skies and mountains and streams and lakes like here. There will be more flat land for growing grains. We will have good horses, cattle, sheep, and pigs; and flowers will bloom and fruit will ripen all year long."

About 60 Highlanders from the surrounding area gathered an hour past noon for the service. Before it started, a local clan leader cautioned that a squad of the bishop's enforcers had been sighted a few miles away and that an alarm would be sounded if they approached the village so that the crowd would have time to scatter. The minister then began his sermon. This time he spoke of the folly of sin. He saw sin in many places but the sins dearest to his heart were those of a sexual nature. Fornication was evil; adultery and sodomy were abominations.

His voice was rising to a crescendo in his condemnation of these vices when the alarm was sounded. Everything came to a sudden stop as nearly everyone hastened to leave the scene. Gill and Rod were nonplused. So was the minister. No one had told them where they should go. With quick thinking, Gill grabbed Johnson's arm and told Rod to follow as they hastened to the secluded hiding place they had found that morning.

Within minutes they heard the clatter of horses as the enforcers galloped to the scene and a loosened a torrent of blasphemies as they expressed their anger at not finding the targets of their raid. As they talked after the enforcers left, Gill asked: "Are curses like theirs a greater sin than murder or the sins you preached about?"

"Taking the Lord's name in vain or having relations with someone other than your wife are most grievous sins," Johnson told them. "With murder, it depends. Killing another Campbell would be a serious sin while killing someone who steals your sheep or a person from another clan can be a lesser transgression."

As they retraced their steps on their return to Wester Kames, the boys talked of their ambitions for the future. Gill thought he would stay on at Wester Kames where he expected to inherit his father's estate. Rod had no such opportunities awaiting him. "Your da owns his land and it will someday be yours. But my da is only a tenant. He can be turned out and if he stays, the tenancy will go to my older brother. It isn't big enough to support two families so I will have to find something else to do. Tenancies are hard to find and I want to be more than a crofter or a grassman. Maybe I'll go to Glasgow and sign on as a seaman."

"What would you most like to do, Rod?"

"I'd like to get a farm somewhere. If I can get the money for passage, I think I'll go to the Carolinas or to New England. I hear there is good land there."

* * * * *

A month after Gill's return, his father received a message from Sir Duncan Campbell, Laird of the Auchinbreck cadet of the Campbell clan. Sir Duncan wanted them to meet with him at his new castle at Carnessary. "I have seen little of him since he became laird"; William told him, "and you have never met him, even though you are first cousins. When you were a wee lad, I used to ride quite often to the big house at Auchinbreck where I was born. But after your uncle Sir Dugald died, his son moved to Carnessary which is much farther from here."

"Why did he move? Didn't he like the old house?"

"There were several reasons son. Ten years ago there was a big fire at Auchinbreck. Sir Dugald, your uncle, who loved the house as much as anyone died while trying to put out the flames. He was not in good health and got so excited that he just dropped over dead. After he died his son Duncan had to choose between rebuilding there or moving to a new site. He had a good property at Carnessary on the sea in southern Lorne that his wife liked so they built the new castle there."

"Have you been there?"

"Only a couple of times. It is a larger place than what we had at Auchinbreck, more of a castle with landscaped grounds and several outbuildings. Duncan's wife was from Stirling and wanted a place for elegant entertaining such as they have at Stirling and Edinburgh.

Sir Duncan extended a hearty welcome to his uncle and cousin when they arrived at the castle. He was in his prime of life, a handsome man of 33 with a tall broad shouldered frame, a strong Roman nose, and a thatch of short blond hair. After expressing regret for not seeing them more often, he showed them his estate. Later as they supped on the oat bread, cheese, beef stew and ale that provided their evening meal, he explained that he wanted them to go with him on the morrow to the earl's castle at Inveraray.

"The earl will be back in Argyll for a week or two. You hold your tenure at Wester Kames directly from him, not from me. And since we are all involved it is important that we learn from him how the recent changes in government will affect us."

Two days later they were at the earl's castle. The earl grabbed William's arm and pulled him into an embrace. "Welcome, welcome, old friend," he chortled. "How is your life as a farmer? Happier and a lot less frustrating than mine has been I'll wager."

Later he explained: "For 20 years the king has picked one after another of the Engagers who murdered my father to govern us as his commissioners. Every one of them has made it a point to ram Prelacy down our throats, to persecute and suppress the followers of the Covenant, and to fill their moneybags at the expense of the Scots people. Holding the line against them has been like fighting off a pack of wolves. Much as I've wanted, I've never been able to take a firm stand for representative government nor for defending the Kirk because there was always a group of powerful lords there hoping I would stub my toe so they could take over all of Argyll.

"With the new order, I fear our situation will get worse, not better. I had a halfway friend in Lauderdale but with his forced resignation that is gone. The king has sent his brother James, the Duke of York, to be our new commissioner."

"What is he like?" William asked.

"The first thing you should know about him is that he is an avowed Catholic and he is Charles' heir apparent."

"How can he serve as head of the Church of England if he is a Catholic," Gill asked.

"That is a troublesome question that a lot of people including those in the Parliaments of both England and Scotland are asking."

"Doesn't King Charles have a son who can succeed him?"

"He has several sons, but they are all bastards he got off his various mistresses. Henry, the Duke of Monmouth is the oldest, the most able and most prominent. Some people think he could be a worthy king but others are dead set against him. He could have a chance if Charles and his cavaliers would support him. Unfortunately, he and the king are on the outs with each other.

"Monmouth was here last year and it was he who put down the Covenanter extremists at Bothwell Bridge. Back in London, he got himself involved with Lord Shaftesburgh and the English Whigs and was ordered into exile. The situation regarding the succession got tense last year when Charles got sick and it was feared he might die. James dashed back from his exile in France and Monmouth was ready to come from Holland. When the king recovered, James was there but Parliament did not want him in England, so Charles dumped him on us."

"Charles had a grudge against your father but had good reasons for favoring you, my lord. Can you count on James for any favor?" William asked.

Argyll shook his head. "Let me tell you about the meeting I had with the Duke when he came to Stirling and then you can decide for yourselves. He came to my lodgings where I entertained him as best I could. After he was there for a while, he said: 'I know of your service to my brother and welcome you to my favor. He then asked what he could do to show the faith he had in me. I thanked him and told him that his favor was all the recompense I sought. He then said 'My Lord, if you will do one thing you may be the greatest man in Scotland.' When I humbly asked what that was, he replied that all he wanted was that I 'exchange the worst of religions for the best; His request caught me off guard. I did not use diplomatic language in telling him what I thought and His Grace stamped out of my house in a huff."

* * * * *

When Scotland's new Parliament met at the end of July 1681, it was Argyll who carried the royal crown in the parade of dignitaries that marched from Holyrood House to the place of meeting. His selection for the honor was recognition of his prominence. But the weakness of his position with respect to the new government was soon exposed.

With its first act Parliament ratified all of Scotland's earlier laws that had been designed to protect the Protestant religion. Argyll proposed the addition of a clause, which would have indicated opposition to Popery. The proposal had the support of several lords and bishops but irritated the duke and was set aside as being implied and thus unnecessary.

Two legal actions were quickly taken to punish the earl. One of them sanctioned a monetary claim against his estate while the second challenged his hereditary right to serve as Sheriff and Justice General of Argylshire, the Isles, and some other areas. Both actions were designed to embarrass him and it was only after he presented his royal charters that his name was cleared.

Argyll faced a larger challenge in dealing with the Test Act, which was enacted to exclude all persons from civil and ecclesiastical offices who would not be subservient to royal will. The Act which was hastily drawn up and passed contained provisions that were both complex and in some cases self-contradictory. One provision required persons holding civil and ecclesiastical offices to swear that they "sincerely professed the true Protestant religion, contained in the Confession of Faith of King James VI and that they would adhere thereto, educate their children therein, and never consent to any alterations of the same." A second part of the Act called for "oaths to swear and affirm that the King's Majesty was the only supreme government over all persons in all cases, ecclesiastical and civil, that it was unlawful for subjects on any pretense whatever, to enter into covenants or leagues, or to assemble in council or convention to treat of any matter of Church or State, without his permission..."

The Test Act was hurriedly passed before most of its signers read it or realized what they had endorsed. While it seemed to endorse Presbyterianism, the provisions concerning the Confession of Faith involved contradictions. Sir John Dalrymple, President of the Court Session and one of the most notable legal authorities of the day, observed that the Act inferred "an obligation upon those who took it, to conform to any religion the King pleased, and yet adhere to the Presbyterian religion; to oppose Prelacy and yet to maintain the present constitution of the church, which was Prelacy; and to renounce and yet affirm the doctrine of non-resistance,"

One of the first questions referred to after the Act was passed concerned whether the Duke of York, a confirmed Catholic, should be required to sign. The Duke refused and his royalist followers supported his claim of special privilege. No other exemptions were to be allowed. Most of the lords signed without any troubling of their consciences, many with only a superficial understanding of what they were signing. Several Episcopalian bishops and ministers, however, showed reluctance to sign.

Much to the Duke's annoyance, Argyll argued that the law should apply to the royal family as well as to others. He had until the end of the year to decide whether he would sign and chose to delay his decision. Pressure was soon brought to bear on him to sign. On a trip to Inverary in October, he and Sir Duncan asked William to return to Edinburgh with them to be on hand if it appeared necessary to send him to King Charles with a request for intervention. Gill's mother was ill and William expressed his desire to stay with her but agreed to send Gill, who was now 18, to serve in his stead.

At Glasgow while in route to Edinburgh, Argyll received word that he had been arbitrarily dismissed from his position as Extraordinary Lord of the Court of Session, a position he had held since 1674. He received a hostile reception from the Duke when he protested his dismissal. A day later he was summoned to a meeting of the Council to sign the Test.

After first being assured by the Bishop of Edinburgh that he had the Duke's permission to sign the Test with a letter of explanation, Argyll went to the Council Chamber in early November, knelt down, and signed with the explanation: "I have considered the Test, and I am very desirous to give obedience as far as I can. I'm confident the Parliament never intended to impose contradictory oaths. Therefore I think no man can explain it but for himself.

Accordingly, I take it, as far as it is consistent with itself and the Protestant religion."

James seemed satisfied with the earl's action at the time; Argyll's enemies were not. The next day the Duke indicated dissatisfaction. A few days later the earl was required to sign the oath again this time as Commissioner of the Treasury. Before the Council, he again signed the oath and added the words "as before". His critics demanded a more detailed explanation, whereupon he read the reservation he had stated earlier. In the proceedings that followed he was dismissed from the Council and informed he could not serve as Commissioner of the Treasury.

Argyll was ordered not to leave town and a few days later on December 8 was sent to prison and orders were sent to the Lord Advocate to prosecute him for treason. The charge of treason rested on his act of "lease making" that is of making a statement that reflected on the integrity of Parliament.

Argyll's first choice of a lawyer to handle his defense declined because of fear that acceptance of the case would subject him to a similar charge of treason. Suitable counsel was found, however; and a strong defense, which included the earl's eloquent account of his long years of service to the crown, was presented at the trial.

The trial itself consisted of two parts, the first of which dealt with the relevance of the charge that Argyll had libeled Parliament and the second with the question of guilt. The first half was conducted before a panel composed of the Justice General and five judges. One of the judges was Lord Nairn, an old man who slept through part of the trial and retired to his bed before the judges conferred. Two of the judges found the charge relevant and two were for dismissal. The Justice General could have broken the tie but chose not to do so as he himself had signed the Test with an explanation. Lord Nairn was raised from his bed in the midst of the night, persuaded to hear a summary of the proceedings, which he had missed, during the reading of which he again dozed off, and finally voted that the charges were relevant.

The second portion of the trial was conducted the next day and ended with the jury's verdict that the earl had stated a reservation in signing the Test and accordingly was guilty of lease making. Conviction carried a penalty of death by execution. The earl was thereupon remanded to imprisonment at the Castle and a message was dispatched to the royal court at London seeking the King's approval.

Gill went with Sir Duncan to the Castle prison. He was ready to ride to London. Duncan objected: "I have already sent one of my own men," he said. "It is best that way. He has been over the route several times, knows the post stations, and knows whom to contact in London. It is better that you stay here in case the earl has need of you."

Then started the wait for an answer from London. Would Charles remember Argyll's past services to him and choose to void the sentence? Argyll was confident he would. But any of several mishaps could affect the final answer. Argyll's messenger could meet foul play or suffer from an accident; Charles could be away from London and unavailable; the earl's activities could be misconstrued as a personal affront to the king. Even under the best of conditions the rider would need three full days to get to London. Assuming a ride of three and a half days each way and a full day spent in London awaiting the king's decision, Charles' answer could not be reasonably expected to arrive before December 22.

As the days of waiting passed, Argyll remained calm and cheerful. He was confident that Charles would remember his years of faithful service. His supporters began to feel alarm, however, when James was reported as saying that he would wait until December 22 and then order the execution if no word came from the king. Argyll was still confident that he would be freed when the guard at the castle was doubled on December 20 and he was informed that he would be moved the next day to the common jail where felons were usually sent to await their execution.

Sir Duncan's rider rode into Edinburgh that evening. He was a full day ahead of the official who was bringing the king's decision to Duke James. The message he brought was far from what Argyll had expected. Charles had agreed to the death sentence with the proviso that execution was to be delayed during the king's pleasure. Until then, the earl had resisted every suggestion that he try to escape. Now with the knowledge that he would legally be no more than dead, that he would probably remain in prison, and that the king could have him executed at any time, he saw no reason for staying to face his judges.

Plans for his escape had already been made. Horses were to wait for him from dusk until ten o'clock at the Bristo Port city gate. From there he was to ride to Lauder where fresh horses would await him. His major problem called for getting past the guards and out of the castle. The plan decided upon called for Lady Sophia Lindsay, the daughter of his second wife, to come to his prison quarters that evening with a page in livery to carry her train.

As one of her stepfather's favorites, Lady Sophia was eager to play her role as a deliverer. Gill offered to go as her page but Duncan objected: "You would never get by, Gill. You are almost a head taller than the earl and even if you were to change clothes with him, none of the guards would be fooled. We will send Gilbert as the page. We can use you though as the lantern bearer who will light her way."

Lady Sophia went to Argyll's cell at the Castle after dusk with her two servants. Gilbert and the earl then exchanged clothes and the earl put on Gilbert's wig. When the guard came twenty minutes later to tell her that the time had come for her to leave, she burst into tears and cried out a tearful farewell. As she left the Castle, she stopped twice within sight of the guards to castigate her page for his awkwardness and for letting her gown touch the floor. The first sentry questioned them but was satisfied and let them pass. A second guard at the Castle entrance let them pass. Outside the great gate another guard grabbed Argyll's arm and looked at him as though he might recognize him. At this point, Gill asked what the page had done wrong. The inquisitive guard then dropped Argyll's arm and waved them on.

Once they were out of view of the guards, Gill took Argyll by several back streets to the Bistro Porto gate where they found the companion and horses that the earl then used to ride southward. Argyll did not change clothes until he was well out of Edinburgh. By riding all night, he established a good lead on possible pursuers and with the help of friends he was able to cross into Northumberland

and then go on to London where he stayed several weeks before going on to Holland.

* * * * *

Argyll's escape meant that his life was saved; but it was a harbinger of hard times for his family and clan. Lady Sophia was sent to prison for the role she had played. His title was vacated, his estates confiscated. The administration of most of his offices and properties was turned over to a long time adversary, the Marquis of Atholl.

Gill returned to Argyllshire with Sir Duncan where they had their hands full protecting their properties from Atholl's unsympathetic oversight. Their problem was aggravated by adverse weather conditions. A late spring in 1682 followed by weeks of dismal weather led to crop failures all over Scotland. Argyllshire was no exception. The oat crop barely yielded enough to justify its planting and with people everywhere depending on oatmeal as the principal item in their diets thousands of people faced hunger and starvation. Meg Campbell suffered from declining health throughout the year. Months of privation and malnutrition took their toll early the next year when she died from one of the fevers that infested the land.

Most of the Campbell clan suffered from hard times and discontent in 1683 and '84. With no single leader to protect them, the various lairds found it difficult to protect their cadets from the abuse and high-handed thievery of the rival Highlanders Atholl had set among them. Fortunately for William and Duncan, Atholl's cadre of leeches found life easier around Inverary where they enjoyed a safety in numbers not found in outlying areas. Even so, many Campbells found reasons to look with favor on possible migration to settlements in the new world.

Argyll suffered no loss of loyalty from his clan during his exile. It was known that he was in Holland and probably short of funds. Subscriptions were taken to send money to him. There also was common talk that he would lead an invasion and try to regain his place in Scotland. His enemies in the government were aware of this threat; a watch was placed on his friends; their mail was intercepted and read;

and people were subjected to public examinations when letters from Argyll were suspected of being written in code.

Few people in Argyll's old domain had specific knowledge of his plans or the success he was having in putting them into effect. All of Argyll was suddenly abuzz with rumors though when word reached them that Charles II had died on February 6, 1685. His brother James claimed the crown as his successor. James was widely distrusted because of his absolutist views and because he was an avowed Catholic. Now, if ever, was an appropriate time for his opponents to strike a blow for what they thought was right.

Argyll had indeed been planning an invasion of Scotland. He interpreted the widespread indignation expressed about his trial and conviction as a sign that the Scots would accept him as the leader of a new more representative government. He had discussed the prospect of an invasion with friends among the English Whigs and had provided them with a realistic estimate of the amount of financing and military support he would need for a successful invasion and then had foolishly given way when they pared his estimates down to unrealistic levels. With the news of Charles death, he joined in a hastily arranged alliance with Monmouth who wanted to return to England as king. Together they agreed that Monmouth would lead an invasion of southern England while Argyll led an invasion of Scotland.

The two invasions were ill fated from the start. Neither leader had adequate funding, men, or materiel. They shared a common objective, but their efforts were poorly coordinated. Argyll's progress in putting his expedition together was complicated by differences and backbiting between his officers and advisors. Still optimistic about his chances for success though, he sailed with three ships and 300 men from the Zuider Zee on April 28. Adverse winds and a need to wait for clearance of their sailing permits forced a delay when they reached the North Sea. The little fleet finally started its invasion voyage on May 2.

The ships enjoyed fast passage to Scotland and were within sight of the Firth of Moray on May 5. Rather than land, however, they sailed on to the Orkneys toward their planned destination in the Western Highlands. A dense fog in the Orkney passage caused them to send two men ashore to find a competent pilot who could guide them through the straits. The men unfortunately were captured and sent as prisoners to Edinburgh while an attempt by the crew to rescue them was rebuffed.

After some delay, the three ships sailed west and then south down the Minch inside the Outer Hebrides to Mull where they anchored on May 11. Mull was in Campbell country and was soon under the earl's control. From there Argyll's son Charles went on to Lorne on the west Scottish mainland to seize the castle at Dunstaffnage and dispatch letters to friends requesting a rallying of their forces to Argyll's cause.

* * * * *

The first definite news Gill had of the invasion came in early May when his father returned to Wester Kames after a business trip to Glasgow. Worried and obviously disturbed, William told his son that the picture was dark. He had to avoid guards patrolling the roads on his trip home. An alarm had been sounded that Argyll had left Holland with an invasion force. Atholl had doubled his number of guards at Inverary. More than that, the government had 60,000 troops - 20,000 in Northumberland, 20,000 at Stirling, and 20,000 at Glasgow - posed to stop the expected invasion. Watches also had been set on many of Argyll's friends.

"But can't he count on people rising to support him?"

"No, I am afraid he has miscalculated. Should he arrive here with 10,000 well-armed men, several thousand Scots would line up to support him. But after 20 years of being beaten down, most of them will sit it out. The royalists still want our blood. The Covenanters we have left appreciate his leadership but remember how he supported the crown and stood aside while they were being slaughtered at Bothwell Bridge. People dislike James but are not ready to accept Monmouth."

"What I don't understand is how the earl could have been a close friend of Charles and not get along with James."

"You know from what I have told you, son, that the earl and I were both members of the king's household when he was crowned as king at Scone 30 years ago. I was with him when he took his army to England and again when he escaped from Cromwell's army. We stood with him during the years of the Protector's rule and again after his restoration.

"I can see now though that our love and trust were misplaced. In his 20 years as king Charles never showed any regard or respect for his subjects in Scotland. Never once did he come here after his restoration. He turned our government over to one loyalist tyrant after another. He tried to dismantle the Covenant and force us to submit to Episcopalian rule of our religious life. His lieutenants taxed us, oppressed us and bullied us at every turn. Then he sent his brother, an avowed Catholic, to govern our Protestant land.

"I plainly see it now that Charles was out to punish us for pressuring him to accept the Covenant. He hated us for that, tried to force us to accept his views, and went on to impose trade and other restrictions on us that have kept us from enjoying a good life."

"What are you telling me, da? Must we join the earl in his revolt even though he has little chance of winning?"

"That is our problem. I have always supported the earl even when I questioned his policies. But I'm of the old school. I am a Campbell and give my full support to the head of our clan. Years ago, I would have insisted that you do likewise. We are freer now in our thinking. You should do what you think is best for you."

"Then I will stand with you in supporting our lord."

"Remember when you say that that Argyll is no Hannibal or Caesar. I think he has been misguided in his decision to join with Monmouth and that following him will probably bode no good for either of us."

"What would you have me do?"

"That depends on what happens. If Argyll can win or hold his own, we will survive. If his support falls apart, James will want his head, and probably mine. You will lose Wester Kames and be thrown out with nothing if you aren't killed.

"I am proud of you for supporting the earl, Gill, but I am only being realistic in telling you we must have a plan to fall back to if worst comes to worst. I've saved some money for emergencies. It isn't much, only 80 pounds, but it can make the difference between life and death if trouble strikes."

"Is it at Wester Kames?"

"No, that is one of the first places Atholl's brigands will pillage once they get the signal. The money is hidden in a safe spot near the castle at Ellan Gheirrig. I will show it to you tomorrow. If a time comes when you need it, take it with my blessing and get someone to ferry you over to Ireland or better still join a party that is migrating to North America."

"America, why there?"

"With money, you can buy land in America, clear your own farm, believe as you want, and make a good life for yourself without all the hatred and restraints we have here."

* * * * *

Argyll's call for volunteers had a disappointing response. Far from 5,000 or even 2,000 recruits, barely 200 new men came to join his tiny army. Hoping that more would follow, he established a headquarters at Sir Duncan's Carnessary castle, had his men chase Atholl's troops off Islay and had his ships sail to Campbelltown in Kintyre. From there, he sent out a declaration that listed governmental misdeeds and examples of tyranny during the past 25 years, which he had come to rectify. Again he was disappointed by the lack of public response. Some additional recruits joined his ranks, but not many. Promises of aid were given but not fulfilled. People listened but were reluctant to act. James was not a popular king, but neither was the prospect of Monmouth as his replacement. Moreover, with a royal army near at hand, most Scots found it prudent to stand by without taking sides.

Argyll landed his force near the southern tip of Kintyre and led them north to Tarbot. Progress was slowed at that point partly because he was inclined to wait for the Highlander support he hoped would soon come his way and by conflicting advice from his officers. Had he had the usual powers of a general, he could have acted decisively. He was hampered though by the insistence of his officers that every major decision be decided in council. Now when a definite strategy was needed, some wanted to march eastward while several others insisted that they should cross the Firth of Clyde to Ayr where they thought his army would be welcomed.

A small force of his Highlander supporters, commanded by Argyll's son Charles, tried to take Bute where they were met and repulsed by some of Atholl's troops. Stung by this defeat, Charles crossed from Bute with a force of 100 men with the intent of marching to Cowall. As his party reached the shore, another body of Atholl's men attacked it. In the brisk skirmish that followed, Argyll's men found themselves short of ammunition; Charles retired to the rear to get more supplies; his action was misinterpreted by some of his men who thought he was deserting them; and a disorganized rout followed.

As the men started to panic, William Campbell, who was riding with them, tried to stem the tide. About 30 men stayed with him to blunt Atholl's attack. But they too gave ground and fled when a well-placed musket shot crashed into William's brain. Leaving William and the other casualties behind, the survivors in Charles' troop escaped to Castle Ellan Gheirrig which, located on a small islet in Loch Ridden, is connected by a narrow shallow channel to the Kyles of Bute.

Gill did not hear of his father's death until two days later. By then he had been dispatched with a dragoon of horse under Colonel Rumbold and 300 foot under Major Henderson to take Castle Ardkinglass. Their small force faced 5,000 men commanded by the Marquis of Atholl. Atholl did not choose to give battle and after some maneuvering the invaders returned to Ellan Gheirrig. Meanwhile, Argyll sent part of his army across the Firth of Clyde to assault Largs and Greenoch in Ayr. A temporary success was realized at Greenoch but the landing at Largs met armed resistance that forced the army to withdraw.

Argyll had ammunition and supplies stored at Ellan Gheirrig. It seemed to be a safe and easily defendable site because it was located beyond the firepower of the English warships, which were now filling the Firth of Clyde. It was not long, however, before it became obvious that the castle was vulnerable and that the main body of the army would have to move. Morale was low and more and more desertions were reported every day. By June 11, the day the army moved inland only 500 Highlanders and 700 Lowlanders remained of the possible 2,500 to 3,000 who had once been in the invading army.

Argyll led his men to the head of Loch Striven and then to Loch Long. While there, they were joined by the remnant of their force that had been left to garrison Ellan Gheirrig. They had deserted the castle when an English warship edged its way up the shallow channel from the Kyles of Bute to a point within firing range of the castle. Orders had been issued to blow up the cache of arms, powder, and food stored at the castle if the castle was abandoned. This plan was foiled, however, when deserters extinguished the burning fuses and surrendered the castle to the attacking English marines.

Argyll led what was left of his army from Loch Long to the head of Garloch with the intention of marching the 12 miles from there to Glasgow where he could find food for his hungry men along with possible support. Progress again was delayed by bickering between his officers. The army finally camped along the shores of Garloch and spent the night of June 16 three miles above Dunbarton.

The next day they marched to Kilmaronock where they found food and rested. They then followed the high road that led from Dunbarton to Stirling. Along the route, they met a detachment of soldiers. Both armies stopped; neither was inclined to fight; and both bedded down for the night. Meanwhile, desertions brought the size of Argyll's army down to 900 men. Argyll talked bravely of battle and possible success but seemed far from convinced.

The remnants of his army spent the night near Dunreath Castle. Fears were expressed of a dangerous night attack and it was decided that the army should leave fires burning while it stole away during the night to Glasgow. The army marched away in good order but found the next morning that their guides were taking them away from rather than to the city. When this mistake was discovered, the remaining force panicked. Soon only 500 were left.

Argyll called for a meeting with his son John, Sir John Cockran who was one of his chief advisors, Sir Duncan Campbell, and Gill at a farm house at Kilkpatrick ten miles south of Glasgow. On Sir John's advice it was decided that Argyll should take his Highlanders and ride to the Highlands where he could hide and maybe recruit another army. The officers rode on toward Glasgow and split up an hour later. Duncan and Gill turned north with the intent of going to the Highlands while Argyll and his son turned south rather than north.

Argyll found a peasant with whom he changed clothes in the hope that he might avoid detection. Unfortunately for him, he was apprehended and recognized by two militiamen who turned him over to the local authorities who in turn took him to Edinburgh on June 20. His capture was reported to James II who quickly dispatched an order from London that he be executed within three days. No trial for treason was needed as his execution could be based on the verdict that had been passed on him four years earlier.

* * * * *

Argyll's capture brought an early ending to the insurrection in Scotland. Sir Duncan and Gill considered the prospect of trying to recruit a following in the Highlands to continue the struggle but soon dismissed the idea as having little prospect of success. The trusted friend they met near Inverary told them that the Earl of Atholl, the Duke of Gordon, and the Earl of Breadelbane had seized Argyll's castle at Inverary and had already sent armed bands out to exert vengeance on the entire Campbell clan. Regardless of actions taken by the national government in Edinburgh, their orders called for pillaging Campbell properties, killing the men who had supported the earl's invasion, imprisoning and moving their families, burning their buildings, and confiscating their properties.

The two men went into hiding only to learn on the third day that Atholl's men had stormed and gutted Duncan's castle at Carnessary. That same day they saw a posted public notice that listed the names of 30 Campbell leaders who had prices on their heads. Sir Duncan's name headed the list, followed by those of the two William Campbells. With this information, Duncan and Gill knew they had little chance of surviving if they stayed in Argyllshire. Guards had been posted at all of the western ports to seize refugees who might try to escape by sea. Their best chance for escape called for a bold ride to Edinburgh and embarking from there on a ship to Holland or some other country.

Taking the little money Duncan could raise, they rode to Edinburgh a week after the earl's execution. All went well until they reached the city gates where one of the gatekeepers recognized Duncan. While he was calling for guards to arrest them, a sympathizer whispered that they should follow him. Together they left on a fast trot from the gatehouse, dodged out of sight behind several buildings, followed a twisted path along back lanes, and soon were issued into the courtyard of a Covenanter safe house. The proprietor readily agreed with Duncan's view that his earlier plan for escape by sea must now be abandoned.

"They will have guards checking every boat," he said, "and by tomorrow, they will be watching for you on the Berwick road. If you feel up to it your best chance for escape is to take two of our horses now and head south to McCoy's place. He can give you fresh horses and show you where you might best cross the border into Northumberland."

Fifteen minutes later, Duncan was leading Gill out of Edinburgh. To strangers, they looked like two farmers going home from a day at the market. Once the burgh's last cluster of houses was behind them, Gill expressed relief. Duncan, however, urged continued vigilance and caution. "We are probably safe if we keep moving; and you cousin are in luck because I have been over this trail before and know where we are going. Fortunately for us, our friends made careful plans several months ago that people like us could use if we had to get out of Scotland in a hurry."

* * * * *

Three days later Gill and Duncan knocked at the door and were issued into the house of Hugh Oakham, a prosperous householder in Newburn. Oakham was an English Presbyterian and a Whig, both callings of which gave him logical reasons to dislike and be critical of King James. But he was a pragmatist guided more by sound thinking than by emotions or speculation. Once he heard Duncan's account of Argyll's defeat and of their hurried flight from Scotland, he said: "You are welcome here and can stay until it is safe to go on. That may not be for some days yet."

Gill started to protest but stopped when Oakham added: "As you probably know, Monmouth landed an invasion force on our channel coast two weeks ago. James has sent an army to deal with him. Until we hear something of the outcome, it will be best that you stay out of sight. Don't count on much from Monmouth. As I see it, the odds are stacked against him. James has had plenty of time to prepare for him; and while the duke hoped otherwise, there just isn't any ground swell of support here to make him king."

Gill and Duncan were happy enough to remain in hiding and make themselves useful with work on Oakham's estate. Ten days later, Oakham came back from the village with news that Monmouth's army had been defeated and that he and his chief supporters had been charged with treason. Closer to home, he had learned that James' supporters in Scotland were having second thoughts about their rush to justice in pushing for Argyll's early execution. They now wished they had delayed his execution long enough to allow them to use torture to extort a confession from him that could implicate his friends. More than that, basing his execution on the 1682 verdict meant that his estates would not be attained to the crown.

"After all that the earl did for Charles, I was hoping that James might forgive him," Gill said.

"Your hopes had little basis. Charles claimed that the marquis and the Covenanters used him. The truth is, he used them. Instead of thanking them for keeping his claim to the throne alive after his father's death, he agreed to Argyll's execution and tried to force the Scots to accept Episcopacy.

The only difference with James is that he has a long run goal of making us all Catholics."

In their conversations with Oakham, the old gentleman displayed considerable knowledge of the king's character and shortcomings. "James is haughty, arrogant, and is stubborn in holding to his beliefs," he told them. "One of his worst features is that he refuses to listen to advice and firmly believes he is God's anointed who can do no wrong. He has no use for our form of government and sincerely believes it is Parliament's solemn duty to approve his every whim."

"What kind of a man is he?" Gill asked.

"From what I have been told, he is greatly devoted to his Catholic beliefs, attends mass almost every day, but at the same time lives a life of debauchery. His closest advisors are priests and yet he has had more mistresses than Charles had. People say he has the pox and that next to his priests his closest associates are prostitutes. We could live with that though if he were a popular king who had our interests at heart."

"We all know he is a Catholic; but how can he favor them when it is against the law for Catholics to hold public offices?" Duncan asked.

"He simply ignores the law by giving his choices exemptions from the religious requirements of the Test Act. Half the members of his Privy Council are Catholics and he has started a drive to replace officers in the army and navy with Catholics. The bishops of the Church are unhappy with what he is doing. Thus far though, they have done little to oppose his plan to get Parliament to repeal the Test Act and the Habeas Corpus Act.

"If he gets Parliament to repeal the Test Act, won't that help our Covenanters?"

"Don't count on it. He wants to open offices in the government and in the army and navy for his fellow Catholics. He has no intention of doing that for Presbyterians. As far as he is concerned, we are heretics and it is only through his goodness of heart that he does not burn us the stake."

A few days into August, Oakham returned from Newburn with the news that Monmouth had been executed and that upward of 500 of his officers and associates had been hanged. "It is a pity," he opined, "but not unexpected. I can see now that we will have to put up with James for awhile. You can mark my word though, he will overstep the patience of his subjects one of these days and we will overthrow him one way or another.

"This action narrows your options," he continued. "Neither of you can expect to live safely either here or in Scotland. You might have a chance in Ireland or you can head for Holland. France is out of the question. It is no place for Protestants."

In the days that followed, Duncan chose to go to Holland where he had friends at the court of William of Orange. Gill wondered if he might not be better off in Northern Ireland where he could lose himself among the Scottish settlers. Duncan remembered that his father had told him of a former officer now living in Ulster who had been a fellow officer in the Campbell corps that Duncan's father had commanded back in the 1640s. As Duncan remembered, the former officer lived on an estate that had been confiscated from Irish rebels.

Armed with a letter of introduction from Duncan, Gill prepared to leave for Liverpool the next morning. At their last meal together, Oakham bid him Godspeed and added: "There is something I have wanted to ask you. I know your given name is William. Here in England we would call you Will or Bill but your friends call you Gill. Is that a shortening of Guillaume, the French equivalent of William?"

"One might think that sir, but that is not the case with me. No one in my family spoke French. When I was born, my father wanted to call me Gillispic, which is one of our old family names. He was away at the time of my birth and got home to find that I had already been christened as William. He argued that one William in our family was enough and started calling me his little Gillispic. That was shortened to Gill and I've been just plain Gill ever since."

* * * * *

Gill picked a large red apple from a fruit laden tree, polished it with his hands, and then sat on a log as he sunk his teeth into the apple and savored its crunchy goodness. As he looked out at the distant hills and the harvested fields near the orchard, he realized he was happy, happier than he had been since those days when he lived with his parents at Wester Kames. That was only a few years back, but it seemed long ago.

It was more than two years now since he had fled from certain death in Scotland. He had ridden with his cousin Duncan to Northumberland and then made his way to Liverpool where he took passage to Belfast and came north to Malcolm McBane's farm near Coleraine. McBane was an old man, crippled by a recently broken leg and wrinkled with age. These frailties notwithstanding, he had greeted Gill with cheer once he discovered who he was.

McBane eagerly recounted memories of the year he had served as a young captain in the Campbell corps commanded by Gill's grandfather Sir Duncan Campbell and of the months he had served after Sir Duncan's death with Gill's uncle Sir Dugald. He wanted to hear what had happened to Sir Dugald's family. It was not until after he had talked of these matters and had insisted that Gill share supper with him that he asked about Gill's plans for the future. When Gill indicated that he was seeking employment, McBane inquired about his experience as a farmer. When he learned that Gill had worked with his father in farming the Wester Kames estate, he said: "You have no need to tell me more. Since my accident I've been pretty much put on a shelf. I need a steward who can supervise my tenants and manage my day workers. The job is yours if you think you can handle it."

In the months that followed Gill had employed his youthful vigor and imagination to show that he could manage McBane's estate to their mutual advantage. More than once he had felt a painful yearning to go back to Argyllshire; but recognition of his status always left him convinced that it was best that he stay in Ulster. Further evidence was provided by snatches of information McBane received of conditions in Scotland.

From these reports he learned that Argyll's two younger sons, Charles and John, had been imprisoned and then banished while Archibald, the eldest son who had not participated in the uprising and who had even offered to fight against his father, was free and now pressing the crown for restitution of the Argyll estates and titles. A few of Argyll's associates had been arrested, tried and executed at Edinburgh. The most hurtful vengeance against the clan had come in Argyllshire where 23 of the Campbell leaders whose names had appeared on the wanted list had been captured and then hanged. Many others, both men and women had been slaughtered, imprisoned, and in several cases shipped to the West Indies to serve as slave laborers. Soldiers also had been allowed to seize women and girls and take them to their homes where they were expected to live as hostage servants and wenches.

Gill enjoyed his work with McBane. Reluctant to flaunt his status as a refugee, he stayed close to McBane's estate during the first year after becoming its steward. Desire for companionship with more people of his own age led him to explore a larger community and seek a wider group of friendships during his second year. It was then that he met Jamie McLean. Jamie was a young man of about his age. He had been born on the Isle of Islay and lived there until his father moved to Ulster where he now operated a farm three miles away from that of Malcolm McBane.

Gill and Jamie took an early liking to each other. They were of similar build, both better educated than most of the young adults around them, and both pleased to learn that they shared similar interests. Gill felt himself pulled as by a magnet to Jamie's charming company. The two young men soon were riding together to explore the countryside, to hunt in the nearby woods, fish in its streams, and swim in the River Bally.

As Gill finished eating his apple, he smiled as he remembered his latest promise to Jamie. Jamie had told him that the kirk in his village had a new minister, a "preacher who belts out a real message". Gill had never been to Jamie's home, or to his kirk, but he would tomorrow.

The church service the next day was all Gill had expected. After the service, he found Jamie standing with his father, Sam McLean. When Jamie introduced them, the elder McLean took a stern look at him and then said with a twinkle in his eye: "So you are the Campbell my son keeps talking about. Considering what you Campbells did to the McLeans on Mull, I should be organizing a party to run you off this island. As a Campbell, I suspect you are here to grab my land and steal my daughters."

"My mother was a McLean, sir," Gill answered, "That should make me a safe Campbell. I can assure you that I am not after your land. As far as your daughters are concerned, I can tell you better after I get to meet them."

Sam laughed, reached out to pump Gill's hand and said: "Come home with us then, my whole family is waiting to meet you."

Gill was greeted at the McLean home by Jamie's mother, his two sisters, Mary and Margaret who were 17 and 16, and by a younger brother Charles who was 14, and was soon treated as a member of the family. After a pleasant afternoon of visiting and eating, Gill left for his ride back to McBane's with a satisfied feeling that this was one of the happiest days of his life.

Gill's trips to the McLean cottage did not stop with his first visit. Ten days later he casually stopped by to exchange greetings. The visits then became more frequent; sometimes to talk to Jamie, sometimes just to exchange pleasantries with the womenfolk. By the time his horse had memorized the route to and from the McLean's, Jamie and the others in his family sensed that it was the two sisters who were the real attraction that kept drawing him back to their abode.

The unanswered question was which of the two girls was the honeypot that attracted this young gallant. Gill did not raise the question with himself at first. If he had he would have confessed that he had not decided. He liked them both; and having enjoyed little companionship with the fair sex during his teen and early manhood years, he was now enjoying the attention of two lovelies too much to care about making a choice.

For several weeks Gill enjoyed the company of both sisters as he met them at the kirk, visited with them at their father's farm, and joined in the revels of local social gatherings. His first push toward choosing one over the other came one afternoon in August 1688 when he was riding toward their house and saw them coming toward him in an open carriage. For some reason the carriage horse spooked and started to gallop away paying no heed to the commands of the girl who was holding the reins. Gill spurred his horse forward with the intent of catching and stopping the runaway horse. Before he got within shouting range of the gyrating carriage, the horse changed directions, one wheel of the carriage dropped into a deep furrow, the carriage overturned, and the horse fell entangled in its harness.

Gill reached the scene just in time to pull the two sisters away from the overturned carriage. Both were bruised and badly shaken from the ride and their fall, but both were still very much alive. Margaret got to her feet and started to survey the damage to the carriage. Mary was not so lucky. As she tried to stand she felt a double pang of pain and fell back to the ground. One of her ankles was twisted. Worse still, the ulna in her night forearm was broken. She tried to remain calm but the throbbing pain she felt soon had her fighting to keep from screaming.

Gill saw she was in pain and quickly moved to help her. Once she told him of where she hurt, he carefully raised her to sitting position and told Margaret to comfort her while he unhitched the horse from its tangle of twisted harness, tipped the carriage back onto its wheels, and rehitched the horse. After checking to make certain that the carriage was in working order, he lifted Mary back into the carriage. For the first time he could remember, he was holding a girl in his arms and she was clinging to him. He enjoyed the sensation and might have prolonged it had it not seemed more important that he get her to someone who could care for her injuries.

Margaret rode his horse and he drove the carriage with a protective arm around Mary as they made their way to the cottage of a part-time surgeon who set her arm and bandaged both the broken arm and the twisted ankle. Back with the two girls at the McLean cottage, Gill carried Mary into the house and laid her on her cot. As he was about to leave, she thanked him and raising herself from the cot, put her arms around his neck and kissed him.

Gill was startled by this display of affection. Maybe it was only a way of expressing her gratitude, but he interpreted it as a forerunner of something deeper, as an invitation to love. Flustered and somewhat embarrassed, he excused himself after entrusting her to her mother and Margaret's care only to ask himself as he rode to McBane's place why had he left so soon.

The next afternoon found him back at the McLean house inquiring about her recovery. Busy as he was with his farm work, he rode to her side almost every day in the weeks that followed as she recovered from her injuries. He, the McLeans, and most of their neighbors knew that his concern involved more than her recovery. He was in love and wanted the whole world to know it.

Mary enjoyed the attention he gave her and was quick to assure Margaret and their mother that Gill was the one man for her. Left alone with her, Gill found unexpected pleasure in holding her hands and caressing her checks. He enjoyed running his fingers through her long black hair with its tinge of auburn that made it shine like dark mahogany. Much of their conversation consisted of sweet nothings; but though neither was quick to say it, there was an unspoken agreement from early on that they soon would wed.

* * * * *

When Gill told McBane in early October of his plan to marry, the old gentleman snorted his approval: "It is about time. I'm not complaining because you have been giving me good service and you haven't been slacking off any. But you have been wasting a lot of good time riding back and forth to see your lass. I say it is time to bed her down, bring her here to share your quarters so you won't spend so much time on the road."

A wedding date was set for mid-November; the bans were posted at the kirk; Mary's family gave their full-hearted consent: and plans were made for the happy day. Two weeks before the wedding, Gill was reminded while visiting with Sam and Jamie at McBane's house that the future may not be as rosy as he had hoped. The dark cloud McBane saw coming was not of his or Mary's making. Ireland was in turmoil to the south of them and the trouble was coming their way. While Gill had been courting his bride-to-be, he had completely ignored the changing political climate around him.

In far off London, King James had encountered increasing opposition to his tyrannical rule. He was still packing the army and navy with Catholic officers, listening mostly to the advice of Catholic counselors, and rationalizing his every move. His plan to make England a Catholic nation was encountering stiff resistance but the similar plan he had for Ireland was falling into place.

Prior to 1686 England's policy for Ireland called for stationing a Protestant army on the island and filling all public offices with Protestants. This policy was undermined when Richard Talbot, an Irish Catholic, wormed his way into James' confidence, was named Earl of Tyrconnell in 1685 and was sent to Ireland the next year with authority to administer Ireland's military affairs. Tyrconnell embarked on a program for converting Ireland's 7,000-man army into a Catholic striking force. Protestant officers, many of them veterans of years of service and most of whom had purchased their commissions, were replaced by Catholics and frequently discharged without their back pay and also without their uniforms, arms, or horses. Catholics replaced more than 6,000 soldiers.

By 1687 the army was reconstituted. Money, however, was in short supply; and with insufficient funds to pay officers and men, the army became the oppressor rather than the defender of property rights as soldiers were allowed, even encouraged, to compensate themselves by looting the homes and properties of Protestants.

With reform of the army underway, Tyrconnell muscled in on the administrative domain of James' brother-in-law, the Earl of Clarendon, who was Lord Lieutenant for Ireland. He engineered the king's recalling of Clarendon and his replacement of him as Lord Deputy in 1687. With his added power he set about replacing almost all of the country's civil officials with Catholics. Catholics were put in charge of the courts and law enforcement. A strenuous effort also was made to revise the corporations that governed the establishment of the leading towns. Londonderry, for example, which had had an all-Protestant government and legal restrictions against Catholics living in the town, was ordered to accept a new charter, which reserved 45 of its 65 civil offices for Catholics.

The reaction to these changes in policy shook the foundations of Ireland's economy. The native Irish Catholics, who represented 80 percent of the population but who owned only a fifth of the property, were exuberant. In their eyes, justice at last was at hand. The English intruders and members of the Anglican-associated Church of Ireland and other Protestants could be thrown out.

For the Protestants, the new order invited panic. Hundreds of long time residents decided they could best move to England or Scotland. Most left their properties with only those goods they could carry with them. Seeing what was happening around them, many torched their crops and buildings rather than abandon them to Irish marauders. With opportunities for sailing away definitely limited, thousands fled northward with what property they could carry in the hope that they might find peace and protection in Ulster where most of the residents were Scots or English settlers.

"Why don't they organize themselves and fight back?" Gill asked.

"They are scared and well they might be." McBane replied. "Tyrconnell started by taking our arms from us. Then he deprived us of the protection we have come to expect from the army and the police and now we are facing another massacre of Protestants like that our people suffered in 1641."

"I'm not going to just wait for them to murder us," Gill said. "We still have some weapons. We can get organized and fight to keep what we have."

"You are right," McBane answered. "The folks here can do more than those at Cork or Dublin could. We still have Protestant control of Derry. But if we are to fight with any success, we will need leaders who can inspire confidence in our men and we will need soldiers who know how to fight."

"We can find the men," Jamie joined in. "You are an old army officer. Can you teach us to fight?"

"I'm too old to do much fighting, but with Gill's help I will do what I can." the old man replied.

Mary McLean and Captain William Campbell were married as they had planned on November 15. The ceremony at the kirk was followed by a military reception attended by all 80 of the young men who had volunteered to fight for the Protestant cause. Throughout the month before the wedding McBane had drilled the men as intensively as he could considering the fact that most of them were also working on their farms and had some distance to ride for their training sessions. He taught them the rudiments of fighting both on horseback and as foot soldiers. He insisted on tight discipline and subjected them to hours of drilling. He also told them to elect their officers. From the beginning, the men had looked to Gill as their leader and when the time for voting came he was their unanimous choice for captain. Jamie and four others were chosen to serve as first lieutenants.

News that William of Orange had landed an invasion force in southern England and that James had shown little ability to repulse him cheered the wedding guests. Their high hopes were dampened though by the report that Richard Hamilton, the Scot who had been sent to Ireland to persuade Tyrconnell to shift his allegiance to William, had joined forces instead with Tryconnell in a plan to rid Ireland of Protestant influence. Further bad tidings came with the news that Tryconnell had ordered Lord Mountjoy, commander of the Protestant regiment still quartered at Londonderry to march his force to Dublin from whence they would sail to England. The Earl of Antrim had orders to recruit a Catholic army to take their place at Londonderry.

Gill's honeymoon was cut short as the Protestants in northern Ulster reacted to the order for the Catholic vesture of Londonderry. A group of young apprentices in Derry closed the town's gates and refused entrance to the vanguard of Antrim's army when it reached the town and demanded admission. Concerns about the probability of an armed attack rose when McBane and several other landowners received letters that warned that an unspecified Irish group was planning a countrywide massacre of English and Scottish Protestants on the night of December 8.

The massacre did not occur but the threat alerted Protestant residents to an imminent possibility that a massacre like that had taken place 47 years earlier could be repeated. Panic spread as refugees from southern Ireland fled into Ulster. Seeing trouble ahead, town officials at Londonderry scrambled to lay in supplies of food, arms, and gunpowder. Hundreds of people who had lived in more rural areas moved to Londonderry.

Gill and Mary stayed on at the McBane farm. They were happy together and confident that McBane's troop could join with other bodies of troops that had been recruited in the Coleraine area to forestall an Irish takeover. Their spirits were buoyed in late December when they heard that James had fled to France and that William and Mary now ruled in England. They knew a message had been sent to England asking for military aid and also that Tryconnell in Dublin had sent Mountjoy back to Londonderry to seek an agreement with the town's officials.

Mountjoy's troop was not allowed to reenter Londonderry. He met with the local officials, however, and agreed to terms that would allow the town to organize its own defenses, provide pardons for its leaders for their earlier defiance, and allow the town's citizens to keep their arms. Mountjoy left his lieutenant, Colonel Robert Lundy, to serve as mayor of the town while he returned to Dublin where Tryconnell promptly sent him as an emissary to France with an associate who carried a letter that asked King Louis to confine him in the Bastille.

Tyrconnell used Mountjoy's articles as a play for time, time to train and reposition his army of close to 50,000 men which he hoped would soon end the opposition to his rule in Ulster. This army was already pressing north with hundreds of Protestant refugees fleeing ahead of it. Northern Ulster, however, was still free from attack during January and February 1689. The most distressing news of the moment concerned Governor Lundy's lack of leadership, his refusal to take advice, his pessimistic conviction that all would soon be lost, and his open encouragement that people flee from Londonderry.

Meanwhile James II was in France organizing an invasion force to occupy Ireland. He landed at Kinsale in southern Ireland with a contingent of French officers and materiel on March 12. His party then proceeded to Dublin where he received a royal welcome. All Ireland was soon aware that his first order of business was to subdue Ulster so that he could go in triumph to Scotland from which place he planned to invade England and reestablish himself on the throne. Hamilton, his commanding general, advanced with James' army on Coleraine on March 27. Thanks to the preparations Gill and his colleagues had made, the advance guard of Hamilton's army met determined opposition and was driven back in confusion. In this first encounter with the Irish army, the Ulstermen showed they could defeat their enemy.

Fear of an impending attack by a larger force that might cut his communications with Londonderry caused the governor of Coleraine to split his defensive army into two forces. One was sent to defend and hold Moneymore which was located several miles to the south while the other was sent to Magherafelt. Gill led the force sent to Moneymore, found that his small force was too badly outnumbered to conduct a successful defense, and led his men in an orderly retreat across the Sperrin mountains to Londonderry.

With its defenders gone and the Irish army again moving north, Coleraine was abandoned on April 8. McBane could have fled with the McLeans to Londonderry. Instead, he found passage for him and his wife on a small ship headed for Kintyre in Scotland. "I'm too old to fight", he told Sam McLean, "and it's not safe for us here. This farm was taken from an Irish owner and he'll want it back with my blood when he really should be paying me for making a productive farm out of the patch of weeds he left behind."

* * * * *

Gill reached Londonderry with his body of horses on April 10. On this, his first visit to the town, he took pains to appraise those of its features that affected its vulnerability to attack. The town had close to 20,000 residents and refugees crowded into the space occupied by only 3,500 people the year before. It was an old town, first settled close to a thousand years earlier and more recently incorporated as a town 80 years earlier by some companies of the City of London as the Londonderry Plantation.

The town occupied an oblong shaped area of less than a half square mile on the west bank inside a curve of the River Foyle. It together with an adjacent area outside its walls had once been an island surrounded on both sides by branches of the river. The western branch had long since been clogged with a silt deposit that left a stretch of bogland which now provided a western boundary to the town. On its eastern side, the town was served by the River Foyle which was navigable at high tide and which flowed five miles north to Lough Foyle, a salt water lagoon which was seven miles wide and stretched 15 miles farther north to a narrow channel entrance to the sea.

A thick wall protected the town. It had four gates: Ferryquay gate to the east, Shipquay gate to north, and Butcher's gate and Bishop's gate to the west and south. As a thriving market center it boasted a variety of shops and tradesmen and it had a cathedral built on a hill that rose almost 200 feet above the area around the town's walls.

As soon as he had acquainted himself with the lay-out of the town and reported his arrival to the governor, Gill undertook the task of locating his wife and her family. He found them quartered in a single room assigned to them by the town authorities. His reunion with them was a happy one as they all were pleased to know that the others were alive and well. Mary and Gill also appreciated the effort of her family to arrange times when the newlyweds could enjoy periods of privacy.

The joy of Gill's reunion with Mary was dampened by his inability to explain the cloud of confusion and disarray that blanketed the town. From all he could see Londonderry had the manpower and arms to defend itself. It had a fair stock of food supplies and most of its citizens were determined to defend the town. True, many of its defenders needed training and discipline. That problem could be handled. What was lacking was evidence of real leadership in high places.

Governor Lundy was a military colonel but displayed ineptness as a commander. He refused to take advice, insisted on secret conferences with his staff, was evasive when fellow officials asked if he had taken his oath of allegiance to William and Mary, did nothing to discourage officers and leading citizens from fleeing from the town, and often seemed to be rushing hither and yon for no purpose. To the surprise of most everyone, he had ordered the defenders of several outlying Protestant strongholds that could have stemmed the oncoming march of the Irish army to abandon their positions and come to Derry.

A critical phase of Lundy's tenure as governor came at the end of the second week of April. Lundy was advised by several men who understood the town's predicament that he should send men to secure the river passes across the River Finn at Lifford, Claydford and Long Causey. Control of one or another of these fords would allow Hamilton to send a besieging force of Irish troops to the area west of Londonderry. Under pressure, Lundy agreed to send the needed men on April 15. He was urgently warned on the 14th that a defensive force must be sent immediately because the Irish army was already posed to seize two of the key passes. But Lundy held stubbornly to his plan; and when he led a large Protestant army to the fords on the 15th, he found several thousand Irish troops already crossing the fords at Claydford and Lifford.

Gill took no part in the defense of Claydford. He and his troop of horse were sent north the day before to inspect the small fort at Culmore, which was located near the point at which the Foyle flows into Lough Foyle. When he returned two days later after finding that there had been little reason for his ride, he was shocked to hear that Lundy's army had abandoned the two fords almost without a fight.

Told of the defeat, he sought information concerning the whereabouts of Jamie and Charles who had ridden to Claydford with Lundy's army. After an hour's search, he found Charles sobbing in an alcove along the town's wall. Between tears, Charles expressed hopeless anger. "The coward, the traitor," he cried. "We could have stopped them at the ford had we only got there ahead of them. Jamie mounted a charge that had several hundred of them running back to the river. Then Jamie was shot dead by one of their marksmen. Lundy saw it and instead of coming to our support cried out: 'We can't hold them. You are cut off. Shift for yourselves.' He then fled in panic to Derry. With him galloping away to save his neck, no one else was willing to stay on and fight so the day was lost."

Gill was devastated by the news of his best friend's death. As a soldier he forced himself to maintain his composure as he did what he could to solace the grief of Mary and her family. He was angered by Lundy's behavior. Was their governor a spineless figurehead or might he be a secret agent of King James? He wished he knew; but while he waited for answers to his troubling doubts, he maintained his loyalty to the cause by not raising irritating questions with his colleagues.

The loss of the fords across the River Finn opened the way for Hamilton to send several thousand troops to occupy the high ground that fringed on the town's bogland western boundary. Big guns, a few at first and more later, were hauled into place to bombard the town. The outlook for surviving a siege appeared glum and Lundy along with many residents was ready to surrender. People became more hopeful the next day though when watchmen in the cathedral tower saw an English fleet of eleven ships enter the Lough Foyle. Deliverance from the threatened siege and defeat of the Irish army now seemed to be at hand.

Colonel John Cunningham brought a stock of supplies with his fleet and had orders to land his 1,600 trained soldiers if he could do so safely. After waiting two days for favorable winds to sail up the river and also for a response to the letter he had sent to Lundy, he had his men row him upstream for a meeting with the governor. Lundy met with him in a private session attended by a few of his close friends. No word of their discussion was reported to the townspeople. It was learned later that Lundy assured the colonel that the town was surrounded with upwards of 30,000 Irish troops, that they had at most a ten day supply of food on hand, that Londonderry was no fit place to land two regiments of soldiers, and that the town would fall within a matter of days. With this gloomy advice and without bothering to check with others, the colonel returned to his ships and led his fleet out of the lake and back to England.

* * * * *

James Stuart, recently deposed as King of England, was in a foul mood. His accommodations at Dublin Castle were definitely inferior to those he had enjoyed for years in England, Scotland, and France. The mistress who had shared his bed these last two weeks bored him with her endless talk and had further irritated him the night before by insisting that he should make her a countess. "Ungrateful wench," he thought, "doesn't she know that it is for me to grant favors, not for her to ask for them. Someone should tell her it is honor enough for me to sleep with her and that it is royal policy not to give noble rank to the likes of her until she has borne me a son or daughter. Anyway, I'm through with her. She is more interested in wheedling favors from me for her Irish friends than in giving me pleasure."

The thought of her serving as part of the Irish lobby that surrounded him added to his annoyance. From the time of his arrival in Cork and Dublin, he had become more and more aware of the gulf that separated his goal with this invasion from those of Tryconnell and Count d'Avaux, the watchdog Louis XIV had sent along with his invasion force to watch after the interests of France.

Tyrconnell and his Irish colleagues wanted James to give them independence from England. They were pressuring him to void Poyning's Law, the old English law that required English approval of legislation passed by the Irish Parliament. They wanted to see Catholicism established as the sole legal religion in Ireland and programs started to deprive English and Scottish investors and settlers of those properties that had once been taken from Irish owners.

James had no sympathy for his Irish subjects. He endorsed Tyrconnell's program for opening civil and military appointments to Catholics. But he had no intention of giving the Irish all they wanted. To do so would defeat his purpose for undertaking the invasion. For him, victory in Ireland was a necessary prelude to a successful invasion of Scotland and his restoration to the English crown. Accepting the demands of the Irish at this point would destroy his credibility in both England and Scotland as a defender of established property rights.

D'Avaux gave him less trouble than Tyrconnell and the Irish, but he was trouble enough with his annoying advice. He could not ignore or offend d'Avaux because he knew his hope for military success was heavily dependent on the military leadership provided by French officers and the arms and supplies he had brought with him. Without French support his cause would be lost. Yet he was definitely irritated by the Count's reminders that he could and should bypass Ulster and go on Scotland where he might attract a successful following before William could finally establish himself in England.

Yes, d'Avaux's arguments did make sense. But James felt he could not go to Scotland knowing that a significant portion of the population in Ireland still defied his authority. D'Avaux assigned no merit to his argument, but this did not shake James' confidence in his own judgment. It was apparent to him that France would just as soon have him out of the picture. France had no particular interest in having him rule these three nations again, not if it could have Ireland as a subject state where the government would pursue the interests of France.

James received word in early April of the success Hamilton and his French generals were enjoying as they pushed past Belfast into northern Ulster. His Irish advisors wanted him to stay in Dublin where they hoped he would grant them more concessions. His military advisors insisted though that he join his army before its assault on Londonderry. He and D'Avaux started their trip north on April 13 and were shocked as they rode to Armaugh and Charlemont by the evidence of waste and desolation around them. The retreating Protestants had left a scorched earth behind them that offered little support for the invading army.

At Armaugh a report was received from Hamilton that an English relief fleet had been sighted off Londonderry and that a body of the army had gone over to the enemy. In a curious display of confused leadership, James decided to return to Dublin and then reversed his decision when he learned that the army had not deserted. He then rode on to Strabane and to Hamilton's camp on the southern outskirts of Londonderry. Upon his arrival at the camp on April 17, he found that Hamilton had sent emissaries to Governor Lundy to arrange for the surrender of the town. Lundy had sent a message to Hamilton asking for surrender terms and Hamilton had answered with a written promise that the garrison would be allowed to depart in peace if they surrendered their arms and horses.

Lundy and his hand picked council decided in secret council to surrender the town on April 18. When James approached the Bishop's gate at the southern wall later that day, he had his colors flying and fully expected a respectful reception. The town's garrison, however, had not been informed of Lundy's plan to surrender and reacted by firing on the advancing army.

Far from cheering James and yielding to him as their rightful king, the royal approach was greeted with outbursts of musket fire and cries of 'No surrender'. A few of James' soldiers were killed and he withdrew in bewilderment and disbelief. "What ails these people?" he thought, "We have offered them honorable terms to accept me as their anointed king. If they prefer certain death to justice then that is what we will give them."

On April 19, a trumpeter brought a letter to the gate with a message demanding an answer as to why the town had not responded to the offer of surrender terms sent two days earlier. The garrison refused to respond. They wanted no further negotiations. Mortified by their response, James chose to return to Dublin. The siege of Londonderry had begun.

* * * * *

It was not until April 18 that the defenders and townspeople of Londonderry learned the full extent of Lundy's treachery. It was then that Lundy's clerk leaked the details of the governor's meeting with Colonel Cunningham, his insistence that the town would surrender within a week, and his recommendation that the colonel sail away with his fleet. He reported that Lundy had persuaded his council to accept Hamilton's surrender terms and had tried with mixed success to get several leaders in the town to endorse his decision. The clerk's report stirred up indignation all over town as its defenders realized that their appointed leader had been working for over a month against their avowed interests.

Gill was as indignant as anyone, particularly so as he blamed Jamie's death on Lundy's cowardice. "I've suspected his loyalty ever since I got here," he told Mary. "I should have protested but have held back because he is our governor."

"Then you should make your protest now," Mary assured him.

The need for a suitable opportunity was not long coming. Adam Murray, a Protestant leader from the area, was observed from the watchtower riding with a strong body of horse from his station at Culmore fort to the Pennyburn mill, which was located west of the Foyle, only a mile and a half north of the town. Lundy sent a message to him with an order that the troop come no closer. But Murray came anyway and the guards at Butcher's gate were pleased to let them enter the town.

Shortly after his arrival, Murray asked to see Gill whom he had met the previous week at Culmore. "What is going on here?" he inquired.

Gill gave him a brief account of Lundy's misdeeds and expressed his indignation at the failure of the town's leaders to take action. When Murray asked if the town's defenders were pleased with Lundy's leadership, Gill assured him that they were not. Murray gritted his teeth and growled: "Then it is time for us to put some mettle in their bones. Before we do anything we must first make sure we have the garrison behind us. Once we are sure, we can turn the traitors out. Here is a way we can find out. You and I will go around town this afternoon and ask all who oppose Lundy's plan to surrender to tie white handkerchiefs around their left arms and march to the governor's office tomorrow morning. That will tell us whether or not we have popular support."

Gill solicited the support of his company and every colleague he encountered during the next two hours. They spread through the town and advised people on every street and alley of the need for a show of support the next morning. Come April 19, over 90 percent of the more than

20,000 people in Londonderry were on the streets wearing white handkerchiefs on their arms.

Murray led them to the room where Lundy was meeting behind closed doors with his tight clique of advisors. When he broke into the room with Gill and several other officers, Lundy demanded that they leave. When they refused, he asked that they state their business. Murray then enumerated a list of Lundy's questionable decisions and demanded his resignation. Far from defending his actions, Lundy tried to persuade Murray to sign the draft of his agreement to surrender the town. When Murray refused, he asked several churchmen to back his stand. When they too refused, he fled to the safety of his house. A few days later he left Londonderry, worked his way through the Irish lines, and returned to England.

The townspeople proceeded to select a new mayor without waiting for Lundy to resign his post. Murray was a popular choice but refused to accept the honor and the choice of the voters went to Major Henry Baker, a stalwart soldier who at the age of 42 had earned the respect of the voters. Baker accepted the office and asked that Reverend George Walker be appointed to administer the town's stores. Provisions were quickly made to reorganize the town's defenses. The military defenders were assigned to six regiments, each headed by a Lieutenant Colonel who had shown ability to lead and willingness to fight. The several companies of soldiers quartered in the town were allowed to elect their own officers and also chose the regiments to which they were assigned. Somewhat to his surprise, Gill at 27 was selected as the youngest of the six regimental commanders.

* * * * *

Gill had good reason to be proud of the recognition given him by Derry's new authorities. He enjoyed the preeminence his position gave him and his family. He was resolved, however, to stay on as a humble and compassionate leader of his regiment. Being admitted to the topmost meetings of the town's leaders, he had special reasons for assessing the town's capabilities to sustain the siege that was now underway. The town had sufficient food supplies, arms and munitions to care for it for several weeks. Water was a problem because people had to go outside the town walls to fill their containers and the sources closest to the town were soon polluted with mud and refuse. Their major problem as he saw it concerned how long the town could withstand a siege. If King William could send them relief within the next few weeks, they could hold the town provided the French officers who were directing the Irish artillery did not bring in enough big guns to blast down the town's walls.

Colonel Campbell was not greatly concerned about his own welfare. He had learned in Scotland how he could survive on little more than a handful of oatmeal a day. His chief worry concerned his family. Mary was in her third month of pregnancy and he knew that mothers-to-be needed more than scarce handouts of oatmeal to survive and produce healthy babies. He felt Sam McLean and his wife and daughter Margaret deserved better treatment than the town could provide. Young Charles, whom he had selected as his military aide, could get by on his soldier's rations, but as a lad whose body was still growing to manhood he would surely suffer from pangs of hunger. All of them could get by for the time being; but King William's relief expedition must come soon if they were to survive.

Most of Gill's responsibility as a colonel involved a boring routine of supervising watches, keeping his men alert and ready to fight on short notice, and keeping peace within the town. He found himself constantly on call to handle unexpected complications. These pressures on his time kept him busy; and while he had reasons to worry, he realized as April turned to May that he was happy with his work. True, he missed the green fields of Coleraine. He hated the containment of the town's walls; he missed Jamie's affable companionship and also that of his father who had been killed four years before; but these negatives were balanced by the towering love he had for Mary.

Mary was such a good scout in accepting the inconveniences of their lives without complaint. On those occasions when he could, in their room or in some secluded corner of the town wall, he loved to hold her in his arms.

Somehow, now in the early months of her pregnancy, she seemed more beautiful than ever. How they enjoyed strolling arm in arm through the town, looking out from the walls at the new growth of grass and shrubs in the boglands, and talking of a future when they could return to McBane's farm or have a farm of their own where they could harvest crops, fattening their livestock, and watch their children grow.

* * * * *

Garrison duty in the besieged town offered few opportunities for heroics. During the first days of the siege, Gill and the other officers frequently sallied out from one of the town's gates with their men to find forage and other supplies in the nearby countryside. Improvised attacks also were made on small segregated groups of Irish soldiers that sometimes ended with the capture of valuable supplies. Opportunities for these attacks soon disappeared as Hamilton and his French officers tightened their strangle hold on the town. The town's approach to the sea was cut off on April 20 when Hamilton captured the fort at Culmore, proceeded to build a boom across the Foyle and sent a detachment of troops to establish a base at Pennyburn Mill.

Only four pitched battles were fought between the besieging army and the town's defenders during the siege. On May 5, one of Hamilton's officers led 3,000 troops in an attack on Windmill Hill, which was located in the area south of the town's walls between the Foyle and the bogland. Gill was one of the garrison commanders who counterattacked the next day and succeeded in driving the Irish besiegers from their newly dug entrenchments. Five days later Gill rode with Colonel Murray and 1,000 men to dislodge the enemy force at Pennyburn Mill. A temporary victory was won but Murray's men had to retreat when a large detachment of Irish reinforcements was sent to the site from Culmore.

A third battle, for which Gill received special commendation, occurred on June 5 when a besieging army of 6,000 men again tried to take Windmill Hill but was fought off with high casualties by the defenders. The fourth and final battle occurred on June 28 when the besiegers raided and took the outer works of the wall at Bishop's gate but were dislodged with considerable loss of life to the besiegers by a segment of the town's garrison.

As week followed week, the two principal topics of speculation were when would William send an army to relieve the siege and would relief arrive in time. An answer to both questions seemed at hand on June 7 when observers in the watchtower sighted three English warships entering Lough Foyle. By June 11, 30 ships were at anchor with the fleet. Cannons were fired to let the ship officers know that Londonderry was still holding out. Aside from this, however, the fleet officers had no means of knowing the predicament faced by the town.

Lieutenant General Kirke, the commander of the relief force, had orders not to proceed up the River Foyle beyond the Culmore fort until he had information about the status of the besieged town. He saw the boom across the river and chose not to breach it. With Hamilton's army controlling both banks of the river neither the general nor the town officials had a way to communicate with the other. The enemy intercepted messages sent by land. One of Kirke's men finally swam up the river to the town that signaled his arrival by firing one of its cannons. Unfortunately, he brought no code for further communication and was drowned as he tried to swim the five miles back to his ship. Kirke stayed with his fleet in the lake for two weeks and then sailed away to effect a landing some miles to the west on Inch island.

The end of June was an especially trying time for the beleaguered town. Kirke's departure meant it was abandoned for a second time by the navy that should have supported them. Governor Baker was taken ill the middle of June and died on June 30. Colonel Michaelburne was chosen as his successor and Gill was selected as one of the officials who bore his pall to a burial site at the cathedral. Hamilton, who was well informed by deserters about the precarious state of the town's food reserves, added to the town's problems by lobbing a message enclosed in a hollow bombshell into the town which demanded the town's surrender. When this demand was rejected, General Rosen, the French commander of a branch of the Irish army chose to use terrorism to force the town's capitulation.

Rosen sent out orders on July 1 for rounding up all the Protestants, men, women and children, that could be found in the area around the town. They were then herded without food or other supplies to the town's walls. A crowd of upwards of 7,000 people were uprooted from their places of refugee and forced to stand before the town's gates on July 2 and 3. With no food for them within the town, the garrison guards refused to allow them entrance.

Responding to this challenge, Governor Michael-burne's council ordered the construction of a huge gallows on the Double Bastion within clear sight of the entrenched Irish army. The council sent out an announcement that the Irish captives within the town would be hanged one by one if the horde of hungry Protestants beneath the walls were not fed and allowed to depart in peace. A request was sent to the Irish army to send priests to the town that could administer last rites to the condemned prisoners.

The responsibility for taking the first 20 Irish from the places where they were confined to the town jail was assigned to Gill. "I am not doing this because I have any disrespect for you or your people," he told them. "You have been condemned to hang because that is the only way we can insist that your officers treat our people justly with compassion for their misery. If you wish to appeal the decision that has been made, you can write to General Hamilton and ask that he send our people to their homes. Should you choose to write such a letter, I will make certain that it gets to your general."

The hoped for request for clemency was written and sent to Hamilton who rejected it with a further threat of revenge on the beleaguered garrison. Rosen, however, relented and ordered that the amassed Protestants be freed. He had concluded that his use of terrorism was counterpro-ductive, a stand that was supported by James whose order for releasing the Protestants was received the next day.

The freeing of the horde of people under the walls provided Gill with a welcome opportunity. Hunger was fast becoming a serious problem within the walls and the prospects for relief were decidedly dark. He wanted somehow to get Mary and the McLeans out of the town and outside where their prospects for survival would be better. He found by happenstance that a few of the uprooted Protestants wanted to join the defenders and that some people from the town could be slipped among those who would be leaving.

Quickly gathering his family around him, he explained his plan for their departure. Gaunt and emaciated, Sam McLean said: "I'm not a quitter, Gill. If there was anything I could do here to save the town I would stay. All Maude and I can do though is provide two extra mouths to tax our food reserves. You are right as near as I can tell about our chances of surviving so we will go. The girls will have to decide what they will do for themselves."

Mary and Margaret refused to consider the prospect of leaving. Mary insisted that she must stay by her husband's side while Margaret said: "I'll stay here to help Mary. It's right for you to go, mamma and poppa, but you can imagine what those soldiers will do with me if I try to go. Anyway, there are things I can do to help relieve the suffering here."

It was a sad and tearful parting as the elder McLeans prepared to pass through the Ferryquay gate and join the hundreds of fellow Protestants who were huddled there while waiting to start long walks back to their houses. Sam and Maude were thinner and weaker than most of the people around them but they were determined to find their way back to the farm they had abandoned more than six months earlier.

* * * * *

The plight of the besieged behind the town walls became increasingly precarious with every passing day after the departure of Sam and Maude. Reverend Walker had been steadily reducing the allocations of food from his diminishing stores for over a month. By now, all of the cattle, sheep, pigs, and chickens had been slaughtered. One by one all but a few of the horses that had provided mounts for the cavalry had been eaten. Cats, dogs, and even rats and mice had become prized food supplies. With the supply of meal almost exhausted and stark hunger facing them, some people suggested the possible need to start eating their Irish prisoners. Reverend Walker had turned to issuing small allotments of tallow and starch to people that they could eat with their meager rations of meal. Bits of dried hides that could be chewed were issued as a substitute for meat.

Some people went out from the walls in the face of enemy fire to find herbs and edible greens in the bogland. In a desperate sally from the walls, Lieutenant Colonel Fitzgerald led a party of guardsmen in a successful attempt to capture a small store of meal and mutton but in an effort that cost him his life.

Everyone in the town was suffering from lack of nourishment. They were starved and weak; their bodies lacked energy and were slow to react. Soldiers would fall or collapse while on guard duty. Yet with all their suffering, many of the besieged sensed a feeling of euphoria. Theirs was the righteous cause; they were determined to triumph; and they somehow were able to call forth surges of energy and vigor when such were needed to withstand those attempts that were made to storm the walls.

By the second week in July pestilence became the twin companion of famine in undermining the town's ability to defend itself. For 90 days the town's residents had lived crowded together with inadequate water supplies and sharing an increasingly polluted environment. Until now there had been few signs of disease; but sickness had suddenly came to the town like a plague. Hundreds were confined to their beds with fevers that in most cases led to early deaths.

Mary was one of the unfortunate who were marked for death. Gill had worried for weeks about his inability to provide her with a more adequate diet. All along she had protested that she was all right but her emaciated figure told him otherwise. On July 8 she felt the ravaging effects of fever. All the next day he sat by her side, fanning her to give her comfort, and praying for her survival. As the fever wore her reserve to its breaking point that evening, she gave up hope of living to deliver their child. Sensing that death was at hand, she begged that Gill and Margaret promise her that they would care for each other after she was gone. With their promise given, she closed her eyes and smiled as her spirit left its earthly body.

So many people were dying that the survivors faced problems in disposing of their dead. Gill's popularity with his regiment was such though that they provided a military service and internment for their Colonel's lady. Bereaved though he was, Gill found himself quickly pressed by the need to handle other duties. On July 10 Hamilton lobbed a second message into the town demanding its surrender by July 14 and indicating willingness to negotiate favorable surrender terms. Gill was commissioned by the town council to join with Colonel Lance in working out the surrender terms.

The garrison's hopes for rescue by a relief force were buoyed at this crucial moment when General Kirke returned with part of his fleet to Lough Foyle and succeeded in sending a boy through the Irish lines with a note asking for information on the town's status. Governor Michaelburne sent the boy back with an answer, which he had presence of mind to swallow when Irish troopers captured him. Released, the boy returned to the town where he was provided with a second answer, enclosed in a suppository, which he was able to deliver to the general's staff.

Playing for time, Gill and his partner responded to Hamilton's demand on July 11 with an offer to surrender if the garrison and townspeople could be guaranteed full freedom; be left with their arms and munitions, have their property rights restored, receive a guarantee of religious freedom, have the Irish soldiers near the town disarmed so they could not seek revenge on the besieged population; and have the Irish prisoners held in the town moved to General Kirke's ships. They set the nearest date of possible surrender as July 26, the date when the town's supply of food would be exhausted.

Hamilton's Jacobite officers mulled over this far-fetched list of terms and sent a message to the town agreeing to all but three of the stipulations. They would not permit the transfer of the Irish prisoners to Kirke's fleet. They would allow the garrison to leave the town with their arms but not the townspeople; and they would not postpone the date of surrender beyond July 15. In it's response on July 14 the town council renewed its refusal to surrender before July 26. With this reply, negotiations ended and Hamilton's army resumed its bombardment of the town.

While these negotiations were continuing, General Kirke finally received the message concerning the town's plight and the likelihood that its food supplies would be exhausted by July 26. Breaking forth from his lethargy, he ordered his frigates to bombard the fort at Culmore and Hamilton's shore emplacements near the mouth of the River Foyle.

The *Mountjoy* sailed directly up the mouth of the river in an attempt to smash the boom that blocked entrance to the Foyle. The rebound from its impact caused the ship to go aground. An attempt by the Jacobite soldiers to board the grounded ship was rebuffed by a burst of cannon fire that dislodged the ship. Meanwhile, a party of English sailors attacked and cut the boom with their axes. With the entrance to the river open, the *Mountjoy* and two supply ships were then able to make their way, firing at the Irish shore batteries along the way, to the gates of the town.

The supply ships were met with a frenzy of excitement, but order was kept as they unloaded barrels of meal, cheeses, butter, bacon, peas, biscuits, and brandy. No one went hungry in Londonderry that night though many had to be cautioned about the dangers of overeating after their long fast. With food in their stomachs and more at hand, the town's survivors could now start their climb back to normal health.

Hamilton's army continued its sporadic bombardment of the town for three more days. But after 102 days, the siege was broken. Troops from the landing at Inch reached the town on August 3 and four days later Kirke brought in three regiments of soldiers who were quartered at Windmill Hill away from the pestilence of the town. Soon after, the Irish army which was suffering from low morale and wretched living conditions started its withdrawal from the Londonderry area, a withdrawal to the south that was speeded when King William's General Schomberg landed a force of 10,000 Dutch, Huguenot, and freshly recruited English soldiers near Belfast.

No exact counts were made of the number of casualties. Most accounts however indicated that the size of the defending garrison dropped from 7,000 to only 3,000 at the end of the siege. Of the 20,000 to 25,000 people who were packed into the town at the start of the siege, a few thousand slipped away while between 10,000 and 15,000 died from starvation or pestilence.

* * * * *

Gill stayed on at Derry for two weeks after the lifting of the siege. There was nothing to keep him in Londonderry once his service was no longer needed. As soon as he and Mary and Charles felt their bodies restored to reasonable health, they took a supply of food together with a few meager possessions and started their long hike back to the McLean farm. Except for their telling of Mary's death, it was a happy homecoming for them and the elder McLeans when they reached the family's house on August 16.

Sam and Maude were in fair health though Sam was now bothered with a cough he could not shake. Their house had been entered in their absence but little was taken or destroyed. None of their fields had been tilled during the spring or summer but there was a lush crop of forage that could be harvested if they could find horses or cattle to eat it. Enough volunteer oats were growing in two fields to warrant harvesting operations. Food supplies would be hard to come by for the next several months but with fish from the river and an occasional deer from the nearby woods they expected to survive,

When Gill told Sam of his promise to his dying wife to take care of Margaret, Sam answered: "That's logical. Both of my daughters were in love with you from the day you met them. Fact is I wasn't sure for awhile which one you would ask to marry. As I remember, I once accused you of coming to steal my daughters. It appears now that you have and you do so with my blessing."

Margaret was delighted with the idea of marriage to Gill. She had indeed been in love with him when he chose her sister and now after living with them in Derry she was sure she wanted to spend her life with him. Gill was less

132

certain. He knew he had made a vow to Mary that he should keep. He loved Margaret; but he loved her more as a sister, not in the passionate way he had loved Mary. He was disturbed with the idea of substituting one sister for the other so soon after Mary's death. When he mentioned his concern to Charles, the boy looked at him in wonder. "Don't talk like that, Gill," he implored. "I need you for my brother and pop and mom and Maggie would be heart broken if you left us."

Margaret favored setting an early date for the wedding. Gill thought the date should be postponed a few months out of respect for their bereavement. The McLeans objected when their advice was sought. "You've been living together, all of us in one room and then you, Margaret and Charles in the room, for months" they reminded him. "Make it legal as soon as we can get a minister to say the right words."

When Gill walked to McBane's farm, to see how it how fared, he was distressed to find the buildings in shambles. They had been wrecked, torched, and the property abandoned. Marauders had stolen what property items they wanted, driven off most of the cattle and other livestock, and gone their way. He was able to construct a temporary dwelling place for himself and went to work harvesting a field of volunteer oats that was ripe and ready to fall. Scouting around the property and the nearby woods, he found a few cattle and sheep that had somehow been missed by the marauders. He also found two horses that, though somewhat wild after months of freedom, came to him and yielded to his dominance when he put halters around their heads.

McBane's tenants and workers were nowhere to be found. Gill judged from the state of their houses that they had been victims of a raid and were either dead or had been scared off. He decided to leave their properties alone for the time being until they either returned or he got instructions from McBane. For now though, he knew he needed help in starting the job of restoring the farm to its earlier productive status. Help came when he found a man wandering through the area who was seeking food and possible work. Daniel Frazier was not the brightest or most imaginative worker, but he was reliable, willing to work, and satisfied when Gill told him that he might have to work for his keep for a while until they could get the farm back into working order.

Most of Gill's attention in September was spent on getting the McBane farm back into production and rebuilding enough of one of the houses to provide living quarters for Margaret and him during the coming winter. He made it a point to ride over to the McLean's house three times a week to check on his in-laws' well being and provide his input for the wedding which was planned for October 4. Most of McLean's neighbors had suffered as he did from the spring and summer of war. With a promise of peace at hand, they got together at their kirk and committed themselves to a community self-help plan. Gill was proud to cast his lot with them and working together they were able to provide every household with some livestock, at least one horse, and an assurance of plentiful food supplies for the winter.

* * * * *

While Gill and Sam were struggling to reestablish themselves, King William's Duke of Schomberg landed his polygot force at Belfast where they established a base for further operations. Schomberg showed little interest in engaging the Jacobite army during the fall or winter months that followed. His presence, however, caused James to pull his forces out of northern Ulster. While Schomberg waited, the strength of James' army was bolstered by the arrival in March of 6,000 well-trained soldiers from France who were exchanged for a similar number of Irish troops who were transported to service in King Louis' war in Europe.

England was allied at the time with the Dutch and was fighting with them on land and sea against the might of France's Louis XIV. Hoping for an early victory that could end the war in Ireland, William came in person with a large body of reinforcements on June 14, 1690. On his landing, a call went out to the Protestant settlements in northern Ulster to send additional troops to support his drive for victory.

Preparations for military action had been delayed by wet and miserable weather conditions during the spring and early summer. William's arrival brought with it a shift to hot dry weather that enabled him to lead his army of 20,000 men south to Hillsborough, to Laughbrickland, Newry, and then on June 27 to Dundalk. Meanwhile, the Jacobite army retreated farther and farther south. James reached the River Boyne, the last natural barrier north of Dublin, on June 28. He had his men cross and then destroy the bridges at Dragheda on the coast and three miles upstream at Oldbridge and then had them dig entrenchments along the southern banks for a final stand against the expected assault by William's army.

Gill arrived at William's camp at Dundalk on June 28. The king was busy planning military operations but seemed pleased to take time to thank Colonel William Campbell for this addition to his striking force. On hearing his name, William said "Campbell, were you by chance one of Argyll's men?"

"That I was your majesty. I fought with the earl's command and was with him until the day he was captured."

Gill noted somewhat to his surprise that his new king was both short and slender. He was no taller than Argyll had been and lacked the earl's stocky build. He had dark hair, pleasing features, and carried himself with regal pride. Unlike King James, he showed no signs of haughtiness. Instead, he had a likeable charm and an eagerness to mingle with and share adversity with his men that endeared him to them.

When Gill saw the king's bright orange sash, he remembered that William had a double claim to the throne. As the son of Charles I's daughter, he was after the deposed James, the most direct male heir to the English throne while Mary, his queen, who had been raised as a Protestant, was James' eldest daughter.

"Happy to have you and your men with us," William said. "I could wish though that you had brought a larger troop. We can always use more cavalry."

"There would be more of us your majesty, had we been able to supply ourselves with horses."

"Horses? Why Ulster must have plenty of horses."

"Not us, sir. We were at Londonderry where we had to eat them."

"Londonderry eh? You did well there, Colonel. It was thoughtless of us to ask that question. We will be riding against the Irish tomorrow, so plan to ride with us."

Gill's troop rode with William's vanguard to the Boyne on the 29th. As they came within view of the river at Oldbridge, they could see the Jacobites busily preparing their defenses on the opposite bank. The site they had picked offered definite advantages for the defenders. It was situated on high ground in a bend of the river; the banks on both sides were steep; and the river, while fordable at low tide, had an uncertain bottom and narrow boggy beaches.

William had his army make camp just out of gunshot range. Big guns would be needed before he could force a crossing and it would be night before his artillery would arrive and could be put in place. Meanwhile, the king, with characteristic disregard for his own safety, rode close to the river to better appraise his opportunity for attack on the morrow.

Later in the afternoon after the king had issued orders for the placement of his cannon, he rode upstream with Gill and some of his other officers. They were within sight of the enemy but always just out of musket range. William called a halt when they reached an attractive glen and announced that this would be a good place for them to enjoy a picnic. While the officers were standing around and their food was being unpacked, a French gunner on the south bank brought his hidden 6-pounder field piece to bear on the picnic site. His first shot startled the group and a second shot grazed the king's shoulder while tearing away a tuft of his uniform.

William seemed unruffled by the shots; but holding his shoulder barked: "That is a bit too close. Let's get out of here." Later when he found that his flesh wound was not serious, he added: "Apparently, they would rather that I not fight tomorrow, but I'll be here in person."

James' defense plan called for placing two regiments on his right flank to prevent a crossing of the Boyne at the port town of Drogheda. Most of his troops were concentrated at his center at Oldbridge while a small force in his left flank was spread out along the river to prevent his army from being encircled and cut off from its supply route to

Dublin. William in turn kept most of his army across the river from Oldbridge while sending 8,000 men, about a third of his army, upstream with orders to ford the Boyne at Slane or at the closer site of Rosnaree if the river proved crossable at that point.

Count Schomberg, the Duke's son who commanded William's right flank, started marching his cavalry, dragoons, and infantry upstream well before dawn on July 1. News of their movement alarmed James who concluded that the bulk of William's army was on its way to cutting off his escape route to Dublin. To counter this move, he ordered almost half of the troops in his center to support his left flank. The shift, while well intended, had less effect than anticipated because Schomberg's force forded the river at Rosnaree rather than Slane and found itself protected by deep ravines from cavalry attack.

Meanwhile, William remained with the bulk of his army at Oldbridge. He started his bombardment of the enemy's positions at 9:00, hid a regiment of his crack Dutch assault troops in a ravine and ordered their assault on the Jacobite positions at 10:00 at the moment when the river was its lowest low tide level. The assault force succeeded in establishing a footing on the southern shore. A second assault covering a wider area followed at 11:00. An hour later a third assault force crossed all along the river from Oldbridge to Drybridge.

Gill's troop joined a cavalry unit from Enniskillen in crossing the Boyne at Drybridge as part of the third assault. They found the crossing perilous because of rising water levels and the boggy nature of the shore. Once across, they were challenged by the stubborn defense of an infantry unit and by a countercharge of Jacobite cavalry. Fighting was fierce but Gill's unit suffered only limited casualties as they forced the enemy to give up ground. By mid-afternoon the Jacobites realized that their battle was lost. They abandoned their defensive positions and started a retreat that could easily have become a rout had it not been for the courageous action of the French officers who were able to maintain discipline in the retreating army. Great quantities of arms, munitions, food, and other supplies were captured as the Jacobites fled to Dublin.

Mopping up operations kept William's army busy on July 2. Altogether James lost about 2,000 men at the battle of Boyne while William lost 200. James' plan for capturing Ireland was now in shambles. Recognizing his failure, he hastened to Dublin and then hurried on to Waterford where he boarded a frigate, which took him to France. The defeated units of his army split at Dublin, some going on to Waterford and a larger number heading west to Limerick.

Gill rode south with the king to Dublin and then on to Waterford where the Jacobite fort surrendered in mid July. Fighting continued in western Ireland where the stubborn Irish defenders did not finally surrender until a year later. The prospect for an early ending of hostilities seemed sufficiently good after the fall of Waterford though for William to release Gill and his fellow Ustermen and send them back to their homes.

* * * * *

Six years after William's victory at the Boyne, Gill left Margaret and their three children- James born in 1690, Mary in 1693, and the infant Sam, born in 1695- on a short trip to his homeland in Argyllshire. It was a short voyage and he wondered as he landed at Campbelltown and rode on north why he had not come earlier.

It was good to be back in familiar country amid sites and a countryside he had cherished and loved in his youth. But it was not the Argyll he remembered. In the ten years that had passed since he rode away with a price on his head, many things had changed. The scenery was there but numerous buildings and improvements he remembered had been ravaged and never restored. There was less evidence of individual tenant holdings and fields once planted to crops were now covered with grass.

"It is the new way of handling estates," Sir Duncan of Auchinbreck told him when he reached his cousin's rebuilt home. "In the old days, the Earls of Argyll saw themselves as chiefs of the Campbell clan. They worked to advance the interests of all of the clan's members. They needed men who could fight for the clan and felt it was their duty to sustain and protect those who supported them. Our new earl has a different philosophy. He has accepted the English view that he is by right the owner of the clan's land and that it his prerogative to use it for his personal benefit. He no longer needs a personal army so he does not care whether his clansmen live or die as long as he can use the land to his benefit."

"You mean he is pushing families off their holdings?"

"That is exactly what I mean. They call it an enclosure movement. He is not trying to do it over night and in our less productive areas he couldn't care less whether people stay or leave for work in the towns. But as tenancies expire and he has opportunities to squeeze people off our better lands, he puts units together, plants the tillable land to grass, and brings in flocks of sheep that can provide him with wool he can sell in the markets."

"That doesn't sound promising for me. I had planned to see if the earl might reinstate the rights my father had as proprietor at Wester Kames."

"I wish you success Gill but doubt you will get very far with the earl. Argyll's grandfather gave the land to your father. Then Atholl confiscated it, claimed you had abandoned it when we rode away from here with prices on our heads. The same thing happened to my estate but my wife was able to hold onto it while I was in Holland. The earl got your land back through a royal grant and can legally insist that it is his not yours.

"If he were more like his father and grandfather, he would probably give it to you with thanks for past services. But that's not the way our present earl thinks. He stood aloof and even offered to fight against his father while we were risking our lives for him. If his brother Charles were the earl instead of Archy, you would have a chance but it would be against Archy's grain to acknowledge your claim."

Gill spent a day and night with Sir Duncan during which time they rehashed memories of their past exploits. The next day, he rode on to Inveraray where he was able to visit with Sir Archibald Campbell, the new Earl of Argyll. Sir Archibald received him in much the way Sir Duncan had foreseen. As he saw it, Gill had abandoned his property and all future claims he had to it when he had left Scotland. More than that, there was an unsettled question as to what rights he had as a refugee who had fled from the area with a price on his head. The earl offered to help clarify his legal status and find him a place as a possible tenant but that was all. Burning with frustration and knowing that the offer lacked substance, Gill kept his temper while he politely thanked the earl for his offer and went his way.

On his way back to Campbelltown; he stopped at his boyhood home at Wester Kames. Much was changed; the buildings he remembered were gone, probably torched by Atholl's thugs; one house had been restored but in a questionable new style; only half as many tenants as his father had had were at work in the fields and none of them were related to or even seemed to remember the neighbors Gill had known so well.

He rode on to the place where he thought his father had been killed and said a short prayer where he thought he was buried. From there he went to the ruins of the old castle of Ellan Gheirrig. It was abandoned and looked more like a pile of rubble than a one-time fortification.

Getting his bearings at the site of the old castle, he went alone to the cove where his father had buried the secret cache of 80 pounds. He found all of it there in the half decayed leather bag his father had hidden beneath a large stone. "Da told me to use it to sail away," he remembered, "but so far I have gone no farther than the short distance to Ireland."

Gill rode to Campbelltown the next day and fortunately was able to book passage on a ship that would sail to Coleraine the following morning. As he entered the dining room at his inn that evening, he was hailed by a familiar voice: "Gill, Gill Campbell, is that you?"

The speaker was Roddy MacDowell, Gill's boyhood neighbor and friend. Rod had a long tale to tell of his adventures as a sailor. His family at Wester Kames had completely disappeared while he was off at sea. Pushing his memory of them aside, he was eager to talk of his travels all over the Atlantic, to Spain, West Africa, Brazil, the West Indies, and the American colonies. "Do you remember, Gill, that I once told you I might some day migrate to one of the American colonies. I've had my chance to see them and that is where I am going when I am ready to settle down."

"Where do you intend to go?"

"Lots of Scots are going to Pennsylvania. They have mountains like ours and there is plenty of good land in the backcountry that is almost free for the taking. For me though, I'm going to New England. It's a lot like Scotland only the farming is better. The Puritans in Boston look down their long noses at Presbyterians like us but there are settlements that are all Scots. You should go there, Gill. You'll have more chances to get ahead there than here."

"Maybe I will," Gill answered thinking of his father's advice. "Maybe I will, but it won't be until my Jamie and Sam are old enough to stand on their own."

* * * * *

Campbells Came

Part Four

Sam

1728 - 58

"Those two boys, bless their souls, are as different as black and white." Granny McLean was voicing her often-repeated refrain about her daughter's two boys. "Oh, they are both grown men now, healthy and strong as two young oxen. People say they look alike even though Jamie's hair is blond like straw while Sam's is dark like his mom's. The thing different about them is the way they think and act. Jamie is the steady one. He is cautious and thinks things out before he acts. Sam expects Jamie to lead and usually follows but like as not chases off after some wild idea without ever a thought to the consequences.

"When they were little tikes Jamie had to look out for little Mary, who died when she was five, and for Sammy who was the baby of the family. It stayed like that as they grew up with Jamie always watching out for him and Sam following in his own wild way. When they rode in the woods, Jamie would stick to known trails but had to watch every moment to keep Sam from wandering off into the undergrowth where he could be lost for a week."

"Did he ever outgrow his wildness?" the widow Bowers asked.

"Sam is still the little boy looking for adventure he always was. Near as I can see, he hasn't settled down yet. When Duke Argyll sent out that call three years ago for volunteers to keep the Earl of Mar from putting the pretender on the throne, Gill told his sons he wasn't going to leave his farm to fight another war. But he allowed that the duke might restore the family's right to their old estate at Wester Kames if Jamie or Sam chose to fight."

"Tell me again about the duke. Didn't Maggie's husband fight for his father?"

"No. No, that was the duke's grandfather. Gill fought for the Earl of Argyll who was captured and beheaded before Gill came to Ulster. The earl's son got his family titles back and became a duke after William took the crown. The duke now is his son. He made his name in the military where he and Marlborough were King William's two top generals. Queen Anne put him on her Privy Council and when she died he was one of the lords who got Prince George to come over from Hanover to be our king. Right after that he had to hurry back to Scotland where he put down the Earl of Mar's plan for putting King James' son on the throne."

"Now I remember. Did the boys join the duke's army?"

"Both volunteered but in different ways. Jamie got an officer's commission for lining up a troop of Ulstermen to support the duke. When Sam heard that Jamie was going, he caught the first ship to Glasgow and joined as a common soldier. He was only 19 and said he didn't want to be an officer. All he wanted was to see some action.

"He got to Scotland two weeks before his brother just when Argyll saw a need to send his cavalry to Perth. The duke thought his body of horse was too small to make an impression on Mar's supporters so he put Sam and about 200 other untrained recruits on horses and had them ride to Perth with his dragoons. That quick action kept a lot of Mar sympathizers from joining his army.

"Both boys were with Argyll when he defeated Mar's larger army later at Dunblane. The two armies did not meet each other head on in that battle. Jamie's troop was with the duke's right wing, which found itself facing no enemy when it charged up over a hill. Sam was with the other wing, which came near to being smashed. He saw bloodshed and killing all around him but came through without a scratch."

"Did their service get them any favors from the duke?"

"No, he brushed them off as though their service was due him as the head of the clan. Jamie came home in disgust after the big battle. Sam stayed on to force peace on the Highlands. We thought he was wasting his time; but to hear him tell it, the six months he spent there was the greatest experience of his life."

"What did Gill and Maggie think of it?"

"They were plenty happy to get their boys back unharmed. Gill was disappointed, of course, with the duke's attitude about his ownership rights. But he was not surprised. As he saw it, it was just another reason why he should go to America."

"Too many of our good Scots have been leaving for America. I never thought it would happen to him though because he was one of our best farmers."

"He had all the reasons anyone needed for leaving. After what he and our other Ulstermen did to keep William on the throne and save England from another civil war, he had good reason to resent the way Parliament has treated us like third class citizens. The restrictions they set up to limit our sale of farm and textile products in England and their prohibitions against our trade with other markets have left us living from hand to mouth.

"Worse than that, Parliament didn't give us the same right to religious freedom it gave to England and Scotland under its Toleration Act of 1690. The Church of Ireland with its Episcopalian hierarchy was vested with all the powers here that the Church of England used to have in England. People say Parliament did that to keep a tight rein on the Irish Catholics. But the Episcopalian bishops have vented their wrath more against we Presbyterians than against the Catholics. We cannot hold civil offices or go to schools. They say the marriages and other rites performed by our ministers have no legal standing. They have even arrested and imprisoned some of our men for living with their wives."

"You are right dearie. They don't treat us good. On the sunny side though, we can thank God we are not persecuted as much here as in some places."

"Yes, with everyone here being Scots Presbyterian, we have been able to resist the bishops' drive to make us join their church. There was another reason though for Gill deciding to go. Like all of us, he was hurt by three years, one right after the other, of crop failure. He lost most of his sheep to foot rot. Still, he got by as well as the rest of us except for one thing. Unlike his neighbors who owned their land, he was the steward of an absentee owner's estate."

"You mean that the landlord turned him out?"

"That is what happened. Mr. McBane who first took Gill on as his steward died in Scotland without ever coming back after the siege of Derry. Gill ran the farm for his widow and then for the nephew who inherited the property. The nephew sold the farm to an investor who seemed satisfied with the rents he received during the good years, but he refused to go along with any reduction when times turned bad. Somehow, he just couldn't understand that no rent is earned when you have a crop failure. When Gill couldn't pay what he expected, he got a new steward who soon found that he could not pay any rent at all."

"Did Gill find another opening?"

"He probably could have. By then he was ready to leave. He had been putting a little aside to buy a farm of his own. When he was kicked out without even a thank you, he decided it was time to seek his fortune in America."

* * * * *

The crisp morning breeze had a freshness about it that cleared Sam's foggy head. Overhead the predawn eastern sky was lit with a rosy glow that signaled the coming of another sunrise, sunrise this time in a near cloudless sky. It had stormed during the night. The little ship *Arbella* had rolled and tossed on the wild sea. The turbulence had wrecked havoc in the large galley where most of the 120 passengers tried to sleep. Many had tied themselves to their cots to keep from being bounced to the floor and all but the most hardy had suffered the misery of seasickness. Exhausted after the fitful night, most of the passengers were now trying to get a few hours of peaceful rest. Not so with Sam Campbell. Once the storm subsided, he had fled to the deck to enjoy fresh air and some privacy while escaping the sickening stench of the puke-covered galley floor.

Sam ambled aft to the stern of the ship. As he gazed out over the vast expanse of ocean, he marveled at how the wild turbulent waves that had almost engulfed the ship a few hours earlier had now leveled into a smooth almost placid sea. The howling wind had given way to a gentle breeze. Far from reefing in the sails, the ship's crew was now unfurling them to take full advantage of the wind.

As Sam stood at the stern looking to the east and captivated by the ballet like grace of three dolphins that leaped and glided in rhythmic precision in the ship's wake, he was startled by the "Morning" greeting of a cheerful crewman. "Captain says that more of this and we will see land within a week."

Sam acknowledged the greeting with a nod while keeping his gaze on the eastern sky where the sun would soon appear above the horizon. His bearded companion

147

took no offense at his failure to speak and added in a philosophical vein: "I'd expect a young fellow like you to be up front looking at where we be going rather than back here reflecting on where you been".

"You are right, friend. I should be looking at what is to come. But what's behind me is important too. It makes me wonder why I'm here."

As the sailor moved on, Sam continued his reverie and his musing over the life he had left. He could easily have been on this voyage a dozen years ago when his parents had migrated to New England. Why had he stayed on in Ulster when both da and ma had wanted him to join them? His reasons now seemed pointless. But they had seemed important at the time. He had had his heart set on marrying Isbel and going into business with her father. His infatuation had lasted until after his father migrated to New Hampshire and had suddenly ended when she chose to marry to another man.

Isbel had been his first but not his last serious love. There had been three other lasses in succession in the five years after Isbel who had caught his eye and let him build up expectations of possible marriage. With each of them, he had found after really getting to know them that their interests were too different from his to provide a firm basis for a happy marriage.

Then he had found Alice and his entire world changed. She was a lovely lass, an orphan without close family, and just as penniless as him. Somehow they had struck it off from their first meeting. Sam was never sure what she saw in him. In his eyes she was beautiful, witty, and fun to be with. She had a natural wildness about her that matched his own. Like him she had no driving desire for status or wealth. Instead she cherished life close to nature and saw freedom in nonconformity.

Sam and Alice had enough respect for the rules of society to be married at a local kirk. Beyond that they lived a gay free life together. She rode a horse like a man, fished and hunted with him, and thought nothing of shedding her clothes to swim with him in secluded lakes and streams. In three different summers they rode into the Highlands together and lived there as much like wild goats as people.

Children would have been welcome but none came. Then their joyful life together ended one afternoon a year ago when Alice was riding in rough rocky country.

Her horse stumbled near the edge of a precipice. Alice was thrown and the horse crushed her skull when it fell on her. Sam was devastated by her premature death. His mental state worsened a few weeks later when Jamie told him he was migrating to America.

The two brothers had been working together as partners. Of the two, Jamie was the steady one who ran a successful farming operation. He was married and had a growing family. Unlike most of his neighbors he had put some savings aside. But he had not prospered because of his farming. No full time farmer could make money in Ulster with England's trade restrictions. With Sam's help, he ran a semisecret trading business.

Sam had been a farmer too; but while Jamie expected his farming operations to pay for themselves, Sam was a wee farmer. He had a house, a small bit of land, and hardly tried to do more than raise some potatoes, a few vegetables and keep a cow. He and Alice had lived on his earnings as Jamie's trading partner.

Sam had far more interest in buying and selling things than in growing crops. He had a congenial charm and a desire to visit and communicate with others that made him a born salesman. His chief failing was that he was ever prone to sell his goods and services for too little. He would buy goods for resale and then sell them to others for little more than he paid for them.

Jamie and Sam had started their trading about the time their parents left for America. They had operated on a small scale at a time when Ulster suffered from hard times, crop failures, and trading restrictions that allowed English merchants to monopolize local sales without buying Ulster products in return. The brothers had found sympathetic merchants in Ayr who were willing to exchange manufactured goods for the cloth and produce they could bring across the narrow Irish Sea from Ulster. The trading arrangement was logical, profitable for both parties, but unfortunately illegal.

Their trading business was always small, but it had thrived over a ten-year period. They made no secret of their activities among their neighbors, neighbors who supplied the products they sold and who bought the goods they brought back in return. They had to be ever cautious though of whom they talked to and whom they dealt with. Quite early in their operations they found they could buy noninterference with a few well-placed contributions to local officials. But this practice led to problems as more open palms were extended to them and as the greed of the recipients called for larger and larger payments.

Matters came to a head shortly after Alice's death. Jamie had come to Sam's house with the unpleasant news that Angus McGinty, an official they paid to be blind to their activity, had been recalled, that reports of their activities had been rumored in England, and that the new governor had proclaimed his intent to put an end to illegal trading.

"What are our choices?" Sam had asked.

"There are three things we can do," Jamie had advised. "We can go back to full time farming and starve; we can keep on trading and take a chance of surviving without being sent to the gallows; or we can pull up stakes and ship out to New England."

"Christ in Heaven, man, I'd starve for sure if I turned to farming and I don't fancy wearing a noose so what is the chance of us getting to Boston? Tell me again what da wrote in his last letter."

"His letter is three months old now. He wrote that they were pleased with their lives in New Hampshire. He and ma joined up with some Scots settlers in a town about 50 miles north of Boston called Londonderry. He wrote that the settlement was expanding and that they have a small house and have cleared some land that the town voted to give them. He also said that the land is as good as any we have here and that the town has voted to give them more land. The colony there has good prospects and there are thousands of acres near them that settlers can claim.

"Did he write anything about Indian raids or massacres?"

"Da wrote that there are no Indians near them and that living there is no more dangerous than what we

Campbells put up with living alongside other clans in Scotland."

The two brothers agreed that they should restrict their trading operations to an almost invisible minimum while they made preparations to sail to Boston. Three months later Jamie turned his farm over to a young buyer and embarked with his family on a voyage to the New World. Sam's predicament was more complicated. He had no savings to pay for his passage. With Jamie gone, he skimped by as best he could while he explored possibilities for joining his parents and brother at the new Londonderry across the sea.

A lucky lead came his way when one of his merchant friends told him that James Hunter, another merchant, had decided to sail to Boston where he planned to open a store. Sam visited Hunter and found that the merchant was looking for an assistant. Sam took the position and soon impressed his employer with his sales ability. Not long afterwards Sam told Hunter of his desire to go to America and of his fear that he could never afford to do so.

Much to Sam's delight, Hunter proposed a work passage arrangement under which he would pay for Sam's passage if Sam would agree to work for him for five years for subsistence keep and a dismissal grant of ten pounds. The arrangement was not unlike the indentured service contracts thousands of poor people in England, Scotland and Ireland were using to open new doors of opportunity for them in America. Sam's arrangement differed in two respects from the usual service contract. Sam would sail with Hunter and his family as their servant and not be sailing with a group of potential workers whose services would be auctioned off to bidders at their arrival pier and his term of service was limited to five years rather than the customary seven.

Sam's departure followed in due course. It was not until after he was on board and ready to sail from their Scottish port that he met the Hunter family. His employer, James Hunter, was a broadchested, stern and hardheaded businessman, about ten years older than Sam, who had a keen eye for profits. His wife, Matty, was a plump and friendly lady who promptly took a motherly interest in Sam's welfare. The Hunters had two children, Mary, a pretty girl who was approaching her eighteenth birthday, and Jamie, their 13-year-old son.

Living close to them on the crowded ship and sharing his meager food rations with them, Sam soon became a member of the family. His relations with James Hunter remained formal. Hunter could never forget that he was the employer, the master. The others in the family though were quick to open their arms to him. They enjoyed his conversation, his stories, and his company.

Matty adopted him as a second son; Mary regarded him for awhile as a brother and then as something more; young Jamie looked to him for company and companionship, something he sorely missed after he left those he had played with in Ayr.

"Yes," Sam said to himself as he cast a glance at the boundless waters of the Atlantic, "that is why I am here. What can the future hold for me?"

Turning around, Sam saw that several of the passengers had followed him to the deck of the *Arbella*. Among them was the smiling face of his master's daughter. Seeing him, Mary strode to his side with the greeting: "Good news Sam. That sailor with the red beard says if the breeze holds we can expect to see Boston soon."

* * * * *

Sam arrived in Boston in 1728. Five dreary years followed during which he fulfilled the terms of his agreement to work as James Hunter's indentured servant. Unlike many others who served under comparable contracts, Sam wasted little time complaining about his lack of freedom. The possibility that he could run away to the frontier where he might escape capture never entered his mind. He had agreed to his contract of his own free will and was determined to fill out his tenure with cheerful and cooperative service. He liked his master but soon learned he could expect no concessions from him. James Hunter was a just and fair-minded employer, a devout Presbyterian, yet at the same time a hardheaded penny pinching businessman who insisted on getting everything he thought was his.

After a first few months of sputtering, Hunter's business started to prosper. Hunter realized that his success could be credited in large measure to Sam's good-natured camaraderie and to the skill he displayed in pleasing customers. He accepted Sam as his unofficial partner in his buying and selling operations without ever modifying his official status as the master's servant. Sam recognized and respected the rigidity of Hunter's position. He could have bargained for change but chose to ignore the issue. Actually, he could not have cared much less. He lived with the Hunters, had his own room and privacy, and was treated as a member of the family. He had no complaints about how he was fed or clothed and generally enjoyed the limited freedom he had.

The one aspect of Sam's life that irked him most was the fact that his work kept him inside laboring in a busy port town while his heart yearned for activity in a more natural world. Much to his satisfaction, Hunter gave him a week off every year to visit his parents and Jamie at Londonderry. While there, he found joy in working on their farms and rapture in tramping through the nearby forests and fishing in local streams. Settled again in Boston, he always had the feeling that although that 100-year old town still had nearby woods and opportunities for outdoor activities, it was more urbanized than he liked. He promised himself that once he completed his term of service he would leave Boston and find a home closer to the fringe of settlement.

Living as he did with the Hunters, Sam had close daily contacts with Matty Hunter and her daughter. From the very beginning, they treated him more as a member of the family than as a servant. Sam soon found himself bound to the family both by his loyalty to the master and by fondness for its womenfolk.

Once they were settled in their new home, Sam frequently handled the chore of buying food supplies for the family. He went with them to the local kirk and was soon escorting Mary to social gatherings. By mid 1729, most of their Scottish friends regarded them as a pair. This appearance was not apparent to Sam. In his eyes, he was treating his master's daughter much as he would a younger sister. The remorse that still clung to him after Alice's death closed his thinking to any prospect of a new loving relationship.

Sam's reluctance to initiate a courtship disappointed Mary. She had already decided that he was the man she wanted to marry. Knowing the reason for his hesitation, she decided to wait for his hurt to heal. She avoided pressing him for a commitment, continued showering him with affection, and kept up her hope that he would soon see her in the light she wished. For more than a year, the two kept enjoying each other's company and occasional teasing by others without Sam seeing her as more than a dear and delightful friend.

His attitude gradually changed during his second year in Hunter's employ. He knew he was fond of Mary, liked her company, and that there was room in his life for a loving wife. He was bothered though by three reservations. First, he realized that his feeling for her was not on par with the wild and compelling love he had had for Alice. Second, it seemed somehow wrong for him to court his master's daughter; and third, he sensed that there was something incestuous about him proposing marriage to a member of his unofficial family.

Commonsense finally prevailed. After a few months of more intensive courtship, Sam and Mary were married in May of 1731. James Hunter was pleased with Mary's choice of a husband and gave his blessing to their union. But only 35 of the 60 months of Sam's contracted servitude had elapsed and he saw no reason for releasing his new son-in-law from the terms of their agreement. The young couple continued to live, now in the same room and the same bed, in Hunter's house. The final two years of Sam's servitude were punctuated by the birth of his first son, Daniel, in March 1732 and a second son, Samuel, in October of the next year.

Sam's tenure as an indentured servant ended in June of 1733. It had been his intent to move as soon as he was free to Londonderry. Two considerations made June an awkward time for him to leave. His wife was experiencing problems with her second pregnancy and it seemed best that she stay on in Boston where medical care and advice was available. James Hunter also was experiencing a health problem that required several weeks of bed rest during which he was unable to give more than passing attention to his business. He had been grooming his son Jamie to take over Sam's work but the boy, now 18, was not yet ready to shoulder sole responsibility for running the family business. A solution for both problems was found when Sam agreed to stay on one extra year, this time at a reasonable wage that allowed him to put money aside to help pay for his move to New Hampshire.

Mary and their two boys were with him when he finally moved to Londonderry in the summer of 1734. The town council voted him a building lot and a tract of farmland, part of which he cleared to plant vegetable crops. After a few weeks, Mary, now pregnant again, returned to live with her parents in Boston while Sam set about building a house.

Sam had help from Jamie and several neighbors in building his house. As he worked with them Jamie noted that Sam frequently punctuated his remarks with exclamations of "Cheese 'n rice". "What's this 'Cheese 'n rice' business about?" he asked.

"Oh, that is something Jim Hunter drilled into my head." Sam explained. "He didn't go for my usual cussing, said I was using the Lord's name in vain; and threatened to raise hell if I turned to using gutter language. Jim said our language is too precious to be tarnished with that kind of garbage. I thought it out and decided there was no way I could expect to quit cussing but that it was just as easy to say Cheese 'n rice as Jesus Christ."

* * * * *

The golden rays of the late afternoon sun cast a warm comforting glow over the Hampshire countryside. Sam paused as he leaned on his scythe and looked with pride at the product of his efforts during the summers of 1735 and '36. A few yards away was the rough timbered house he and his neighbors had built the preceding year. It was a small abode, neither as large nor as fancy as the Hunter house in Boston, but it was large enough for the needs of Mary and their three boys. Dan was four and a half, Sam would be three in October, and little Joel had been born in Boston during the winter of 1735 while he was still building the house. Close to the house was a barn with his horse, two cows, some sheep, hogs and chickens.

On the outskirts of the village was the little farm the townspeople had voted him. His father and brother had already been voted more land. In a way he envied them but he expected that he too would be voted additional land once he cleared and brought his tract into use. Clearing land of trees and rocks was a hard and challenging task for even the strongest men and now after months of toil, Sam could look with pride on what he had accomplished. He had completely cleared one field that was now covered with a crop of golden wheat almost ready for harvest. There was a smaller field planted to corn, potatoes, and garden crops; and he had a partly cleared tract that provided forage and pasturage for his animals.

Sam sensed a satisfied exuberance. He could look forward to a winter of self-sufficiency. He would not have to lean on da for food supplies to see his family through this winter. Reverend Macintosh had already congratulated him on the progress he had made in the two years he had been with the Reverend's Scottish flock. As he wiped sweat from his brow, Sam knew he should be content and happy. He told himself he was, that in another year or two he would have more land and maybe even build a larger house. That would be enough to keep most men happy, but what about him? Mid all the satisfaction he felt about his status, he had a restless feeling that he wanted something different. He had been content to give his full attention to making a home for his brood. Now that challenge seemed met, he wanted to broaden out.

"Cheese 'n rice", he expostulated as he explained his unrest to his father that evening, "I keep yearning for the life I had back in Ulster when Jamie and I were buying and selling stuff on the side."

"Back when you were smuggling under the king's nose," his father snorted. "Smuggling isn't something you can very well do here. I suppose though that there are opportunities for buying and selling things like you did in Boston. Why don't you wait until your crops are harvested and then ride over to Salem to see if you can work out something to satisfy your craving?"

* * * * *

It was a warm near cloudless day in late September when Sam mounted his horse for the ride to Salem. His route took him through a long stretch of heavily wooded countryside. With the autumnal burst of glory, his view of nature matched nothing he had ever seen before.

Every kind of tree known in New England was present and the riot of colors they displayed was enough to astound him. Every imaginable shade of yellow, orange, red and green could be found in the underbrush. Towering above were the bright yellows and reds of the elms, beeches and maples, the rust browns and purples of scattered oaks, and the deep greens of hemlocks and pines. Together they provided a fantasia of vivid color. No scenery in Scotland or New England had ever impressed him as much as this display of the forest's annual farewell to summer.

Once he reached Salem, Sam made a round of the shops and taverns along the harbor front. He knew the type of person he was seeking and was not disappointed when he met Jeremiah Wringer. After assuring himself that Jeremiah was a man with whom he could confide, he inquired about prospects for carrying on the type of buying and selling that most interested him.

"Oy git yur point mate," the old man told him. "Oy did me bit of smugglin back in Bristol afore the king's agints started askin questions. Twas'n excitin life. But tis ard ter copy ere. We'rn too far from dur ole country. Nun can cross der waters in small ships an one needs coin to sail dur big uns. Ad yer own ship, yer could sneak goods ere from England ur main Europe but Billy Bones kin allays stop yer un ask ter see yer bill a ladin. Many a lad as loss is ship when der navy caught im wit illegal cargo.

"Yer best bet if yer got a ship is ter trade wit the sudern colonies er dur Wes indies. Trouble is we ain'tce got nuttin but dried fish and cut trees to trade to em. Some capins are sperimentin wit tree way trade now. Dey bring

157

sugar er molasses from der Indies ere: ye turn it inta rum, and dey ship der rum to Africa where dey trade it fer niggra slaves dey en sell in der Indies so'n dey can buy more sugar n molasses. It can be a money makin deal cept der sea captins from England, France and Spain and der royal navies see us as illegals."

Sailing the ocean doesn't appeal much to me," Sam interjected. "I want to keep my trading on land."

"Den oy can't promise yer much," Jerimiah responded. "Yer could git a stock a goods to peddle from village ter village. Der's plenty people who wants tings. Trouble is dat dey have no money to pay. Dey have nuttin to sell save some grain, cheese, or·weavin an what bit a coin dey git goes fer taxes."

Sam felt discouraged as he admitted failure and started his trek back to Derry. The blaze of color in the forest seemed less glorious than it had been when he rode with hope to Salem. His feeling of gloom was accentuated as the day passed by a rising wind with a deluge of rain that soaked him to the skin and ripped what seemed like millions of leaves from the trees.

The storm grew in intensity as he rode on. The force of the wind made it difficult for him to stay on his mount. As his horse stumbled forward, he realized they must seek refuge from the elements. Worrying about his welfare and that of his horse, he almost shouted for joy when he saw a cabin in a small clearing beside the road. He went to the cabin and asked the man who came to door if he might tarry in the man's shed until the storm abated.

"What kind of Christian do you take me for," the man responded. "Put your horse in the shed an come in here out of the wet. If I am any judge of it, this storm will get worse before it passes over. We don't rightly get many of them here but I'd say this one has all the markings of one of those hurricanes that sometimes come up the coast from the Indies. I seen them a couple times down there when I sailed with Capin Berry."

Sam was more than happy to accept the warmth and protection of the cabin. During the next few hours, he enjoyed the hospitality of Joseph Austin and his wife as the storm continued to blow out its unabated fury. Austin's house was sturdy and well made. Except for the howling of the wind and the sounds of driving rain and the tearing of branches from nearby trees the storm caused little concern for the Austins other than their decision not to light a fire in their fireplace to warm their evening meal.

The two men had much to discuss after Sam got around to explaining his disappointment over his failure to find the answer he wanted at Salem. Joe listened to his account with interest. He asked a few clarifying questions and then observed: "Sam you seem like a likely lad. It could just be that I have your answer. That man you talked to was right when he told you that most folks around here have no money. He didn't tell you everything though when he said all we have for trading is fish, lumber, and weaving. That might be true when we trade with Virginny or the Indies, but the most valuable thing we have to sell in Europe is furs."

"Furs. I hadn't thought of that. That calls for trapping and shooting. Can't say I've heard much of that at Derry."

"You wouldn't at Denny. There's not much room left for furbearing critters when an area gets settled. In the outlying settlements though, lots of folks do some trapping to get extra income. But the real money and fun for folks like us comes when we leave the trapping to others. We can get a stock of trading goods and go up different rivers to Indian or white settlements where we can exchange our goods for prime pelts we can bring back for resale to the jobbers at Portsmouth or Salem."

"That outdoor living sounds fine. When do you do it?"

"Some traders make it a full time business. They are as like as not to spend their summers and winters living with the Indians, cavorting with some squaw and raising a batch of half-breeds. That's not good for Christian family life. If one plans it right though, he can take goods up in the early spring, trade them for furs, bring the pelts back for resale and have most of the year left to raise a few crops and live here with his family."

"Wouldn't it be better to go up stream during the summer when it is warmer?"

"It doesn't work that way. The Indians know that winter is the best time to trap on shoot beavers, martens, and other varmits. Their fur sets then. Later on the quality drops off and the pelts can be worthless. The furs are ready for trading around the end of March; the Indians are hungry for new supplies. If you wait for warm weather, some other trader will buy the pelts before you get there."

"You've sold me on the idea, Joe. I'd like to try it. How do I get started?"

"You may not know it Sam, but I think the Good Lord sent you here with that storm. So happens, I am looking for a partner. It is usual for two men to travel together. My last partner is down with lumbago. Old Ezra says he can't go any more. Rheumatism is too bad. If you want to make a try of it I will take you on. We can get together and line up our inventory between now and when spring breaks in March. I'll show you the ropes so you will get 40 percent of the profits to my 60 percent the first year. If we go on after that it will be fifty-fifty."

"How long will we be gone and where are we going?"

"I reckon we will be gone for eight to ten weeks and should be back by the end of May. The best river for us is the Merrimack. You must know about it because it flows not far west of your settlement at Denny. We'll go up the river paddling when we can and portaging around the falls and rapids till we get to mountain country and then go up one of the branches. All told we will probably go a hundred miles upstream."

A bargain reached, Sam returned home a happy man with dreams of exciting adventures to come. It hardly occurred to him until he reached his house that he had not counseled with Mary before making his commitment. Mary was not happy with the prospect of him being away from her and the boys for several weeks. But she loved her man and understood his untamed craving for adventure. She had already spent two extended periods away from him while he was building their house and told herself this separation would be no different. Reluctant as she was to have him away, she saw the good sense of giving his plan her blessing. If this is what Sam wants then it is what Sam should have.

An inventory of easily packed trade items was as-sembled and on March 20, a raw day with snow on the ground and bits of ice still floating with the current of the

Merrimack, Sam and Joe started their first trip together as fur traders.

* * * * *

Seated on the gnarled trunk of a fallen tree, Joe Austin gazed attentively across a small clearing along the Winnepesaukee river as he gently tamped out the ashes from his corncob pipe. He was by nature a man of cheerful disposition. Few things bothered him. For him, hand work was man's accepted lot in life. Rigorous tasks such as long summer days of scything an oat crop or poling a boat upstream through icy waters were nothing more than tests of a man's valor.

Today he was as happy and contented as he had ever been. His canoes were loaded with furs, some of the finest he had even seen. More than that, it was a warm glorious day in May. The forest around him was alive with the pulsing of spring. Tiny green leaves were bursting forth from the naked branches of the trees. The advanced season had brought forth a wonderland of small wild flowers but thankfully not yet the swarms of black flies that often made life miserable. A few feet away two gray squirrels stopped to peer at him before one chased the other up the trunk of a towering oak. Birds added to the rustic charm as they flitted about amid the trees.

Joe liked what he saw. He had no names for the different kinds of birds. Most of them were of various shades of gray. But there were exceptions. What name, he wondered, fit that yellow bird with the black markings? And what kind of bird was that little beauty with plumage the color of ripe red strawberries? With its peaked ducal crest, it could easily claim a commission in the king's service.

As Joe marveled at the beauty of nature's bounty, he felt a surge of satisfaction. This was a great day for him. The toughest part of this fur-trading trip was behind him. He and Sam had worked their way upstream and bartered their stock of goods for a pile of pelts they could now sell to their jobber at a price that would bring them a good profit. Most of the credit for their success was due to him, but much also belonged to Sam Campbell.

"It sure was my lucky day," he thought, "when Sam came to my door. For a greenhorn at this business, he turned out to be a fast learner. By the end of our first trip a year ago, he was talking Indian lingo better than I do. More than that, he has a way about him that makes strangers like him. He remembers people's names and looks, greets them like real friends, and is always polite and even tempered even when they get excited and want to start throwing things at him. Somehow he makes people feel he is a man they can trust, someone who wants to please them.

At half the villages we have visited the head men have offered him his choice of their women for the night. That is a temptation most traders accept. But not Sam. He always just shakes his head, says 'No', but says it in a way that causes no one to take offense."

Thinking of Sam, Joe wondered how much longer he would have to wait for him. The two traders had spent the previous night at Enoch's cabin only a few hundred yards upstream. They had stopped to warn Enoch about the probable presence of a party of hostile Indians that a friendly native had told them was in the area. Enoch had laughed at the idea of danger and had invited them to stay awhile to do some angling in a nearby brook before going on their way. Mention of fishing was all it took to excite Sam's interest. He was an avid angler and had insisted on delaying their departure this morning long enough for him to catch a fat trout for their evening meal.

The relative peace of the primeval scene was suddenly shattered by a shriek, a banging sound of wood hitting wood, and an excited babble of human voices. It could not be Sam returning. He had a gift for moving as silently through the woods as any Indian. Joe wondered for a moment if Sam had encountered a bear. He knew otherwise when Sam burst into sight and came running toward him. Once he got within speaking distance, he signaled for silence and whispered: "Hurry. Bring your gun. Enoch has visitors."

The two men raced toward the cabin, watching with every step for signs of trouble. As the cabin came in view they saw four Indian braves pounding at the door. Enoch was barricaded inside with his wife and child. For now they were holding the attackers at bay. The question was how long could they hold out before the Indians set fire to the cabin or broke down the door. Two of the savages carried guns; two others were pounding at the door with their tomahawks.

As Joe and Sam crept closer to the cabin, Enoch fired a musket from the window. No one was hurt but the firing brought howls of fury from the savages. Two of them picked up a log, which they proceeded to use as a battering ram against the door.

"Shoot the one nearest you while I aim at the other," Sam directed.

Their muskets were fired at the same moment. Both targets let out blood curdling cries of pain as they fell mortally wounded. Joe quickly reloaded his gun while Sam stood ready to beat off the attack if either of the two remaining braves should turn on them before he could fire again. One of the savages turned toward them in startled wonder and then threw his tomahawk in Sam's direction. Both then saw the wisdom of retreating outside of musket range. Only one, however, got away as Joe's shot felled the other before he could reach the forest's protective cover.

Enoch was profuse in his thanks. "Another ten minutes and me and my wife and kid would be missing our scalps," he told them. He examined the attire of the three dead Indians paying particular attention to the pattern of stitching on their moccasins. "They ain't local Indians," he concluded. "Must come from Canada or Maine. Bet the Frenchies are paying for scalps again."

"Cheese 'n rice," Sam exploded. "How can you stand living up here by yourself?"

"Ain't bad," Enoch assured him. "You get used to dangers that most never happen. Anyway, its better than having to live with other people."

* * * * *

Sam's life settled into a simple routine during the three years that followed: off with Joe Austin on a fur trading junket every spring, then back to clearing and farming his small holding of land. Two more sons, Nathaniel and

163

Jonathan, were born to join his expanding brood. Fur trading provided almost all of his cash income and the annual treks into the upstream wilds of the province satisfied his craving for out-of-doors adventure.

While Sam and Joe were starting to make plans in November 1740 for their next season, Reverend Samuel Dunlap, an ordained Presbyterian minister, visited the kirk at Londonderry. The Scots in the village opened their homes to the visiting divine and responded favorably to his sermons. It was soon noted though that Dunlap was driven by more than just a desire to preach the gospel. He had sailed up the Hudson River in New York province and had been promised a large grant of land near a river called the Mohawk that flowed from the west to the Hudson if he could induce others to settle in the area.

"The soil there is more fertile than here and it is not filled with stones like here. More than that, there are thousands of acres waiting for settlement and there are no proprietors or charter rules that limit the size of the acreage you can own."

James Campbell with his six children, most of them already old enough to help with the farm work, was intrigued with Dunlap's assurance that he could acquire a large estate if he chose to move to the new frontier. Unlike Sam, Jamie had always wanted to be the proprietor of a large domain; and with sons almost old enough to strike out on their own, he welcomed the promise of bountiful opportunities for them to clear and operate farms nearby.

Jamie found it easy to sell Sam on the idea of moving. Their father, however, shook his head when he was told of the prospect. "Go ahead if you must," he told his two sons. "Your mother and I have done our share of moving and I'm not ready to make any more farms. We will stay here for awhile and then maybe move to Salem to do something less strenuous when we get older."

Only two weeks after Sam agreed to consider the possible move to New York, Joe informed him that the fur-trading jaunt they were planning for the coming spring would probably be their last venture together. "Three things make me say this. I'm getting older and my rheumatism is getting worse. Peggy blames it on me getting cold and wet so often on the river. Maybe she is right.

"Then as you know, the Mason people who hold the royal charter for fur trading in these parts are tightening up their controls. Orders have come from London for their jobbers to limit the credit they give us for outfitting our supplies and they want the jobbers to lower the prices they pay for our furs. On top of all that, I learned last week that the French devils in Canada have decided they will do whatever they have to take the fur trade away from us."

"Take away our trade! Cheese 'n rice, Joe, with the White Mountains between us and them, how can they do that?"

"That is not where they are coming from. It is the new French governor at Louisburg who is raising hell for us. He has his black priests out telling the Algonquins that we are devils. Then he gives them guns and sends them over from Brunswick to raid and destroy our settlements in Maine and here and he pays them off with bounties for all the English scalps they bring him."

The two men were doubly careful as they headed upriver in March with their stock of goods for the Indian villages at which they were now used to trading. They heard rumors that hostile Indians were prowling in the area but they encountered no problems of consequence during their first month in the north.

Trouble met them on April 20. They had left a native village and were floating down the narrow channel of a small river when two savages dropped from an overhanging branch of a large tree onto their boat. Sam, who was in the front of the boat watching for rocks, logs and tree stumps that could impede their progress, was hardly aware of their sudden appearance. Joe, who was steering the boat, shouted a warning and used his paddle to strike the closest brave with a blow that toppled him into the icy waters of the stream. Alerted by Joe's shout, Sam turned, gun in hand, just in time to see the second Indian poised above Joe with his tomahawk raised for a fateful strike.

Sam fired at the very moment that the brave's lethal weapon was starting its downward swing. The shot took off part of the assailant's head and deflected his strike so that the tomahawk struck Joe's shoulder rather than his skull. Sam saw that his partner was wounded. His first impulse was to stop; but sensing the possibility of further attack, he quickly speeded the boat to an open area downstream before stopping to examine the damage done.

At the scene of the attack, one savage was dead while the second was soaking wet and suffering from a fast swelling jaw. Further downstream, Sam found that Joe had a deep gash in his right shoulder. Sam washed the wound and bound it as best he could. He then took stock of what they best could do. It was obvious they could go no farther north. That would call for sturdy paddling and poling and Joe was in no condition to do either. They had disposed of two thirds of their stock and had a neat pile of pelts to show for their efforts. With Joe wounded, they must be content with what they had and hurry down the Merrimack to a place where he could get medical attention.

Recognizing the need for prompt action, Sam tried to make his partner comfortable, turned their boat into the stream and started paddling downstream. Two days later they arrived at a village where Joe received medical care. Before the week was out Sam pounded on the door of Jamie's house in Londonderry. When his brother came to the door, Sam grabbed his hand and said: "Count me in. I'll be ready to move to New York as soon as you are."

* * * * *

Moving families west from Derry to Cherry Valley in the New York colony posed a challenging problem in 1741. Horsemen could work their way through the rough wild country. With no roads and much of the area still regarded as Indian territory, it was a different situation for families that wanted to drive their cows and other livestock while they traveled with oxen-pulled wagons piled high with household goods. Could they have afforded it, it would have been easier to sail to New York harbor and then up the Hudson river to Albany before going on by land to Cherry Valley. With no plausible alternative, the two Campbell families followed the overland route going south into Massachusetts, then across the rugged Berkshires to New York.

It took almost a month for them to get to Albany where they stopped for a day to buy needed supplies; The Dutch merchants of that town were eager to supply their needs but the Campbells were repulsed by what they saw as the merchants' greedy and self seeking demands. Only half satisfied with their purchases, they made their way west from Albany for about fifty miles across undulating hills and valleys to their new home in Cherry Valley.

Their choice of a settlement site lay in a fertile heavily wooded valley set between imposing hills and drained by Cherry creek, which flowed south into the Susquehanna river. Only a few miles away was a watershed divide beyond which water flowed north to the Mohawk river.

Cherry Valley was only one of several new settlements that were springing to life in the Mohawk strip, the name given to the 50-mile wide grant of land along the Mohawk river, stretching from Niagara in the west to Albany on the Hudson, that the Province of New York had acquired from the Five Nations in 1723. Several large grants had been and were still being made by the governor and his aides to individuals. One of these was the grant of 8,000 acres at Cherry Valley that Lieutenant Governor George Clark made to John Lindesay in 1738.

The sight of deep valleys in the area had intrigued Lindesay, sparkling streams gurgling their way over rocky beds, and moderately steep hillsides that reminded him of his native Scotland. He moved to his grant after it was surveyed in 1739 and might have starved during the bleak winter of 1740 had friendly Indians not brought food for him on snowshoes. It was after that experience that he induced Reverend Dunlap to help find settlers to develop the area.

The Campbell brothers housed their families together in a single house in 1741 while they directed their efforts to clearing land for planting crops and erecting their first rudimentary buildings. David Ramsay, William Gallt, and William Dickson joined them as settlers and by year's end there were 30 people, all immigrants from Ulster, living in the pioneer community.

Sam gave full attention during his first year at Cherry Valley, as he had earlier at Derry; to clearing land and putting up needed buildings. He took pride in his work because he knew he was providing for his family's survival. It was not work, however, that he enjoyed. His brother Jamie wanted to acquire part of Lindesay's land grant. Not so with Sam. He had no interest in slaving to clear land of trees, stumps and stones if that was what it took to become the proprietor of a large estate. His inclinations being what they were, he soon found himself pining for adventure like that he had enjoyed as a fur trader who kept a farm only as a home base for his growing family.

Sam stayed on at Cherry Valley for three years during which two more sons, Levi and Reuben, and a daughter, Mary, were born. During the winter that followed his arrival, he tried his hand at trapping. There were numerous beaver and marten in the valley and his work yielded a pile of pelts he planned to haul overland to Albany where he was sure he could find a buyer. His plan changed for the better in April when he chanced to meet a westbound traveler near the Mohawk river who told him there was no need to go to Albany. There was a closer and better market for his pelts at the Johnson store located a few miles further east on the north side of the Mohawk.

"Tell me about this man Johnson," Sam asked, "is he an honest dealer or is he out to squeeze every last penny he can git from you?"

"William Johnson is a wonder in these parts," the traveler reported. "If you expect to live round here you had best get to know him. It won't be hard cause he is of an accommodating sort, hale, and well met. He likes people and goes out of his way to help them. Doesn't make any difference to him whether you are a settler, some Indian, or the governor. He is a young chap, still in his twenties. But you can believe me when I tell you he is going places. He has energy and vision. Not like the politicians in Albany and New York, he does more than just talk. He sees what needs doing and goes ahead and does it."

"How can a young sprout like that get to run a store in these parts?"

"From what I've heard, he came across from England or Ireland four years ago. He was sent up here by his uncle, Sir Peter Warren, who is an admiral in the king's navy, to manage a big estate the admiral somehow picked up. The admiral doesn't know any more about clearing raw land than I know about sailing one of his ships. He keeps sending orders on what Johnson should do. Johnson just does what makes sense and so far has kept the admiral satisfied. He has gone beyond that though to get land of his own and to open the biggest store for settler goods west of Albany. He can sell for lower prices than the Albany merchants because he has figured a way to place his orders in London, ship his goods up the Hudson, bypass that waterfall where the Mohawk flows into the Hudson near Albany and bring them here for sale. With his London connections he pays more for the furs settlers and traders bring in than what the Dutch merchants pay."

"Sounds like the settler's friend. But what kind of a man is he?"

"He is tall and built like you. Like I said, he likes people and most folks like him. He is doing his bit to encourage new settlements. At the same time, he is staking fur traders and has gone out of his way to keep peace with the Mohawks and the other Five Nations of Iroquois tribesmen. Unlike most white settlers, he likes Indians and treats them as brothers. He's learned their language and even goes out ever so often to live with them. He wrestles and hunts with their young braves and trades advice with their old sachems. He has their confidence because they can trust him to keep his word."

Sam followed the stranger's advice a week later when he floated his pelts down a creek to the Mohawk and then down the river to the Johnson store. He was surprised to find several boats headed both up and down stream. Four bateaux were docked near the store. He soon learned that they were flat-bottomed canal boats manned by boisterous crews that poled loads of cargo both east and west of Johnson's store. Falls near the mouth of the Mohawk where it flowed into the Hudson river kept the bateaux from going all the way to the Hudson. By using a portage point near Schenectady from which goods could be hauled overland to and from the Hudson, Johnson had found that he could bypass both the falls on the Mohawk and the town of Albany where Dutch merchants would have insisted on handling his trade.

The store was comprised of a few rough buildings surrounded by a stockade. Outside the storehouse was a campground where settlers, traders, and Indians could spend the night. No group was favored over another. Sam was impressed when he found that a dozen Indians were camped there along with a party of newly arrived Moravian settlers who were going on to a settlement at German Flats.

Sam's biggest surprise came when he visited the store. Inside was a veritable trove of goods. Not since he had left Boston had he seen such a variety of wares in one place and even in Boston they were not so reasonably priced. Around him was an array of British manufactures. He was particularly impressed with the supply of goods that fur traders could use in their trade with Indians. There were stacks of blankets, brightly colored rolls of calico, stockings, garters, ribbons, barrels of gun powder, boxes of lead, gun flints, knives, shags of tobacco, strings of beads, jars of body paint, glittering combs, buckets of molasses, and wampum. Rum also was available though Johnson discouraged its sale to Indians.

Johnson was at the store when Sam entered and came forward to meet him. He introduced himself, examined Sam's furs and surprised him by offering a higher price for them than Sam had expected. In the conversation that followed Sam found that they shared many mutual interests. He soon decided that this man was everything he had been led to expect while Johnson sized Sam up as a likable compatriot whose company he would enjoy.

"So you are from Ulster," Johnson exclaimed. "Welcome to Mohawk country. We have a bit of everything here: Indians, Dutchmen, Germans, English settlers and soldiers, an occasional Huguenot, and our countrymen from Ireland and Scotland. I love them all, all that is except the black Jesuits who send the Frenchies in Canada and their Indians against us. Most of all I love our settlers from Ireland."

"Does that mean you favor Catholics?"

"No, no. Religion has nothing to do with it. Our people can believe anything they like. Christians I hope. Fact is I'm Church of England but anyone Episcopalian, Presbyterian, Catholic, Massachusetts Puritan, Quaker,

Moravian or what have you is welcome as long as he is law abiding and willing to help settle the country."

The emerging rapport between the two men was tightened when Johnson invited Sam to have supper with him. Johnson took a liking to him partly because he was better educated and had more worldly knowledge than most settlers, because he displayed little interest in acquiring land, and mostly because of his enthusiastic comments about fur trading and his tale of adventures in Scotland and New Hampshire.

"Look Sam," he told his guest, "I'll stake you for the supplies you need any time you want to go back to fur trading. For now though, I have another deal for you. I'm taking a stock of goods to our fort at Oswego on Lake Ontario next week. Why don't you come along? Coming will give you a good look at the country. You might even see some places where you can do some trading."

Sam was with him the next week when he left with four batteaux that were loaded with an assortment of goods for western New York. A burly crew of strong boisterous men who sang and cussed as they poled their flat-bottomed boats up the river manned each batteaux. Sam was impressed with the speed with which they propelled their cargo along the more gentle stretches of the river. Progress was slower when they had to work their way upstream through minor rapids. At eight different points men or oxen on the river's bank used ropes attached to the boats to pull them up through river rapids.

At Little Falls, almost half way upstream from the Johnson store, the boats had to be unloaded and their cargoes hauled up around the river falls before they could proceed further. A little over 30 miles farther upstream they reached a carrying over place where they transported their cargoes over a short portage to Wood Creek. With their boats reloaded they traveled the 60 miles downstream to Oneida lake, across the lake, and then down the Oneida river to Oswego.

Johnson's party did not ride on the boats. They rode instead along what could be called a road that bordered the water route. Used as a road during the drier season, it was nigh impassible for wagon traffic after the spring rains.

"This is a miserable road," Johnson said. "It will get more passable as we go farther west because there will be fewer settlers to abuse it. The route goes all the way to Fort Niagara, and it follows what was once just an Indian trail. No one has done it of late, but Indians tell me that they once had runners who could carry messages all the way from Niagara to Albany in under three days."

When Sam asked about the settlements they passed, Johnson explained that they were traveling through the large Mohawk strip grant the Five Nations had made 20 years before to New York. Since then governors and their associates had sold or given substantial grants to various individuals. "My uncle purchased an estate from the widow of a governor who knew how to transfer land titles to his own account. Like most of the others who received grants, he is holding on to most of his land, selling some, but hoping mostly that settlers will come in and create a market for future sales.

"The Dutch patroons who got land from the old Dutch government set up several manorial estates along the Hudson. Some of our new grant owners had dreams of doing the same thing. The breed of settlers who are coming now though have no stomach for being life long tenants or manorial workers. They want to buy land and build up estates of their own. If they can't afford to buy, they just settle on vacant land and use it as their own until an owner shows up to run them off."

As the party made its way west, it encountered fewer and fewer settlements. Johnson explained: "This is good land and with settlers coming in it won't be long before we have towns and villages. Then we'll have better roads. We will even have teamsters along the river to pull the bateaux up through the rapids. We may even build locks like they have in Europe to make the river more navigable."

Johnson left the road at several points to visit Indian villages. At every stop he was greeted with enthusiastic cheers. It was obvious the natives saw him as a friend they could admire and trust. These were Mohawk villages he explained. The Mohawks were the largest and most easterly of the Six Nations of Indians that spoke the Iroquois language. Farther west in New York were the villages of the

Cayugas, the Onondogas, the Oneidas, and the Senacas. A southern tribe, the Tuscaroras, used the same dialect and had for the last 20 years been allied with them as the sixth of the Six Nations.

Legal title to the land was claimed by the royal colony of New York and by the recipients of its grants, but it was the Indian givers who still occupied most of the land. Johnson understood more than the officials in Albany that the security of the settlers and fur traders depended in large measure on the cultivation and maintenance of good will with the Indian nations. He saw it as his responsibility to work for this end. In so doing, he treated the Indians as his equals and was accepted in turn as their blood brother. He bowed to and saluted the old men, hugged and wrestled with the younger ones, and was regarded as a hero by the women of the tribe.

On their second night on the road, they stayed in an Indian village. Sam was offered a comely maiden as a bedmate, an offer he deftly declined. Johnson, however, accepted a similar offer and spent the night with his maiden in a private tent while Sam slept with most of the tribe in their long house.

It took ten days for the party to get to Oswego. The town there was a bustling trading center frequented by 150 fur traders and several merchants who looked to Johnson as their wholesaler. Located as it was on the south shore of Lake Ontario, it stood as a British bastion that challenged the presence of the French operators at Fort Frontenac across Lake Ontario and at Fort Niagara located 120 miles to the west near the end of Lake Ontario.

The importance of the base at Oswego to the British cause was obvious. It provided the one big market in the west country where Indians and traders could exchange their furs for British manufactures. French traders were intent on capturing the same trade and had some advantages in that they had reached the area first, had a direct water route on the St. Lawrence river to the French towns at Montreal and Quebec, and had sent their black robed priests out to convert the natives and school them on the virtue of trading with representatives of France. Many Indians followed the advice of the priests but more and more traveled great distances to sell to the English traders who paid more for furs than the French and who offered better selections of trading goods at lower prices than the French charged.

At the end of their first day at Oswego, Johnson pointed at the activity around them and said: "You see here the need we have for an enlightened Indian policy. Half the time those fools back along the Atlantic act without having any idea of the effect of their policies on the fur trade. The trade is vital to our interests. Furs and tobacco are the two most valuable products we can send to Europe.

"We have room for more settlers here but we must also protect the fur trade. To do that we must counter the efforts of the French to take over the west. We need to strengthen our fortifications and at the same time treat the Indians as partners. Some of those East coast asses talk of removing the Indians. That talk is foolish and dangerous. Friction with the Indians is one thing we must avoid. Driving them into the arms of the French is the last thing we should do."

* * * * *

Sam respected his wife. He was not sure he really loved Mary. At least he did not regard her in the same wild and reckless way he had pledged his plight to Alice. Yet she was a good mother to his children and he felt a firm commitment to his marriage. Even with her husband gone for extended periods, Mary had maintained a happy home for their seven sons and one daughter. She had borne more responsibility than most wives while he was away. Yet she accepted his yearning to be afoot and was always there with open arms when he returned.

Unlike Johnson and many other traders, Sam put aside any temptation he could have had to cavort with Indian maidens. It was not that he lacked opportunities. His genial good nature made him a welcome visitor in the villages he visited. On his first visit he was frequently offered a choice of partners, His tactful refusals, however, soon convinced his hosts of his commitment to his monogamous status. It was not that he condemned the willingness of his fellow traders to plant their seed among the Indians. His Presbyterian upbringing and six years of living in Puritan Boston had left him content to curry the favor of only one woman.

His attitude about fidelity and marriage was affected by his love of family. Poor Mary had had the job of raising his kids. He loved every one of them and often felt he had neglected them. He should be teaching his sons things they would need to know as men. Ever so often he would devote himself whole-heartedly to the task. Whenever he settled down he soon became bored and started to yearn again for life in the wild.

They had lived at Cherry Valley for three years when Sam suggested they move closer to the Johnson store. Much to his surprise, Mary eagerly agreed. She had found life at Cherry Valley with its five families confining. In Scotland, Boston, and Londonderry she had been able to attend regular church services. She wanted to live in a place where she would have more neighbors, opportunities to visit stores, and hopefully see her husband more often. There was another unspoken reason for moving. She liked Sam's brother and his family but was heartily tired of hearing people compare Jamie's success in now owning a grant of 2,000 acres with her husband's apparent lack of interest in land ownership.

The family moved in 1744 to a settlement near the Johnson store. At the new location Sam had a small farm, which he operated much as he had in Londonderry. Fur trading was now his principal occupation and he worked hand in hand with Johnson. The storekeeper had staked him for his first two years of operations and he had saved enough to now operate without credit. Johnson saw enough of him to note that he had a knack for gaining the confidence and cooperation of Indians. He hired Sam to work with him from time to time on Indian affairs. He also suggested that Sam concentrate his fur trading operations in the area north and east of the store that was located near the big crook in the Hudson river.

1744 and 1745 were years of tension along the Mohawk frontier. Britain and France were facing off against each other in Europe's War of Austrian Succession. Their

175

standoff in America was limited mostly to French inspired raids on the British colonies. The French governor at the great fortress at Louisburg on Cape Breton island sponsored predatory raids in northern New England. An army of irregulars from the threatened area retaliated by storming and seizing the supposedly impregnable fort in June 1745. Meanwhile, the French powers in Canada organized and provisioned raids by warriors from Canadian tribes against the settlers and Iroquois villages in the Mohawk country.

Settlers and Indian villages along the Mohawk were left on their own to face the challenge from the north. Johnson and others petitioned the colonial authorities in New York for support but they chose to sit on their hands and ignore the valley's need for defense appropriations. The colony's Board of Indian Commissioners let itself be bogged down with concern over trivial matters when there was real need for resolute action.

Johnson discussed the situation at a conference with Indian leaders at Albany in 1744 and got them to extend the covenant under which the Iroquois nations pledged their support to the British cause. The Indians refused, however, to make war on their Canadian cousins unless they were further provoked. They also used the occasion to complain about several injustices including the high prices they were charged for the goods they bought.

A change for the better came in April 1746 when Governor Clinton discharged the Commission of Indian Affairs and appointed William Johnson as the lone commissioner to supervise Britain's relations with all of the Indian tribes from Canada south to Georgia. Johnson took prompt action to strengthen the military fortification at Oswego. He was commissioned as colonel of the valley's militia and was soon prepared to meet the French challenge. War in America was avoided, however, when the peace of Aix la Chappelle was signed in Europe.

Johnson's appointment added to his duties but brought financial problems as he found it expedient to advance his own funds to pay for needed military supplies. With his added responsibilities, he found it necessary to seek assistance. Sam was one of those he turned to for help. For the next dozen years, Sam was a valued and loyal assistant, not a holder of great authority or a flashy title, but always a competent and patient workhorse who could on short notice carry messages to or negotiate with Indian chiefs or accompany shipments of defense materials to Oswego and other sites.

While the war in Europe ended with the signing of the Treaty of Aix la Chappelle, tensions continued between the French officials in Canada and their British counterparts in the northern colonies. Both had settlers to protect. Both were supporting rival Indian tribes and competing for furs in the unsettled west. Britain's commissioners at the peace conference had foolishly given up the fortress at Louisburg which the citizen militia from New England had captured without help from the British army. And the new French governor at the fortress was again encouraging Indian raids against the British settlements.

Sam was now a frequent traveling companion of William Johnson. Many trips were for business, many also for recreation. Both men liked to hunt and fish. One of their favorite retreats was at a lake and brook located in the Adirondack foothills some miles northeast of the Johnson store.The mountain vista, nearby crags, and cascading waters reminded Sam of the Scottish Highlands.

On one of their visits Sam talked of possibly building a house near the lake. Johnson responded by offering him land. "I can get a claim for you," he promised. "This place is part of a grant the governor made some years ago. The claim is dormant because the owner cannot get a clear title until I get the Mohawk sachems to sign some papers. I'll get the title transferred to you when the time comes. Until then, you can go ahead with your building. While we are at it, what will you call the settlement?"

"Cheese 'n rice, Will. I haven't thought of that. It is sort of like a gift from heaven here. Let's call it Providence."

* * * * *

Sam never got around to moving to Providence though two of his sons started a small settlement there in 1753. For Sam, Mary and their family, the decade that followed his move to the site near Johnson's store was a happy period. The farm that Mary and his boys operated provided the family with adequate food while Sam's earnings as a fur trader and scout provided a steady source of income. As the boys grew older, they too added to the family's income by hiring themselves out for various types of work.

The British colonies were officially at peace with France during most of this period. There was never a season though when the settlers along the Mohawk felt really safe from possible raids. Reports came year after year from Oswego and Niagara of the growing influence the French were exerting with the Indians of western New York, Pennsylvania, and the Ohio country. France was succeeding with its policy of cultivating the good will, friendship, loyalty, and trading preferences of the western natives. As Indian commissioner, Johnson was keenly aware of what was happening. He foresaw the inevitability of armed conflict but had only limited success in selling the colonial officials who lived in port cities along the Atlantic coast on the need for concerted action.

A major conference involving representatives from seven colonies and the principal Indian tribes met at Albany in 1754. There was much talk there of developing a unified strategy for dealing with the French and Indian issues. The delegates listened to the complaints voiced by Indian spokesmen and received a renewed pledge of loyalty from them. But little was accomplished in securing promises of coordinated action by the colonies.

A surprising development came, however, when Benjamin Franklin proposed the organization of a union in which delegates selected by the assemblies of the several colonies would have the power to manage Indian affairs for all of the colonies and be empowered to raise troops and levy and collect taxes to support any wars in which the colonies might be involved. The proposal was applauded by some delegates but was rejected by the majority who regarded it as too democratic.

The prospect for war became real in July 1754 when George Washington, an enterprising young officer in Virginia, was sent with a few hundred soldiers to western Pennsylvania to warn the French garrison at Fort Duquesne that it should vacate the fort and give up France's claim to the area. The small force was met and soundly defeated by a larger force of French and Indian fighters. Britain responded to this rebuff by sending General Braddock to Virginia with an army of British regulars to enforce Britain's claim to the west.

Commonsense would have had Braddock march west along the Mohawk trail where his heavy gear and ordnance could have been transported much of the way over relatively level terrain and by water. Braddock, however, acted under orders issued by the Duke of Cumberland, George II's son, who headed Britain's War Ministry. The duke, who had commanded the army that defeated Bonnie Prince Charles at Culloden, was highly regarded as a military strategist. But seated in London with little appreciation of American advice, geography or travel conditions, he made a grievous mistake in ordering his general to follow the mountainous overland route from Chesapeake Bay to the headwaters of the Ohio river.

Braddock marched west with a larger army than the French had but soon lost most of his Indian scouts who felt slighted by the condescending attitude of the British officers. A painful result was experienced on July 9 when what was left of his army was caught in a disastrous ambush in the hills of western Pennsylvania.

Britain's grand strategy in 1755 called for two other military expeditions. A contingent of troops was to march west along the Mohawk trail to capture the French installation at Fort Niagara on Lake Ontario. Another army was to move up the Hudson river, cross over to Lake George, and go on from there to capture the French fort at Crown Point on Lake Champlain.

As the officer most familiar with the Mohawk trail area and with the best-established record of being able to work with Britain's Indian allies, the command of the Fort Niagara expedition should have gone to Colonel William Johnson, now Major General Johnson. Similar logic favored the designation of Governor Shirley of Massachusetts as commander of the Crown Point venture.

As the plans for the two expeditions were being developed, Governor Shirley concluded that more glory would be associated with a victory at Niagara than at Crown Point. He then used his political clout to claim the Niagara appointment. Johnson was relegated to the Crown Point command and soon found himself at odds with Shirley who insisted on the transfer of Johnson's militia and Indians to his command.

Shirley was late in starting his westward march. His lack of familiarity with local conditions along the route gave rise to unexpected delays. His problems were further aggravated when his condescending manner in dealing with his Indian allies caused most of them to return to their villages. Before ever reaching Niagara, Shirley declared the expedition a failure and dispatched a report to London in which he placed the blame for his defeat on Johnson and the Indians.

* * * * *

The summer of 1755 found Shirley marching west up the Mohawk valley while the militia Johnson had been able to keep crossed Shirley's force as they marched east toward Albany, then up along the Hudson river to a base near the southern tip of Lake George, still known to the French as Lac Ste. Sacrament.

Sam and his eldest son, Daniel, insisted on accompanying Johnson's force. "It's not that I don't want you, Sam," the general told him, "but you don't need to do this. I won't say you are too old to fight, but you have certainly earned the right to stand by and let younger men carry the load."

"Cheese 'n rice, Will," Sam retorted, "wild animals couldn't keep me from going. You are going to need scouts. Shirley has made sure you won't have as many Mohawks to help out as you'll need. I can help cause I know every crag and swamp in those woods as good as any scout you'll find."

Johnson was not able to start his drive until August. By then Shirley had asserted his seniority and taken his pick of the available supplies leaving only meager remnants for the Crown Point expedition. More supplies were needed. Wagons and scouts had to be found. Shirley's meddling with the Indians had left many tribesmen undecided about whether they should participate with either army.

On August 8 Johnson and the Mohawk chief Henrick started to move north with their supplies and artillery from Albany. The New York and Rhode Island militia that had been promised had not yet reached them. Johnson saw it as important, however, that they get to Fort Edward at the crossover point between the Hudson and Lake George where the colonial militia from Massachusetts and Connecticut commanded by Brigadier General Lyman were to meet them.

Within days, 200 more Indians and the New York and Rhode Island militia arrived. The size of the colonial force rose to 3,500 men. It was an untrained citizen army with only one officer who was a trained British regular. Morale was high and the men were eager to fight.

There was no discernable loss of enthusiasm or determination when news reached the army of Braddock's defeat. Many were convinced that this strictly colonial army could gain victory where the British regulars had not. Johnson's major challenge was that of gaining the confidence of his New England troops. This he did by charming their officers with his cordiality, by insisting that they join him in his military councils, and by asking one of their ministers to preach to them on the Sabbath.

Moving on from Fort Edward, Johnson took his men to the southern tip of Lake George where he established a camp large enough to accommodate 5,000 men. The site of the camp had military disadvantages for a garrison lacking boats for escaping by water if the camp were attacked from the south. It was a good site though for Johnson's army as it provided unlimited supplies of pure fresh water as well as a good launching site for sending the army north by boat to attack the French held points located on Lake George and Lake Champlain. By the end of August, the camp was in working order and Johnson had crews at work cutting timbers and building boats for the expected attack.

The French garrison at Crown Point was forewarned by papers captured from the British during Braddock's defeat of the plan to attack the fort. The garrison there was commanded by General Ludwig August von Dieskau, a

German baron and French marshal who had earned a distinguished reputation in the European wars. Learning of Johnson's encampment on Lake George, Dieskau decided to transport his force of 216 French regulars, 700 Canadians, and 700 Indians up the ribbon like narrows of Lake Champlain's South Bay which lies a few miles east of and parallel to Lake George for what he hoped would be a surprise attack on Fort Edward. He assumed the fort would be held by a small band of green troops that could be easily overpowered before he would turn his force north to attack Johnson's lakeside camp from the south.

Unknown to Dieskau the garrison that had been left at Fort Edward had been reinforced and was well able to care for itself. The plan for the attack was disrupted, however, when Dieskau made the mistake of following the wrong road after his men disembarked at the tail end of South Bay. His army soon found itself located between the two colonial garrisons rather than farther east on the direct route to Fort Edward.

While scouting in the area, Sam was one of the first to discover that a French army had landed. He returned to Johnson's camp with the information that night. Johnson and his staff concluded at a council at dawn the next morning that Dieskau would attack Fort Edward first. A force of 1,200 men was dispatched to stall the attack. Meanwhile, Dieskau changed his plan and turned his force about to attack the lake encampment.

Dieskau was able to ambush the colonial militia that was moving to support Fort Edward. In the skirmish that followed, the provincials were thrown back and several of their officers including the Indian chief Hendrick were killed. The survivors retreated in good order to a barricade Johnson had had the foresight to prepare. Reinforcements soon arrived from Lake George and the colonials quickly demonstrated their superiority. Artillery was used to intimidate the Canadian Indians and the French regulars were firmly repulsed when they tried to storm the barricade, General Dieskau was severely wounded and captured as the remaining French soldiers fled back to their boats.

Sam fought at Johnson's side and helped to cover him when he was taken to his tent after falling with a bullet in his thigh. When evening came on September 8 the Americans were content to lick their wounds as they celebrated Britain's lone victory of the year over the French. With no boats of their own on South Bay, no attempt was made to pursue the French army. Most of Dieskau's retreating soldiers were able to return to Crown Point. A combination of supply problems and bad weather then caused both armies to discontinue hostilities.

News of the victory was celebrated both in the colonies and in England. Johnson, now an acclaimed hero, was awarded a knighthood by royal order in November. Bothered by his wound and weary of military action he resigned his commission as major general that winter while retaining his rank as colonel of the Albany militia and his position as commissioner of Indian affairs.

* * * * *

War clouds darkened the scene in late 1755 as both sides made preparations to continue the struggle. Britain sent Major General James Abercrombie and Major General Thomas Webb to the colonies at the end of the year with 8,000 troops and plans for strengthening the garrison at Oswego and launching another drive on Crown Point. Meanwhile, command of the French forces in Canada shifted to Louis Joseph de Saint Veran, the Marquis de Montcalm, an officer who captured public attention as a man of charm and imagination.

Montcalm took an army west to Lake Ontario in 1756 and captured Fort Bull, a small British fortification located near the portage point between the Mohawk river and Wood Creek. This action threatened the security of the trading post at Oswego. Dispatches were sent to Abercrombie asking for help. Abercrombie, however, was slow to act and decided to await the arrival of the Earl of Loudown who had been appointed as Governor of Virginia and commander-in-chief of the British forces in the American colonies.

At Governor Shirley's insistence a small force under John Bradstreet hurried west along the Mohawk trail and through a gauntlet of French and Indian attacks to deliver needed supplies at Oswego. His party brought back information in mid July that Montcalm was massing an army with artillery to take Oswego. General Webb was dispatched to aid the defenders but the besieged garrison surrendered before help could arrive.

With the loss of Oswego, all of the settlements along the Mohawk were endangered. The Iroquois tribes in the western portion of the valley assumed a neutral stance as the French tried to entice them to join in a drive that could take the valley over for France. The Mohawks alone remained loyal to their alliance with Britain.

Sir William was bedridden at a time when his negotiation skills were most needed. It took tact and forceful persuasion on his part and on that of Sam and his other agents to keep the Mohawks and other tribes from repudiating their British alliance. Hostile Indians from Canada roamed almost at will throughout the valley while Governor Loudown kept 10,000 troops in camp with no constructive plan for their use.

Loudown was suited neither by tact nor military expertise for his position. He talked big and did little. His inclination to look down on the colonists and berate their ability and accomplishments made him an unpopular and repulsive figurehead. He sailed with much of his army to Halifax in 1757 with the intent of besieging the French installation at Louisburg. Once there he waited for a month, then gave up the quest and returned to New York. During his absence, General Webb was stationed with 6,000 troops at the new Fort William Henry located at the site of Johnson's earlier encampment on Lake George.

Sam chanced to meet Johnson in June. Both lamented the sorry state of affairs. Hostilities in the area had brought fur trading to a standstill. People were coming to the Johnson store only for necessities. While they were together, Johnson said: "You'll be interested, Sam, in a letter I have just received from the commander at William Henry. He knows Montcalm is preparing for a run on the fort and that he will be outnumbered. He has only 2,200 men in his garrison counting the help he can get from Fort Edward. He wrote that he has an urgent need for scouts and even ordered me to find some Indians for him.

"Cheese 'n rice, Will, why didn't he call on me. Two of my boys live only twenty miles from that fort and I know every mountain, every crag, every swamp and creek in the area."

"It's a job for a young man, Sam. Stay here where you are safe."

"I ain't that old and infirm yet, laddie. Tell him I'll come." And he did.

Sam reported for duty to Colonel Monroe, the commander of the British garrison at William Henry at the beginning of July. He organized Munro's small cadre of scouts and reported two weeks later that Montcalm had brought a large army together with water borne artillery up Lake Champlain and then over onto Lake George and that he was also moving troops to South Bay on Lake Champlain along the same route Dieskau had used two years earlier. The French had already established a temporary camp on Lake George at a point two miles north of William Henry just beyond the firing range of the fort's guns. Sam estimated that Montcalm was commanding a force of 7,000 men and that within a week he would have enough cannon in place to give him superior firing power.

Asked for his recommendations on strategy, Sam shook his head and said: "I'm not a military man, sir, but I do know something about fighting the Frenchies. If Montcalm brings his gunboats to bear on us, he can stay out of range of our guns at the fort while he sinks every boat and scow we have on the lake. Then he can turn his guns on the fort, which doesn't have a hope of being able to stand up to bombardment by big guns. Should he get his army behind us like Dieskau almost did, he can bottle us up here where we will have no choice but to surrender or die."

"What would our chances be if we tried to escape?"

"We can't go anywhere by water. Montcalm controls the lake and anyway going that way would only take us to Canada. If he cuts off the road to Fort Edward, we will be stuck here. There is a road over to the end of South Bay where he has an army. Our chance of going the other direction is cut off by a swamp that no army could cross."

"Are you saying that the swamp is impassable?"

"It is for women and children and for most men too. I have crossed it but most Indians see it as a death trap."

"Then we had best get word to General Webb at Albany 'cause we are not planning to withdraw or surrender."

During the week that followed Sam brought one gloomy report after another to Colonel Munro, so many that the colonel was tempted to accuse him of being in league with the enemy. Every report indicated continued advance by the French forces. On July 23 a detachment of French and Indian troops tangled with the garrison from Fort Edward and came away with 32 scalps. Four days later Montcalm brought his artillery to bear on the cluster of British boats and scows anchored at the southern tip of the lake in front of Fort William Henry. The boats were picked off like sitting ducks. Within two hours 22 boats and scows were either sunk or captured.

Montcalm now had full control of the lake. He could bring his big guns to bear on the fort at any time. First though, he sent half of his army to take and hold the road to Fort Edward. With Munro's line of possible retreat cut off, the bombardment of the fort began. It was soon evident that the garrison at the fort was outgunned and that its timber walls and blockhouses provided slim protection from enemy assault. The fire from Montcalm's big guns ripped timbers apart as though they were nothing more than matchsticks.

Munro found himself in an impossible position. He was unwilling to give up the fort. Yet his only hope of holding it called for attack by a British relief force. Messages had been sent to General Webb requesting aid. Yet Webb, who was stationed a few miles to the south with a sizable body of troops, hesitated to act without first receiving orders from Governor Loudown. Far from sending a relief force, Webb sent back a recommendation that Munro surrender the fort. The message was intercepted by a French patrol and then sent on to Munro who after five days of fierce bombardment concluded that he had no alternative but to surrender.

Sam met with the colonel and his officers in a final council session the night before the surrender. What would happen if they surrendered was the question on everyone's' mind. Some, used to the European rules of war, assumed that Munro and a few of the officers would be taken as prisoners to Canada while the regulars, colonials, and Indians would be disarmed, marched a few miles south of the fort, and then sent on their way.

Asked his opinion, Sam said: "What you say could prove true if we were faced with just French regulars. Trouble is that the Frenchies have a thousand Indian savages with them. They came here looking for scalps and booty and Montcalm will have a devil of a time keeping them under control. We know from what they did here two years ago and then again at Oswego last year that they will strip clothes and scalps off their own dead if they have a mind to. If you can, you should insist that Montcalm take away the Indians' weapons until we are safely away from them."

Sam's recommendation, though sound, was not honored by the French commander. The truth of his expectation became apparent the next day when the dejected garrison hauled down its flag, stacked its weapons, and marched slowly outside the fort. Colonel Munro led his army while Sam and three of his Indian scouts were among the last to leave. As they started down the road to Fort Edward, Sam noted that while a body of French regulars had entered the fort, the main body of Montcalm's army was not in sight. He sensed a need for extra caution when he noted the presence along both sides of the road of several hundred Indian warriors strutting with their body paint and feathers; shaking their fists, and waving their tomahawks in defiance of the orders called out by the few officers who were present. Sam knew the retreating army was in for trouble.

The dejected men and women from the fallen fortress hurried forward in fearful silence as the Indians continued to jeer and curse them. They were already spread out over almost a half-mile of the forest-lined route when Sam heard the expected shout of vengeance. Somewhere ahead a Canadian Indian had tried to snatch a red shawl or some other desired item from one of the departing women. She had resisted the taking and the savage vented his fury by striking her with his hatchet. Soon the cry was taken up all along the route as the Indians moved in with their weapons to take the booty and scalps they wanted.

As Sam surveyed the situation, he saw that there was nothing he could do to save the people ahead of him from the carnage he knew was at hand. Without weapons he could not even defend himself. Fearing for his life, he looked to the surrounding woods for an opportunity to escape. Off to the right some fifty yards beyond its border of trees was the swamp. If he could get there he might be safe.

Noting a sudden movement ahead of the Algonquin braves who had been in his immediate area, he called for his Mohawk scouts and the others near him to follow him. He then ran through the trees to the swamp and jumped into its uncertain waters. The swamp was covered with the slimy green scum of summer and offered a doubtful promise of escape to those who followed him. Of the group, his three Indian scouts were the only ones who entered the swamp with him. The others chose to look for hiding spots in the woods where they might escape the attention of the howling Algonquins.

Sam led his scouts through the more shallow portion of the swamp to a wilderness island in its midst. They stopped there to rest at a place where they heard the continuing cries of people killed and wounded in the massacre intermingled with the shouts and victory chants of the Indian contingent of Montcalm's army. Two hours went by before the sounds of the tumult subsided. Sam was half inclined to return to the scene of the ambush but chose not to when he realized that hostile Indians were probably still there stealing the clothing and scalps of the dead.

It was with extreme care that Sam led his Indian friends across the swamp. The going was slow as they moved through the water testing almost every step to avoid mishaps. After four hours of wading through uncertain waters they reached the western bank and went on to a familiar Indian trail. It was there that Sam said goodbye to his Indian friends and went on after a night of sleep in the woods to Providence where he was happy to find that his two sons and their families had been untouched by the violence at William Henry.

* * * * *

Sam sat on a crude homemade bench in his three-room house. Spring was breaking forth out of doors. This should be a happy time for him, time for his annual excursions to pick up furs for his trade with Sir William's store. But he was miserable. He had a throbbing toothache and knew he faced the agony of another molar extraction. The prospect made him wince. Pulling out a molar was no picnic.

He had already lost most of his teeth and was not looking forward to a toothless future. Yet he had no alternative. His jaw would keep on throbbing until he rooted out the offending member.

The only good thing about having an aching tooth was that it took his mind off his other troubles. Widespread fear of unprovoked raids by hostile Indians had made life unpleasant for all but the most complacent settlers in the valley. Just last November raiders had struck at settlements at German Flats, massacred settlers, pillaged and burned their homes, and driven off their cattle. With the suspicion and distrust many settlers and Indians had of strangers, his fur trading had come to a standstill.

Sam was undecided about who was responsible, who should be blamed for the valley's problems. He could blame the French who were still waging a war to expand French Canada and France's claims to the west country. Their Jesuit priests deserved his ire because it was they who instigated most of the raids against noncombatant settlers. He was inclined to point his finger at that coward General Webb who had stood by doing nothing when he had an army almost within hearing range of the cannons at William Henry. More worthy of blame though was John Campbell, the Earl of Loudown, a disgrace to the Campbell name, who had dilly dallied and turned his back on the people he governed while making wild accusations about the short comings of his colonels, of the Americans, and of their Six Nation allies.

Sam was still commiserating when Samuel Campbell, a son of his brother at Cherry Valley, rode up to his house. "Good news, uncle," he called in greeting. "Those lame brains in London have finally seen the light. Webb and old Loudown have been recalled. Abercrombie is now in charge and a big army is on its way here from England. With them we can take Crown Point before summer is over."

Samuel went on to explain that Abercrombie had agents out recruiting local militia for the summer campaign. He had been promised a lieutenancy if he could supply a troop. He already had lined up a dozen prospects including his cousin Daniel. They needed scouts to round out their force. Would Sam be willing to serve again?

Sam was not quick to volunteer. Abercrombie's prospects looked good, but there were risks to consider. In any case he had to take care of his aching jaw before he could think straight about a decision as important as this. He congratulated his nephew on his promised commission and agreed that he would give serious thought to his request.

A week later with the offending tooth out and his composure more back to normal, he received a message that Johnson wanted to meet with him the next morning. The request surprised him because he knew Johnson had been bedridden much of the winter and had been far from well when he led a troop up the valley to counter another hostile Indian hit and run raid on a German Flats settlement.

When he got to the store Sam found Sir William talking to an elegantly dressed officer from the royal army. Johnson introduced him as Viscount Howe of Abercrombie's high command. It took only a few minutes of cordial conversation to convince Sam that here was a gay spirited British officer he could like and admire. George Augustus Howe was an affable young nobleman who gave every appearance of enjoying life. Unlike most of his blooded colleagues, he readily accepted Americans like Sam as his equals. He wanted their friendship and was willing to look to them for advice.

Johnson explained that Howe was there to assess what the valley could provide in men and military supplies for the coming campaign. Settlers in the valley were expected to help provide Abercrombie's army with wagons, oxen and food. He was also recruiting and training a troop at Canajoharie that would join the army in another month or two. General Howe went on to explain that the army was critically in need of scouts. "From all I've heard, you are one of the best, Sam. You know the country up near Lake

George and we can really use you. Would you consider coming on board again?"

With a more demanding and less congenial officer Sam might have said 'No'. General Howe, however, had an engaging manner that made him anxious to oblige. Without ever a thought of first discussing the prospect with Mary, Sam agreed. Six weeks later he was back in the king's service speculating on the success Abercrombie could expect in the summer of 1758.

Abercrombie, who had spent an undistinguished year in America, came to his post with a favorable reputation earned during his years of military service in Europe. Much was expected of him and as a fellow Scot; he should have made a favorable impression on Sam. He did not. As Sam discovered, he was a cold pickle, obstinate in his views, overly confident of his infallibility, too committed to the principles of European warfare, and totally unwilling to accept advice from his American advisors and scouts.

After only a week in Abercrombie's camp, Sam found himself talking to other Americans and agreeing with them that it was unfortunate that command of the army had not been given to Viscount Howe. He at least was willing to accept advice from the American officers and learn from the bitter experience of others such as General Braddock. With Abercrombie, they felt they had run into a stone wall. Hopefully, the situation might change to for the better.

Abercrombie's first goal was to capture Ticonderoga, a new fort the French were erecting at the southern end of Lake Champlain. Abercrombie led an army of 16,000 men, the largest body of troops yet assembled in America. Opposing him was General Montcalm with an army of only 3,600 men. As the British army moved north, Montcalm had his men entrench themselves in front of the as yet only partially built fort. His men hauled timbers, brush and tree stumps into place to create an abatis, a barricade the British enemy would have to cross in attacking the French.

As the British army rolled north, Abercrombie sent Howe and a small troop ahead to secure a campsite for the army. As they crossed through a forested tract the advance guard was unexpectedly attacked by a larger contingent of

French regulars. In the ensuing skirmish, Howe and several of his men were killed and the troop was forced to retreat.

Giving little heed to the loss of his most talented officer, Abercrombie continued to move his army north. The next day they came within sight of Montcalm's hastily prepared line of defense. Sam and the other scouts reported that the British army had a five to one advantage over the French in numbers. They cautioned though that storming through Montcalm's abatis would lead to an unnecessary loss of lives. Vast holes could be blasted through the protective barricade that shielded the French army from attack if Abercrombie would wait a few hours for the British artillery to be hauled into place.

Abercrombie snorted when he received this unwelcome advice. What did these Americans know about military strategy? They chose to cower behind trees when the tried and true tactics developed and proved in Europe called for frontal attacks. He wanted to get the battle over. He had enough manpower to crush the French, so why wait? Confident of the infallibility of his reasoning, he ordered a frontal attack on the enemy line.

Four columns of Britain's best troops charged through the brush toward Montcalm's defenses on that bloody afternoon on July 8. Most of them got as far as the abatis and then faltered as they tried to twine their way through the tangle of brush and logs. Thrown back by enemy fire, they tried again as their angry general bellowed with rage. The second time they came running back should have been enough to make Abercrombie a believer. But he stubbornly ordered his men to charge forward again.

When the third assault failed, the battlefield was covered with dead and dying soldiers. The air was filled with the cries of the wounded. Abercrombie was crushed. He still had three mobile soldiers for every fighter in the French line. He had big guns on the road that could blast their way through the French defenses. But he had lost his stomach for further fighting. He ordered his army to disengage and retreat.

As the retreating army moved southward away from Ticonderoga, it was met by bands of new recruits coming from the south. Among them was Johnson's contingent from

Canajoharie and the troop commanded by Lieutenant Sam Campbell from Cherry Valley. Sam met with his nephew and his son Daniel that night. He soberly told them details about the bloody battle they had missed and silently gave his thanks to heaven that his kin had been one day too late to have participated in the carnage.

* * * * *

Back at Canajoharie a week after the fiasco at Ticonderoga, Sam decided that the time had come for him to quit military service. Abercrombie's stupid leadership and lack of concern for the lives of his troops had undermined the limited respect he had for the king's officers. There were other reasons too for his decision. He was 63, no longer the athlete he had once been. He now found himself weary and exhausted after a day's march and he had a worrisome rheumatic pain in his left leg that added to his misery.

He rode to Johnson's store to explain his decision to Sir William. Johnson, however, was not ready to listen to talk of quitting. "Give it one more shot, Sam," he explained. "After all the service you have provided, you deserve to go out a winner. Here's your chance to do it. I'm sure you remember how Colonel Bradstreet saved the day for our army and prevented what could have been a rout when he took charge after Abercrombie lost his nerve. He is in charge now and with him we have an officer who has some lead in his craw. He is organizing an expedition to stage a raid on Oswego where I don't think the French are expecting trouble. He needs scouts with your skills to pull off the deal. This might be your last campaign, Sam. I say give it a try because closing down the French at Oswego can slow down and even end the Indian raids in the valley."

Persuaded by Sir William's logic, Sam went along. In early August he rode with Johnson, Colonel Bradstreet and a small contingent of troops to German Flats. From there the party went on to the portage point between the Mohawk and Wood Creek. They then hurried the 60 miles down the creek to Lake Oneida, across the lake and down the Oneida river to Oswego. Surprised by their sudden appearance, the

193

French garrison at the Oswego fort surrendered and Oswego was again a British bastion on Lake Ontario.

With Oswego so easily captured, Bradstreet put his force on some available lake craft, crossed the lake and captured Fort Frontenac and the nearby French trading post at Cadaracqui. France still controlled Fort Niagara many miles further west; but as the victorious officers and men assured themselves, that was a detail that could be dealt with later.

Bradstreet invited Johnson, Sam and some of his officers to a special celebration after the capture of the trading post. As they congratulated each other and drank toasts to the king with champagne captured with the French stores, there was general agreement that the strangle hold the French had held on the west country was finally broken. In an optimistic estimate Bradstreet proclaimed: "This is only the first of what will be a chain of British victories that will free this vast country of French rule."

Sam had reasons of his own for enjoying the elation expressed by the officers. For years he had been defending his family and neighbors from raids inspired by the officials and priests of France. Now at last he had helped carry the war to Canada; now at last he was a victor standing on foreign soil. More, of course, needed to be done; but he knew there were others, younger men than him, who could and would carry on.

While Bradstreet was leading his victorious troops back to Albany, Sam had the misfortune of slipping and falling on a rock at the portage place. An army surgeon bound up his badly twisted ankle and he returned to his home a passenger on one of Johnson's bateaux. As he limped from the canal boat to his house, he knew his carefree days were over. From now on he would be home bound. He would be there helping Mary with the farm and garden even though he would surely dream of further adventures in the far country.

So it was that Sam resigned himself to working in his garden while Sir William led the force that took Fort Niagara in the summer of 1759. He was there too when his nephew Lieutenant Sam Campbell led his troop north with Lord Jeffrey Amherst's army as it stormed its way from Lake

George and Lake Champlain to the St. Lawrence river. With these victories, General Wolfe's triumph over Montcalm on the Plains of Abraham at Quebec, and the fall of Montreal the next year, France lost its claim to Canada and the West and life along the Mohawk returned to tranquil order.

* * * * *

Campbells Came

Part Five

Joel

1752 – 78

The afternoon seemed uncommonly warm as the two teenagers finished hoeing the last rows of corn. "Glad that job is done," Sam the older of the two remarked. "Let's go for a swim before supper."

"I'm for it," Joel his younger brother agreed. "It will be cool in the shade and that water will feel so good. Samuel Campbell, Junior, was 19 and Joel 18 months younger. Tall, broad of shoulder, narrow waisted, with classic features and brown hair like their mother, the two brothers were a handsome pair who looked almost enough alike to pass as identical twins.

They were brothers, close pals, both attentive to the other's needs, yet definitely competitive. From little on Sam had been Joel's model. There was nothing that Sam could do that Joel was not willing to try.

As the two approached the pond where they usually swam, they heard voices, not the boisterous jocularity of men or boys but the softer giggling of girls.

"Darn," Joel swore. "Now we will have to give up our swim."

"No we won't," Sam replied, "that is Jane's voice.

"Let's surprise them."

Joel's first reaction was to say 'No'. Their mother had taught her sons to respect the bodies and privacy of girls. This meant that they stayed away from the pond while the girls bathed. His little sister was the only naked girl he had ever seen and that had not happened again since she was two. Always ready to follow Sam's lead though, he followed his brother through the thickets and brush to the water's edge.

Before them in the water were two girls, Jane with her blond tresses and a second girl, a brunette, Joel had not seen before. The girls dropped down into the pond with only their heads above water when they heard the young men approaching. "Go away, go away", they shouted.

"No way," Sam retorted, "we came here for a swim so you will have to invite us in or leave."

"I dare you to come in," Jane teased.

"You do, do you? Well, we will show you."

With that response to Jane's challenge, Sam stripped off his shirt, slipped out of his shoes and buckskins, stepped out on a projecting log and dived into the pool. Not to be outdone, Joel followed his example and was soon swimming about completely in the buff with the similarly unclothed girls.

After paddling about, splashing water on each other and some good-natured frolicking in the water, Sam and Jane crawled up on the bank and disappeared in the brush. Jane's friend hoisted herself onto the log from which the brothers had dived into the pond and bade Joel to join her. Joel was jolted by her brazen invitation to have him sit bare naked beside her.

Looking up at her, Joel saw that she had a slim attractive figure, an uncommonly pretty face, and long black hair. The feature he could not keep his eyes off of though was her pair of milky white breasts, both full but not too big, and both peaked with nipples that looked like ripe raspberries.

Pulling himself up beside her, Joel felt a thrilling sensation throughout his being. She was the most beautiful, most desirous thing he had ever seen. He felt an urge to throw his arms around her and hold those two beautiful breasts in his two hands. At the same time he was embarrassed by an unwelcome stirring in his loins that caused him to reach out and grab Sam's shirt from an overhanging branch to cover his nakedness.

"Why did you do that?" she asked. "I like the looks of your body."

"I like yours too. But sitting here like this isn't right. We are asking for trouble. Who are you anyway?"

"I'm Nancy. Nancy Leonard, Jane's cousin. You must be Joel. Jane told me all about you, except that you are better looking than I expected."

"Well thank you for that. You are mighty pretty too. How come are you here?"

"My pa has just moved here to work for Sir William."

"He has! Then you will live here and we can go to parties together. Can I take you to the next one?"

Nancy nodded her affirmative and the two young people talked for a few minutes before Joel got up, pulled on his buckskin pants, and said: "It's time for Sam and me to start our chores. Where is he?"

Nancy stood unashamed on the log and pointed off to the left as she answered: "Over there."

"What are they doing?"

"You know."

"Well they shouldn't be doing that."

"It's all right. Jane told me what they do and about their plan to be married."

"Well, they better be careful or they will be getting hitched before they plan to."

* * * * *

Joel saw much of Nancy in the weeks that followed. At 16, she was 17 months younger than him. New in the community, she attracted the attention of several men both young and not so young. She was gracious in her treatment of all of them. Only two months passed before it was generally understood that she was Joel's girl.

At the end of the second month Sam informed his parents and family that he had to get married. Jane was pregnant and he proudly admitted that he was the cause. The big question was not whether they should set up housekeeping together but where.

Joel supplied an answer when he proposed: "You know about that country up near the fish camp where pa goes with Sir William. Sir William offered to get some land for us up there. If you want I'll go there with you. We can clear enough land this summer and fall for next year's crops and we can put up a house suitable for Jane and the baby. It's a good spot with lots of game to supply you with meat. There are wild critters there for fur trapping and in good weather you'll have the lake and streams for fishing.

So it was that Sam and Jane made the first settlement at Providence. Joel worked with them the second summer clearing additional fields for cultivation and building a second house. Much of his time though was spent back at Canajoharie and Johnson's store. The frequency of his migration back and forth ended with the coming of spring in 1754 when he and Nancy were married and the two went to live next to Sam and Jane in Providence.

Life held no great surprises for them during the thirteen years that followed. Neither they nor the single family that joined their settlement ever had much in the way of worldly possessions. Their houses were small but livable. They raised enough corn, wheat, and hay to feed their families and livestock. They accepted hard work without complaint. Joel's father and brothers visited them on frequent occasions and they went back to Johnson's store from time to time to trade fur pelts for needed supplies, to renew their ties with family and civilization, and when they could to attend church services. Life on the whole though was good and both families were content to accept it as it came as they lived close to nature.

Joel and Nancy's first child, Joel Junior arrived a year and a half after their marriage. The baby was born at a tense time for the family. General William Johnson was leading an army composed mostly of colonial militia on what was expected to be a drive on Crown Point in the summer of 1755. Joel's father accompanied the army as a scout and his eldest brother Daniel served with the militia. Joel and his brother Sam both talked of enlisting. Their father was adamant, however, in insisting that they stay with their wives. "Your wives are heavy with child," he argued. "It is your duty to stay here with them. This is not a time to leave women or children alone out here with no neighbors while you are off somewhere playing at being soldiers."

Two summers later, Nancy and Jane were again pregnant when word reached them of Montcalm's advance to seize Fort William Henry. Again Joel and Sam talked of joining the British defensive force. Joel's father objected again this time on the ground that Munro's garrison was composed mostly of British regulars. This time, however, he also insisted that the threat of a possible Indian raid on the Providence settlement was such that the two wives should move to Mary's house for their deliveries. Thus it was that Joel's second son, Nathaniel, was born at Canajoharie a week after the fall of Fort William Henry.

The continuing threat of French invasion gave all of the settlers in the Mohawk country cause for concern during 1757, '58, and '59. Joel and Sam enlisted as members of the troop led by their cousin Lieutenant Sam Campbell from

Cherry Valley and were on their way to join General Abercrombie's army when the general was defeated in 1758. Lieutenant Sam went on to triumph with Amherst's army the next year when it fought its way north to the St. Lawrence river. Neither Joel nor Sam was with him though. Both remained at their homes in Providence where their wives were again expecting deliveries.

Four more children, Benajiah in 1759, Jonathan in 1761, Jemina in 1763, and Benoni in 1765, were born to Nancy and Joel at Providence. The couple experienced some disappointments. For reasons they never understood, prospective settlers bypassed Providence. There also was the matter of acquiring clear title to their land. They lived on a corner of a land grant that had been made in 1741, the title transfer of which still needed the approval of some Mohawk sachem. Sir William had promised he would arrange for transfer of the title to Joel's father. He was still assuring them that the needed approval would be forthcoming; but it was not yet in sight.

Neither Joel nor Nancy was bothered by the relative isolation they endured at Providence. Sam and Jane were close neighbors. Both couples liked their homes and their location and both felt happy. Sam and Jane had an occasional spat while Joel and Nancy lived together in peaceful harmony. Joel's love for his wife grew with every passing day. He enjoyed spending time talking with her, holding her in his arms, doing little favors for her. After more than a dozen years together, they were still a couple very much in love with each other.

Tragedy struck in 1765 after the birth of baby Benoni. Within a matter of days Nancy's robust health failed. Her body was racked with fever; and worn out from years as a frontier wife, she lacked the reserve strength to fight the infection. Joel was alarmed. He offered to take her to Johnson's settlement where she might find medical help. Nancy declined knowing that she could not survive the rigors of the trip.

For two days Joel sat by Nancy's side wiping her brow with a cool damp cloth and stroking her arms. It was then that she said: "Joel darling, I know I am dying."

"You can't", he objected. "If you go I must go with you."

"No, you must stay here for my sake to care for our children, I've been thinking. There is one thing you must promise me before I go."

"Anything you want, my love."

"After I am gone, find my cousin Becky and ask her to help you care for the children. Marry her and give our children a mother."

A few hours later with Joel's solemn promise given, Nancy drifted off to eternal sleep leaving her distraught husband with six children, all of them under ten.

* * * * *

Rebecca Leonard was a maiden lady close to 30 years of age when Joel approached her a few weeks after Nancy's death. She had been disappointed in love some years earlier when the young man she had expected to marry was killed in an accident. She was still living in her father's home where she had cared for an invalid mother up until the time of her death a few months earlier.

Becky was still a handsome woman, but Joel paid little attention to her appearance when he sought an audience with her. He was much impressed though with the cleanliness of her person and house and with her expression of remorse when she heard of Nancy's death. Becky was genuinely surprised when Joel told her of Nancy's request that she care for her children. She was stirred and a little amused when he went farther to propose marriage.

There was nothing unusual about Joel's proposal. Along the frontier, love was usually the deciding factor that influenced young men and women in their decisions to marry. Once one had been married and had a growing family though, marriages of convenience often provided the only practical way in which a widow or widower could meet the challenges of frontier life and survive along with their dependent children.

Not to be rushed into a decision she might regret, Becky asked for a few days in which she could consider

Joel's proposal. Three days later she informed him that she would be happy to care for his children and would marry him on two conditions. She insisted that he move from Providence to Canajoharie or some other more settled area and she also wanted to live in a place where she and the family could attend church services on a regular basis.

Joel agreed to Becky's terms and returned to Providence where he talked Sam and Jane into moving with him to places closer to Johnson's store. The lone family that had settled near them at Providence stayed there for two more years and then left when it receive threats of an Indian raid. True to his word, Sir William finally secured tribal approval for the land grant of 1741 in 1768. By then, however, the fields cleared by the Campbell brothers were already growing a new crop of brush and trees.

Joel was never able to sink his roots very deep at any place after Nancy's death. He and Becky had three more children, Ezekiel, Joshua, and William, and they moved to Cherry Valley where they lived near their Campbell cousin for awhile. Hoping he could use his father's influence with Sir William Johnson to get another homestead, he moved back to Canajoharie in 1773. His plan came to naught, however, when Johnson died unexpectedly the next year. The Johnson empire then passed to Sir William's son Sir John, a man of far less ability and foresight than his father.

* * * * *

Joel could read and write. Like many others in the society in which he mixed, he did little of either. As a boy and young man he accepted physical labor as his lot in life. Beyond that he usually followed Sam's lead in seeking the benefits of a not overly exacting life. His mother was religious, but he cared little for religion and gave scarce a thought to politics. All of this changed when he married Becky. As a matron much devoted to reading her Bible, she took immediate steps to make certain that the youngsters she was raising would be properly taught how to read, write, and handle their numbers. At her insistence Joel started attending church and took note of politics.

Nancy's death came as a serious blow to Joel, a blow that reminded him of his own mortality. While he had believed generally in God, he had never given much thought to the hereafter. That had been a matter that would take care of itself in the distant future. Nancy's death forced him to bring his thinking into focus. He blamed his earlier indifference for her death. God had taken her from him as a warning that he must mend his ways. His greatest desire now was to live a life that would allow him to be reunited with Nancy after his death. To bring this about and with Becky's encouragement, he became a frequent reader of the Bible and was soon displaying his newfound knowledge and zeal in conversations with others.

As far as politics were concerned, Joel had grown up in a family that gave its unquestioned loyalty to Sir William Johnson and his views. Sir William was one of the most prominent men in colonial America and certainly the best known of those who lived along the western frontier. He had frequently been at loggerheads with the provincial officials in New York who seemed to be more interested in land speculation and reaping a harvest from the resources of the west than in showing willingness to provide funds for the protection of settlers or the building of needed roads.

Sir William had done wonders in encouraging set-tlements along the Mohawk, in maintaining amicable relations with Indians of the Six Nations, and in helping Britain and the colonies overthrow the threat of French domination. But with the French and Indian War won, a new situation had developed.

British soldiers had been needed to garrison the forts and carry most of the load in ousting the French. But with the threat of French domination gone, their continued presence throughout the colonies became an irksome nuisance. Citizens resented the condescending attitudes of the 'lobsterbacks'. They resented the practice of quartering soldiers in private homes and the insistence of officials in far off London that they pay sufficient taxes to finance their military occupation.

The merchants and tradesmen who lived along the Atlantic coast castigated the Navigation Acts and the Sugar Act for unfairly channeling the benefits of colonial trade into

British hands. Even Sir William, who served as an agent of the crown, had misgivings about the rules that limited his ability to ship grain to the West Indies where he could exchange it for sugar and molasses.

Factors such as opposition to trade regulations, the imposition of new taxes without colonial sanction, and the substitution of a royally appointed government for the earlier locally elected officials inflamed opposition in places such as Massachusetts. Settlers along the Mohawk shared these grievances but were more vexed by their lack of effective representation on New York's colonial council, which year after year ignored adequate funding of backcountry needs. And they saw their future interests imperiled by the royal proclamation of 1763, which established a western boundary for land settlement.

The Proclamation of 1763 was particularly offensive because it designated all of the area held by Britain west of a boundary connecting Lake Champlain and Fort Stanwix in northcentral New York, Fort Pitt in western Pennsylvania and then down the crest of the Appalachian mountains to Florida as Indian country. New land grants and colonial settlements west of this line were prohibited. The area was to be saved permanently for Indian occupancy; The Quebec Act of 1774 went a step farther by entrusting the administration of this vast area to the Province of Quebec.

Settlers along the frontier such as Daniel Boone in Virginia stood ready to defy the royal order. Years of frontier self sufficiency had imbued them with a spirit of independence that made them a breed apart from their European ancestors who had been accustomed to accepting the instructions of their rulers. Along the frontier, settlers wanted access to the ever greener pastures beyond the boundary and legally or not many were determined to have it.

With growing dissention, popular opinion along the Mohawk divided into separate camps. On one side stood the reformers, those who wanted changes and a larger say in the determination of public policies. These were the people who cheered when they heard of the Boston Tea Party in 1773 and who protested when Parliament retaliated by enacting the Intolerable Acts the next year. Posed against them were the Tories, conservatives mostly who supported the status quo and placed high value on their loyalty to the crown.

Between these two extremes was a middle camp of citizens who were not yet swayed by the arguments and bickering of the radical spokesmen on either side. Some from these groups were genuinely neutral; others took no position because they did not care. A substantial number of those who had been neutral shifted to the reformist side when word reached them in April 1775 of the victory of the Massachusetts minutemen over the British at Lexington and Concord.

With the outbreak of hostilities, the reformists or Whigs throughout the province moved quickly to set up county Committees of Safety to advance their agendas. The Tories took similar action to protect their domains. Tories and loyalists outnumbered the reformists in southern New York. The opposing camps in the Mohawk valley had about equal support. With the Tories and the Whigs clamoring and making threats against each other, those who had been neutral found themselves under increasing pressure to commit themselves to one side or the other.

The emerging conflict drove wedges between long time close friendships and kinships as neighbors, brothers, fathers and sons were guided by their sentiments into separate camps. People who had shared cordial relations for years forswore past commitments and memories as they started to criticize, soon to condemn, then to despise, and finally to hate each other. Joel had acquaintances among Johnson's Scottish Highlanders with whom he had socialized since his boyhood days who now turned on him and treated him as an enemy when he failed to endorse their loyalist bias.

All through 1774 and the early months of 1775 Joel and Sam were perplexed by the swirling controversy that was ripping the fabric of their society. They had no deep-seated convictions that pointed them to either camp. To clarify their thinking, they went to their father who at 80 still lived in the valley. "What do you think pa? Tell us what you think we should do."

"Cheese 'n rice, lads." he responded, "this is going to end in a fight and I'm too old to be in it. I ain't planning to favor either side."

"No one expects you to fight," Joel exclaimed. "You must have some feeling though on where we should stand."

"I got feelings. Wish I could sort them out. I fought for the king back in Scotland. Then I made my living ducking around his duty collectors. Your uncle Jamie and I came to this land because the blasted British wouldn't let us live in peace in Ulster. Once we came here from Hampshire, I got along by trading with Sir William who was a real gentleman and who worked for the king. If he was still living I reckon I'd favor who he favored."

"Do you think he would have been a Tory now?"

"People say he would but I'm not convinced. Most men of property are loyalists and have good reason to be Tories.

"Sir William was about the richest man in America so he could have been. He owned more land than anyone I ever heard of. The king gave him a title and he ran the Indian service for the king. On that side he looked like a Toryman. But the Sir William I knew was always ready to condemn the stupidity of British generals and of policies dictated by men in London who had no idea of the messes they were making. He often said we could do better making our own decisions right here. Besides that, he was as much interested in the welfare of settlers as doing the king's business. If it came to choosing between Indians and the fur trade on one side or advancing the settlers interests, I reckon he would have gone for the settlers."

Joel and Sam took pleasure in discussing reports of emerging developments with each other and when they could with their cousin Sam Campbell who lived in Cherry Valley. Captain Sam, as his neighbors called him, owned a large farm; much of it carved out of the land grant his father had received more than 30 years earlier. Unlike most large landowners, however, he had little sympathy for the royalist cause. "We need to be free to run our affairs," he insisted, "Britain has done its part in helping to get us started but it should stand aside now like an understanding parent while we show the world we can stand on our own."

Joel's conversations with Sam and his cousin together with self-examination of his feelings led him to the conclusion that he should support the reformists. He was reluctant at first though to take a definite stand. Even after hearing of the flare-up at Lexington and Concord he harbored a fear that the colonials could not stand up to a British attack.

All thoughts of continued neutrality vanished when news reached him of the military standoff at Bunker Hill and of Ethan Allen's success in taking Ticonderoga. The colonists had shown they could stand up to and even defeat the British. With more widespread support, he was now convinced they could win the struggle for independence.

The three Campbells had no illusions about the task ahead. Captain Sam said: "It's war and whether we like it or not we are going to be in the middle of it. It won't be like the last war. In that one, we were together here while the enemy was over there. This time it will be civil war with neighbor fighting neighbor and the enemy living next to you. Things can easily go wrong simply because we will not know who our real friends are.

"General Washington needs all of the recruits we can send him for the Continental army. At the same time though we must keep men here for our defense. We have a long border both to the north and the west that we must defend without much help because Washington will have his hands full handling the fighting along the coast."

"Should we be joining up?" Joel asked.

"Only if they offer you a fat commission," Captain Sam answered. "Wars are for young men, not for old farts like us. Here I am at 50 and you two are only year or two younger. If we had the resources to recruit and supply a troop or so, the army would take us on as officers; but as old men who would have to fight in the ranks, they would find us more bother than we are worth. Anyway, the place where we can do the most good is right here. The settlements here in the valley need protection from the fury of the Tories and the Indians who will be in league with them."

"Why do you say that? Do you really think the Tories will fight?"

"I couldn't be more sure of it. Look where those who are being uprooted around here are going. They are heading for Fort Niagara where Dan Claus and Guy Johnson, our new Commissioners of Indian Affairs, are using their authority as Sir William's successors to line up Indian support for war on us. They will have the support of the British governor in Canada; but it is the Tories who will cause the most trouble. They hate us and with good reason because we are the ones who are crowding them out, taking over their properties, and keeping some of their families here as hostages.

"They will be looking for revenge and that's the worst kind of enemy to fight. Even if we succeed in checking them, they can cause problems, big problems. If the Yankees who are sending troops to take Montreal succeed, there will be less threat of invasion from the west. If that effort fails, we can look for invasions both from Lake Champlain in the north and Oswego in the west."

"That can be devastating."

"If worse comes to worse, it will be. In the meantime we cannot just sit here on our hands. Some of our men can go off and join the army. With those who stay here, we must line up recruits for the militia, give them some training, supply them with weapons, and get them ready to fight on short notice."

Advice like that spoken by Captain Sam was passed on and adopted by the local Committee on Safety. Bodies of volunteer militia were organized in most communities. Tory sympathizers also took action to defend their interests but the pressures for reform gradually forced the more outspoken Tories to flee north to Canada or west to Fort Niagara or Oswego.

Many others, who were loyalists at heart, stayed on in the valley ready to show their true colors if a favorable situation should arise. Among the most prominent of those who left was Sir John Johnson, Sir William's son and principal heir, who after weeks of indecision, chose to cast his lot with the Tory cause.

* * * * *

The summer of 1775 and autumn that followed was a time of tense awareness. Sentiments favoring the reformists gained strength throughout the valley and the remaining loyalists found themselves under increasing pressure to leave. Meanwhile the overall situation was grim. Two bodies of troops from the northern colonies, both with too few men and not enough supplies to accomplish their goals, launched unsuccessful attacks on Montreal and Quebec. General Gage tightened his stranglehold on Boston while Washington, who commanded the colonial army outside the city, seemed powerless to force British evacuation of the port city.

Better news for the rebellious colonists came during the winter and spring of 1776 when volunteers from New England and New York succeeded in hauling heavy cannons from Fort Ticonderoga to the Hudson river and then overland across the Berkshire mountains to Boston where they were mounted on Dorchester Heights. From that commanding position, the threat of bombardment of Boston and its harbor was enough to prompt a speedy evacuation of the British army from the occupied city.

General Gage took his army to Halifax. A few months later, the reinforced army, now under the command of Sir William Howe, a younger brother of the Viscount Howe who had died 18 years earlier in Abercrombie's unsuccessful assault on Ticonderoga, sailed to New York. His success there in forcing General Washington to give up Long Island and the city of New York struck directly at the security of the colonial patriots who lived along the Mohawk.

1776 was a year of political decision but also a year of growing uneasiness. The Continental Congress meeting in Philadelphia declared the independence of the thirteen colonies from their mother country. This was big talk, brave talk; but could the colonies work together and succeed in throwing off the yoke of military occupation. It was not without reason that New York was one of the last of the colonies to subscribe to the declaration. New York City, its largest town and its gateway to the Atlantic was occupied by the king's troops.

Peace prevailed throughout the Mohawk valley during the spring, summer, and fall of 1776. War, however, was nearby. It took the valiant effort of an out-manned and outgunned navy in Lake Champlain to stall the advance of Sir Guy Carleton's southward thrust across the lake. Everyone was aware that a war was being fought both to the north and to the south of them. There was no occasion for relaxed vigilance. Next month, next year, the British would surely strike again. British regulars could move up the Hudson or down from Canada with their Hessian mercenaries. An attack also was expected from the direction of Fort Niagara where Sir John Johnson was said to have a thousand British and Hessian troops massed ready to march with an uncounted number of Tories, Indians and Canadiens in a decisive attempt to reclaim the valley for British rule.

* * * * *

General John Burgoyne was one of the officers who sailed to Boston with Sir William Howe in May 1775. He left there when Gage's army was evacuated, went on to Canada, and returned to England in late 1776 about the time that Howe was storming his way into New York.

Gentleman Johnny, the illegitimate son of a British nobleman, was an affable character noted for his charming manners, his dalliance with the ladies, his literary talents, his skill as a politician, and his willingness to think big. Back in England, he visited with Lord George Germain, the British Colonial Secretary, and outlined a grand strategy, which if followed to conclusion could bring a speedy end to the colonial revolution.

Burgoyne proposed that a three-pronged attack be launched on upper New York. He would return to Canada with an army that would move up Lake Champlain to Ticonderoga and then down to Albany. Meanwhile, a detachment from his Canadian army would move eastward from Fort Niagara or Oswego through the Mohawk valley and General Howe would lead an army up the Hudson from New York City. With the joining of the three victorious armies at Albany, New England would be cut off from the other colonies and the two now separated clusters of colonies would lose their will to continue the war.

The grand strategy was endorsed by Germain as a stroke of genius. There was little doubt in London that Burgoyne could triumph over the feeble opposition the colonials could be expected to muster. The British regulars with their Hessian, American Tory, Indian, and Canadien supporters would earn their crowns of glory with the taking of Ticonderoga and Fort Edward after which there was nothing to stop a victorious march to Albany. A smaller force could easily handle the invasion along the Mohawk. After all, the only obstacles there were a few outmoded forts that were known to be poorly manned and in disrepair. Howe's success in coming from the south could also be counted on. He had already defeated the provincial army at White Plains and the opposition led by Washington was quartered south rather than north of New York.

Burgoyne sold his plan to Lord Germain and the top British officials and returned to Canada in early 1777. With him were an additional 6,000 British regulars and Hessian mercenaries. Shortly after his arrival he nominated Lieutenant Colonel Barry St. Leger to serve as acting Brigadier General and commander of the force that was sent up the St. Lawrence river to Oswego on Lake Ontario.

Wet weather and impassable roads forced a delay in Burgoyne's plan to move his army southward during the early months of 1777. Even so, his force was able to move south through Lake Champlain and to occupy all but the southern end of that lake during May and June. Meanwhile, St. Leger made his way up the St. Lawrence with a smaller army to Oswego where he took over the command of the garrison and Johnson's assembled Tories and Indians.

Half expected and not kept secret, the approach of the two armies struck terror in the hearts of many along the Mohawk. Some were ready to surrender without putting up a fight, a sentiment that many loyalists who still lived in the valley played upon to slight avail. The patriots faced the challenge with determination. Men and military supplies were dispatched to Fort Stanwix at the portage point between the Mohawk and Wood Creek. Pleas also were sent to General Schuyler who was commanding at Ticonderoga and Fort Edward and to General Washington asking for military support. No one was really surprised when both reported that they had desperate needs for troops and supplies where they were and that the settlers would have to shoulder their own defense.

Fort Stanwix, though undermanned in the past, could no longer be considered a pushover. The fort, established in 1758, had existed at the site more as a trading center than as a true military establishment since the end of the French and Indian War. Recognizing the threat of an invasion, Washington had sent orders in 1776 for garrisoning and strengthening the fort. Colonel Peter Gansevoort had been sent to command the garrison in May of 1777 and had taken quick action to strengthen the battlements. He also sent crews to clog Wood Creek with fallen trees so as to slow the progress St. Leger's force could make from Oswego.

While Gansevoort was strengthening the defenses at Fort Stanwix, St. Leger established his army at Oswego and then started to move up the Oneida river, across Oneida lake, and then up Wood Creek. Scouting reports kept the garrison at Fort Stanwix aware of his approach. They also alarmed them because much yet remained to be done in the rebuilding of the fort's battlements. The relaying of these reports to patriots down the Mohawk alerted them to realization of Gansevoort's need for reinforcements if he was to successfully resist the expected siege.

By the end of June Burgoyne's army commanded the entire route to the southern end of Lake Champlain. Thus far he had faced only light opposition. Before him was Fort Ticonderoga. This once great fortress had been reinforced by its garrison and was thought to be impregnable. The fort was undermanned but General Schuyler had supplied it with a considerable stock of food and military supplies.

Burgoyne's advance could have been stalled at this point. Luckily for him one of his engineers was able to build a road up the supposedly inaccessible steep incline of Sugar Loaf Hill, a cone shaped mound about a mile southwest of the fort that rose 750 feet above the surrounding terrain. With a road built and cannon drawn to its top, the British were able to rake the fort with fire. Recognizing his inability to cope with this threat, the American commander at Ticonderoga wisely chose to evacuate his garrison from the fort and abandon those supplies they could not easily carry away.

Many were dismayed by the news of the fall of Ticonderoga on July 6. Throughout the valley, there were hundreds of weak hearted folk who were ready to give up in despair. The news cheered St. Leger's force. It inflamed their expectations. Some on his staff, including several Tories, thought the patriots could now be stampeded into surrender. It was obvious though that they would have to hurry with their part of the invasion if they were to reach Albany in time to claim their share of the glory of victory.

* * * * *

Joel was with his brother Sam near Canajoharie when a passerby told them about the fall of Fort Ti and the approach of St. Leger. The news struck him as a double calamity. The two brothers had lived for many years in an area that surely would be overrun by British regulars and their allies if Burgoyne continued his advance further south. Both felt a sudden urge to encourage their older sons to join Schuyler's defenders. Both also were deeply troubled about the threat of a Tory led invasion from the west.

Before the day was out, the two brothers were on their horses riding to Cherry Valley. The news they brought confounded Captain Sam. For a couple of minutes he just shook his head in disbelief. As a veteran of the French and Indian war who had spent time at Forst Ti, he found it hard to believe that the fort could be taken without a long siege. Once he regained his composure, he said: "And I suppose you are wondering what we should do about it. Some men would have us rushing off to join the patriots near Saratoga. It is better though that we do first things first. With the news of this setback, General Schuyler should get all the new militia he needs from New York and New England to hold Gentleman Johnny in check. Our first job is to reinforce Fort Stanwix. After we roll Johnson's Tories back we can send help to stop Burgoyne."

His advice seemed sound. It was only after Joel and Sam agreed with him and volunteered to help persuade their neighbors to join them as recruits that Captain Sam

215

explained: "I've been expecting an emergency like this. Some of us out here have been working with the Tryon County Committee on Safety. We have lined up a roster of men to serve like the Massachusetts minutemen. We have been stockpiling supplies of guns, powder, and lead along with swords and knives and we have met for some military drills. General Schuyler knows about us and has picked Nicholas Herkimer from over at German Flats to be our Brigadier General."

"A Dutchman. Is he worth following?" Sam asked.

"He's first rate," Captain Sam replied. "He is a leading citizen who lives in a big fortified house over near Little Falls. People around there look up to him as a leader. I've met him and know he is one of the best we've got. He is capable, level headed and doesn't seem like one who will panic or go to pieces when the first gun is fired. He'll make a good general. Like as not, he is sending out instructions right now for us to assemble so we can march to Stanwix."

Joel and Sam spent the night at Cherry Valley. General Herkimer's proclamation of July 17 reached them the next morning just as they were preparing to start their return ride to their homes. Herkimer advised the residents of the valley that an army of 2,000 Canadiens and savages was encamped at Oswego preparing to assault the settlements of the valley. He sent out a call for all men between the ages of 16 and 60 to repair immediately with arms and needed supplies to Fort Dayton, which was, located a few miles west of the Herkimer homestead.

Joel and Sam had several matters to discuss as they rode back to their homes. Both felt themselves committed to march west with the militia. There were questions though about which sons they should take along. Sam said: "With all my girls, Paul is the only son I have of fighting age. He will be raring to go; but I'm not sure I want him to. Do you remember how pa talked us out of joining Sir William's army back 20 years ago? I'm like that now. I'll be proud if Paul wants to fight but more than that I want to keep him safe so he can raise a family of his own."

"I know exactly how you feel," Joel agreed. "Pa ordered us to stay in Providence to take care of our wives. I suppose I could tell that to my Joe but he is away working in

Albany and won't be affected. Nate is 20 and will insist on going especially if Paul goes. Ben will argue that he should go too if Nate gets to go and I don't see that I can stop him. Jonny will have a tantrum when I tell him he must stay home. He wants to do everything his older brothers do but I can put my foot down with him. He isn't 16 yet and I need to have someone of that age at home to help Becky care for our place."

Joel's announcement to his family that he would be marching to Fort Dayton met with the reception he expected. Becky accepted his decision with the reluctance of a wife who cared for her husband's welfare but saw the need for men striving to protect their families. Nate and Ben insisted that they must join while Jonny was loud in his protest that it was unfair to keep him at home, that the war would be over before he would have a chance to fight. He calmed down and agreed to stay at home only after Joel assured him that there would be other opportunities to fight and that his presence on the farm was essential for the support of his younger brothers should disaster somehow strike.

Many residents ignored Herkimer's order for the assembly of militia, but by and large the response was enthusiastic. Some men were able to march immediately to Fort Dayton. Most though needed a week or so to set their affairs in order. By the end of July the road leading to the fort was filled with men, wagons and supplies designed for the relief of Fort Stanwix.

While the valley militia was making their way to Herkimer's headquarters, Colonel Gansevoort was working his garrison of 650 soldiers to the limit. Trees were felled to further buttress the strength of the fort while other trees were cut to clog Wood Creek. At the same time, St. Leger was moving his army of 1,400 men, 600 of them Indians, up Oneida river and across Oneida lake to the mouth of Wood Creek where he started his slow progress up the last 14 miles that separated him from the fort.

Four bateaux, loaded with supplies and guarded by 100 soldiers from Fort Dayton, worked their way up the Mohawk to Stanwix and had hardly more than unloaded on August 2 when the first troops from St. Leger's army came within firing range. The supplies were hastily moved inside the fort while St. Leger's men started taking positions just outside the fort's firing range. Captain Tice from the besieging army approached the fort under a flag of truce the next day and delivered St. Leger's demand that the fort surrender. Gansevoort promptly rebuffed the order.

The scene was set for a siege. St. Leger, however, was unable to proceed because his men had not yet been able to bring their heavy artillery up the still partly clogged creek. Both sides exchanged small gunfire during the next two days. Little damage was done by either side and Gansevoort's men were even able to continue construction work on the fort's new parapet.

Some 900 men, all high-spirited volunteers but none of them professional soldiers, assembled at Fort Dayton on Sunday, August 3. Herkimer divided his force into four regiments commanded by Colonels Ebenezer Cox, Joseph Klock, Peter Bellinger, and Frederick Vischer. When Captain Campbell arrived with his troop of 30 men from Cherry Valley and the 12 others who came with Sam and Joel and their sons, Herkimer directed that they serve with the Canajoharie force headed by Colonel Cox.

The patriot army started its 40-mile march to Stanwix the next morning. They marched 14 miles that first day. On the second day they traveled 15 more miles during which they forded from the north to the south shore of the Mohawk river. As the army was making its slow westward progress, Herkimer sent three men ahead to Stanwix to advise Gansevoort of their approach and to ask the garrison there to fire three cannons in quick succession the next morning as an indication that the messengers had arrived.

After the army camped that night General Herkimer called his officers together and recommended that the army remain in camp until their scouts could report on what lay ahead and also until possible additional recruits might catch up with them. The recommendation was met with a storm of protest. Some officers lost their tempers and even went so far as to infer that Herkimer was a coward and that he might even be a Tory sympathizer. With their refusal tio listen to his logic, the general relented and conceded: "All right gentlemen, we will march on to the fort tomorrow."

St. Leger learned of the approach of Herkimer's army on August 5. The scouts he had sent to check on activity along the road to Fort Dayton brought back pertinent information about the approaching army. They also reported that they had allowed Herkimer's three messengers to pass them unmolested. With the night of August 5 drawing on, St. Leger met with Sir John Johnson, Captain Walter Butler and several other officers and devised a plan for an ambush that could send Herkimer and his men reeling back down the valley and at the same time convince the garrison at Fort Stanwix of the futility of its refusal to surrender.

* * * * *

Most of Herkimer's citizen soldiers were up and moving about shortly after dawn on August 6. In the light of early morn the air was already heavy with the summer dog day mugginess that signaled the coming of an uncommonly hot and sultry day. Several men were anxious to start this final day of their march to Fort Stanwix before the sun got very high in the sky. Even with their desire to get going, though, it was almost 8 o'clock before the men were fed, their gear loaded on the supply wagons, and the campsite cleared so the march could begin.

Almost everyone was fidgety and nervous with the anxiety men feel when they face the uncertainties of possible battle. Nate Campbell had spent the night sharing a blanket with his brother Ben. When Paul shook his two cousins to awaken them at dawn, his first question was: "How do you guys feel this fine day?"

"Scared as hell," Ben responded, "but don't you say nothing to my pa. Anyway we have nothing to worry about except another long day of marching." His sentiment was shared by most of the men; but even so, most felt more confident and at the same time relieved when they heard the distant boom of three cannons fired in succession.

For an hour and a half the now strung out army marched along a narrow road bordered with patches of heavy timber and occasional oak openings. Colonel Cox and his Canajoharians marched at the head of the long line. Klock and Bellinger's regiments followed while Vischer's regiment was the rear guard that advanced with the slow gaited oxen that pulled the wagons loaded with gear and supplies.

A short distance beyond the Indian village of Oriska, Cox's men followed the road down an incline into a steep sided ravine that bordered Oriskany Creek. As they crossed the bridge and started their upward climb on the western side, Captain Campbell heard a rustle in the deep forest that surrounded and towered over them that sent a chill down his spine. Turning to Joel who was marching beside him, he said: "I don't like what I see. This could be a perfect setting for an ambush." Turning to his contingent, he barked: "We may be in for trouble, lads. Make sure every one of you has your gun loaded and ready for firing. Get your knives ready for action too. Be on guard. If you hear a shot dodge behind the closest cover. And remember to fight in pairs, two men behind every tree, one to watch and shoot while the other reloads."

The captain's order was hardly more than uttered when the men heard the firing of a gun ahead of them. This distraction was followed by a cascading din of savage yells and quickly after by the firing of a few hundred muskets along both sides of the ravine. What had appeared as a peaceful forest now became a living hell as Tories and painted Indians emerged on both sides of the road just long enough to pour their murderous fire on the marching militia.

Herkimer's army received almost half of its casualties during the first five minutes of the attack as most of his men were caught completely unaware. Colonel Cox was killed as he tried to marshal his men into a fighting formation. Other officers went down along with dozens of men who were too startled to think clearly when the firing started.

General Herkimer spurred his horse around once the fighting started to give directions to his men and was promptly grounded as his horse was shot, reared up, toppled him to the ground, and then fell on him. The general's left leg was crushed beneath the knee by the falling horse. Unable to stand and seemingly indifferent to the pain, Herkimer had his men prop him up against a tree a few feet from the road and from that spot continued to direct the defense of his now struggling army.

Only a few men witnessed the general's fall and his response. For most of them, those first few moments were a time of maddening despair. Brave men wondered if they should stay or run. Many who never thought it possible suddenly found they had wet their buckskins. Some even had unexpected bowel movements. In every regiment, raw recruits were left without leaders at the very moment they had desperate need for calm advice that could still their urge to panic.

Thanks to their commander's warning, Captain Sam's troop suffered fewer casualties than any of the nearby contingents. Even so, three of his men from Cherry Valley along with Joel's son Benijiah were killed in the first minutes of fighting. Nate and Paul Campbell suffered minor wounds but kept on fighting. While the more severely wounded men were being pulled to the safety provided by trees of the forest, Captain Sam called out: "Sturdy, lads. Get behind a tree or log, two to a tree. Don't shoot until you see their ugly hides. Cover your partner while he reloads."

After the tumult and near panic of the first few minutes of the surprise attack, the action slowed down to a trading of deliberate shots between an aggressive army of near naked Indians and revenge seeking Tories and the determined patriots. As faces and bodies appeared amid the forest growth, the patriots saw that every Indian they faced was stripped of all his clothing except a breechcloth and sandals. Their only adornment was the body paints that had been liberally applied in designs of yellow, red, blue, and black.

With the rising temperature and the mugginess of the day, Joel wished he too could fight without the sticky encumbrance of his shirt and buckskins. He knew though that his bare body was not suited to brushing against twigs, thorns, and brush. More than that, he realized that body paint could be a liability. Flashes of yellow, red, and blue amid the forest's green signaled the presence of an enemy that otherwise might have remained unseen.

From time to time during the next two hours Indian braves would creep forward with tomahawks and knives to take scalps from the dead and wounded. Every time they showed themselves in the open, they were driven back by murderous fire to the shelter of trees from behind which they continued their firing. Neither side seemed able to assert an advantage over the other. The Indians and Tories kept up their attack while the patriots held their ground.

The fighting had gone on for two and a half hours when the participants were cooled by a brisk breeze. A dark cloud appeared overhead. Flashes of lightening filled the sky and rumblings of thunder were heard. Even before the first drops of rain were felt, Captain Sam ordered: "Pass the word to all the lads. Hold your fire but make sure your guns are loaded and that your powder is dry. We are in for a soaker. The enemy won't do much firing but they may use this as an opportunity to get our scalps so don't let your guard down."

He had hardly finished speaking when rain came down in a torrent that soaked everyone to the skin in seconds. For the moment, all signs of fighting stopped. Then as the captain had expected, dozens of savages suddenly streamed out from behind their trees and came into the open area of the road in their search for scalps, scalps that could be taken to their villages as tokens of victory, scalps that could be traded for the king's gold. It was the moment the patriots had waited for. With deadly accuracy they fired their covered muskets at the approaching savages. Fifteen Indians were killed by Campbell's troop while dozens of others quickly broke and ran away carrying wounded colleagues into the protective forest.

As the heavy rain continued to fall, an unofficial truce prevailed. With neither side inclined to carry on hand-to-hand battle in the rain; Captain Sam used the break to assess the damage done to Cox's regiment. He was astonished to find that almost half of Cox's men were either dead or wounded and that the colonel had been killed in the first minutes of fighting. Walking back to General Herkimer's position, he found the general sitting with his back against a tree, his injured leg wrapped with a bloody bandage, and the general calmly shielding a corncob pipe, which he was puffing away.

Herkimer ignored the captain's query about his wound and insisted instead on a report about the status of the army further up the road. When Sam completed his report, the general said: "We've taken a rough blow, Sam; but with our boys following your order that they fight in pairs and especially after the way you met that charge during the rain, the odds are now more even. This rain ain't going to last long and when it gets dry enough for the boys to open their powder bags the fight will go on.

"Cox is dead. Klock is down and Bellinger is missing, probably captured. God only knows what has happened to Vischer. I need officers so you are the colonel now. So get along and get your men organized so we can win the day."

News of Sam Campbell's field promotion to colonel quickly spread. The new commander made a speedy visit to each of the three regiments and left orders with the remaining officers for their continued fighting in pairs until the enemy was known to retire from the field. He also ordered them to hold their defensive positions until they had clear evidence that the enemy was giving up and leaving. "We'll hold our own here instead of trying to flush them out of the woods," he argued. "That way we can avoid being caught in another ambush. Anyway they will make better targets coming to us than if we try to hunt them down."

After 55 minutes of continued downpour, the rain stopped, the skies cleared, and men looked again to the use of their muskets. Fifteen more minutes elapsed before the Indians and Tories resumed their sporadic shooting from their hiding places amid the dense foliage of the forest. Sam was one of the few patriots who were wounded when a bullet grazed his upper arm. The attackers felt most of the limited damage that was done during the next two hours.

Two hours later the firing from the woods petered out. Were the Indians out of ammunition? Might this be a ruse to get the patriots to rush into the woods where they could be picked off by enemy fire? Colonel Campbell needed information before he could formulate a plan for action. He dispatched two small troops to converge on a spot from which there had been considerable firing. The troops moved in without difficulty and came back with two prisoners, both wounded, one an Indian and the other a Tory.

With a bit of persuasion the two admitted that what remained of the attacking force was withdrawing to their camp outside Fort Stanwix. Colonel Campbell then ordered his men to search the woods. The stragglers they found were allowed a choice between death and surrendering. With the way ahead of them cleared of opposition, the colonel sent part of the militia to the high ground west of the bloody ravine cut by Oriskany Creek. After more than six hours of fighting, the citizen army had thrown back the ambushers and emerged victorious.

With the fighting over, Joel sank down on a log beside his brother Sam. He felt exhausted by the labor of the day. He was emotionally drained. The body of his son Benajiah lay a few feet from him. He had stood with Sam beside it for the full four hours since the downpour. He had lost a son and had vowed that no Indian would take his scalp without taking that of the father too.

Colonel Sam found Joel half sobbing, half in a non-comprehending trance. He thought it best to have him accompany him as he walked back to ask General Herkimer for instructions. They found the general looking haggard in obvious pain but still reposed in the protection of his tree and still smoking his pipe.

"What orders general," the colonel spoke.

"Orders? First tell me your casualties."

"We lost bad. Of the 45 men I brought in my troop, eleven are dead. My cousin here lost his son. Another 15 or so are wounded and all the rest have their scrapes and bruises."

Herkimer leaned toward them and took Joel's outstretched hand in his. "As a father, I feel for you," he said. "I'm most sorry for his death and for those fine men who lost their lives fighting for our cause here today."

Turning to Colonel Sam, he said: "I'd say your outfit came through better than most today. Between being killed, wounded, or captured, I lost all of my colonels. More than half of our officers are dead and no one has counted how many men.

"That should tell you what we will do. The men are hungry and exhausted. It would be suicide to keep going ahead when we don't know what we might run into. Order the lads to make camp back where the wagons are. We'll rest there tonight and then do the Christian thing tomorrow in burying our dead."

* * * * *

Unbeknownst to Herkimer's army another phase of the war in the west took place at Fort Stanwix on the same day as the bloody battle at Oriskany Creek. Advised of the approach of the valley militia, Colonel Gansevoort sent Captain Willett with 250 men of his garrison out of the fort to harry St. Leger's besieging force. They charged into the campground used by the Indians and found much to their surprise that the warriors who had gone to fight at Oriskany had left hardly anyone to defend their camp. They proceeded to appropriate a considerable quantity of useful supplies including military equipment, food and cooking utensils, blankets, and most of the Indian's clothing. With the removal of the booty to the fort, the garrison had reason to celebrate a mild victory.

When the survivors from the ambuscade returned to their camp in the late afternoon, they were dismayed to find that they had no food to fill their empty stomachs, no clothes to cover their near naked bodies, and no blankets to keep them warm at night. They quickly raised a howling clamor of protest. St. Leger did what he could to placate their demands. Meanwhile, he also was plagued with the report that he had lost upwards of half of his Indians in the battle and that his regulars were still facing difficulties in moving his artillery up Wood Creek.

A few prisoners were brought back to the British camp after the battle. St. Leger saw an opportunity to use them to his advantage. Two were induced to write letters to the commander at the fort which claimed Herkimer had suffered terrible defeat and begged the defenders at the fort to capitulate before their fate would be sealed. Gansevoort received the message and a second demand for his surrender on the day after the battle. He blatantly refused to consider the surrender offer but did consent to three days of truce. That same night he sent two officers through the besieging enemy line with a message for General Schuyler at Albany in which he detailed the garrison's predicament.

The armistice agreed to on August 8 was broken the next day when St. Leger's batteries started firing on the fort. The guns were not of sufficient calibre to do much damage. Intermittent firing by both sides continued for another twelve days. During this period the British tried to approach the fort on several occasions but were always thrown back by the defenders.

With the passing days and little evidence that St. Leger could prevail, his Indians lost heart. They were chagrined by their failure to gain scalps and booty, disheartened by the killing and wounding of most of their numbers, and offended by the treatment they received in camp. In disgust, large numbers of them took their meager supplies of clothes and blankets and headed west toward Fort Niagara.

A report reached the British camp on August 22 that Burgoyne had lost a crucial battle and that a provincial army of 2,000 men was marching to relieve Fort Stanwix. Realizing the scant chance he now had for victory, St. Leger gave orders for lifting the siege and for his army to abandon all but its most portable equipment as it scampered down Wood Creek to Oswego.

* * * * *

Herkimer's army stayed on a day at the camp near the battle site. It was a day spent binding up its wounds and burying its dead. The extent of the carnage was appalling. No battle in America that anyone could recall had ever had such a high percentage of fatalities and casualties among its combatants. There was not a soul among the survivors who had not lost a son or brother or a close friend. Many a heart was breaking, many a silent tear shed as brave fighting men fought to maintain a stoic calm.

Joel gritted his teeth and steeled his emotions as he shared the common grief. He had a son who deserved an honorable burial. His brother Sam and his nephew Paul had minor wounds that called for attention. There were others in the troop who were more seriously wounded and two who lingered on even though it was apparent that they soon would die. And like everyone else in the camp, he was concerned about the general's crushed leg. A camp surgeon had treated him but had bungled the job. Herkimer was still losing blood and was getting noticeably weaker.

On the second day Colonel Campbell ordered the survivors to break camp and make their way back to Fort Dayton. Herkimer rode with the more seriously wounded in one of the luggage wagons until they reached the Mohawk crossing. At that point he and the wounded that could not walk were put on a bateaux and floated downstream to Fort Dayton and beyond. Herkimer was taken to his family homestead where he died a week later.

Reports of the battle raced down the Mohawk ahead of the withdrawing army. The first reports, carried by deserters who were fleeing from the battle scene spoke of devastating defeat and the utter destruction of the patriot army. General Schuyler received a report on August 8 that the army had been overwhelmed and that General Herkimer was dead. The next day he received a report from Herkimer about the army's victory after more than six hours of fighting.

Victory or no victory, it was clear to Schuyler that a second relief force must be sent to lift the siege at Stanwix. With this objective in mind, Major General Benedict Arnold was dispatched with a regiment of Continental troops stationed near Albany to march west to relieve the harried fortress at Stanwix.

Arnold was a resourceful, daring and somewhat reckless leader whose fervor for fighting endeared him to his men but whose saucy independence often annoyed fellow officers who regarded him as an overly ambitious, self-centered opportunist. There was no doubt in anyone's mind as to his courage. He had participated in the taking of Ticonderoga in 1775, had suffered a severe leg wound during the repulsed attack on Quebec later that winter, and had supervised a make-shift naval operation that had stalled a British attempt to take over Lake Champlain in 1776. In his present assignment, he was gung ho in his intent to move ahead, to free Fort Stanwix, and then hurry back in time to defeat Burgoyne.

Arnold left Albany with 800 soldiers on August 10. A call was sent ahead for militia volunteers to join his force as it marched west. Joel and Sam induced several of their neighbors to join them in their march to the assembly point at Fort Dayton. Arnold arrived there two days after their arrival on August 18. He was still there on August 22 when a carrier brought a message from Colonel Gansevoort that St. Leger's Indians had deserted and that St. Leger had issued orders for breaking camp.

Arnold responded by ordering a forced march that brought his 2000 troops to Fort Stanwix on August 24. By then the retreating British force was already miles ahead of them on its way back to Oswego. No attempt was made to pursue them. After a short stay, General Arnold turned his army around and had his men march east, dropping the militia off along the way, to join the Continental army that was facing Burgoyne.

* * * * *

Back home again, Joel received a hostile reception when he entered his house near Canajoharie. Becky had almost always been a patient and sweet tempted wife as she had cared for and made a home for his children. Today she was in a fighting mood. "You thoughtless men," she stormed, "you think you can take off and play soldier any time you feel like it while leaving me here to wonder if I will ever see you again and with only me and your kids to handle the crops and chores. Wasn't losing one son enough? Do you think you must join him in the grave? I don't like it no matter how important you say it is. For half a pence I would walk away from here and leave you on your own."

Joel realized he had indeed left Becky without first discussing the matter with her and at a time when his wheat crop was golden ripe and ready for harvest. He was sorry and promised to make amends. Becky had been a good wife and a good mother to Nancy 's sons. She was his friend and a faithful companion. Both knew there was no bond of passionate love between them. As so often happened on the frontier, young men might be passionately in love with their first wives, as he had been with Nancy. But death had a way of coming early to young wives; and when a man was left with small children to raise, a marriage of convenience to an available widow or old maid offered the only practicable solution. Becky had accepted the load of raising his boys. He owed her for that and promised to be more considerate in the future.

While General Arnold was marching back to Albany and Joel was restoring peace in his household, a war was still being fought in the forested terrain north of Albany. Burgoyne's army had rolled steadily southward during the summer, its progress slowed mostly by the valiant efforts of patriots in felling trees across roads along his route.

The army of British and Hessian regulars supported by Indians and Tories reached Batten Kill on August 9. From that place it appeared ready to launch a quick drive on Albany. With the time consumed in getting that far south, however, the army was suffering from a shortage of food and other supplies. Scouts reported that the Continentals had a stock of food and war materiel stored some miles to the south and east at Bennington. Colonels Baum and Breymann were accordingly dispatched with regiments of Hessian troops to capture the needed supplies. Much to Burgoyne's chagrin, both detachments were met and repulsed along the Walloomsac river on August 16 by New England troops led by General John Stark.

During the month that followed, Gentleman Johnny's army continued its forward movement but at a slower and slower rate. General Horatio Gates was sent by the Continental Congress as a replacement for General Schuyler. Gates appointed Arnold as commander of the left wing of the army when he returned from Stanwix and charged him with responsibility for fortifying a defensive position known as Bemis Heights.

In mid September Burgoyne crossed the Hudson river with his army near the settlement at Saratoga. That he did not have firm control of the country behind him was demonstrated on September 18 when General Lincoln raided the British held fort at Ticonderoga. One day later Gates' army faced Burgoyne's attacking force at Freeman's Farm near Saratoga and succeeded in throwing the enemy back.

News of the Continental victories at Bennington, Ti-conderoga, and Freeman's Farm caused a frenzy of excitement up and down the valley. Here at last was evidence that the colonists could meet and triumph over the best Britain had to offer. This news combined with anger over Indian atrocities brought a boost in pro-independence sentiment. With most of their crops harvested for the year, hundreds of settlers packed their guns and set off to help General Gates put an end to Burgoyne's invasion.

Joel marched with his son Nate, this time with Becky's approval and blessing. Colonel Sam invited them to join the troop he was leading from Cherry Valley and Canajoharie. They left their home on October 2 and finally reached the American encampment north of Saratoga on the afternoon of October 6. Arrangements were made there for them to join General Ten Broeck's brigade of New York volunteers.

The newcomers arrived on the battlefield at an opportune moment. The Americans had already dislodged the British and Canadien force from the line it held in a second battle at Freeman's Farm. Burgoyne's army had retreated to a defensive line on the west bank of the Hudson where it was protected by the Belcarres and Breymann redoubts. On October 7 the two armies were posed for a final test. Burgoyne's men, now the defenders, were lined up behind the trenches and log barriers of their defensive line and behind their two fortified redoubts. Each was protected by a tangled abatis of brush and broken branches through which the charging Americans would have to come if they hoped to win in a frontal attack. General Arnold and General Gates had conflicting ideas about how the attack against the British army should be pursued. Arnold insisted that the patriots should attack while Gates wanted to wait for the British to come to him. The argument between the two generals became heated, led to words and an exchange of insults, and culminated with Gates' dismissal of Arnold from his command.

As the two armies faced each other after his dismissal, Arnold heard the booming cannon, saw messengers riding to and from General Gates' headquarters, and saw the British army start to move out to meet the Americans. At this point he threw caution to the wind, leaped on his horse, and shouted: "No man will keep me in my tent today" as he rode off to command the left wing of the American army which faced to the two redoubts.

As self-appointed commander, Arnold led several hundred troops in a frontal assault on the larger Belcarres redoubt. The assault was thrown back once and then again. With both rebuffs, the attackers simply withdrew for the moment to an area outside of the enemy's firing range before trying again. While the battle continued there, Arnold suddenly saw opportunity further to his left. He rode at full gallop between the two armies to a position in front of the extreme left flank of the Continental line where Dan Morgan's corps and the brigades led by Generals Ten Broeck and Learned stood ready to enter the fray.

Pointing his arm toward the enemy, Arnold called for a forward charge, not to the Balcarres redoubt, not to Breymann's redoubt, but to three log buildings located between the two fortified sites. The charge brought the barging brigades alongside and then behind the defenses of the two redoubts. Within minutes flanking attacks poured on to the surprised loyalists. Panic followed as men threw away their arms and ran for safety. It was only with stern resolve that their officers were able to marshal them into an organized retreat.

The messenger General Gates sent with orders for Arnold to return to his tent did not reach him until after the victory was won. By then Arnold was down for a second time with a serious wound in his left leg. He was wounded further in the aftermath of the battle when the vindictive General Gates gave him scant credit for the victory in his report to the Continental Congress.

Joel and the others of his troop were under fire for only a scant few minutes before victory was won. None of the Canajoharie men were harmed and some had not even had opportunities to fire their guns. All, however, rejoiced in the success of their feat. Little fighting took place during the next two days as Burgoyne's army retreated. A week later on October 17, Gentleman Johnny surrendered. The grand strategy for using a three pronged pincher movement to split the colonies had failed. The Americans had demonstrated their ability to hold their own both in the west and at Saratoga. Sir Henry Clinton, who had finally started to move on the plan for bringing troops up the Hudson from New York, saw that it was too late, abandoned the campaign and returned to New York.

With victory at Saratoga, the outlook for the future of the American states brightened. France now came into the war as an ally against Britain. The centers of contention between the rival armies moved south to Pennsylvania, Virginia and the Carolinas. The Campbell families were happy to have their men back unscathed. But any hopes they may have had that Saratoga would end the war along the Mohawk were badly misplaced.

* * * * *

St. Leger's withdrawal from the siege of Fort Stanwix did nothing to stem the hatred the Tories felt toward the patriots who had caused them to abandon their homes in the valley. Joining them in their continued opposition to the new order were the disgruntled Senaca and Cayuga tribesmen from the western nations who sought revenge after their defeat at Oriskany.Important among the leaders of this opposition were Sir John Johnson and Colonel John Butler and his son Walter. Colonel Butler, a veteran of the French and Indian War, had been a substantial landowner and settler in the valley. Walter had been trained as a lawyer and had been one of the first Tories to flee west to Oswego. He had joined St. Leger in the siege of Stanwix, had helped plan and execute the ambush at Oriskany, and had later been captured by soldiers of the Continental army while trying to induce settlers to join the Tory cause. He was tried for treason as a spy, condemned to death by General Arnold, his sentence reprieved, and then imprisoned at Albany from whence he escaped and returned to Canada during the early part of 1778.

There was much rejoicing in the valley after the victories of 1777. Some felt a sigh of relief, thought the threat of violence was over. Saner heads, however, realized that peace was still a distant mirage. The enemy would come again and defenses had to be strengthened and readied to meet any coming challenge. Colonel Sam Campbell and some of his neighbors took their case to the Marquis de

Lafayette, one of Washington's new lieutenants. Lafayette agreed with their request and ordered the construction of a defensive fort at Cherry Valley. The anxiety and lack of ease felt throughout the valley during the year after Oriskany was compounded by a general breakdown of law and order. Indians, ruffians, and strangers wandered here and there throughout the valley, some of them on honest business, many watching for opportunities to steal or do other mischief. No one knew if it was safe to trust a stranger. Fears of unprovoked violence were kindled and aggravated by reports that the western Indians and the dispossessed Tories were coming back with guns and tomahawks to exert their idea of justice.

* * * * *

The family reunion had all the markings of a gala occasion. Joe brought greetings from Grandfather Samuel Campbell who at 83 lived on a small farm near Middleton about 100 miles south of the Mohawk valley and 40 miles northwest of New York City. As Joe explained, grandda would like to have come and be with his sons and their families but was too infirm for the travel.

Food was there aplenty. The wives had made competent provision for the occasion by baking rolls, bread, cakes and cookies. Pails were filled with crusty fresh fried chicken, bowls with baby potatoes and peas cooked in cream sauce, lettuce salad with a vinegar and sugar dressing, platters with fresh corn on the cob, ripe red tomatoes, deviled eggs, and generous slices of home grown melons. It was a clear warm afternoon with plenty of shade, no mosquitoes and few flies or ants. The children had a boisterous happy time playing with their cousins. All things considered, the afternoon should have provided a perfect setting for a memorable family get together were in not for the general gloom shared by the grown up participants.

Far from the cheerful banter enjoyed at earlier reunions, the conversation dragged. There were topics everyone wanted to discuss but which all seemed intent on avoiding as unfit for picnic fare. Even when some led forth with comments about the weather and their farming operations, most of the others seemed inclined to quickly drop the subject. Joel finally broke the relative silence with a comment about the Indian raids. This was the topic everyone had been trying to ignore. With the damn broken, everyone had an account to tell, a rumor to dwell on, a fear to express. Far from calming the tension everyone felt, the sharing of views only added fuel to the flames that were licking at the sense of security the families enjoyed.

"Why do we sit here like sheep surrounded by wolves?" Sam's wife complained. "We act like a flock of scared hens facing a fox in the coop."

"Yes, why? Why?" was the lament taken up by several of the women?

"Why indeed," Sam answered. "Would you have us leave all we got and run like scared rats from the varmints?"

"No," Becky snorted, "you men think it is heroic to stay here and wait for the Indians to come for our scalps. You think you can chase them off, but they always come back looking for vengeance. They want more than an eye for an eye and it is we women who bear the burden of worry and grief while you men think you can play it out like a game."

"What would you have us do?" Nate asked.

"Leave. Pack up your things and go some place where there are no Indians or avenging Tories."

"But this is our land, the fields we broke our backs clearing. Would you have us walk away from this fruit of our brows, from what we have spent most of our lives working for?" one of the men asked.

"I say we should move to some place closer to the old settlements where there are no Indian neighbors," Becky answered. "It makes no sense staying here to hold on to a few acres when they can all be lost along with our lives and our scalps."

Becky's challenge unloosed a babble of comment as a dozen people tried to express their views. Joel, who had been sitting quietly during the outburst, suddenly pounded the table for attention. "The women have a case, lads. Maybe we have been asking too much of them. Lord knows, I'm scared and I think most of you are too. Life is for living not for going around fearing that every day will be your last.

No matter how brave we think we are, we should at least put our women folk and young ones out of harms' way. Now let's consider what we can do. Joe, you live down at Middletown, can we make a living down there? Would we be any safer there than here?"

Middletown was still a land of opportunity as Joe saw it. There was good land there, developed farms one could buy or rent and also some areas awaiting settlement. The Delaware Indians were sometimes in evidence, but they were friendly and not allies of the Tories. "The town there is a long hike from here because you'll have to go east toward the Hudson before turning south to get around the Catskills. We are south of the mountains and west of the Hudson. Moving there will put you a good bit closer to the British army than you are here. New York City is only 40 miles away and is the chief market for what we can sell."

"How much danger are you facing from the Brits?" Sam asked.

"So far, General Clinton has shown no more interest than Howe did in coming out our way. The threat is always there if they decide that we have something they want. Till now they've shown more inclination to chase off into Jersey or Pennsylvania than to march west. Choosing between the threat of redskins here or of redcoats there, I think Middletown is your best bet."

Sam and Joel looked at each other for a moment. Then Sam nodded his consent and Joel brought the issue to a conclusion with the announcement: "Let's check it out. If the prospects are good and life doesn't turn for the better here, we can move down there this winter."

* * * * *

Joel rode south to Middletown with his son Jonathan and his brother Sam in early October. Their crops were harvested for the year. The patches of trees they passed displayed their annual riotous festival of color. Their ride took them east of the Catskills then south and west into the Delaware River country. Joel, who had seen nothing other than land along the upper Hudson and the Mohawk, was surprised to find that other areas had their assets too. What

235

they saw around Middletown pleased them. Farms were for sale and for rent; but with little money, Joel was particularly pleased when he found that raw land was available for settlement.

When they returned to Canajoharie later in the month they had detailed plans for packing up their families and belongings and moving south. Several chilly rainy days at the end of October and in early November made the roads generally impassable for wagon traffic. Their plans for moving were placed on hold. The bad weather though did bring a relaxation of tensions. With weather like this, families up and down the valley could surely enjoy more security than they had from hostile Indian attacks.

Colonel Alden at the fort at Cherry Valley was as convinced as anyone that there was no longer need for vigilance. That he was poorly suited for his command was shown by the decidedly slipshod manner in which he supervised the fort. He had a garrison of well-trained men, mostly from Massachusetts, under his command but gave little attention to maintaining tight discipline. Through lack of interest, he had allowed the fort to become dangerously short of both food supplies and powder.

All summer he had responded to rumors and reports that Johnson or Butler was leading bands of Tories and Indians to storm the fort. A warning, carried by a friendly Delaware, had come only yesterday, that an attack was imminent. But like the defenders who had responded needlessly to cries of 'Wolf, wolf' many times, this was a cry that he dismissed and disregarded.

It rained on November 9. With an approaching blast of winter weather, the rain turned to sleet and the next day to snow. Surely with weather like this there was no reason for caution. Nevertheless, Alden did send scouts out to check on possible hostile activities along the two principal roads that led to the Cherry Valley settlement. A third route, a seldom-used trail leading to the Susquehanna valley was left unchecked.

Colonel Alden, several of his officers, and about 40 of his men spent the evening and night of November 10 at the large Wells house. Located some 400 yards from the fort, the Wells house provided better accommodations for entertainment than the fort. Mrs. Wells and her servants had a well-earned reputation for providing tasty fare.

Totally unexpected by the colonel, Walter Butler and his rangers made their way up Cherry creek from the Susquehanna river on November 10. Their progress was slowed by the frightful weather and by the fact that the 200 Tories and Indians in the attacking force had little to eat other than grains of corn. Late in the day, they captured one of Alden's scouts who had been sent out to observe them on a nearby road. Taken to Butler's camp that night, the frightened scout gave the rangers an inviting account of the sorry state of affairs at the Cherry Valley fort and of the colonel's penchant for spending nights at an unfortified private house located almost a quarter of a mile from the fort.

The morning of November 11 found Cherry Valley covered with a blanket of snow. What had been a snow storm changed to icy drizzle around 10 o'clock as Butler's rangers moved from their camp to positions around the settlement and its fort. A first shot was fired around 11:00, not at the fort but at the Wells house. Colonel Alden and his men reacted quickly, grabbed their guns, and started to run in the direction of the fort. It was too late. Butler's men were ready for them. Alden and 12 of his men were shot down like sitting ducks as they tried to make their way to the safety of the fort.

Butler and his Tories then turned their attention to the fort where the suddenly alert garrison opened the gates to allow the entry of 28 of the fleeing soldiers, some of them wounded, and then settled down under the command of a few competent master sergeants to withstand a siege. The Tories and some of the Indians started firing at the fort. Firing and counter firing from the fort went on till mid-afternoon with little damage done to either side.

While part of Butler's force was attacking the fort with little visible signs of success, most of the Indians together with some vengeful Tories turned their fury on the men, women and children who lived in the 40 houses that comprised the Cherry Valley settlement. Rangers broke into almost every house, pillaged them of whatever plunder caught their fancy, and proceeded in many cases to slaughter and tomahawk noncombatant residents. Dozens of men, women, and children ran into the woods for safety. Butler, much to his credit, tried to dissuade his savage allies from their frenzy but was not able to stop them until 40 settlers, many of them women and children, were killed with their scalps taken by the excited Indians.

Around 3:30 Butler called a halt to the firing on the fort. It had become evident that the outnumbered garrison could defend itself from attack from outside the fort and that they had no penchant for coming out into the open to fight. At that point, Butler felt his rangers had gained their needed measure of revenge. More than two score of the rebellious enemy had been killed, more than a dozen were injured, and about 40 others had been rounded up as prisoners who could be taken to the west country where they would be assigned to different Indian villages to be kept until arrangements could be made to exchange them for imprisoned Tories.

Butler camped with his rangers and prisoners amid the still smoking ruins of the now burned out Cherry Valley settlement that night. A huge fire was built and a cow captured with the booty was killed and roasted for the assembled throng. It was snowing again the next morning when Butler ordered his rangers to take their booty and prisoners and start their homeward trek down Cherry creek to the Susquehanna River, on to its confluence with the Chemung, and then up that river on a 300-mile march back to Fort Niagara.

Colonel Sam Campbell was saved from what would probably have been certain death in the Cherry Valley massacre by an unplanned absence from his home. He had ridden in the rain on November 9 to Canajoharie to visit with his cousins Sam and Joel and to talk to them about their plans for moving to Middletown. In the back of his mind he was considering the prospect of offering them a tract of land he had been planning to sell if they would agree to continue to live in the area.

The two brothers felt flattered by the colonel's proposal and agreed to consider it. Two hours of pleasant conversation and good-natured banter followed. It was not until the colonel's planned time of departure to Cherry Valley that they noted that the rain had turned to sleet. Joel insisted that he stay overnight. Colonel Sam agreed and decided to extend his visit for another day when they awoke on November 10 to find the ground covered with snow.

The Campbells received their first news of the massacre on November 12 when a half frozen survivor who had hidden in the woods limped into Canajoharie with his tale of horror. Colonel Campbell's first inclination was to mount his horse and gallop off to Cherry Valley. Joel and Sam insisted that he wait until they could assemble a posse of a dozen men who could ride with him. They knew it could be suicide for a single rider to return to the settlement. It was hazardous too for a small troop such as theirs to go where a larger enemy force had been only a day earlier. No one wanted to encounter Butler's rangers, or to ride into an ambush. Yet everyone realized that could be just what they were doing. Still everyone was willing to put his life on the line if that could help the survivors of the massacre.

Much to Joel's relief, the posse met no opposition on its way to or on its arrival at Cherry Valley. They found the ruins of a dozen houses still smoking. Most of the 28 remaining houses were still habitable though repairs would be needed with most of them. All had been pillaged and household items were scattered around the settlement. It was obvious that the Indians had taken things and then thrown them away when they considered the prospect of having to carry them the long way back to Niagara. The raiders had taken what horses and cattle they could along with a considerable amount of grain.

The men were surprised to find that the raiders had left several horses and cows, animals that may have fled into the woods when the firing started. Stocks of food remained along with sheep, hogs, and chickens. Men from the garrison were already trying to make order out of the chaos. Survivors who had returned after spending the night in the woods and prisoners who had been abandoned at the last moment had been taken into the fort where they could be housed and fed. Some fires had been extinguished and steps were being taken to lay out the dead for burial.

Colonel Sam hurried to his own house, which he found in ruins. The bodies of his mother-in-law and one of his daughters lay among the dead. Both had been scalped. He was overcome with grief with these discoveries but even more concerned with the absence of his wife and four of his younger children. Where could they be? They obviously had been taken as prisoners, but to what end? Their bodies could be lying out there slaughtered in the snow. If they were not dead, they could be facing a living hell as Butler's rangers fled westward in frigid weather toward far off Niagara.

Joel and Sam did their best to console and comfort their cousin. They shared his anger and grief but could do little more for him than assure him that Butler would surely try to keep his wife and children alive and safe so that they could be exchanged for Butler's wife and sister who were being held as hostages by the patriots at Albany.

Colonel Klock came with a detachment of Continental troops from Schoharie two days after the massacre. By then the snow was beginning to pile up. It was already two feet deep along the roads. From all appearances, the raiders were long gone. Klock called off plans for a pursuit. His decision, however, did not prevent General Ten Broeck at Albany from ordering 2,000 troops from nine different regiments to prepare themselves for pursuit of Butler's retreating rangers. With the temperature dropping and more snow falling, it soon became evident that the proposed pursuit would prove fruitless.

The tragedy at Cherry Valley and the early onset of winter left the Campbells unable to proceed with their plan to move to Middletown. The weather moderated for a while in mid December and Joel and Sam talked of the possibility of leaving their families in their snug houses while they rode south to start building new houses for them. Their speculations were brought to an abrupt end just before Christmas when cases of smallpox were reported at Canajoharie. Whether they had been exposed or not, there was no chance now that they could leave before spring. Everyone in the community was subject to quarantine. No one from any other community would welcome travelers from a settlement where they could have been exposed to the dreaded disease.

The spring of 1779 was fast coming when Joel and Becky finally left with their family from the valley where they had spent most of their lives. Traveling with them was a caravan of Campbell families as most of Joel's brothers decided that they too would move to the Middletown area. At their new settlement they started over as settlers. The change was not hard to make. Working together and with others of the Campbell clan, they cleared new land, erected new buildings, and within a few months were living very much as they had in the Mohawk valley.

They had reason to wonder if they had found security when Joseph Brant, a Mohawk chief led a raid on nearby Minisink on the Delaware river in July. Casualties from the assault were few and Brant quickly fled from the scene with his small warrior band. Final relief from fear of Indian attacks came in 1779 when General 'Mad Anthony' Wayne led a military expedition west to deal with the Indian problem. He met and defeated Butler's army in western Pennsylvania, after which the tribesmen fled to their base at Niagara.

* * * * *

Campbells Came

Part Six

Jonny

1786 – 1818

Flickering light from 20 lanterns, the boisterous laughter of a merry crowd, and the rasping twang of music from three fiddles filled the great room of Campbell Hall as two young men entered the hail. Across the room three musicians scratched out a rhythm as a caller chanted out his 'Dosey do' instructions to two groups that were dancing a Virginia reel.

"Looks like the usual crowd," Jonny observed to his to his brother Reuben. "No, wait a minute. Who is that girl over there in the blue dress? Don't think I've ever seen her."

"She's easy on the eyes. I 'spect that means you are going hunting".

And he did. Two dances later, Jonathan Campbell, Jonny to his friends, introduced himself and asked Eunice Button for the next dance. Twice more he danced with her, and when time came for refreshments, he was there at her elbow to treat her to cider and cookies. He was there again later to ask if he could see her home. When asked why he had not seen her before, she explained that she had just come from Connecticut to live with her brother John, a recent newcomer to the area.

The young couple found it easy, almost natural, to talk to each other. From the time of their first dance, each was drawn to the other like bits of magnetized metal. Jonny made no secret of his feelings. He liked what he saw, felt he had scored a victory over all the men present when she agreed to let him see her home, rejoiced when she agreed to see him again, and clasped her to him while he gave her a good night kiss as though they were already romantically involved when he delivered her to her door. He wasn't sure at first whether his actions were driven by emerging love or lust. He was sure though that he liked what he saw and wondered as he ambled home after leaving her if she might indeed be the girl he had been looking for.

Jonny spent considerable time with Eunice that summer in 1786. Day after day his mind was filled with thoughts of her. He saw her as beautiful, charming, an ideal companion, as the girl he wanted to marry. Eunice, who was surprising attractive for a maiden still unmarried in her mid twenties, was as much interested in him as he was with her. It was not long before their friends saw them as a couple.

Quite without realizing it, Jonny found himself doing things to please her and going places with her where he would not otherwise have gone. He even started taking her to church, something he had resisted doing since childhood.

Eunice wanted to know everything about him. "There are so many Campbells around here, you must own this place," she said." When did you come here anyway?"

Jonny explained that his father had moved to Mamakating in Ulster county eight years earlier with his four sons and with four brothers and their families to live near his grandfather and that between them they now accounted for 37 Campbells in the area.

"Tell me about your grandfather. Did they name Campbell Hall for him?"

"Campbell Hall was here long before we came. My grandfather lived for only a few months after we moved here. He was an interesting old man. At least I always thought so. He was raised in Ulster but came to Boston from Scotland after his first wife died. He lived in New Hampshire for awhile and then moved to the Mohawk Valley where he made his living as a fur trader."

"A fur trader. That must have been exciting. And along the Mohawk too. Were you there during the Indian raids?"

"We sure were. Getting away from them was the big reason for coming here."

"And your people came from Ulster. Did that have something to do with naming this Ulster county?"

"No, nothing like that. Someone in Britain named it Ulster long before we got here. The Duke of York, who later became James II, named the colony after himself when the British took it over from the Dutch. He divided the colony into several counties. One was named Kings and another Queens after his parents, two others were called Nassau and Orange after two Dutch princes who were married to his sisters, and Ulster was named after his brother who was the Duke of Ulster."

Jonathan was just as anxious to learn details about Eunice's background. She told him she was from Connecticut where she was the next to youngest of the eight children born to Captain Matthias Button and his wife

Phoebe. Her baby sister had died young and she had grown up as the youngest in the family.

"You say your father's name is Matthias. Isn't that a Dutch name?"

"It sounds Dutch but our family isn't Dutch, The first Matthias Button came to New England with Endicott's settlement 160 years ago. We've had Matthias Buttons in every generation since. I have one cousin who claims he is Matthias Button the fifth by direct descent. Another cousin Matthias died as a British prisoner during the Revolution. We've had lots of soldiers and merchants as well as farmers in the family but the first Matthias was the most interesting."

"What did he do?"

"Not very much besides wearing out four or five wives. The interesting part was that he got in trouble with a neighbor he accused of being guilty of witchcraft. The court let the neighbor off. Then the neighbor got revenge by burning down Matthias' house with his sick wife in it."

"That was murder. Was he punished for it?"

"Not for murder. Her death was ruled an unfortunate accident. But the court allowed Matthias to sue his neighbor for his loss of property."

"If your father was a captain during the war, he should be sitting pretty, so how come you are here?"

"My father and my oldest brother Joseph went north from Connecticut to Vermont during the war to help General Stark fight the British and the Hessians at Bennington and then retake Ticonderoga. They liked the country up there so much they decided to move there once the war was over. Daddy took his second wife and their seven children with him to Vermont leaving my three other brothers and sister, all of them married, and me at Voluntown. As the only single person left, I went to live with my brother John and his wife. When they moved here from Connecticut, I came with them."

"Did your other brothers fight in the war?"

"They were in the Connecticut militia. Except for us girls, we were a 100 percent military family. How about your family, Jonny, did you fight in the war?"

"I wanted to fight at Saratoga but I was still just a kid. My father and two older brothers went but they wouldn't hear of taking me along. My father and two of my brothers were at Oriskany. That was where my brother Benajiah was killed."

"So you didn't get to fight?"

"I tried again in '81 when our militia marched west to stop Butler and his Tories on their last rampage. Our troop arrived at the river crossing where Butler was killed only an hour after the last battle of the war was fought."

"Did you lose any close friends in the fighting?"

"Losing my brother Ben was the worst. He was just a year and a half older than me. We had played together all of our lives. He was my best friend. Losing him was like losing an arm. Except for Uncle Jonathan, he was the only one in our family who was killed. Pa's cousin in Cherry Valley was in the middle of it though. He was promoted from captain to colonel in the field at Oriskany. Later he was visiting with pa and my Uncle Samuel when the Indians and Tories struck at Cherry Valley. Some of his family were scalped and killed and his wife and four of their children were taken as prisoners to western New York."

"Did they ever get back?"

"They were farmed out to different Indian villages where they lived for seven years until the war ended."

"Were any of them hurt?"

"Not that I know of. They had to live with the savages but were not harmed because the Tories planned to trade them for some Tories held by the patriots. Their chief abuse was that they were separated from each other. Funny thing, the youngest boy was only three when he was kidnapped. He grew to ten speaking just the Indian lingo. When he finally saw his mother again, he did not know her. Something about her though caused him to go to her and throw his arms around her."

Jonny thought of Eunice as his bride-to-be almost from the evening of their first meeting on. He was reluctant to press his case though because he felt he should have more substance to his name than he had before asking her to join him in matrimony. He had 20 acres that he cleared in '86 and on which he planned to build a house. But he had not yet started to build it and he held to the view that a man should not marry until he had a threshold to carry his bride across.

By the spring of '87 he was ready to start building. Lack of money was his major problem. Money was in short supply all over the united states and particularly so in the west country. The paper continentals that were in circulation had depreciated so much in value that most merchants refused to accept them. They wanted hard currency and coins of any sort were as scarce as hen's teeth.

Jonny was still living in his father's house when he was shocked to hear that John Button was planning to move to another community. The announcement, forced him to make a decision. For the next two days he asked himself time and again should he ask Eunice to marry him now or hope she would be willing to wait for him while he built a house for them. The possibility that he might lose her if she moved away with her brother was just not acceptable.

With some reluctance, he broached the subject with Eunice. She was quicker to respond than he had expected. She had no desire to become an old maid. They were already best friends; she loved him, wanted to spend the rest of her life with him and would not mind living under Joel Campbell's roof until their house was ready for occupancy. With the decision made, arrangements were made at the church, and Jonathan Campbell was married to Eunice Button, both 26, in 1787.

* * * * *

The Jonny Campbell who introduced himself to Eunice Button in 1785 was typical of hundreds of other men who had grown up along what was still the western frontier. Unpampered by past exposure to luxuries, he was a rugged son of the woods and soil. Thanks to the watchful care of his stepmother, he could read and write though he did little of either. With little interest in scholarship, he was ill inclined to join his parents in their Bible readings. He was a hardy worker, a jack-of-all-trades but had thus far shown no inclination to be anything other than a farmer. He hoped to someday have a farm as large or larger than that operated by his father and never for an instant doubted that he would live and die as a farmer.

Of medium height and sturdy build, he was a healthy specimen of young manhood. He was congenial, adventurous, and courageous by nature, intensely loyal to his family, and ever willing to bear his share of the workload. His one major weakness was his vile temper. All of his life he tended to explode if he failed to get his way. His parents had noted this weakness while he was but a child and had carefully weaned him to a practice of counting to ten before venting his rage on others. With self-control, there were fewer and fewer outbursts as he reached manhood. There were times though when he had to fight with himself to contain the flames of sudden anger that still flared up from time to time,

Unlike many others, Jonny also suffered from a vague feeling of insecurity. It was not a fear that kept him from participating in the reckless chance taking indulged in by his fellow young immortals. Yet it was always there, a feeling that the unhoped for would happen. Losing his mother when he was only four, his boyhood years afflicted with frequent reoccurring tensions over possible Indian and Tory raids, and losing Ben, the brother who was his role model and best friend, had left a permanent mark on him, a suspicion that fate was ever ready to deal him an unwanted hand.

As a boy and teenager, Jonny had displayed a gregarious nature, an exuberant desire to enjoy the give and take of growing up in a large family of boys amid numerous cousins and friends. He liked girls and enjoyed dancing with them. His major interests were centered though on sports, outdoor living, and hanging out with other boys. The course of his upbringing took a wayward turn when he was fifteen.

It was about that time that he and Ben started to associate more than they had with his older brother Nate and their cousin Paul. In their quest for fun loving activities, the four lads were careful to stay out of trouble. They never stole or swiped anything more than an occasional apple from an inviting orchard. Their exuberance led to occasional mischief such as the tipping over of outhouses and the hoisting of a neighbor's wagon onto the roof of his barn one

Halloween. It was they though who induced Jonny to smoke his first pipe of tobacco, to drink his first swig of hard liquor, and to place his first bet on the turn of a card. It was with them too that he first heard men boast of their sexual exploits. As a farm boy, Jonny learned about the animal side of sex early in life. Throughout his early teens, he often wondered about human sexuality, but it was a subject his parents and friends did not discuss. Becky had schooled all of her sons to the view that their bodies were to remain clothed in the presence of others and that the bodies of girls were to be admired but remain untouched and unseen by men until after they were married. With his father keeping a closed mouth on the subject, Jonny assumed that it was his moral duty to stifle his sexual yearnings and that it was somehow sinful for him to even think about sex.

A change in this situation came during the October after Oriskany while Jonny's father and older brothers were off fighting at Saratoga. Rumors had passed from man to man that summer that Miz Buckley, a young widow who lived at Canajoharie, was willing to spread her legs for men for a price. Paul heard the rumor while marching back from Oriskany. After repeating it to Nate and Jonny, he dared them to visit her. The three lads laughed about the challenge but did nothing more. After his father insisted that he stay home while the others marched to Saratoga, Jonny decided he should prove his manhood by taking the few coins he had and visit the widow.

Miz Buckley received him with a hardy welcome. She quickly detected his inexperience and decided to make his initiation an event of significance. She pampered him as she undressed him and took him to her bed, Unsatisfied with their first coupling, she insisted that he stay on with her so she could teach him to perform as she wished. As he finally prepared to leave, she gave him a parting kiss and said: "I like your young body Jonny. Come back next week as my guest. There will never be a charge for you."

Jonny's response, though predictable, came as a surprise to him. His experience was not something he would ever forget. Nor was it something he wanted to brag about to Nate or Paul or anyone else. He certainly did not want to discuss it with his parents. They would object on religious grounds and he wanted no lectures on morals. He knew what he had done was unconventional, but he was in no way ashamed. More than anything, he wanted to return. And return he did, almost every week during the next year and a half while his family stayed on in the Mohawk Valley.

Others in his family complained from time to time of things they had given up when they moved to Middletown. Jonny thought every day of what he had left behind and of which he could not speak. He had tasted the joys of sex. He wanted to continue his secret philandering. The problem as he saw it was where and with whom. There was no Widow Buckley to his knowledge in Middletown. He went to a prostitute but left after inquiring about her charges. He left primarily because he had no money. Later, he told himself he left because he wanted no relations with such as her.

Jonny abstained from sex during the months that followed because he had no apparent opportunities for doing otherwise. He went to dances and parties and soon found that nice girls did not extend sexual favors to men until they had firm assurances that they would be married. He suspected that there were wives or widows who might welcome his advances but he had no means of identifying them.

He found a temporary outlet for his yearning when he was nineteen while he worked in a nearby town where he met a voluptuous blond at a party. She was an immigrant from somewhere in Europe who spoke terrible English but who seemed pleased to take him to her bed. He had a pleasing encounter with her at a second party at which he met her brother. The brother's menacing threats when they spoke to each other convinced him it was time for him to leave for home without saying goodbye.

Jonny marched with the New York militia on its Niagara campaign in 1781 and visited New York City two years later after the British army, which had been quartered there for seven years, was finally evacuated. The Continental army with Washington at its head had moved in to take its place. Jonny was drawn there partly by his desire to see the great general but also because he had hopes of finding employment.

He stayed with his cousin Paul and spent his first few days there looking around. With its 30,000 residents, New York was much the largest city he had ever seen. He was surprised but not impressed by the amenities and numerous shops it offered. Dozens of the larger houses and places of business were boarded up, deserted by Tory owners who chose to leave the city with the British. Good jobs were scarce and he soon concluded that while he probably never would be able to afford living in one of the better houses. He was unwilling to accept the prospect of having to live in the housing available for workers of lower income.

He decided that New York's problem was that it had too many people. He wanted to live some place where there was more open space and fewer women and children. Not finding any work that appealed to him, he took Paul's advice and went to the shipyards to test his potential as a sailor. He signed on to work on a coastal transport. His first short voyage to Newport convinced him that his fear of heights would forever limit his ability to assist in furling and unfurling sails. A turbulent sea on the return voyage left him terribly seasick and prompted him to walk away from the ship, from the port, and from the city, once he found himself again on dry land.

Back in Middletown in midsummer, Jonny worked on his father's farm and found such pleasure as he could at parties with friends. He left in October to work for six weeks on a job at Goshen. He was shocked on his return at the end of November to learn that Tom Erskine, a bachelor friend with whom he had frequently partied, had been forced into a shotgun marriage.

"Tell me about it," he demanded when Nate told him of the marriage.

"It is a simple thing," Nate answered. "You know Grace Ebling. Tom knocked her up last summer. When she found she was pregnant, she told her family that Tom was the father. Her father and brother decided that Tom had to take on her support and make an honest woman of her. Tom objected at first and insisted that some one else was the father. He admitted though that he had been with her. That was enough for the Eblings. They tapped him with their guns and he agreed to the marriage."

"Ouch. What a lousy break for him. Sure am glad I wasn't here."

"Are you telling me something?" Nate demanded. "You spent a lot of time with Tom and his friend Jake last summer. Do you know something I don't about what happened?",

"Yeah, and they are details I should keep my mouth shut about and tell neither you nor anyone else."

"You've said too much to keep quiet now. What really happened?"

"All right, I'll tell you but you must promise not to repeat any of it to anyone else, least of all to pa or ma or any girls I may want to meet."

Nate's promise given, Jonny admitted that he had horsed around with Tom and Jake at a few parties in August and September and that they had met Grace at one of the parties. Nothing unusual happened at the first party. At the second one though she had invited them to come to her father's barn the next afternoon where she promised to serve them fresh doughnuts and home made brew. Not expecting anything more than some fun loving banter, the three young men had come as promised. For awhile, they ate, drank and told stories. Then Grace had insisted that they roll around in her father's haymow. They rolled around on the hay laughing and bumping into each other for several minutes and then she rolled down an incline onto the barn floor. Jonny followed and his body landed on top of hers at the bottom of the slope.

"Before I ever realized what was going on, she was all over me, kissing me, stroking my cheeks, rubbing my chest, opening my shirt and pants, and putting her hands down there. I tried to stay calm, but you know how it is; my soldier was taking no orders from me; he just stood at full attention. By then the other guys were sitting there taking it all in. But that didn't bother her. She just yanked my pants off to get a look at you know what.

"She didn't stop at that. She rose up enough to slip out of her dress and underclothes, laid them on some hay, and spread out with not a stitch on her. Then she asked me to make love to her. I kissed and rubbed her in the right places. She was soon bouncing around like a rubber ball and moaning like she was having a wonderful dream. Then she spread her legs and said: 'Give it to me, Jonny'. I should have got up and run, but that wasn't how I felt. I figured if Gracie was asking for it, it was up to me to give it to her and that is what I did. It wasn't long before I shot off and pulled out. As soon as I did, she turned to the other guys and said: 'It's your turn next Tom. Then I'll take Jake'."

"So the three of you gang raped her."

"No, it wasn't rape. No one forced anyone to do anything. It was her idea and we were there by her invitation."

"Was she a virgin?"

"I don't think so. 'Least I don't remember feeling any maidenhead."

"Is that the whole story?"

"No, that was just the beginning. After Jake had his turn, she had us sit next to her, all of us stark naked, while we drank more brew. Then she said she wanted each of us to give it to her one more time. By the time Jake shot off again, she had our seed seeping out and all over her bottom."

"Was that the end of your serving her?"

"I can't speak for Tom or Jake. I was with her two more times before I left for Goshen."

"Well all I can say is that you are dammed lucky Jonny. You had your fun and didn't have to pay the piper. If they had come to you with their guns, would you have taken her?"

"Maybe yes if they really pointed them at me. She is not the sort I want to marry though."

"It's good for all of us that she didn't pick you rather than Tom for her husband. With her choosing you to do her first, she likely would have picked you if you had been here. Poor Tom got picked because he was available. There is a bigger reason too. He is an only son and his old man has a big farm and a herd of cattle while you have little more than yourself to bring to a wife."

Nate kept his promise not to talk to others about Jonny's experience. Jonny heard more about it two days later though while talking to his father. Joel used Tom's marriage as an example of why his son should be careful in choosing his associates. "When an unmarried girl around here finds herself in a family way, it is her word against his if she picks him to be the father. Grace Ebling is not the first woman who has put her finger on the most eligible of the men who knew her. Just to be safe, you should never go around with any woman you would not be willing to marry. The rule we go by is pretty plain. If people have seen you with the girl and she says you are responsible for her condition, you must either be a good sport and marry her or make yourself a target for any man in her family who decides to take a shot at you."

The lesson learned from his affair with Grace had no effect on Jonny's frequent yearning for sexual contacts. It did convince him, however, that he must accept abstinence as his way of life until he was more ready to consider marriage. There was no more fooling around in the year and a half before he met Eunice. The most positive effect the experience had on him was the prompting of a dawning realization that he must start saving money if he was to someday have a house and farm to which he could bring a wife.

* * * * *

Jonny and Eunice lived for more than a decade on the little farm located next to his father's larger farm at Mamakating. They were poor like most of their neighbors and often survived on a hand to mouth basis. Still they were happy as they built their house and enlarged it to accommodate their expanding brood. John Button's talk of moving remained a dream until 1792 when he took his family to Renssalaer. By then Eunice and Jonny had two daughters, Susanna and Hannah, and their first son, Benajiah, was on the way. The departed Buttons were hardly missed as Jonny and his wife found their lives filled with contacts with brothers and cousins of the Campbell clan.

Important events went hardly noticed around them. The 13 states that had gained independence during the Revolution had stumbled through a confused inflation riddled era under the unworkable Articles of Confederation. A convention had met in Philadelphia the year Jonny and

255

Eunice were married and drafted a constitution for a federal union.

The proposed constitution, which delegated many powers exercised by the states to a single national government, had been adopted by New York after a fiery campaign. Jonny wasn't sure whether the new arrangement was a good idea. He liked keeping the power of government close to the people. At the same time though, he wondered if there was merit in the argument that the country should have a king. Was there some reason why not a single democratic government had survived since the days of ancient Greece and Rome? Even with them, the republics had been taken over by dictators and kings. Britain's experience during the last century showed what could easily happen. The parliamentary democracy introduced there with the removal of King Charles had given way to Cromwell's dictatorial rule as Lord Protector and to the later restoration of the monarchy.

The Campbells approved when General George Washington was called out of retirement to serve as first president of the new United States. With his firm hand on the rudder, he and John Adams were able to steer the ship of state through turbulent waters. It soon became apparent though that there was no unanimity of opinion among the citizenry of the new republic on questions of public policy.

Washington had started as president with the almost unanimous backing of the members of the new Congress. As different policy issues came to the fore, the members gradually attached themselves to two opposing political camps. One group called the Federalists tended to support the interests of merchants, investors, and big landowners. The other group, called anti-Federalists at first, then Republicans or Democratic Republicans, and still later as Democrats, was more inclined to support the interests of small farmers and average citizens.

Both parties favored reasonable appropriations for national defense and for the preservation of law and order. Wide differences existed, however, on issues such as tariff levels, the funding of state debts, establishment of a national bank, and the distribution of public lands. The Federalists in the northern states supported the concept of using protective tariffs to encourage the growth of domestic industries. They wanted a national bank that could underwrite a national currency. They saw the undeveloped western lands that the states were turning over to the national government as a resource that could be sold to pay off the debts the states and the Continental Congress had incurred during the Revolution.

Jefferson, Madison and the other prominent Democratic Republicans saw high tariffs as harmful to the small farmers who accounted for more than 90 percent of the population. They feared that a single national bank would exert monopolistic powers that would favor the moneyed class at the expense of average citizens. They favored liberal land disposal policies and opposed the proposal that the state and Continental debts should be paid off at their full listed value.

Paper money had been issued in vast quantities by the states and the Continental Congress at a time when there was little revenue to support it. By 1790 the bills still in circulation had become so discredited and nearly worthless that few merchants would accept them. The phrase 'Not worth a Continental' amply described the value most people attached to them.

Alexander Hamilton, a leading Federalist, argued that funding this debt at its listed value would bring prestige and respectability to the new government. His critics saw the proposal as a give-away to those rich investors who had accumulated large stocks of the near worthless currency on the chance that it might be funded and who would now stand to reap substantial profits at the expense of the general public.

None of the Campbells were much concerned with national politics. They had been patriots during the Revolution and had survived like most citizens amid the confused state of affairs that followed under the Confederation. The government was providing them with peace and order and they expected little else from it. Like most families living in the backcountry of rural America they lived in a largely self-sufficient society in which people could find happiness and contentment without much use of money. Hard money was scarce; most families had little to sell and satisfied most of their needs with bartering and the cooperative sharing of labor with their neighbors.

With New York's adoption of the Federal Constitution Jonny and the others of his family had hopes, stirred up by the promises of politicians from New York City, that times would become better. He was inclined to support the Federalists because Washington, the nation's hero, was a Federalist. It was not until after the two political parties became established that he realized his interests were represented more by Jefferson's followers than by the Federalists.

There was no need for Jonny to declare his political preference. The shift in his thinking though was a matter of some concern to him. Somehow he still wanted to be a Federalist. He felt he was being disloyal in his leaning toward support of the critics of General Washington's party. As he thought about the major differences between the two parties though, he found himself agreeing more and more with Jefferson's vision of need for a government of small farmers.

He was little concerned with the tariff issue because he bought few items that were subject to duties. He was generally opposed to the national bank idea because he suspected that it would be used to advance the interests of the moneyed class. The two issues that concerned him most were the funding of the state debts and the disposal of the public lands. As he saw it, it would be unfair to pay off the debts at full value because the investors who held most of the near worthless currency had acquired it for the most part at a fraction of its face value.

Land disposal was the issue of greatest importance to him because ability to acquire cheap land on the frontier offered him his best option for breaking out of poverty. Leaders from both parties wanted to have the lands surveyed and then offered for sale at public auctions with a minimum price of $2.00 an acre. They differed greatly, however, in their ideas as to the appropriate minimum size of the sale tracts. Men like Hamilton wanted to sell most of the land at substantial discounts in price to investors who could afford to buy large tracts while the Democratic

Republicans wanted sales of smaller minimum size to actual settlers.

What the state of New York and its counties were doing was a matter of less concern to the Campbell brothers. The politicians in New York City and Albany had never shown much interest in what happened in the backcountry and Jonny didn't expect them to start doing so now. There was talk of the state undertaking a program for building public roads and constructing locks along the Mohawk to provide a navigable canal that could link traffic on the Hudson river with Lake Erie. Such talk seemed more a pipe dream than something that that might be accomplished in his lifetime.

The one accomplishment of state and local government that affected the Campbells most was the legislature's recognition of a need to organize new counties and towns in its west country. With boundary adjustments and the creation of new units, Jonny and his father found that their farms in Ulster county were now part of Orange county and that a subdivision of Mamakating town made them residents of the new town of Deerpath.

* * * * *

Jonny and Eunice had been married for 17 years when summer came in 1804. Mostly they had been happy years even though they were years of scrimping poverty. Their farm was too small to afford them much opportunity for enjoying prosperity. Neighbors on larger farms could sell their surplus produce to buyers from New York. Jonny seldom had any surplus to sell. He worked when he could for other farmers. The few coins he earned were always swallowed up by family emergencies. There were no savings he could put aside for the purchase of the additional land he needed to support his family.

Jonny would never have agreed, but the major reason for his problem was the steadily increasing size of his family. In their 17 years of married life, Eunice had borne him nine children. After their daughters Susanna and Hannah, their first son Benajiah had been born in 1793. Joel in '95, Ruth in '96, John in '98, Benoni in 1800, Ezekiel in

1801, and Frederick in 1803. Both parents were intensely proud of their brood and neither saw anything unusual about its size. Both had come from large families and the Campbell brothers seemed to be competing with each other to see who could make the largest contribution to the nation's expanding population.

Their common need for more land was a frequent topic of conversation between Jonny and his brothers. It was on one of these occasions that Nate introduced him to Martin Halprin, a newcomer to Orange county. Halprin had attended Yale University and was scouting the area with the intent of possibly starting a legal practice.

After hearing their complaints about insufficient land and its effect on their inability to get ahead, Halprin said: "It seems to me that the root of your problem is that you fellers have too many kids."

"What do you mean?" Jonny bristled.

"No offense to you, my friend. Just look at it this way. You have been married for say 15 years. Your farm is the same size now as it was when you first moved on it, but your wife has been a lot more fertile than your fields. While your fields have been wearing out and yield less now than they did at first, your wife has been dropping an extra kid for you to feed every 18 months or so."

"There is nothing wrong with that. I love my kids."

"Of course you love them. There is nothing wrong with having a large family either if you have the resources to give them all a good bringing up. The problem is if you have ten kids, each of them has ten kids, and your grandchildren all have ten kids, it doesn't take long before you have more than 100 times as many people to support."

"We could never take care of them on the land we've got, so what would you have us do?"

"There is a man in England named Malthus who has done some writing on the subject. He says the problem took care of itself in the past. Back then we needed large families because wars, plagues, and famines killed off most of the population. He says that the clearing and settling of new lands like we've been doing here will take care of the problem for awhile but that sooner or later we will be back to the point where our surplus population will die from starvation if they are not killed off by diseases or wars. According to him, we must practice abstinence and have fewer children if we want to avoid or postpone the survival problem."

"When you say abstinence do you mean that we men must be a bunch of eunuchs who cannot have sex with our women?"

"Malthus wouldn't go that far. You could have sex but only enough to maintain population numbers."

"That is not fair," Jonny retorted. "Servicing my wife is the most pleasurable thing a poor man like me gets to do."

"You are speaking for all men or at least nearly all of those I know. There is no reason to go that far yet though. Jefferson has more than doubled the size of the United States with his Louisiana Purchase. There is a lot of good farmland waiting to be settled between here and the Mississippi and even more beyond the big river. Even with big families, we have enough land out there to care for our settlement needs for 100, maybe even 500, years."

"After the land is settled, do you think Malthus will be right?" Nate asked.

"He could be. His logic sounds good. There are some offsetting factors though that can postpone the day of reckoning."

"Like what?"

"We might learn how to grow better crops and get higher yields from our fields. Some farmers are planting better seed and are liming and fertilizing their fields to get bigger yields. Some others are using selective breeding to improve their livestock. Things like that can increase the ability of farmers to produce the surpluses needed to support a larger population."

"With all of these new developments, do you think we will ever get the point where we have something that will let men and women enjoy having relations without having to worry about having babies?" Jonny asked.

"That will be the day," Halprin added.

"But when it comes it will give our ministers fits," Nate added. "They will make a moral issue out of it."

"Well, don't hold your breath on it," Halprin continued. "Those possibilities are still a long ways down the road.

Some day we may get to a point at which we will want to limit population because having more people will cause problems we want to avoid. But that day is a long way off."

"This is all interesting," Nate observed, "but does it give us any answers to our land problem?"

"If you are asking me, I'd say you are in a dead end here. Go west. There is a big country out their waiting for settlers and I'd say you are the sort of folks it is waiting for."

* * * * *

Halprin's suggestion started a chain reaction. Jonny and Nate speculated on the possibility of moving. They discussed the possibility with their father and their four brothers. All of them agreed that their opportunities for getting ahead were limited where they were and that serious consideration should be given to a possible move.

Two critical questions were raised. Where could they go and what costs would arise. Each of them had small farms that could be sold or leased out but no one had savings that could be used to buy land. Buying land in an already settled area like Deerpath was out of the question. Public domain land was for sale in the Ohio country for $2.00 an acre, but that too seemed a steep price for them to pay.

The question of where they should go was upper-most in everyone's thinking when Jonny met with his father and his brothers and their wives on a sunny warm day in August.

"I wish to hell the government would let us have small tracts at a price we could afford," Ezekiel opined.

"How much land are you talking about?" Nate asked.

"I'd be satisfied with 30 or 40 acres. If the land has to be cleared, 20 acres might be all I could handle with the tools I've got, but I'd like to have some extra land to keep my boys busy while they are growing up."

"As for me, I'd like to get 200 acres," Joe replied.

"Why do you want so much?" Nate asked.

"I guess I am thinking ahead. I have four boys and who knows how many more I may get. I'd like enough land to start every one of them off with 40 acres. If I had to cut from that, I'd say 60 or 70 acres. That way I'd have enough to keep at least one of my boys living near me in my old age."

"That is the kind of thinking I like," Joel senior observed, "but how much land we get depends on how much an acre we have to pay for it. The government wants $2.00 minimum an acre. Is there any chance we can find good land for less?"

"Not from the national government, at least not yet," Joe answered. "Land hasn't been selling very fast and some people think they will be cutting the price but that could be years away. They are willing to sell on credit, one fourth of the $2.00 when you buy and the rest within four years. There is talk of allowing discounts if buyers pay cash."

"One fourth down. That means I could buy 40 acres for $20 down. I think I can raise that much cash," Zeke said.

"It's not that easy," Joe continued. "That price calls for minimum purchases of half sections. That's 320 acres."

"Half sections? What is that all about?"

"It means that the government does not allow buyers to go out and locate their own boundaries. The old metes and bounds descriptions are complicated and cause too many problems with isolated unclaimed tracts. Congress solved the problem by setting up a rectangular survey system that calls for public surveys of the land before it can be sold. The surveyors lay the land out in six-mile square townships. Every township contains 36 one-mile square sections each of which contains 640 acres if the survey lines are straight. The half section minimum sized tracts that are for sale have 320 acres and are one mile long by a half mile wide."

"Are you saying that I cannot buy just 30 or 40 acres?"

"Not at one of the government land offices. You might be able to buy odd sized tracts from investors or speculators. Most of them though now think in terms of full half sections or quarter sections."

"Between the price and acreage requirements," Joel continued, "we are left pretty much out in the cold. We could pool our resources and maybe come up with the $160 down payment plus the $20 or so in filing fees that it would take for us to get a half section. But then we would have to worry about getting enough money to make the later payments. Don't any of those Congressmen realize that settlers have no extra income during their first years? It takes all of their energy and all they can make just to feed their families while they are clearing land and putting a house on it. Even if nature cleared the land for them, most settlers live too far from markets to be able to sell enough to cover the follow up payments."

"What happens if you buy on credit and then cannot come up with the later payments?" Jonny asked.

"We won't know for sure until more settlers start defaulting. If a buyer defaults, the government has the right to repossess and resell the land along with all of the improvements made on it. We will have to wait and see whether it will go that far. It will be hell to pay in some places if they do."

"What would happen if we moved out there ahead of the surveyors and just settled down on some choice land?" Ben asked.

"You mean if we went out there as squatters?"

"Yes, is there anything to stop us? Would we be breaking any laws or have the army run us off?"

"The land office agents take a dim view of that, but I guess it is happening more often than they like to admit. My guess is that they would be tolerant; but you would have problems. You would be living next to Indians on land where you weren't supposed to be. When the surveyors come around they will run their lines where they should be even if their lines split your holding into different townships or sections. Then when the land goes on sale, you will have to take your chances on buying it. Speculators could outbid you for it and take over your clearing with all of your improvements."

"That's not fair to settlers," Jonny complained. "If they go ahead and clear land and make improvements on it, the government should give them a chance to buy their claim at its minimum price."

"I agree; but so far the land laws make no provision for it. Congress may change the rule if enough people complain. That is going to take some time though."

"You may be right about the government taking a lenient stand with squatters," Joel senior interjected. "I'm not expecting any favors from them though. The government sent General Harmer out to run squatters off their claims in the Ohio country about 20 years back. Then when those farmers in Pennsylvania refused to pay that tax on hard liquor a few years ago, Washington and Knox said 'The law is the law ' and sent the army out to collect the taxes. If the law says squatting is illegal, I don't put it past the government using the army to keep even deserving families off the land."

"This is a heck of a situation," Jonny concluded. "If we can't buy or squat on government lands, what can we do?"

"Shouldn't we start by looking at the land New York has for sale?" Nate asked.

"The best tracts in this state are already held by investors and speculators," Joe reported. "Most of them are willing to sell and some of their prices look reasonable, but they are all out to get cash if they can. More than that, once the feds put that minimum price of $2.00 an acre on the western lands, every speculator here decided his lands were worth at least that much. Any land they offer for less is apt to be swampland, rough hillsides, or land that is miles and miles away from roads and markets."

"What about those areas claimed by Massachusetts and Connecticut?"

"How did they get any right to claim land out west of here?" Ben asked.

"Their claims come from the original charters they received from the British crown," Joe reported. "Back then the two colonies were given claims to all of the land between their northern and southern boundaries running west to the limits of British jurisdiction. The Dutch came later with their settlement of what is now New York. Connecticut and Massachusetts were willing to let the Dutch settlement take out a slice of land on both sides of the Hudson river but have argued that the strip of land west of there in northern Pennsylvania is by rights Connecticut land while the strip in southern New York just to the west of us belongs to Massachusetts."

"Can claims like that stand up in court?"

"I don't know whether a case was ever argued in the British courts. It was settled here before anyone tried to take it to the Supreme Court."

"And?"

"When Virginia and the other southern states were under pressure to turn their unsettled western lands over to the federal government, New York gave Massachusetts the sales rights to some of the land it claimed. That took care of Massachusetts. As for the Connecticut claim, the colony authorized some of its people to move out there and start some settlements about 40 years ago. Pennsylvania's colonial government didn't take kindly to that and sent a homemade army to oust them. Since then Pennsylvania has maintained its charter claim. The case didn't stop there though. When the states were asked to cede their claims to western land, Connecticut argued that it held title to a strip of the Ohio territory that runs west between an extension of Connecticut's northern and southern boundaries. Concessions were being given to other states so Congress followed through by giving Connecticut sales rights to that portion of the land it claimed called the Western Reserve."

"What kind of sales arrangements do Massachusetts, Connecticut and Pennsylvania have on their public lands?" Josh asked.

This was a question for which no one had answers. They decided after some speculation that the three states were probably holding to the minimum price set by Congress. "They will probably cut their prices later if they have to unload their less desirable lands," Joel rationalized. "But for now they probably argue that what they have is worth as much as the government land in Ohio."

"I don't see that we have made any progress," Jonny said. "Every way we turn runs into a dead end. Isn't there some place somewhere we can go where we can make a decent living?"

"Guy I talked to awhile back may have had the answer," Josh interjected. He was just got back from some place in northern Pennsylvania. He said there were several valleys out there with good land that have not been settled yet. The way he told it, the state made large grants to some investors several years back with the provision that they must settle on their holdings and improve a few acres within a year or two or forfeit their claims. Seems some of the new owners never even visited their grants. With the grants forfeited, the land is just sitting there waiting for settlers to squat on it and make reasonable purchase arrangements later with the state for acquiring title."

"Sounds like a possibility we can live with." Joel observed.

"If the rest of you agree," Joe responded, "let's send Nate and Jonny out to look at the place. If they think it looks good they can stake out a claim and we can move there next spring."

* * * * *

Three weeks later Jonny rode west with Nate and Nate's brother-in-law George Fuller on their inspection tour. Their route across northern Pennsylvania followed a winding route of rough roads and wagon tracks across what seemed like an endless series of high hills and ridges separated by valleys that displayed varying stages of development. At Athens they were directed to cross one more ridge to where they would find the unsettled valley they chose to call Ridgeberry.

Ridgeberry was an unsettled wilderness covered with brush and timber. The land on both sides of Bentley creek was covered with forest growth of all ages. There were few open areas under the taller trees. Most of the ground was covered with dead limbs, decaying leaves, and with brush, young seedlings and larger trees that would call for hours of back breaking labor once settlers started to clear the land to make farms.

The men were not turned off by the presence of the dense forests and undergrowth. Those were indicators in their eyes of soil fertility. True, forests could be seen as the settler's enemy; but they were also his friends. They were hard to cut down; but for some years to come they would provide the settler with timber, with fuel, with game, and sometimes with protection from storms and possible enemies.

The three men concluded from their appraisal that the soil was fertile. The woods were stocked with game. There were no signs of Indian villages or settlements. Two days of exploration in the valley left them convinced that this was as good a place as they were apt to find for their settlement. With this decision made, they started their ride back to Deerpath looking mostly for the easiest route their families could travel on their move to Ridgeberry.

A light rain was falling on the late afternoon of the second day of their return trip when they reached the village of Montrose. They had stopped there on their ride west. Nate favored going on a few miles. George, however, insisted that they seek shelter out of the rain for the night. Jonny agreed with George and the three stopped at a farm and received permission to sleep in the barn. Once they were located Jonny said: "You fellows get comfortable. I'm riding on to that blacksmith's place. My horse is about to lose a shoe and I want to have it fixed so we can start out first thing tomorrow."

Jonny found the blacksmith still at work. He told him of his need and the smith said he would get to it in a few moments. While Jonny stood watching him use his hammers to shape two iron rods on his anvil, the smith surprised him by asking: "Haven't I seen you before?"

"You could have. I passed through here last week with two other men."

A few minutes later, the smith excused himself and went into his house where he spoke to his son. The boy quickly left on an errand while the smith took his time in reshoeing the horse. He was just finishing when four burly men approached the forge.

One of the men looked at Jonny and demanded: "Who are you stranger? What are you doing her?" Jonny explained that he and his friends were on their way back to Deerpath and that he had come into the village to have his horse reshod. The men seemed reluctant to accept his explanation. Didn't he have more to tell them? After responding to several badgering questions, Jonny felt himself on the point of losing his temper. He steeled himself and demanded: "What's going on here? I don't know what you guys are trying to get at but whatever it is I should have a right to know."

No one answered him at first. Then three of the men withdrew a few feet, engaged in a mumbled conversation. When they returned, their spokesman said: "The point is mister that we've had a man murdered in this town, his wife was raped and beat up. Right now you look like the most likely suspect."

Jonny's first impulse was to flee, but he knew he could not get far before he would be captured, maybe killed. He knew it would be futile to try to fight the five men. He protested his innocence and insisted that his two fellow travelers would substantiate his story. This was not enough though to satisfy the men as to his innocence.

The man who had been speaking for the group said: "I'm the deputy here and I am arresting you on suspicion. We don't wish you any harm, mister, especially if you are not guilty. But we've got to be surer before we turn you loose. So you will spend the night here until we can get Judge Witter, our justice of the peace, to hold a hearing on whether we should hold you further."

Jonny enjoyed a good dinner prepared by the deputy's wife and slept in a far better room than George or Nate did that night. They were apprised of his arrest when they came into the village looking for him that evening and they were there at the justice's court when the evidence against him was examined the next morning. Judge Witter dismissed the case and apologized to Jonny for the inconvenience caused when the still bandaged wife assured the court that Jonny was not the man who had murdered her husband.

* * * * *

Back in Deerpath, the three men reported their findings with a recommendation that plans be pushed for the move to Ridgeberry. As the head of the family, Joel Campbell was looked to as leader of the migration. With him and his wife were his seven sons: Joel junior or Joe, Nathaniel, Jonathan, Joshua, Ezekiel, Benoni, and William together with their wives and children. Counting men, women and children, there were 47 Campbells in the party. Moving with them were 21 Fullers as Isaac Fuller, a neighbor with marriage ties to the Campbells, chose to join them in their move.

During the winter months, the men assembled the tools and supplies they felt they must take to meet the challenge that lay ahead. They made certain they had their guns, knives, traps, axes, saws, hammers, crowbars, chisels, awls, spades, hoes, scythes, pitchforks, wooden ploughs, and a harrow. Along with these tools they took seed for their crops while their wives put aside stocks of flour, salt, meal and sugar for their sustenance together with cloth, thread and needles they could use in clothing their families.

Between them, the various families had seven wagons and four carts piled high with household and farming equipment. The men had horses but chose to have their wagons drawn by oxen. Additional cattle and sheep were driven with the caravan. A portable coop was constructed to accommodate two dozen hens and a rooster. After convincing themselves that it would be hopeless to try to herd their pigs over the 100-mile route, five young shoats also were put in a crated pen that could be hauled while the remaining pigs were converted into hams and bacons that could be taken along.

Fortunately for the travelers, spring came early in 1805. The two family groups were finally ready to leave their old homes during the first week in April. The weather remained chilly but dry as they made good time traveling at oxen pace over rutted roads that could have been neigh impassable in wet rainy weather. For eleven days the migrants moved westward before arriving at Ridgeberry.

Once the caravan arrived, the two families split. Separate claims for Jonny and his brothers would be made later. For now the entire Campbell clan worked and lived together as they took quick action to provide a large covered bower that could protect everyone from the rain that was sure to come. Rough hewn logs were notched and tied together around the four sides of the bower enclosure while pine branches were cut to provide a thatched roof. A smaller bower was built a few feet away with a rude fireplace where food could be cooked.

By working together and each concentrating on tasks he could do best, the seven brothers had their two bowers ready for use within a week. Surveying the work done, Joel said: "Good work, lads. This will do nicely for us for now. Once we clear some land and get some planting done, each of you can pick out your own claim and we will start building more permanent houses."

While the men were busy assembling logs and building the two bowers, their wives and older children started the task of clearing brush from the areas they hoped to use for planting crops. Freeing himself from his brothers for a while, Jonny took on the job of girdling the larger trees and chopping down the younger growth that could not be easily cleared away with the brush. Timber from the biggest trees was kept for building purposes while the extra wood and brush was stacked in long windrows that could be burned after the wood dried.

As the settling in process continued, the newcomers had some pleasant surprises. Josh found several sugar maples near the creek and plans were quickly made to tap them for sap that could be boiled down for maple syrup and sugar. Jonny found a stretch of cascading flow on the creek that he thought he might harness to provide possible power for a small mill. The brothers and their older sons also found that the woods contained berry bushes and were well stocked with deer, bears, and rabbits all of which could add to the variety of their food supplies.

With the passing of the first few weeks of settlement, the pristine wilderness yielded to signs of development. Construction was started on three houses, a sawing pit was dug in which two workers, one above and one below could use their crosscut saws to shape timbers and supply boards for building purposes. The fields that had been picked for planting stood apart amid the surrounding wilderness, their earlier cover of brush and young timber removed and the remaining large trees now girdled and standing like silent sentries that could be removed in the weeks to come. Small fields were already planted to corn, wheat, oats, potatoes, beans and vegetables.

The seven brothers knew they faced a busy summer, fall, and winter. They could steal away for some hunting and fishing but each of them knew that his fullest efforts were needed in clearing more land and providing livable houses for each of the eight Campbell families.

No one faced the prospect of going hungry. Everyone could be well fed with bear and venison steaks, with the rabbit and pigeon pies they tapped from nature; their cattle could give them milk, cheese, meat and oxen power; their sheep provided wool for thread and clothes; their chickens and pigs were multiplying and soon would be a source of eggs and meat. With their harvest of wheat and corn they would have meal for sap and jonny cake, potatoes and squashes for baking, honey from wild bees and maple sugar from their trees. They had the makings of a good life; but hard work was needed to put it all together and give every family its own home.

While the seven brothers and their wives were devoted to their several tasks, Joel and Becky were excused by mutual consent from the harder tasks. Both were in good health but both were old, or so their sons thought, and should be entitled to respect and leisure. With free time on his hands, Joel was determined to learn more about the legal status of their settlement. They had moved in and squatted on the land without asking for anyone's consent. After pondering about the matter for several weeks, he decided he should ride over to the settlement at Athens and ask some questions.

Athens was located about six miles east of Ridgeberry across a ridge and in the next valley. A settlement had existed there for several years and numerous cleared fields stretched out from the village. In answer to his inquiries, the first man Joel met directed him to the house of Mr. Bigelow. Bigelow, he found, was a man of approximately his age who had settled there in the early 1790s. Bigelow was happy to tell him about the Athens settlement and the history of the area.

"This whole area," he explained, "is part of Lycoming county and you live in either Smithfield or Athens township, I'm not sure which. This is all temporary of course. Once we get more people out here the county will be split into several counties and you will have your own township."

"What can you tell me about our land grants?"

"We got a mixed up history. Would you believe it if I told you that all this land round here was included under the charter given to Plymouth colony? Somehow it later got shifted to the royal charter given to Connecticut. The Connecticut and Pennsylvania charter grants overlapped. They argued about whose it was back before the Revolution; and when some Connecticutters moved in to start a settlement Ben Franklin and the Pennsylvania legislature decided they would fight for it. They sent an army up here; the Yankees gave in and it has been Pennsylvania land ever since.

"When Pennsylvania finally got around to granting land out here it issued land warrants at dirt-cheap prices to some investors who lived mostly at Philadelphia. The warrants covered grants of 400 acres, more if the buyer agreed to build roads, and provided that the buyers must develop two percent of their area, that would be just eight acres, within two years and live there for five years. The buyers who met these requirements could go to the land offices, ask for a land survey, and get a registered certificate of title. If they didn't follow through in meeting the requirements, they defaulted and the land was supposed to go back to the land office.

"Big chunks of land out here were covered by those land warrants. Most of the buyers defaulted as only a few of them bothered to visit the area and fewer still did any settling."

"What does that mean for settlers who have come in and settled the land?"

"The title situation is a mess. The land officers have been lenient when warrant owners have shown signs of honest intent to settle their lands. Those owners get titles they can sell to others. With those who have defaulted by doing nothing, it can be argued that they have forfeited any rights they had and that the land goes back to the state for resale. I don't rightly know whether that is legal."

"What do settlers do then?"

"Wait for the government to make up its mind, I guess. No, I know what your problem is over with your settlement. We have some of the same problem here. We checked it out with some attorneys and they say we should go ahead and use the land as if it is ours. With mixed up circumstances like you have at Ridgeberry, your best chance for getting clear title is by claiming it by adverse possession. You live on the land as though it belongs to you, pay the taxes on it for seven years; fight off any people who come along claiming it is theirs and then you can go to court and legally claim that it is yours."

* * * * *

Christmas had been a joyful holiday and now two days later Phoebe Button was bubbling with excitement as she stood gazing out the window of her father's house. Outside was a memorable display of New England Yuletide beauty - four inches of snow on the ground, a cloudless blue sky and pine trees dark green with bits of ice on their needles that sparkled like clusters of diamonds in the morning sun. Sleek horses harnessed with tinkling bells drawing colorful sleighs and bundles of pine cones bound with red ribbons hanging from most every door added to the holiday scene.

Inside, her father's house was decorated more lavishly than usual. A Christmas tree covered with strings of popcorn and chains of red and yellow paper stood in a corner. Red candles stood in every window and also above the mantel. A bowl of red apples sat on the table and a sprig of mistletoe hung above the door.

Sally, Phoebe's 15 year old sister, burst into the room and exclaimed: "Oh, Phoebe, it is so exciting. I love weddings and yours tomorrow will be the best. Every girl in town has had eyes for Elias Smith and he picked you. I think he is the best and most handsome man in all Vermont. You must be so happy! I wish you weren't going away though."

Phoebe, a comely lass of 21, hugged her younger sister. "I don't want to leave you either, Sal; but I want so much to be with Elias, to cook for him and make home for him. It would be nice if girls like us could get married and stay on at home forever; but that is not how things are. I'd like to stay here with you and Philura and mom and daddy, but it is only right that I for go where my husband goes."

"I don't mean that. I'd like to have you live here in Wells where we could see each other and visit a lot. It's Elias' plan to move to New York that I don't like. Once you go away from here I might never see you again."

"Nonsense, sis. We'll see each other."

"I'm not so sure. You are moving to New York state. That is where Uncle John lives and where Aunt Eunice was before she moved to Pennsylvania. We have never seen either of them since daddy moved here from Connecticut."

Phoebe Button was married on December 28, 1807 to Elias Smith at Wells, Vermont. The young couple stayed on in Wells until March and then headed westward with two horses and a wagon piled with a motley supply of household goods. They drove the few miles west to the New York border, went on to Glens Falls, drove south to Saratoga Springs, then west to Johnstown, from whence they followed the Mohawk trail to Syracuse. At Syracuse, they turned south and drove 30 miles to Homer where Elias had plans to settle.

The first few months of 1808 were a time of honeymoon bliss for Phoebe. Elias was an attentive and cheerful companion and lover. On the road and at the site of their settlement, he displayed independent determination to get ahead. He was a hard worker who expected his bride to work with him like another workman. Day after day they slaved alongside each other clearing the few acres on their farm on which they planted corn, wheat and potatoes. As time permitted they started construction of the house that was to be their home.

By early July the new house was beginning to take shape. More timbers were needed for the roof; and Elias traded labor with a neighbor who indicated willingness to help him cut and shape the needed timber. Phoebe was hoeing in her garden in mid afternoon while the men were cutting trees in the nearby woods when she heard a scream.

She hurried to the woods and was met by the neighbor. His face was contorted with anguish; tears were streaming down his cheeks as he blubbered: "There's been an accident. The tree fell the wrong way and Elias got hit."

"Is he hurt?" Phoebe cried as she rushed to the side of her fallen husband.

The neighbor helped her stretch out his lifeless body. "He's dead, dead," Phoebe shrieked while the neighbor could find nothing more consoling to say than "He was struck outright. He had no time to suffer."

Phoebe could have fainted, but did not. Later she found it hard to recall what she did or how she reacted. All she remembered was that the neighbors with whom they were acquainted had been solicitous of her welfare. An older woman insisted on caring for her while her two sons dug a grave and prepared the body for burial.

It was not until the day after the brief funeral service that she came out of her daze. The pressing question she had to answer now was what should she do next? Should she try to see the season through on her own and hope some lonely man would offer to take Elias' place? Should she take her horses and wagon and drive back to her father's home in Vermont? Was there some relative, a brother, uncle, or cousin who might live closer she could look to for succor?

A young widow after only six months of marriage, Phoebe realized that she was already in the fourth or fifth month of her pregnancy. She had no desire to take the first man who might come her way, and realized that her pregnancy would not count in her favor if she did. Driving those horses all the way to Wells could be an exhausting experience. Her father's brother John lived somewhere near Albany. That would be a shorter trip, but she didn't know the name of the town where he lived and wasn't sure he would want her to come? Then there was Aunt Eunice who had written such nice letters. She lived in Ridgeberry, Pennsylvania, wherever that was.

Inquiries were made of all the neighbors at Homer. Where is Ridgeberry? No one seemed to have heard of the place. An answer came in early August when a neighbor who had gone to Cortland on business returned with the information that Ridgeberry was located about a dozen miles south of Elmira. With that information Phoebe decided and the neighbor who had cared for her agreed that it would be best for her to take her wagon and household goods to her aunt's home.

Jonny Campbell's family was surprised and delighted when Phoebe drove her team into their yard. Eunice, who had been ailing for several weeks, opened her arms to her. Here was the first relative from her family she had seen in more than as decade. She was delighted with Phoebe's presence and quickly offered to make a home for her. She wanted her there not because she was sorry for her but because she was kin and company and because having her there could lift some of the load of caring for the household from her shoulders.

Jonny, in turn, was not sure at first whether he liked her intrusion. Having her there meant there would be some loss of privacy in his already crowded household. There was something in their meeting, however, that stirred up the dormant interest he had in associating with pretty women. It was not long before he joined Eunice in welcoming her to the family.

Phoebe's arrival meant that there would soon be 14 people living in the household. Eunice's youngest child, William, had been born in 1805. Her three eldest daughters Susanna, Hannah and Ruth, who were 19, 17, and 11, were delighted to have the company of a cousin who was only a few months their senior. The boys liked her and raised no complaints about crowding. They were used to sharing space with others. She found it easy to fit in with the others and when her baby was born near the end of the year, little Matilda too was welcomed as a new member of the family.

* * * * *

Eunice's declining health was already a matter of concern both for her and her husband when Phoebe joined the household. Eunice had been 44 three years earlier when little Billy was born. She had gone into menopause with its heat flashes and other discomforts while she was still nursing the baby. Now that he was weaned, she felt worse rather than better. Like most frontier wives she was tired and worn out after bearing ten children, raising a family, and carrying a heavy work load. Complicating matters further was the onset of a female disorder the likes of which she did not understand.

She knew from the folklore passed on to her in conversations with older women that the itching and soreness she experienced between her legs was not a good sign. Doctors somewhere might have remedies for female complaints but no one at Ridgeberry did. None of the herbal ointments she tried did any good. As the weeks passed, her problems worsened. She was fatigued: there were unaccountable pains in her lower back; she suffered from abdominal cramps. The discomfort and pain she felt with sexual intercourse made that once joyful pastime a fearsome and revolting act.

Jonny felt none of the symptoms or pains that were making Eunice's life a living hell. He loved her and was ready to do anything he could to ease her pain. He wanted to see her health restored but neither he nor any of his associates had any idea of what could be done. He spent his spare hours sitting with her, consoling her, and just holding her hand. His despair over her deteriorating health was further complicated by the void it left for the satisfaction of his sexual yearnings.

Once Phoebe joined the household it was Phoebe who lifted most of the workload from Eunice's shoulders. Susannah was planning to marry one of the Fuller boys while Hannah had her boy friends and was more interested in going to parties than in doing house work. Phoebe, on the other hand, was grateful to the Campbells for the haven they had provided and willingly took over household chores while insisting that Eunice lie down and rest. More than that she became a close companion to whom Eunice could pour out her innermost thoughts.

Susanna was married in March 1809 and moved away with her husband. Eunice's condition worsened. She now felt tired and listless; her once healthy appetite slipped away; the abdominal cramps and pains became more intense. Jonny and Phoebe did all they could to ease her suffering and make her comfortable. Jonny was grateful for Phoebe's help, for her willingness to take charge of the house.

Little by little Jonny's close association with his niece brought a strong bond of togetherness between them. At the same time, Phoebe's participation in the local social scene soon made her a center of attention for the single men in the community. Several of them, some young, some older, soon saw her as a highly eligible young widow who could make a cheerful and competent helpmate. Silas Campbell, son of Jonny's favorite brother Nate, was one of those who fancied her attention.

Silas danced with Phoebe at several parties, but was disappointed when she showed reluctance to be alone with him. For awhile, he assumed that the gradual worsening of her aunt's condition was the factor that caused her to keep him at arms length. On a warm afternoon in May, he chanced to see her walk into a dense wooded area on his uncle's farm. Curious as to what she was doing, he too went into the woods.

Once in the woods, he heard voices. One was Phoebe's; the other sounded like his uncle Jonny. He could not quite make out what they were saying. He chose to remain a silent intruder as he waited to hear more. After some moments during which he heard muffled voices, he heard some wild moaning, quiet at first and then much louder as Phoebe uttered mild shrieks of pleasure and begged 'Don't stop. Don't stop.' Silas peaked through the brush and saw the couple sprawled on the bare earth, Jonny on top of his half dressed niece and both intent on satisfying their lustful desires.

Silas crept away, ashamed in a way that he had witnessed the scene; half wishing that it had been him rather than his uncle who had gratified his pleasure, and now convinced that his courtship of Phoebe was at an end. Silas was not a man who started or repeated gossip or who enjoyed talking about his friends' misbehavior. He liked his uncle and wished him no harm. When his father chanced to ask him about his courtship that evening, however, he told him what he had heard and seen.

Nate saw Jonny the next afternoon. After some words of greeting, he drove directly to the point: "What is this I hear of you rutting with your niece?"

Jonny made no effort to deny that it had happened; did not ask how Nate had learned of it, and after some questioning admitted that he and Phoebe had been exchanging favors for almost two months.

Nate protested: "You should not be doing this, brother. It is not fair to Eunice. You could make life miserable for Phoebe if you get her pregnant; and it is not fair to the young bucks around here who might want to marry her."

"Marry her? Who wants to marry her?"

"You don't know because you have been at home with your wife while Phoebe has been at our parties. It might surprise you that half of the unmarried men here about have been eyeing her as a possible wife. My Silas is one of them."

"Silas? He can't have her. He is too young to marry."

"Come on Jonny. You know better than that. Silas is almost two years older than Phoebe."

"Well, he can't have her. She is my wife."

"Not yet, she isn't. Eunice is still alive and you cannot have more than one wife."

"Pa had two wives and grandpa had two before him. Who says I cannot have two."

"You can but only one at a time."

"Do you know of any law that says I cannot have two? No, you don't. And the Bible is full of saintly men who had more than one so don't try telling me that I cannot on moral grounds."

"Custom says you can't Jonny, and anyway it is not fair for Eunice."

"Eunice already knows about us, Nate, I told her. She knows I love her and would do anything to help her get well; but she also knows she is on her last pins. When she had that spell a few weeks ago, we talked and she asked Phoebe to marry me and take care of the kids. Then she made me promise to marry Phoebe. I love Phoebe just like I do Eunice; and once she got us promised, we figured we were as good as already married."

"Jonny, you are a case. I'm not going to cause you any trouble. Watch out for that cock of yours though. It can get you into a real stew if you are not more careful. And please be careful with what you and Phoebe do. We don't want you setting a bad example for our young folks."

* * * * *

Eunice's condition steadily worsened in the weeks that followed. She suffered from cramps and excruciating pain. Jonny had heard of a drug used in far off China that was said to relieve pain but he and the others at Ridgeberry had no idea of how to get it. By June she was bedridden and strange bumps appeared and grew on her body. Then near the end of the month, her resistance seemed to collapse, she got what her family thought was a cold which changed in two days to a raging fever, and she died.

After a short three months of mourning, Jonny engaged an itinerant minister to pronounce a short marriage ceremony for Phoebe and him. Their neighbors read nothing unusual in the news of their marriage. For them this was just another commonsense arrangement of a widower finding a bride to help take care of his family. Jonny's daughters, one of them already married and the other committed, objected to the idea of their cousin moving into their mother's bed. The boys in the family, however, accepted her with enthusiasm. They liked her and were fearful of what life would be like for them without her. As for Jonny, the marriage ended what had been a clandestine affair and left him more contented than he had been for several months.

Two years passed before Phoebe had her first and only child with Jonny. Their son was born at the end of January in 1812. Phoebe decided that the boy should be named Jonathan after his father. Jonny, who had hardly ever used his rightful name, objected. "Why call him that?" he argued, "It will be confusing. Any way, I already have a son named John."

"That is all right dear. This one will have his father's name and we will call him Jonathan."

The War of 1812 came and went without having a noticeable effect on the Ridgeberry community. The people there were too far from the scene of action to feel much involved. The major concern of most of the men was that of bringing more land under cultivation. Like his brothers,

281

Jonny spent considerable time and energy adding improvements to his house and providing barns, fences and pasturage for his cattle and sheep.

A second project also was commanding much of Jonny's attention. He had noted when he first moved to Ridgeberry that the level of Bentley creek dropped several feet along a stretch of the stream that bordered his claim. This observation prompted plans for damming all or part of the creek to get a head of water that could be diverted through a canal to a point where he could use it to power a waterwheel. With this source of power he knew he could use millstones to grind wheat and corn into meal. More important, he could use the same source of power with gears to operate a circular saw to convert logs into sawed lumber.

After months of idle speculation, Jonny finally acted on his plan in 1813. With the help of his brothers and their sons, he dug the necessary diversion canal to a newly constructed mill site. During the fall and winter months he experimented with different models of waterwheels until he found one that seemed to best fit his needs. With money borrowed from his brothers, he purchased the needed gears, belts, pulleys, millstones and saws and by harvest time in 1814 was able to grind the first meal milled in the valley. Supplying their own ground meal freed the settlers from what had been a 20-mile round trip journey to the closest mill. Once the harvested grain was ground, Jonny turned his attention to sawing timbers; and soon every family was able to think of tighter construction in their houses and of the substitution of plank flooring for the dirt floors they had used since their first days of settlement.

* * * * *

A critical time for the Campbell settlement came in 1817. This was the beginning of the time period history books refer to as "the era of good feelings". Jonny was surprised one afternoon to see two strangers with surveying instruments making calculations on his farm. When he asked what they were doing, they informed him that they had been dispatched by the Pennsylvania Land Office to survey the area and establish boundary markers. They had no further answers to his inquiries but assured him he could secure answers from the Land Office at Williamsport.

Williamport was several miles away. No one wanted to take the chance of stirring up questions by going there. It was far easier to assume that the surveys were associated with some changes in county and township boundaries. This entire area had been incorporated four years earlier in the new county of Bradford and Ridgeberry had been designated as a separate township with the new name of Ridgebury.

Joel Campbell, who was now 81, was not pleased with his sons' complacency. "I'z afraid you lads is playing with fire," he argued.

"Why get excited," Nate argued. "We are here. We've made good farms on this land. We've paid the taxes on it all these years. If anyone comes saying that it is his, we can insist that it is ours by adverse possession."

The day of reckoning came sooner than anyone expected. Less than a month after the surveyors left, three men rode into Ridgebury with a sheriff's deputy. They had legal papers that asserted that they were the legal owners of over a thousand acres more than half of which overlapped Campbell settlements. All of the land cleared by Jonny, Nate and their father Joel was included. Of the seven brothers who had settled in the valley, William was the only one whose claim was not affected.

The new claimants insisted that the Campbells were trespassers who should be immediately expelled. Their demands were met by more than one outburst of anger. Jonny, who long ago had learned the value of counting to ten on such occasions, had to fight with his emotions to suppress his urge to tie the visitors to trees and pelt them with stones. Joel assumed control of the Campbell force, told his sons to be quiet, and then insisted on a lengthy examination of the papers. He inquired about the possibility of making an appeal. When they denied there was any possibility, he pointed out that their attempt to revive long invalid claims to farms that others had developed constituted nothing more than thievery.

Joel's lecture infuriated one of the claimants. It convinced the deputy, however, that an injustice was being done and that no further action should be taken until the Campbells had an opportunity to secure legal advice. The three claimants stormed away but not before assuring Joel that they would be back with a court order for their evacuation. One of them shouted as he left: "All of this land and all of the buildings, fences, crops, and other improvements you have put on it are ours. When we return you are to leave them all as they are or face legal liability for their removal."

At the family council that followed, the brothers, their wives and older children were flabbergasted at the enormity of their catastrophe, Had they lost property to a cyclone or a flood, they could pick up the pieces and go on. But they were being asked to walk away from settled farms that represented a dozen years of backbreaking labor. Truly, no people who had ever been forced to leave their homes were more mistreated. How could a country which bragged about the justice it provided let money minded investors who had done nothing to develop their claims stand by until others converted the wilderness into promising farms and then let them claim the farms as theirs?

Jonny was all for fortifying a portion of the property and daring others to take it from them. Joel counseled a more cautious response. "As I understand it," he reasoned, "their claims are based on the land warrants issued by the state back 30, 40, years ago and they did not live up to the development and residency requirements for making the claims valid. We have good cause to argue that their claims were forfeited a long time ago and that title should be ours by adverse possession."

A lawyer at Athens took their case. Speaking to Jonny and Nate, he said: "I have no questions about the merits of your argument. The state issued dozens of warrants for grants of 400 acres or more all through this area. Most of the grants went to investors from Philadelphia who paid little or nothing for them. The warrants had specific requirements for farm development and residency, requirements that most of the grantees ignored. As a matter of fact, very few of them ever visited their grants. They have been coming out of the woodwork in recent years though claiming the land that was covered by their grants and most particularly land that has been developed by squatters.

"You have sound legal grounds for arguing that they forfeited any claim they had to the land when they did not follow through in meeting the warrant requirements. If the court will accept that argument, you can claim title by adverse possession. If I can make a court case of it, you should have clear sailing because no jury of your peers out here would rule against you."

"Then we have nothing to worry about?"

"It's not that simple. There probably will not be a court case. People at the Land Office will make the decision. Whatever they decide, the judge will have to accept."

"Won't the Land Office insist on fulfillment of its own settlement requirements?"

"They should, but there have been several cases in which the Office has found reasons or excuses for honoring the warrant claims. It is possible that money or favors have changed hands. In any case, it often seems that the Land Office is a better friend of absentee investors than of actual settlers."

"But that is like legalizing highway robbery. They are stealing the fruits of other men's labor."

"Well put. It's wrong, but that is how investor fortunes are made."

Their attorney made an honest attempt to nullify the investor claims. Officials at the Land Office, however, refused to reopen the case by examining the evidence. In due course a judge from a state court signed an order which gave the Campbells seven days to vacate those portions of their farms covered by the warrant claims. The court order also specified that they were to leave all buildings, unharvested crops and other improvements on the land.

A sheriff's deputy delivered the order and expressed his personal regret that he had no choice in serving the notice. All of the brothers were in a sullen mood when he left and were still discussing details on what they should do two hours later when a representative of the warrant holders rode up to Jonny's door. He gave them an oral offer to sell them the property at a bargain price of $9.00 an acre on the same terms as the federal government was selling public land, one fourth down in cash within 30 days and the balance payable in equal payments during the next three years.

With the receipt of this offer the brothers looked at each other in barely controlled fury. Jonny, who had had fought hard to control his temper for several days, exploded: "Get off of this property with your thieving offer. No, wait until I get my gun. I'm going to rid this country of cheating coyotes."

The land agent made a fast retreat and was soon out of sight. Still boiling from the flames of his wrath, Jonny ran into his house, seized his gun, mounted a horse and rode off in fast pursuit before anyone could stop him.

Phoebe came from the house and demanded an explanation of what had happened. Nate and Ben looked down in shame. When Nate described what had happened, Ben added: "We were all so mad that no one gave a thought to trying to stop him. I sure hope he doesn't get in trouble. I won't shed no tears though if he shoots the bastard."

With Jonny gone, Joel said: "Now look lads. Jonny's going to be all right. He will come back after he cools off. For now though, we've got to start making plans for this move."

The brothers knew from earlier discussions what they should be doing. Nevertheless a long afternoon and evening followed as everyone kept a lookout for Jonny. There was no report of any confrontation with the land agent or any one else. But Jonny was missing. He did not come home. When he had not returned by the end of the second day, the brothers talked of sending scouts out to look for him. Everyone was sure he could take care of himself. But why hadn't he come home? Was it possible something could have happened to him? Phoebe was sure something had, that he might be dead or wounded. Concern for her tears and fears caused the brothers to send people out to look for him, Parties rode in every direction but all came back after nightfall with nothing to report.

It was not until the end of the third day that Jonny returned worn out and famished from lack of eating. His anger had run its course. He gave no explanation as to where he had been or what he had done. The first thing he did upon entering his house was to ask Phoebe for food. After he had eaten, he growled: "If we are moving in four days, we had best get started with the packing. First thing though, open that gate so the cattle can get in that corn patch."

None of the families that were scheduled to move had waited for Jonny's return before starting preparations for the move. Joel had insisted earlier when he first learned of the warrant claims that they make contingency plans for meeting this not hoped for emergency.

Together they had examined the papers served on them and determined that all of the land farmed by Joel, Jonny and Nate was included within the warrant claim boundaries. Benoni would lose all of his cleared fields, Joe two fields, and Josh and Zeke one field each. Ben, Joe, Josh and Zeke fortunately had their houses and barns on land outside the boundaries. William was the only one whose entire farm laid outside the warrant claim area.

The brothers had decided that if moves became necessary that Joel, who was now 82, was too old to face the task of clearing another farm. William had offered to add a room to his house to care for his aged parents. Jonny and Nate had no clear idea of where they would move. They were joined by Ben who argued that if he was to lose all of his cleared fields that he might as well move to a totally new area where his prospects for getting ahead might be better. Joe, Josh and Zeke wanted to find new fields that would make it possible for them to stay on in Ridgebury. They also planned to join William and the Fullers in seeking court action to recognize their acquisition of titles by adverse possession before possible new claimants might show up with demands for the surrender of their holdings.

The brothers who were not moving offered temporary refuge to Nate and Jonny. Both answered that as long as they had to move, they preferred to make it a one-time operation. They gave their brothers the chickens, pigs, and extra sheep and cattle they would not be taking with them. Jonny gave part of his household goods to his parents and arranged to move his dried timbers and cut lumber to his brothers' properties.

One of the first questions Phoebe asked after Jonny's return was: "Where are we going?" Ben and Nate had decided that they would go west to Ohio and maybe even as far as Illinois. They had heard there was rich black earth out there on prairies that settlers could farm without clearing. Both had saved enough money to cover the necessary down payments for the minimum sized tracts of 80 acres that the government was now allowing settlers buy.

'Where are we going?" Jonny growled. "Well, it won't be to settle on any government land. Those land offices are run by a pack of thieves. They let you settle the land, clear it of brush, trees and stones, put up houses and fences, and then when it starts to look good, they take it away and give it to some of their moneyed friends who never sweat a drop or turned a clod. The government is run by rich bankers and investors who know how to pull the strings so they can ride high and mighty on our backs.

"Sure they would like to have me clear another farm for them. Well, I've had enough of that game. From now on, I'm through with this business of sinking my roots down to make a home they can take away from me. There are thousands of acres out there we can move onto, much of it with good timber. We can move out there and locate on places that ain't been claimed, go out ahead of the surveyors if we want, fix up a house, and live off the land before neighbors come in. That way, we will be free to kill the wild game and cut down and sell the logs."

"You are planning to go into the lumber business?" Nat asked.

"That is just what I 'spect to do. Let other guys do the plowing and farming. I'll live nearby making a fair living cutting the big trees, sawing and shaping the timbers and boards so they can do their building; and when settlers come in to crowd me out or when I run out of good timber, I will just move on to where there is more of it."

"Then you are not going to leave your saw and grist mill here like they ordered?"

"Hell no, I ain't. Starting tomorrow, we're tearing it down and packing the waterwheel, saws and grist gear. I'm going to tear out that dam too so they will get it back like nature had it. If those robbers expect to have a mill, they will have to build their own 'cause I'm taking mine with me."

"The sheriff said you could be legally liable for destroying or removing improvements."

"Maybe so if I stayed in Pennsylvania: but he will have to follow me to New York 'cause that's where I will be."

By noon on the sixth day, Jonny had two wagons stacked high with farming and logging equipment and with the household items Phoebe wanted to take. His extra farm animals were already feeding in Zeke's pasture. Zeke rode to his house with his wagon near the end of the day with an invitation for Jonny's family to attend a farewell dinner that evening.

As they looked around the now half abandoned house, Jonny said: "Zeke, there is no reason why we should leave the floor boards here for someone who won't appreciate them. Grab some tools and we will put them in your wagon."

The two men went to work and with the assistance of Jonny's sons Ben and John soon had the house stripped of its flooring. With the boards in Zeke's wagon, Jonny then went with his family to Ezekiel's house, more satisfied with himself than he had been for over a week.

On the morning of the seventh day, all of the Campbell clan at Ridgebury assembled with the Fullers and several neighbors in front of the house that had been Joel and Becky's home for the past 12 years. Joel and his wife were already moved to William's homestead but had insisted that the entire family meet there together this one last time to receive their benediction.

Ben and Nate had their wagons packed and were ready to start their long trek west. Jonny was ready to take his family north into southern New York. This was probably the last time they would be together. The significance of their parting was apparent to everyone. Jonny had tears in his eyes as he clasped Ben and Nate to him and wished them well. His youngest son Jonathan also sensed the drama of the occasion as he skirted about, still a child of five, saying goodbye to other children and stopping to give his special toy to his toddler friend, Charity Fuller.

With the parting greetings expressed, the three departing brothers left. While his family waved their goodbyes, Jonny drove ahead looking neither to the right or left. As he passed the house he and his brothers had built for his family, the house that represented a dozen years of his life, he stopped his horses and went inside. He was back driving the lead team when Phoebe looked back and exclaimed: "Look there is smoke. Our house is on fire."

"Yes, I know," Jonny replied as he urged his horses on.

* * * * *

Jonny took his family to an unsettled wooded area about ten miles north of Ridgebury in Tioga county, New York. He returned to Ridgebury from time to time with his family to visit friends and relatives. They were close enough to attend his father's funeral when the old gentleman died at the age of 93. But never again as they moved from one place to another in the next 25 years did they stay at one site for more than three or four years.

Unlike the great majority of the Americans who were on the move westward, Jonny never again admitted a desire to sink his roots in a community which might grow and where in his old age he could hope to pass a productive farm on to one of his sons. He belonged to a different breed of frontiersmen, those who enjoyed living on the untamed fringe, those who squatted on unsettled lands, lived off the country and paid no taxes, always knowing that they would have to move on when the surging tide of settlement reached them.

He differed from this restless breed in one important respect. He took his axes and saws with him, installed his waterwheel and sawmill at likely spots, cut down and hauled or floated choice tall timbers to his mill, sawed them and then sold his product to the settlers who were closing in on him. Without really realizing it, he was a forerunner of the timber barons whose operations gained prominence later in the century.

Campbells Came

Part Seven

Jonathan

1841 – 49

Jonathan was scared. Never before in his 29 years had he had as much reason to fear what might happen next. With their arms bound behind them, their bodies trussed to two trees and a wagon, he and his three Mormon companions had been manhandled, gagged, and forced to stand and watch an administration of mob justice. Like two of the other shackled men, he was a visitor in town who had been invited that afternoon to come to David Croxton's home to meet two missionaries.

Jonathan had come to Hebrun to inquire about his possible rental of a farm. He had friends here and had been pleased when he ran into Brother Croxton that afternoon. Neither man had had any inkling at the time that they would now be tugging against stout cords that bound their battered bodies. Jonathan knew Mormons were not popular, that their missionary system was disliked, that they had been persecuted in Ohio and out in Missouri; but this was the first he had heard of them being subject to violence in New York.

The problem had started that afternoon when Brothers Jenson and Cowley had stood on a street corner in the middle of town and conducted an outdoor church service. Jenson had sang and prayed, while Brother Cowley had preached a fiery sermon to a straggly band of onlookers. It was not the kind of missionary proselyting Jonathan liked. The speaker was too outspoken, too inclined to cite scriptures as proof that his was the proven way, and that everyone must repent and follow his lead if they hoped to avoid an afterlife in hell. Still, he had rather admired the man's nerve and gumption, standing there on a curbstone, ignoring hecklers, and hoping to convert someone among the restless listeners.

With no other plans for the evening, he had gladly accepted Croxton's invitation to come to his house and meet the missionaries. Like the other men who were shackled with him, he had been totally surprised when a few minutes after he arrived at Croxton's house, they found the house surrounded by an unruly mob. About 20 rowdy ruffians forced their way into the house, knocked Croxton down when he objected, ordered his wife and children to stay in a bedroom, and hauled the two missionaries and the others outside where they were bound and gagged.

Jonathan recognized several amid the lynching party. None of them were churchgoers or top citizens of the town. In his eyes they were all reprobates, the dregs of society who hung out in the two local taverns. He had no choice but to stand and hope this horrible nightmare would come to a peaceful ending. From bits of conversation he heard, it was apparent there was no plan for the mob's action. As men bragged and swore about what they would do, it was evident that no one gave a hoot for real justice. What they wanted was excitement, the exhilaration they could feel when abusing others. None of them had been offended by Brother Cowley's sermon because none had been there. They had heard of it though and of the chance that they would be at Croxton's house that night. They had come looking for what they regarded as fair game for their amusement.

What should they do was an oft repeated question. "Horsewhip them", someone shouted. "Ride 'em out of town on a rail"; "Strip them and cut off their nuts"; "Tar and feather them", others bellowed. One of the ringleaders climbed on a wheelbarrow and demanded order. "Jake here has a barrel of tar we can use," he gloated, "and I saw a feather mattress in Croxton's house. Pete, you build a fire while Jake and Jimmy bring a bucket full of that tar over here. Heat it up until it is nice and gooey. Let's start with the preacher. We can go after the others later. You can take your clothes off now Mister Brother Cowley or we will take them off for you. We ain't fixing to hurt you. We only want to find out what is blackest, you when we get through with you or that life in hell you promised us "

Men hooted, swore and joshed each other as they stripped the struggling victim naked and waited for the sticky tar to warm. Jonathan squirmed in discomfort as he felt for Brother Cowley but was halfway thankful his gag gave him an excuse for not crying out in protest. He knew that keeping quiet gave him his best chance for avoiding treatment equal to that being doled out to the unfortunate missionary.

When one of the men tending the fire announced that the tar was starting to run, the impromptu leader ordered them to take the bucket off the fire. "Take it off and get a stick to stir it up. We don't want to burn him. We want no murder charges even though his black heart deserves it. Ain't no point in getting the law after us when all we want is some good clean fun. Now two of you dudes, daub that tar all over him, smear it on his head, and then roll him in the feathers from this old mattress."

Most of the men wanted to keep their hands and clothes away from the tar. There were some though who seemed eager to follow their leader's orders. Most of them laughed and jeered their helpless victim as they painted his body with the black sticky goo and held him down while they daubed liquid tar on his hair and around his face, neck and shoulders. Two of them then tossed his black naked body onto the pile of feathers from the now ripped open mattress. Cowley was rolled over and over on the loose feathers, and then jerked to his feet.

The gristly scene provoked a roar of laughter. The ringleader then called: "You are the prettiest angel out of hell, I ever did see. Let's show him off, boys. Straddle him on one of those planks over there and let's take him down to Harry's place."

Within minutes, the men were off to Harry's tavern, Brother Cowley's body writhed in pain as slivers from the rough plank ripped into his private parts while the men carrying the plank bounced along toward the tavern. Tar was burning his broken flesh but neither prayers nor tears had any effect in slowing the rowdy procession.

The parade was stopped two blocks from Croxton's house by the sudden appearance of the town constable who had heard the commotion and hurried forth to restore order. He ordered the two men who were carrying Cowley to lower him to the ground. Before more could be done, the mob melted away as its members dashed away in every direction. No one wanted to stay and explain what they were doing.

With the lynching party gone, Mrs. Croxton came from the house with a knife with which she cut the cords that bound her husband, Brother Jenson, and the two others. They were soon joined by the constable who entrusted Brother Cowley to their care but who made no offer to help them clean the tar and feathers from his body.

The Croxtons provided what materials they could to clear away the tar and feathers. Cowley took a hot bath and after two hours of scrubbing was able to remove most of the tar. Bits of tar and patches of chafed skin on his face and arms remained as visible reminders of his ordeal. Beneath his clothes, his body was sore and torn.

* * * * *

Jonathan was still shaking when he returned to his lodging place. Once he was in bed with a blanket pulled over him, he wanted to forget the nightmare he had witnessed. He wanted to sleep, but sleep eluded him as his thoughts kept rehearsing the cruel events of the evening. He was able to redirect his thinking only by deliberately concentrating on other things.

He thought of his wife Charity, wished so much she could be here with him. Maybe if she was here in his arms, he could relax and his mind could dwell on more pleasant things. He knew what he had seen this night was only a mild example of what had happened to Mormons many times in Ohio and Missouri. The violence here had not reached the peak reported in western Missouri where hostile mobs had raided Mormon settlements, raped and abused their women, beaten, reviled, and even killed some of their members.

Thinking of Charity, he could not help but feel elated. She was the best thing that had ever happened to him. She was a daughter of Abial Fuller, who had moved to Pennsylvania with his father and who had married Rachel Campbell, one of his father's cousins. He and Charity had been playmates when they were small children. He had seen her three or four times while they were growing up when his parents returned on visits to Ridgebury; but he had had little to do with her until he returned there when he was 21.

He had been living with his parents and working with his father cutting timber and sawing lumber when he had gone back to Ridgebury in May of 1833 on what was supposed to be a short visit. The Charity he remembered as a gawky teenager was now an attractive charming young lady. One look at her, and his whole life changed.

Their courtship was brief. Charity had always liked him and, as she later confessed, had even dreamed of him as her future husband while she was still a girl in pigtails. Their friendship and mutual admiration quickly turned to love. Jonathan cancelled his plan to go back to work with his father, found work instead with his uncle William, and was married in September.

In the years since their marriage, Jonathan had returned to New York to work with his father in the lumber business for three years and had then gone back to Ridgebury to try his hand at farming. His father was moving again at the time and Jonathan had wanted to operate on his own. A crop failure that first year had set him back but his hopes had remained high. It was a time of optimism and high hopes. Paper money had been abundant and was readily accepted by merchants and creditors alike. Land values were rising and business conditions were booming all over the nation, even in backcountry areas such as Ridgebury.

Then came that shocker called the Specie Circular in 1837. President Jackson ordered the government land offices to accept payments in hard currency only. Almost over night, the little gold and silver coinage that had been in circulation was horded away. The paper money that had been issued by banks all over the country depreciated rapidly in value, business conditions worsened, and farmers like the Campbells found themselves pushed back to a barter economy. Another crop failure in 1837 added to their plight but not as much as the nationwide business depression that ran its course during the next few years.

Farmers and businessmen everywhere had been stymied in their operations since the depression started in 1837. Now in 1841 business conditions in the rural backcountry were beginning to show signs of improvement. Jonathan was still optimistic for future success. He realized though that he and Charity had made virtually no progress in getting ahead financially in the eight years they had been married. They had had much more success in acquiring a family. They now had five children. Little William, their first baby, had died while still an infant. Abial, now six, Nephi, almost four, Emma, two and a half, and Alma, still a babe in arms at four months were his pride and joy.

He had known for some time that he must have either more or better farmland if he was to continue as a farmer. His brothers Benajiah and Joel had moved to Ohio and had written that they were planning to go on to Illinois. He and Charity had talked of joining them but had decided they should give their former neighborhood in New York one more try. That was why he was here looking for a farm he might rent.

Ridgebury had not been too bad. But there was rising resentment there against Mormons and Mormonism. He couldn't quite put his finger on the reason. It made sense though to move if you were not wanted. He had hoped that Mormons might be more popular here. But what he had experienced tonight convinced him that moving here would really be a case of one jumping out of the frying pan into the fire.

Mormonism:how, he wondered as he tried to get to sleep, how had he and his family ever become involved with the beliefs and controversies associated with this new religion? He remembered that his grandmother had been a pious and religious Christian and that grandfather Joel had liked to read and quote from the Scriptures. His grandfather had once told him that the Campbells had been Covenanters in Scotland, been persecuted for their beliefs there and in Ulster, and had come to America partly to enjoy religious freedom.

He doubted his father had ever had much concern for religion. Jonny, had attended church services from time to time, but Jonathan thought he did so more to please his wife than for any concern for salvation. Mom was the religious one in the family. She had spent hours reading from the Bible to him and his brothers and sisters.

Although the Campbells had seldom had an opportunity to attend church services at Ridgebury, they had considered themselves as Presbyterians. Grandmother Becky had taught a Bible study class for several years and an itinerant minister came their way two or three times a year, often enough to baptize babies and sanctify marriages. This situation changed when they moved to New York.

Jonny Campbell's move away from Ridgebury coincided with a rise of religious fervor all across the West. It was a time, as one minister described it, of Great Awakening. Churches of one or more Protestant faiths were established in most towns and villages. Circuit riders from the Baptist, Methodist, and Presbyterian faiths rode from settlement to settlement bringing the word of God with a promise of salvation for believers and the threat of eternal damnation for those who did not confess their sins. The west country was also combed by Catholic priests, Lutheran, Moravian, Congregational, and Evangelical ministers who were intent on bringing their versions of the word of God to the people. A new church led by Alexander Campbell, the son of a Scottish Covenanter, who worked out of headquarters at Buffalo, also was attracting converts.

The religious awaking and fervor that swept over much of the country was fed in part by the many summer revival meetings sponsored by the Baptist, Campbellite, Methodist, and Presbyterian faiths. Believers and nonbelievers, saints and sinners were brought together at huge gatherings, sometimes meeting in the open but more and more now under bowers or in buildings that provided protection from sun and rain. Meetings could last for a single day or for most of a week. There was sharing of food and socializing of course, and time allowed for singing, praying and testifying. But the big attraction at the morning, afternoon, and evening sessions was hell fire evangelism. Souls were to be saved and promises of salvation were extended to even the most hardened sinners if they could be induced to publicly confess their sins and pray for forgiveness.

Jonathan's mother Phoebe had loved the camp meetings. The intensity of the religious fervor enjoyed there gave her a feeling of redemption, of having her spirits cleansed. After moving to New York, she made it a practice to attend the camp meetings as often as she could, usually with her children and sometimes but not often with her husband.

Like his father, Jonathan was not convinced he should attend church on a regular basis. He accompanied his mother because she expected him to. He disliked the long repetitious prayers that were a standard feature of most services and sometimes wondered if there might be a heavenly prize for he who could utter the longest prayer. It was the long boring sermons he liked least. He found it hard to keep his mind from wandering to thoughts of other things when he should have been following the logic of a preacher's remarks. He knew he should take the gist of sermons to heart, but it was the excitement evangelists could generate when they had people crying one minute and jumping up shouting "Hallelujah" or "God be praised" the next he liked most.

He was there hoping more for entertainment than enlightenment. Seeing ordinary people get so filled with the spirit of their religious fervor that they would jump up, yell, sing and start dancing in the middle of a sermon was something he enjoyed. One other thing about going to church he liked was the music. He enjoyed singing with others, especially so when they could be accompanied by the rumbling tones of an organ.

While Jonathan had often dragged his feet and found excuses for not going to church, his brother Benajiah loved every minute of it. Ben was the smartest of the boys. He could read and write better than anyone else. Of all his brothers and sisters, Ben was the one who spent the most time reading the Bible, discussing religious themes, and trying to find explanations for questions that troubled him.

Jonathan was not sure what Ben was looking for; but after attending the services of several different churches with him over a ten year period, he was surprised to hear him confess: "Much as I enjoy hearing sermons, I still can't decide on which church I should join. They all agree on basic details such as the supremacy of God, the divinity of Christ, the promise of resurrection and future life, and our need to repent for our sins. They differ some on other items: Are we saved by divine grace alone or is faith without works a blind alley? Are our actions directed by predestination or is our fate determined by our own actions? Are we by nature sinful creatures that must be redeemed if we are to enjoy salvation? What rituals must be abided by with baptisms, takings of the sacrament, or our departure from this life?"

Benajiah found an answer to his quest when he met Joseph Smith in 1835. We had all heard stories about Joe Smith, of how he claimed he found some golden plates in a hillside some miles west of where we lived in New York. He claimed he had received divine guidance in translating the writing on them to come up with the Book of Mormon, which told of a settlement of people from the Holy Land in America and of Christ's visit with them after his crucifixion. No one in the family took Smith's claims very serious. Pa scoffed at the accounts, as did most of the people we knew. Our attitude changed though after Ben told us of his meeting with the prophet.

Smith had been troubled as much as Ben by differences in the beliefs preached by the churches that were competing for his acceptance. After the Book of Mormon was published, he claimed he had a vision in which he was instructed to found a new church, the Church of Jesus Christ of Latter-day Saints. The new church had only six members when it was organized in 1830. Its doctrines were spelled out in 13 Articles of Faith. Its major difference from other churches was that it operated with a restored priesthood without ministers or clergy and accepted both the Book of Mormon and the Bible as the word of God.

Ben's first contact with the church came in 1834 by which time the church had almost a thousand converts. From early on, the church sent out missionaries, ordinarily two men who held the priesthood who donated their time and paid their own expenses to preach the gospel to those who would listen. At their urging, Ben read their tracts and the Book of Mormon and attended some of their services. His conversion took place over a period of several months during which he studied their doctrines, held them to the same standards he had used in evaluating those of other denominations, and met the prophet.

As Ben related the experience, he had not expected Smith to be different than the many ministers he had met. He was surprised and soon captivated though by Smith's friendly down-to-earth manner, by his apparent sincerity, his personal magnetism, and by his unique ability to convey the impression that here was a trustworthy advisor whose counsel could be accepted with confidence.

There were several things about Mormonism that had appealed to Ben. The idea of a restored priesthood bothered him at first but soon won his support. He liked the idea of a church operating without clergy and allowing every man of worth to share in the priesthood. The three level hierarchal organization of the church with a president with a council for the entire church at the top, stake presidents with councils heading its regional branches, and bishops with councils heading the wards to which individual members belonged, appealed to him. "It is organized as tightly as an army," he told Jonathan, "with officials who report to each other at every level; but it is a democratic arrangement with appointments being sustained in open meeting by the members."

Ben had not allowed himself to be stampeded into conversion. He read what he could and carefully considered his decision before asking for baptism in 1835. He was ordained later that year and promptly started a campaign to bring his parents, brothers and their families into the fold. His mother, Phoebe, and Jonathan's wife, Charity, were easy converts. There was something about Mormonism from the very beginning, perhaps it was the promise that couples could be married for time and eternity that seemed to appeal more to women than to men.

Jonathan and his father were slower to yield to Ben's persuasion. With his continued preaching to them and the persuasion of their wives and others, both finally agreed to join the church. Both were baptized as members in 1837.

The conversion of the Campbells and some of the Fullers at Ridgebury did not add to their popularity in that community. Members of other churches suddenly regarded them as outcasts. Adding to their isolation was their commitment of long hours to participation in church activities, a factor that reduced their social contacts with nonMormons and led to charges that they were clannish.

The Mormon practice of sending out missionaries to convert people who were already Christians was resented both by ministers and the members of other sects. Their acceptance of the Book of Mormon was widely misinterpreted by many as a rejection of the Bible. Matters of small concern such as the misdeeds of individual members soon were magnified in some communities into ugly charges against all Mormons.

With their presence not appreciated and storm clouds gathering on the horizon, Jonathan and Charity felt the time had come for them to leave Ridgebury. They knew that Joseph Smith had established a haven for them in Illinois. Maybe they should be going there but Jonathan had resisted the idea. He had wanted to work for a year or so near his father's place in New York. After last night's ordeal, he now knew they must go west and soon.

* * * * *

Jonathan knew as he pulled on his shirt and pants after that restless night that he and Charity would soon be moving to Nauvoo. A return to this place for even a single season was out of the question. The possibility that he could avoid possible difficulties by forsaking Mormonism was a prospect he stubbornly refused to consider. True, he was not a particularly religious person and gave little thought to details in belief. As far as he was concerned, his brother Benajiah had done the necessary research for the family before he joined the church. His mother and his wife were devoted members and he had made a lifelong commitment when he asked for baptism. The Mormons were now his people and come hell or high water he intended to stick with them.

He had planned to leave this morning for Ridgebury. Before going though, he wanted to clear up some questions in his thinking. He had a friend, a fellow he had known as a student more than a dozen years earlier, who lived in the town whom he wanted to visit.

Cyrus Baxter was a quiet mannered observer of the world about him. He had a studious nature, had an inquiring mind, was well read, and worked at a local school. Jonathan found him at his house. After an initial exchange of greetings, Jonathan got right to the point with an inquiry about whether Cy had heard of the lynching party the previous evening.

"Yes, it was the talk of the town this morning. It is the most outrageous and disturbing thing that has happened here in years."

"What do you think of it?"

"I'm a softy, Jon. Acts like that have no appeal for me. As far as I know, Mr. Cowley did nothing that hurt anyone. He broke no laws. The hoodlums who attacked him did a dastardly thing when they took the law in their own hands for no reason other than spite."

"Spite?"

"No, that is not the right term. Let's call it copycat vengeance. They had heard of the troubles Mormons have had in Missouri. The fact that those missionaries hadn't done anything wrong didn't bother them. Cowley just happened to be at a place where he was not wanted and that made him fair game for persecution. None of our upstanding citizens were there. The ruffians who staged the raid on Croxton's house were mostly men who feel the world has cheated them of something. They refuse to admit that the blame for their problems lies in themselves. They may not be ready to blame the Mormons for their problems, but they see them as being different. That is enough to make them the dumping ground for any complaints they have; and persecuting people who can't fight back, like kicking a dog, is one way of getting satisfaction for not getting everything we think the world owes us.

"Cowley really set himself up for what happened. I doubt anyone in the mob who was there heard him do his preaching. They knew though that he had preached a message that was not popular. Some of the ringleaders saw this as an opportunity to demonstrate their brute power to take vengeance on someone they saw as different from them. That was the case for the ringleaders. The others were just followers who were looking for excitement and who saw a good tar and feathering as fun as long as it was administered to someone else."

"I just don't understand that."

"You are a fair minded chap who wouldn't, Jon. You were brought up to respect other people, respect their bodies and their thinking. There are plenty of people out there though who see human misery as entertainment, especially if they can cause it and it is not their misery. How else can you explain going to watch public hangings? We are a lot more like the Romans who went to the Coliseum to see Christians devoured by the lions than we want to admit."

"What I really want you to tell me, Cy, is why are Mormons so unpopular."

"Most of your family are Mormons, Jon. Don't you spend any time in those meetings you have talking about why you are disliked?"

"No, I can't say that we have ever analyzed the question. We know some people hate us and that here and there we are persecuted because of our beliefs. What I really want to know is why?"

"I can give you one man's opinion; and I'll give it to you straight if you promise not to become angry with me."

"That is fair enough. Shoot."

"Let me start by telling you that I have talked with your missionaries, read their tracts, read most of your Book of Mormon, and even heard your prophet speak. It has all been interesting; but for me not very convincing.

"I can see why many people have been taken in by Joe Smith. He is a persuasive speaker and has a manner about him that draws people to him if they are half way inclined to accept his message. He is one of the most remarkable men I have ever seen. He has an unusual ability to turn people on. At the same time there is something about him that turns many people off. Those of us who are skeptical about him see him as too glib, too smooth, sometimes too commonplace. We may misjudge him, but we see him as a charlatan, sort of a patent medicine salesman who promises more than he can deliver."

"What do you mean 'more than he can deliver'?"

"Let me put it this way. Some years ago an old man who lived like a hermit in the woods approached me. He claimed he was the Savior, Jesus Christ, who had returned to rule the world. Did we fall down on our knees and believe him? No, of course not, Joe Smith's case is similar. He says angels visited him, that he had divine assistance in translating the writings on those golden plates into the Book of Mormon; that the priesthood of old was restored to him; and that God directed him to start a new church. The Joe

Smith I saw and heard speak is a common ordinary man like you and me. Do I believe his claims? Well, not quite."

"But it can be as he had said."

"Yes, it is possible, just as it is possible that the medicine a peddler sells might cure my disease. But I still have my doubts about him. Something in me asks: 'What is in it for him?' I agree with you that there is something in his message that has people from all over the northern states, and from Britain too I'm told, flocking to his side. For me though, I see Mormonism more as a cult than a respected religion."

"We are not a cult."

"I'm sure you do not see it that way. Your group has characteristics though that people associate with cults."

"Like what?"

"To begin with, Smith named himself as head of the church. He sees it as his church, so much so that several of his close associates have separated themselves from him and chosen to go their own ways. The power of the church radiates from him and his family. Converts commit their fortunes and their lives to him. Many have left families, friends, and jobs to be with him. Members have given the proceeds from sales of their farms and other properties to Joe Smith to use as he sees fit. Besides all this, he has introduced secret rituals that only the most devout members can experience; and his followers have joined together in suspicious activities that isolate and shield them from contacts with the outside world."

"Shield us? I've never heard of that."

"What I mean is, he has you attending so many church services on Sunday and during the week, doing so much church business, spending so much time studying your scriptures, saying your prayers and bearing your testimonies that you are often cut off from contacts you could have had with nonMormons. If I were designing a system to get people to support one doctrine to the exclusion of others, I could not come up with a better arrangement. People can be led to believe anything if they want to and if they hear its virtues and strengths extolled day after day while hearing little or nothing of why they should question it."

"All right, I can see we have sized Joseph Smith up differently. But I still do not understand why some people hate him so."

"Different people could give you different reasons. For convenience sake, let me split them into three groups, first there are the ministers of other churches, then average citizens and church goers, and finally the rough element that leads the outright persecution of Mormons.

"All of the other Christian faiths place great emphasis on acceptance of the Bible. Some favor acceptance of some parts more than others. The clergy who lead them differ of course on their interpretations of various fine points. Most of them were astounded though when Smith brought forth the Book of Mormon and placed it on equal footing with the Bible. Personally, I do not see the Book as a threat. I am not even sure it plays a necessary part in Mormonism. For me it is a non-issue; but that is not the way those preachers who rant and rave against the fallacies of the so-called Mormon Bible see it.

"A bigger issue for the clergy is Smith's claim that he operates with the authority of a restored priesthood. When he says restored, he means the original authority was lost sometime after the death of Christ. That is a touchy issue with clergymen because almost every denomination claims that its clergy operate with authority that came to them through an unbroken chain of ordinations that goes back to Christ. Smith's assertion challenges the validity of their claims to authority. Their reaction to his challenge is about what one might expect.

"Turning now to the average citizen group, I'd say most of them are indifferent to or skeptical about Mormonism. Some may dislike it, but few really hate it. Some are skeptical for reasons such as mine, some because they have heard and believed vile gossip that misrepresents Mormons and what they stand for. Two things that have hurt you as much as anything with this group are your missionary system and your claim that you are a chosen people."

"What is wrong with them?"

"Most Christian denominations believe in sending missionaries to far off places where they can preach the gospel to infidels and heathens. They reject the idea of sending missionaries to convert people who are already Christians. But this is what the Mormons are doing. I suppose some people enjoy having missionaries come to visit them. Thousands of others resent their visits as intrusions on their private lives and wish you would leave them alone.

"Back to that second point, most average citizens resent any suggestion that you are better than they are."

"Oh, come on, Cy. We don't think that."

"You may not do it intentionally, but you give that impression. Let me ask you: what do you call your fellow members?"

"Brothers and sisters."

"Not that. What is the name of your church?"

"The Church of Jesus Christ of Latter-day Saints."

"Latter-day Saints. And aren't you told that you are a chosen people and the Children of God?"

"Well, yes."

"That's right. And what do you call nonMormons?"

"Gentiles."

"Do you know what that word 'gentiles' means to most people?"

"In the Bible that is what Jews called those who were not Jews. For us it is people who are not Mormons."

"For hundreds of years, Jon, people have equated the term 'gentiles' with heathens. When common citizens who regard themselves as good Christians hear themselves referred to as gentiles and when they hear that you consider yourselves as saints and as the chosen people they see it as an inference that they are not. For them that boils down to a conclusion that you think you are better than they are."

"That is not the way I see it. The Mormons I know don't think they are any better than anyone else. I guess it does make us feel good though when fellow members say we are special."

"You encountered some of the last group I spoke of, the real haters, last night. The only explanation for their attitude is that this world still has a lot of people who see nothing wrong in tormenting, beating, and even killing people who are in some way different than them. They think of you much like many slaveholders in the South think about runaway slaves and Abolitionists.

"A lot of the persecution your people faced in western Missouri came because they opposed slavery and were moving in large numbers into a slave holding state. They came in caravans that looked like invading armies. When you stuck together and did not think and act like your neighbors did, the people who got there ahead of you went on the warpath.

"Much of their anti-Mormon sentiment was based on false accusations and unfounded rumors. The men who led the fight against you saw you as a threat simply because you were different than them and because they feared you could soon out vote them and take over."

"But that doesn't make sense," Jonathan objected.

"I didn't say it did. In a civilized country it should never happen. Yet it has happened time after time in the past. The ancient Romans sent innocent Christians to the lions. During the Middle Ages, people like the Anabaptists were burned alive as heretics. Entire populations of Jews in countries such as Spain and England were forced to migrate or face extermination. More recently in England and Scotland, we have had Anglicans persecuting Covenanters and Catholics along with independent thinkers.

"We've made some progress here in America but it has not been too long since the powers in Massachusetts endorsed the execution of poor women accused of witchcraft. Their courts even went so far as to order the public whipping of Quakers and other religious minorities and shipping them off to be sold as slaves in the West Indies."

"Is there anything Mormons can do to get around this hating?"

"Bits of it will probably last for years. I suspect most of it will run its course if your church survives after the Smiths are gone and if your membership keeps on increasing. Respectability will come with survival. It will come sooner if you have members like the Emperor Constantine who rise to the top and become role models in society. Until then, Jon, your safest place for living will be somewhere where you will be part of the majority, not of a small minority as you are here."

* * * * *

Jonathan returned to Ridgebury fully convinced that he and Charity should pack up their belongings and move to Nauvoo while it was still spring. They soon found, however, that it takes time to dispose of surplus cattle and farm equipment. It was June before they were finally able to hitch up their team and drive to Hornsby where they intended to spend a few days with Jonathan's parents before heading westward.

Their plans changed when Jonathan's father persuaded him to stay on long enough to help Jonny finish a timber-cutting job he had started. "Help me finish this job, son," his father had promised, "and I will fold up my work here and go to Nauvoo with you."

Jonny Campbell still looked hale and hearty at 79 but his son realized he needed help. The experienced hired hand that had been working for him had left and his only helper was his 16-year-old grandson, Sam Campbell, the son of Jonathan's brother Benoni.

What Jonathan had expected at first would be a short-term commitment turned out to be one of longer duration when he found that his father had access to enough timber to keep them busy for more than a year. Jonathan did not complain about the delay because he liked the work, he was able to save a few dollars, and best of all, he and Sam hit it off with each other and found that they enjoyed working together as a team.

It was September 1842 before Jonathan was ready to leave with his family, his parents and Sam on their drive west. With no rail line yet built to the west and the cost of traveling by water on the Erie Canal and the Great Lakes being what it was, they found themselves content to load their wagons and follow the land route that crossed western New York, the northwest corner of Pennsylvania, and northern Ohio, Indiana, and Illinois.

The drive from Hornsby to Nauvoo took three weeks. As they moved westward Jonathan noted that the forested

309

hills and mountains of New York gradually gave way to rolling country and then to the flat treeless prairies of Indiana and Illinois. He found himself missing the trees and hills amid which he had grown up. He had to admit though that the apparent productivity of the soil, together with the absence of forests that had to be cleared and of stones that had to be removed, made this inviting country for farmers.

When the party reached Nauvoo in October they were pleased to find Jonathan's brothers Benajiah and William waiting to greet them. The new town on the Mississippi was experiencing rapid growth. Housing was in short supply. Arrangements were soon made though for Jonathan's parents to stay with William's family while the others moved in with Ben's family. Two weeks later Jonathan and Charity were fortunately able to move into a small newly vacated house located near their Campbell in-laws.

Although less than four years old, the Nauvoo they found in 1842 was already the largest town in Illinois. Joseph Smith had purchased the site of the town from a sharpster land jobber in 1839 as a place of refuge for the Mormon families that were fleeing from persecution in Missouri. At the time the site was called Commerce. It was located at a favorable spot on the Mississippi river with productive highlands to the east but a large area of swampy land along the river.

Almost half of the settlers had died during the first year from fevers contracted from living or working near the swamps. By 1842, however, most of the lowland had been drained and the town had become a bustling community with close to 10,000 residents. Broad straight streets had been laid out. A variety of businesses including banks, stores, a newspaper, sawmill, and a brewery were already established and houses were being built in every part of town.

Hard money was scarce as it was everywhere in the west. The Mormon church was the largest single employer. It had a sizable force already at work constructing a temple. With little money available, a barter system had been devised under which workmen were paid with script that represented work credits that could be redeemed with purchases at local stores. With popular acceptance of the script and the inflow of hard coinage brought to town by the influx of new settlers, Nauvoo enjoyed more prosperity than most western communities.

For the first weeks after their arrival, Nauvoo seemed like an answer to Jonathan and Charity's prayers. Jonathan and Sam were hired to work at the Law Brothers' sawmill. The town offered amenities they had never enjoyed before. Their neighbors welcomed their presence and made them feel wanted. Of course, they wanted better housing, but that would come with time. Meanwhile, they felt they had escaped from the dark cloud of tension they had lived under and could now look forward to getting ahead.

Jonathan's optimism was fed by the bustling activity he saw about him. It was buttressed by Ben's enthusiastic espousal of everything Nauvoo stood for and by his boast that "Nauvoo is the city of saints to which God's blessings will flow." Ben talked Jonathan and Sam into joining the Nauvoo Legion, the local armed force headed by General Joseph Smith. He insisted that they accompany him to church and to the large out-of-doors sessions of the church's general conference.

Joseph Smith was not always in residence in Nauvoo and his associates were often uncertain as to when or where he might appear. Ben and Jonathan were fortunate though in being able to see and hear him speak at two general conference sessions. Viewing him from some distance, Jonathan was impressed at the first session by the prophet's demeanor, his picture of athletic vitality, and the captivating quality of his voice and message. At the second meeting, he was surprised and puzzled when the prophet staggered on his way to the podium and spoke with a slurred voice. Benajiah was sure Smith was showing the after effects of having had a vision. "He is filled with the spirit of the Lord," he observed. Jonathan had reason to wonder though when a lady next to them added: "He is filled with spirit all right, but it is not the Lord's."

Jonathan's day of awakening came a month after his arrival. He and Sam were sitting on a bench opposite the brewery eating their lunch. Pete Boswick, a fellow sawmill worker was with them. As they unwrapped their lunches,

Sam said: "I've been wondering about this brewery. Here we are in the city of saints and Brother Joseph preached just last Sunday that we should follow the Word of Wisdom and avoid drinking beer and strong spirits. If that is church doctrine, how can we have a brewery?"

Pete looked at him and replied: "You must be a new-comer here son. The way the church looks at it, the Word of Wisdom is advice for good health. Breaking the rules by drinking or smoking ain't sinful. Lots of good Mormons have a taste for drinking coffee, or tea, or spirits, or even for smoking or chewing tobaccy and they ain't hurting anyone but themselves if they keep on. Some of Brother Joseph's closest friends like their pipes and cigars and the prophet himself drinks coffee and wine. Porter Rockwell, the prophet's bodyguard, got in a ruckus sometime back when he set up a bar in the Mansion House where the prophet lives. Brother Joseph was ready to keep it as an accommo-dation for fancy visitors but Sister Emma wouldn't hear of it."

"You are telling us something we've never heard," Jonathan interjected.

"If you are new here or if you spend your time with our goody goodies you wouldn't hear of it. It's not the impression the church and town authorities want people to hear. I've been here two years, get around a bit, and read some outside newspapers; and I'm here to tell you that there are a lot of things rotten here. Much more and this town will be ready to explode."

"Can it really be that bad?" Sam asked.

"It is worse than you might think. See that house with the pink door down there. That is our local whorehouse. Brother John Bennett, the prophet's first councilor, used to be a regular visitor there."

"But he is not here any more."

"He's gone all right. He came here full of ambition and soft talk two years ago and inveigled himself into the confidence of the church leaders. Joseph fell for his line and ended up making him his first assistant. He was a real doer. He got a charter for the town from the legislature, organized the Nauvoo Legion and was its chief officer though he had sense enough to make Brother Joseph its general. He had his fingers in several different pies. When his true colors started to show, we saw he was really just a con man working for his own interests. The church gave him the boot last year and now he is out making trouble."

"I haven't heard of any trouble," Jonathan observed.

"You would have if you read some of the newspapers from other towns. Bennett is working with the gentiles now and is accusing Joseph of all sort of misdeeds."

"Like what?" Sam asked.

"Misuse of funds for one thing. The charge that hurts most though is that Joseph is keeping several wives on the side. Joseph denies it, but the charge keeps coming up."

"Sounds like the church should have got rid of Mister Bennett earlier," Jonathan growled.

"Or never have accepted him in the first place. But that is only part of the problem," Pete continued. "This town has its share of bad characters, but Brother Joseph can't get much done in putting things in order because he is hiding out most of the time."

"Hiding out? Why?"

"Trouble is he miscalculated when he got here after he escaped with his life from that prison they had him in Missouri. If he had just forgotten about the affair, it might have blown over. Instead, he went to Washington with a petition to punish Missouri for persecuting our people. Governor Boggs and the other Missouri authorities were offended and have been trying ever since to get him back so they can try him on a trumped up charge of treason. So far our governor won't extradite him, so Missouri is sending thugs here to kidnap him and take him back by force."

"Our Legion should be able to protect him."

"Should be, but that is not a guarantee. Anyway, the Legion is part of the problem. The gentiles see it as Joseph's personal army. No other town in the state has anything like it. The gentiles are afraid of what it might do. They also complain that since most of the saints vote for whoever Joseph favors that that gives him the power to control elections."

"You may not have noticed it yet but everything in Nauvoo is run by and for Joseph Smith. He is the mayor, general of the Legion, operator of Mansion House, and head of the bank as well as head of the church. Several of the top jobs are reserved for members of his family. He runs the show and anyone who questions him is excommunicated. That is not bad when he makes the right decisions but he slips up sometimes by taking the advice of con men and by allowing crooks to operate with the protection of church membership."

Sam was perplexed. "How can he do that?" he blurted.

"What I am saying is that while most of our saints are honest upright citizens we also have some low life who use their pretended membership to protect them if they are accused of defrauding or robbing others. One gang stole produce from some merchants across the river a few months back, then were protected by the town when they denied it, and brought discredit on all of us when they were finally caught red handed with the stolen goods."

"Can something be done to stop that?" Jonathon asked.

"If you are asking my opinion," Pete answered." "I'd say: Get the church out of politics. Joseph treats the church and our government here as the same thing when we would be better off if they were completely separate."

Jonathan was perplexed a week later when he and Sam received a request that they report to the prophet's office at Mansion House. He was puzzled by the reason. Was the prophet going to ask that he drop everything and go on a mission? It was a common request, which he hoped, would not be made of him.

Once the two men presented themselves, they were surprised when the prophet greeted them personally. Neither had seen him up close before. They saw that he was tall, well built with a lithe athletic figure, and had a handsome face. Smith walked with a slight limp caused by the faulty setting of a broken leg when he was a child. He had a pleasant, winning manner and a ready smile, which was marred by the noticeable loss of one of his front teeth.

After a few words of introduction, Smith got quickly to the point. "I've been told." he informed them, "that you have had experience with logging operations. As you must know, Nauvoo has a real need for lumber and we face a problem because we have already cut most of the good timber around here.

"The church saw this problem coming and sent Brother Lyman Wight up the river to Black River Falls in the Wisconsin territory last year to make arrangements with one of the Indian tribes to let us cut timber. Lyman has a crew there cutting trees and dragging them to the river where they can be pulled together into rafts that can be floated down to our sawmill. The operation is still getting under way. Brother Lyman writes that he needs more men and I'd like you to join him."

Jonathan looked at his nephew and then replied for both of them: "We would be honored to go. How soon does he need us?"

"Last week would have suited him fine."

"I'm willing to go but I need to wait for at least a month. My wife is eight months pregnant and is due to drop our babe any day now. She usually has a rough time of it and I figure it is my duty to be here with her."

"I understand your concern, Brother Jonathan. Plan to stay here until after Christmas. I'll send word to Lyman that you will be on your way after the new year."

* * * * *

Early January found Jonathan and Sam heading north by boat on the Mississippi to the mouth of the frozen Black river and then tramping 40 miles over land to the Mormon logging camp. As a crow flies, they were close to 200 miles north of Nauvoo, closer to 300 miles if one followed the twisting route of the Black and Mississippi rivers. Two dozen men were working at the camp. They lived together in a large log structure and were busily engaged in marking and felling some of the nation's best timber.

The two men marveled at the sight when they went into the virgin forest with their fellow workers. Here were hundreds of straight white pines that rose to majestic heights of 50 or more feet. After their earlier experience of cutting gnarled hardwoods in New York, they found it exciting and almost easy to wield their axes and saws in cutting prime timber. They had no need to cut anything but the very best trees and the white pines around them were the very best.

Logging for long hours in the open during a Wisconsin winter can be hard and exhausting work; but Jonathan and Sam enjoyed each other's company and what they were doing. Their routine called for identifying and cutting the best trees, trimming branches from the cut logs, and snaking them to the banks of the river. After the ice in the river melted, they had the often tricky task of tying the floating logs together into rafts that could be floated down stream to Nauvoo.

Work with sharp axes and saws amid falling limbs and trees and maneuvering floating logs in a fast flowing stream of icy water is not a calling for the weak of heart. Broken limbs and serious injuries are a common occurrence and lives are frequently lost. The camp was not without its casualties. Yet during the months Jonathan and Sam spent there, they suffered only one mishap. That came in June of '43 when Sam slipped from a rolling log and hit his head against another log as he fell into the still icy waters of the river. Jonathan saw the accident, quickly realized that Sam could drown if he was not immediately pulled to shore. He jumped into the frothy stream, pushed logs apart and held Sam's head above the water while he worked their way around the milling logs until he reached the river's bank.

Once rafts of logs were assembled, they could not be sent on their long journey down the two rivers without accompaniment. There were too many places where they could wedge against the banks and pile up along the narrow channel of the Black river. Two man crews were sent with them to see that they got to the Mississippi where several rafts could be tied together for their journey down the Mississippi. Crews were needed on this leg of their delivery too to keep the logs moving as planned and to forestall possible high jacking by river men who might be tempted to appropriate undefended property.

While Jonathan enjoyed working with Sam and the fellowship he shared with others of the crew, he was frequently lonesome for the loving presence of Charity and their children. He looked forward to the times when he and

Sam could take their turn in bringing logs down the river. These were times of celebration for him, marred only once when he found that his mother, who had been in ill health, had passed away.

At home for a short break after each return, he and Charity often talked of alternative employment opportunities. The prospect of living full time in Nauvoo appealed to them. But time after time, he returned to the logging camp without regret. He enjoyed living with the other men at the camp and felt that the inconvenience of being away from his family was justified because he was doing his duty.

On his trips to Nauvoo he sensed an increasingly precarious state of town affairs. Nauvoo's population had passed the 15,000 level. Hard money was coming back into circulation; and with revived business conditions most of the residents were optimistic about the future. But all was not well; and much as he tried to shield her from it, Charity was hearing rumors that made her worry about their future well being.

Things were happening that surlied the reputation of the Mormons. Merchants at Melrose, the Iowa town across the river from Nauvoo, complained that Mormons were stealing goods from them. Hard feelings were generated when the land jobber, from whom Joseph had purchased the site of Nauvoo, fled after taking payments from 250 Mormon settlers for home and farm sites he did not own.

Tom Sharp, a newspaper editor at the nearby town of Warsaw, took special delight in ranting against the Mormons in a series of articles that were copied by other papers. He denounced Joseph Smith as an arrogant, coarse, immoral, stupid, and vulgar opportunist. John Bennett added his venom to the growing criticism with published denunciations of Smith and his associates. A hate campaign that vilified the church and its members was taking form and led to mob violence and the burning of a Mormon settler's home.

Two other developments added to the turmoil. After months of hesitation, Joseph proclaimed the church's acceptance in 1843 of polygamy as church doctrine. The announcement was met with dismay and quickly denounced by several church leaders including Sidney Rigdon and

William Law, both of whom had served as Joseph's councilors. Some prominent saints, including the Law brothers, left the church to start denominations of their own which accepted Joseph's earlier, but not his latest, visions.

In a second event, a party of Missourians seized Joseph while on a trip away from Nauvoo. Quick action by officers of the Legion kept them from taking him by force to Missouri. In the legal maneuvering that followed, Brother Joseph agreed to shift his voter support from a Whig to a Democratic candidate for office, a move that brought him the enmity of the Whigs of Illinois without earning noticeable credit from the Democrats.

As the summer of 1844 approached, most of Nauvoo's citizens were elated by Joseph Smith's declaration of his candidacy for the presidency of the United States. Many shared the unrealistic belief that he could be elected. Those who were closest to him though realized that he faced a grim future. Missouri was pushing its demand that he be extradited to that state to face prosecution for treason and for the attempted murder of former Governor Boggs. Governor Ford of Illinois still refused to extradite him but was showing signs of willingness to yield to Missouri's demands.

Back at Black River Falls in May 1844, Jonathan and Sam were still happily at work at the logging camp when Lyman Wight was called back to Nauvoo. Wight was a big, easy mannered supervisor who enjoyed his liquor, coffee, and pipe and whose conversation was sprinkled with vulgar blasphemies. He was popular and liked, by even the most religious members of his crew, and everyone was there to wish him well at a jovial farewell party held in his honor.

Sam had wondered for some time how Lyman could do the things he did and still be considered a leader of the church. In broaching the subject at the farewell dinner, he asked: "Aren't you one of Brother Joseph's oldest friends?"

Wight agreed that he was. "I've known him, for most of the last ten years. Oliver Cowdrey was his scribe when he wrote the Book of Mormon. I took over when Oliver left. I was with him when he went from Ohio to Missouri and then shared space with him and his brother Hyrum while we were prisoners in that stinking jail at West Liberty. I've been with him ever since,"

"While you were his scribe, did you write down his visions or just his letters?"

"Both. I reckon I wrote most of what he put in the Doctrines and Covenants. Joe never liked to do much writing. When he had his visions, he would talk slow and deliberately while I wrote down what he said."

"Did he go into a trance or something like that when he had his visions?"

"Yes and no. He would turn real serious like. I knew it was no time then for joking or asking questions. Those were times when he didn't talk rough or cuss like he often did."

"You say he swears?"

"Oh, don't get wrong ideas about him, Sam. Joe is not your usual sort of guy. In many ways, he is like two different people. He can turn on that charm of his and be as saintly as you please on Sunday or when he is with churchgoers. That is the way most of his followers see him. But when he is out with close friends, he can shed that appearance like changing from a fancy suit to comfortable work clothes and just be a happy go lucky guy."

"Did he ever criticize you for cussing or drinking?"

"One or two times, but not much. You see, he did it too. He can drink like a fish and swear like a pirate and repent a half hour later wishing he had never done it. Another reason why he doesn't complain is that he knows that it was my drinking, smoking, and card playing with the jailers that got us out of that jail in Missouri."

"How did that happen?"

"It's a long story but the point is that they had a half dozen of us in jail on trumped up charges. They had no real case against us so they just kept us in jail without indictment until we gave them a reason by cutting a hole in the jail house wall and getting caught before we could squeeze through."

"Those were bad days for us. One day they brought us some queer meat to eat. Joe wouldn't touch it until he found out what it was. They kept bringing it back for every meal until they finally told us it was part of a dead nigger. I think Joe went three days with nothing to eat and nothing to drink 'cept his coffee.

"Back to me and drinking. The guards at the jail were leery about talking to Joe, afraid I guess that he would convert them. But that didn't go for me. I got real chummy with them, especially with the night guards. We would sit and drink and play cards and tell stories for half the night. It was them that kept me advised on what was going on.

"When the local judge finally decided to give us a change of venue for a trial, it was one of them that told me he had seen the legal papers that called for us moving. Trouble was there was no mention of where we were to go. Right then we knew there was a plan to take us out of jail and turn us over to a mob. The guard also told me the sheriff was willing to let us slip away if we could grease his palm. Joe agreed to pay a big bribe and the next night we found the door unlocked, the guards looking the other way, and horses waiting for a hard ride across Missouri. Joe didn't have any money with him to pay the bribe, but the sheriff took his word and Joe got the money to him later."

"Don't any of the saints object to his drinking and swearing?" Sam asked.

"Some of those who have worked closely with him have just walked away. Most others like me stick with him because we like his message and see him as our man even though he has his human frailties. As for the faithful who follow him, most don't know and don't want to know about his shortcomings. They believe what they want to believe and don't see what they don't want to see."

"What about this polygamy business?" Jonathan asked. "Did Brother Joseph tell you about it before his vision last summer?"

"Oh that. Joe and some of the brothers closest to him have known about that for three or four years. He and a few others already had several wives. They kept it quiet because they weren't sure how the members would take to the idea. Joe has always had a weakness when it comes to women. I think he was relieved when he found justification for satisfying his desires in the practices of prophets from the Old Testament. When he announced that as church doctrine, he really opened a kettle of fish."

"I sure agree with you on that," Jonathan affirmed.

* * * * *

Jonathan and Sam were working in the pineries when word reached their camp in July that Joseph and his brother Hyrum had been murdered at the Carthage jail on June 25. The crew suspended its logging operations, tied together the logs that were piled along the river's bank, and left a few days later on the long float to Nauvoo.

Back in the City of Saints they found that a boiling controversy had surrounded the prophet during the final weeks of his life. William Law, one of the town's principal businessmen and the former councilor to the prophet who had left the church because of his refusal to accept polygamy as church doctrine, had brought a printing press to Nauvoo. The first printing of the newspaper that came out on June 7 denounced Smith and called on him to repent. Brother Joseph was infuriated by this effrontery in his own city. He ordered the closing of the newspaper office and seizure of its press.

Smith's attempt to muzzle the press was a fatal mistake. Editors of other papers in nearby areas joined in the clamor for his punishment. Governor Ford insisted that he submit to arrest for his hasty action. Joseph complied with the governor's order and was imprisoned in the county jail at Carthage along with his brother and two associates. During the night, the jailers stood aside when the jail was surrounded by a howling mob and unidentified mobsters shot Joseph and Hyrum.

The return of their martyred bodies to Nauvoo the next day left the town shocked and in mourning. Many gentiles in nearby communities fled from the area, as they feared retribution by the Legion. But the Legion remained inactive as the prophet's followers contained their grief. Nauvoo had lost its leader and Its spirit. Questions were raised about who was now in charge; but life in the town went on much as usual.

There was no clear indication of who had the right to succeed the prophet as president of the church. Joseph had indicated that the honor should go to his son. But Joseph's son was still a child. Joseph had also indicated on various occasions that the succession should go to former close associates such as Oliver Cowdrey, John Bennett, and Sidney Rigdon. James Strang, one of the twelve apostles claimed that Joseph had promised the presidency to him. Others argued that the presidency should go to the senior member of the Council of Twelve.

Action to choose the prophet's successor was delayed for several weeks. Most of the apostles were away supervising missions in other parts of the United States, Canada, or Europe. When a conference to name a leader was finally scheduled in August it was expected by many that Sidney Rigdon would be endorsed as acting president to serve until Joseph's son came of age.

Brigham Young, the senior apostle, and several of his fellow apostles returned to Nauvoo just two days before the conference was held. Ten thousand members of the church attended the huge out of doors meeting. Rigdon, who suffered from ill health, spoke briefly with a weak voice and asked that hasty action be avoided. When Brigham Young started to speak, hundreds of those around him witnessed an apparition. They asserted later that he spoke with the voice of the prophet. Some even claimed that he took on the appearance of their martyred leader. His comments had an almost hypnotic effect on the assembled crowd; and after he concluded his remarks, he was confirmed as president of the church by acclamation.

With Brigham's choice as president, several dissenters, including Joseph's widow, left the church; but the great majority of the saints held faithfully to their commitment to the gospel. Business conditions continued as usual. But it was soon evident that outsiders in Illinois were determined to force an exodus of Mormons from the area. Legal action was taken to deprive Nauvoo of its charter, its right to have its own judge, and its right to have its militia. The military arms that had been entrusted to the Nauvoo Legion were taken away.

All through the remainder of 1845 and 1846 Brigham slaved to protect the town and its residents until a solution could be found for their dilemma. The leaders of the church knew they had to move; but there was the big question of where. The leaders also were determined that construction of the temple proceed to a point at which it could be consecrated to the Lord's service before they would have to leave it to those who would take over the town.

The stubborn reluctance of the Mormons at Nauvoo to yield to the demands of their gentile neighbors led to mob violence. Mormons settlers were murdered and their houses burned at Morley. This action caused a kindly disposed gentile to recruit a Mormon force at Nauvoo which swept over the nearby country, took Carthage, and set up a guard there. This retaliatory action brought Governor Ford's intervention and a demand on his part that the Mormons leave the state before the spring of 1846.

Like his neighbors, the chain of unhappy events that threatened to strangle Nauvoo disturbed Jonathan. He had what he considered a good job at the sawmill; he liked living in the town and didn't want to move. He could have joined some others who left the church and stayed on in the Nauvoo area. But neither he nor Charity gave a second thought to that possibility. Jonathan might not be a very religious man, but he and his wife had made a commitment when they joined the church. Maybe they were just stubborn; but they would go wherever the church's leaders decided they should.

* * * * *

Wild rumors that Brigham Young would soon be arrested on some charge and that a squadron of army dragoons had been ordered to come north from New Orleans to wipe out the Mormon settlement helped cause the church's new president to move the evacuation date up from the spring of '46. A few saints crossed the Mississippi to the Iowa side in January. Jonathan's family moved with a larger group that crossed on the ice of the frozen river in February. Others delayed their moves, some even until the next year. By late spring, however, the sacred items had been removed from the temple and Nauvoo had become a mostly deserted town.

Most of the saints had only a vague idea of where they were going when they stepped onto Iowa soil. They were headed to an as yet unannounced place where they could find safe refuge. Sam Brannan, an enterprising New Yorker who had joined the church, chartered a ship to take several hundred saints to California, which was still under Mexican control. California also was viewed by many of those who were leaving Nauvoo as a possible destination.

There was some speculation in Washington and the Eastern press that Brigham Young might lead upwards of 20,000 migrants to Oregon where he could support Britain's claim to the Oregon territory. Fears that he might be going to either place prompted demands in several quarters that the federal government act to keep him from crossing the Rocky Mountains.

Brigham Young was well aware of the significance of his choice of a refuge site. He was a loyal citizen of the United States and was anxious to secure an agreement with the federal government that would provide protection for the migrating Mormons. Before he left Nauvoo, he sent Jesse C. Little to meet with President Polk in Washington with an offer to haul supplies to the government's western forts and to establish settlements that could provide food and other supplies for the forts in exchange for protection. Meanwhile, he was intrigued by reports received from western explorers and mountain men about a possible settlement site along the Great Salt Lake.

The first contingent of the migrating party moved forward a few miles at a time across southern Iowa. It was charged with the job of making a wagon trail that later migrants could follow. On the warmer days they were able to drive ahead for several miles. On cold and stormy days, they often stayed in their camps. Jonathan and the other men walked at first over the snow covered frozen earth as they helped push their teams and oxen along. Later when the weather warmed, they had to slog along over wet and muddy turf. Those who had stout wagons and good teams were able to move ahead with few problems worse than coping with the cold and wet weather. Many in the party though were poor people who traveled with horses, oxen, wagons and equipment ill suited for the journey. For them, broken wheels, dying animals, and the ravages of winter maladies added to the misery of their travel.

By the end of March the advance party was about half way between the Mississippi and the Missouri rivers at a place they called Mount Pisgah. Many in the party were suffering from overexposure to the elements. Exhausted travelers were sick with respiratory problems, chills and fevers, and many died. The situation called for rest and recuperation.

Inspection of the area showed it to be an excellent stopping place at which future travelers might also stop for rest. A major camp was accordingly laid out. The party tarried at Mount Pisgah for several weeks. Once the weather permitted, oxen were used to break the prairie sod; crops were planted that later groups of migrants would harvest; and then all but a few of the party hitched up their teams to continue their travel west.

Jonathan and his family were among those of the advance party who drove on to Council Bluffs on the east bank of the Missouri river. Summer was already here when they arrived and attention was quickly given to the need to plow new fields and plant crops that could sustain the large community of saints that would be spending the coming winter here. A large camp was laid out. Men were advised to find employment in the area as the lateness of the season made it unwise for the saints to consider further travel to the west before the coming spring.

Brigham Young was at Council Bluffs, still waiting for word from Washington, when Captain James Allen and four dragoons from Colonel Stephen W. Kearney's army headquarters at Fort Leavenworth, Kansas, rode into the camp at Mount Pisgah on June 26, 1847. He carried an order to recruit 500 volunteers for a special battalion that would march to California to advance the nation's war with Mexico.

News arrived a few days later that Brother Little had met with President Polk on June 5. Instead of concerning himself with the proposal Little had brought from Brigham Young, President Polk was now primarily concerned with the war Congress had declared on Mexico on May 13. He offered to give the Mormons the protection they wanted together with the right to travel through and winter in Indian territory if they would raise 500 to 1,000 volunteers to advance the war effort.

Word about Allen's order for volunteers was quickly dispatched to Brother Brigham. Meanwhile, many saints greeted the order with dismay. Some suspected foul play and many complained that they could not be expected to volunteer for service in an army that had played a significant role just a few years earlier in driving the them out of Missouri. Brigham Young, however, was quick to accept President Polk's proposal. His decision soon won the endorsement of his followers when it was realized that compliance could bring them protection from further persecution and at the same time provide a possible source of funding for the financially troubled church.

Captain Allen rode to Council Bluffs to meet with Young and on July 6. Brigham returned with Heber C. Kimball to Mount Pisgah. In announcing his support for recruitment, Brother Brigham said: "This is the first time our government has stretched its arm to our assistance." He went on to assert that enlistment would prove the loyalty of the Mormon migrants and it would provide wages that could help support the families of volunteers and the church. Sixty men volunteered at the end of the meeting and 68 more the next day.

By July 16, 450 volunteers were gathered at Council Bluffs. President Young promised them they could elect their own officers but they insisted that Young make the appointments. The first four companies of 100 men each marched to Sarpys, a French trading post on the Missouri river, where they were issued blankets, coffee and sugar. Back in Council Bluffs, a battalion was ready to march as soon as sufficient recruits would volunteer to fill out the fifth company.

The recruitment campaign caused some serious mind searching for Jonathan. He had served with the Nauvoo Legion and enjoyed the time he had played at being a soldier. He had a yearning to be with the volunteers. But he was 35, the father of three young children, and Charity was six months pregnant. It might be a manly thing to go, but what husband would leave his wife under these conditions?

Brigham spoke again at a meeting on July 8 of the importance of more men volunteering. The meeting was followed in Mormon fashion by a dance, a festival which celebrated the readiness of the volunteers to leave. The continued drive for enlistments caused many men who had not volunteered to feel a sense of guilt.

Following another plea by Brigham on July 19, Sam came to Jonathan and said: "I know I am needed here, and I don't want to leave you, but I really think I should volunteer." Jonathan nodded as he replied: "I know just how you feel. I'll go with you if we can get your father and your uncle Benajiah to look after my Charity and our kids."

A family council followed. His brothers promised to do their bit while commending him and Sam for making a Campbell commitment to the cause. Jonathan was still uneasy about his offer, but this feeling changed when Charity hugged him and said: "Don't hold back because of me. I'm proud of what you are doing. We'll get by here. What's most important now is that you and Sam do your duty to our country and the church."

* * * * *

Jonathan and Sam were among the 40 men who enlisted on July 18 and 19. Company E was now filled and orders were issued for the battalion to start its 200 mile march to Fort Leavenworth the next day. Tears aplenty were shed as the men marched off in a rainstorm. They were soon soaked to the skin. They had no organized mess. Most had brought along meager supplies of flour and parched corn, leaving food they could have taken for their families at the camp. When evening came, they camped in the open and slept in their wet blankets. For their first meal, they wrapped flour dough around sticks that they baked over coals from their campfires.

The battalion crossed from Iowa Territory into Missouri on July 23. By then some men were already out of food. Many others suffered from hunger, sore feet, and heat exhaustion. Most of them had been without flour for two days when a supply wagon from Fort Leavenworth finally reached them. At that point tempers flared when the

Missourian who commanded the supply detail, a man who had helped drive the saints out of Missouri a few years earlier, refused to release any supplies to Mormons. Captain, now Colonel, Allen ended the dispute by ordering the officer to choose between delivering the supplies and facing a court marshal.

It took five hours to ferry the men and their gear across the Missouri river to Fort Leavenworth when they reached that army installation on August 1. One recruit had died on the march, many others were sick, worn down from heat and exposure. Everyone was excited by the prospect of staying put for a few days.

A roster taken at the fort showed that the battalion contained 496 men. Three additional officers and one private joined them there to bring the count to an even 500. Each company had four officers and nine or ten noncommissioned officers. Company A had a total of 106 members; B, 100; C, 105; D, 102; and E, 87. Thirty-one wives of battalion members, three other women, and 44 children accompanied the fighting force. At the time of their arrival, 470 other soldiers, most of them Missouri volunteers, were stationed at the fort.

During the next two weeks, the men started drilling in formations. Most of them were eager to get the muskets they had been promised they could keep at the end of their enlistments. The flintlock rifles they received weighed more than a dozen pounds. Learning that they were expected to carry them, many soon agreed with Colonel Allen's observation that they might want to throw them away long before they ever got to California.

In addition to their muskets, every soldier was issued a leather belt that crossed his left shoulder to which cartridge shells, which weighed an ounce each, were attached. A bayonet and scabbard were attached to a second belt that crossed the right shoulder. Knapsacks for carrying clothing and necessities were fastened to their chests while rolls of bedding were carried on their backs. They also received cotton havesack bags large enough to carry food rations for a day or two and canteens that could carry three pints of water.

The men were assigned to six men messes each of which received a frying pan, a coffee pot, and a camp kettle as cooking gear. Each of the five companies was also authorized to buy a baggage wagon and a mule team to haul their knapsacks and bedding.

The men received $42.00 each as clothing allowances. From this amount, some bought various items they needed; but most sent their payments back to their families or to the church with the result that most marched in worn clothing that became tatters and rags long before they got to California. The men also sent most of their monthly pay, which ranged from $7.00 for privates to $50.00 for the senior officers to the church. Apostle Parley Pratt visited the battalion at the fort and took $5,860.00 back with him for the church at Council Bluffs on August 8.

The stop at the fort provided a restful prelude to the 860-mile march that lay ahead when they left for Santa Fe on August 13. Colonel Allen, who had taken a kindly interest in his troops, was taken ill before the men left and was not able to accompany them. Marching conditions now became more difficult as the weather was hot; the men were loaded with heavy muskets and gear, and wagon breakdowns frequently left them without food. A violent rainstorm blew down their tents, caused the overturning of two baggage wagons and left everyone soaked. Indians stole cattle from the quartermaster's herd and scores of men were soon ailing.

Sad news of Colonel Allen's death reached the battalion on August 26 and three days later Lieutenant Andrew Smith, a West Pointer, arrived from Fort Leavenworth to command the battalion in Allen's place. The new commander, the men soon found, was cut from different cloth than Colonel Allen. He was a stickler for discipline who displayed little concern for the welfare of his men.

Smith's most grievous decision came when he appointed George W. Sanderson as staff medical officer. Sanderson was a Missourian who held a grudge against the men. His standard treatment for all types of illness was to dose the men with calomel or arsenic. He was abusive in his treatment of the sick, refused to allow them to ride on the wagons, and talked openly of leaving them on the prairies.

Soldiers were soon convinced he was out to kill them. Men sick with chills or fever concealed their complaints rather than take his purgatives. Some reported their ailments and threw away the medicine. When Sanderson learned of this, he ordered that the doses be swallowed in his presence.

In one case, he forced a soldier who was suffering from abdominal cramps to swallow the standard concoction of calomel and arsenic from a rusty spoon. The soldier died the next day. Sick men thereafter chose to stand guard when they could barely stand or get others to answer for them at roll call rather than report to Sanderson. Lieutenant Smith was furious when he learned of these practices, but chose to back up his medical officer even when his officers assured him that Sanderson was giving the same medicine for such varied afflictions as boils, rheumatism, fevers, diarrhea, and lame backs.

The battalion was making slow time because of bad weather and rough marching conditions when it met John Brown, a Mormon several recruits had known at Nauvoo, riding eastward on the trail in mid September. Brown reported that he had taken 14 Mormon families to Pueblo where they were going to spend the winter before going on to meet Brigham Young at Fort Laramie the next year. Upon hearing this report Lieutenant Smith decided to send a contingent of sick and older volunteers along with their wives and children to Bents Fort and from there to Pueblo where they could join the earlier Mormon group.

Smith thought he could save time by shifting to a cut-off route and sent orders ahead to Bents Fort to have supplies sent to the cut-off point. The supplies were dispatched as requested; but when they arrived, the supervising officer, another Missourian, refused to deliver them to Mormons. He changed his mind; however, when Smith threatened to turn the Mormon soldiers on him.

Marching through rough country with no established trail and sometimes going considerable distances without water, the battalion still made good time as it entered Mexican territory. A message reached them on October 3 that General Kearney had taken Santa Fe and wanted them to report there by October 10. Smith complied by taking his officers and his most able men and hurrying ahead.

Jonathan and Sam were in this group that reached the old Spanish settlement on October 9 just 57 days after they left Fort Leavenworth. The rest of the battalion limped into Santa Fe three days later.

* * * * *

Kearney left Santa Fe for California with a cavalry detail before the battalion arrived. Orders had been left for it to follow under the command of Colonel Philip St. George Cooke. Their specific duty now was to lay out a wagon road from Santa Fe to California.

Colonel Cooke was a professional soldier and not at all pleased with his assignment. He had wanted a command that would bring military action. He moved quickly to send a second group of the older and more infirm volunteers together with more women and children to Pueblo. He also made Lieutenant Smith quartermaster of Company E, an appointment that was protested by the men because the displaced officer had earned their respect by standing up to Smith on the march from Fort Leavenworth.

The battalion started its long march from Santa Fe on October 19 with 55 army wagons and 12 private family wagons. Slow progress was made as a road running southward along the Rio Grande was laid out over rough country. Wagons often had to be unloaded and then reloaded as the men helped their oxen pull wagons over imposing obstacles. They soon found they had fewer horses and mules than needed. They had enough flour, sugar, and coffee to last 60 days but only enough salted pork for 30 days. When the officers found they could buy only part of the additional food supplies they needed form Indian and Mexican settlements along their route, the battalion was put on short rations.

Colonel Cooke concluded in early November that it would be folly to continue with the full party. A third group composed of another 54 of the sick and least able men and one woman were sent back to seek a winter haven at Pueblo. With their departure, only 335 men were left with the battalion.

331

In mid November Cooke had to decide between continuing south into Sonora or turning west. His decision to turn west was approved by the men who saw it as the more direct route to California. Turning west, however, meant that the battalion had to build its road over mountains and that it had to find a path to follow, as none of Cooke's guides knew of a way.

Progress was slowed as they crossed desert country and went for up to two days at a time without water. The route ran through patches of mesquite and brush and called for moving rocks and boulders once they reached the mountains. On November 30 they made their way up a canyon only to find themselves at the top of a cliff over which they had to lower their wagons with ropes before they could continue their way.

Early December found them across the mountains and able to supplement their short rations by shooting occasional wild cattle and game. Their growing optimism at this point was dampened though by a report that 5,000 Mexican troops were stationed ahead of them at Tucson.

Three days short of Tuscon the battalion marched into an open area where a large herd of wild cattle was grazing. Colonel Cooke was riding his white mule while most of the men were ambling along, none of them armed as the colonel had allowed them to stack their muskets in the baggage wagons.

Jonathan's curiosity was perked as he looked at the herd. "That's a mean looking bunch of critters if I ever saw one," he observed. "Near as I can see they are all bulls. Do you fellows see any cows or heifers out there?"

Sam looked and admitted he saw none. Another private explained: "Our guide says bulls are often found together like this because the Indians find it easier to kill the cows and calves. Taste better too, I'll bet."

Moments later something agitated the herd. Suddenly 40 bulls were bearing down on the unprotected men. Some made a dash to get behind the wagons, some to get their guns, and some to run for their lives. The battle of the bulls lasted only a few minutes before some men got to their guns and started to fight back. In that short time three men and three mules were gored and several baggage wagons were overturned. Colonel Cooke lost his hat when his mule was nearly gored. Nine bulls were killed and after their fierce charge, the remaining bulls seemed content to wander away.

There was no confrontation at Tucson as the Mexican troops departed before the battalion arrived. A brief stop at that settlement was followed by a harrowing march to the Gila river. When they reached the Gila on December 21, their mules had come 48 hours without water while the men had marched for 36 consecutive hours, 26 of them without water. Most of the men were now exhausted and weak. Their clothes were reduced to rags and many marched without hats or shoes. Some help came when they were befriended by a settlement of Pima Indians that supplied them with much needed food.

Along the Gila, they met a band of Mexico-bound refugees who reported that General Kearney had won a battle and was now in San Diego. Farther progress along the river was slowed when several wagons mired down in the sand and men had to help the oxen pull them free. Other problems came when Cooke tried to float two loads of supplies down the river only to have them stranded on sandbars along the banks.

The battalion forded the icy waters of the Colorado river on January 10 and reached Palm Springs eight days later giving thanks to heaven that they had crossed the California desert in the winter rather than during a summer when they could have died from the heat. News confirming the report of Kearney's victory awaited them at Palm Springs; and haggard and poorly clothed as they were, the men celebrated with music and a dance.

During the next few days the battalion worked its way through San Felipe canyon. Crowbars, picks and axes were needed to widen the narrow path enough to accommodate wagon traffic. At one point the path was so narrow that the men had to take their wagons apart and carry them to a wider spot where they could be reassembled.

Once across the final range of mountains, the men got their first view of the Pacific Ocean at San Luis Rey and then marched to San Diego on January 29. It had taken 103 days out of Santa Fe and five and a half months out of Council Bluffs for them to accomplish one of the longest marches in recorded military history. They had laid out a wagon road and arrived with their oxen and mules still pulling five-army baggage wagons together with three smaller private wagons.

Jonathan and Sam arrived sunburned, tired, without shoes and wearing the ragged remains of their clothes. It had been a hard and exhausting journey but they were still in good health and high spirits. Neither one complained about the privation and duress of the march. For them, the high point of their journey was their memory of the battle of the bulls.

* * * * *

Stationed in San Diego, the men had plenty to eat. Weeks passed though before they were re-outfitted with clothes and shoes. They were quartered at first in an abandoned flea infested mission and later in a second mission at San Luis Rey that required cleaning before they could live in it. Colonel Cooke busied them with daily military drills; but their duties left them with time for relaxation, and regaining the weight they had lost during their long march.

In March the men in Company B were detailed to San Diego while the others four companies were sent north to Pueblo de Los Angeles where trouble soon threatened when they were quartered next to a squadron of Missouri volunteers. Bloodshed was averted when they moved to a campsite farther from the town. More controversy followed when some officers in the Missourian contingent refused to accept General Kearney's selection of Colonel Cooke as commander of the military forces in California. Rumors were heard that they would attack the four Mormon companies. Trouble again was averted, however when the battalion built a fort to protect themselves from attack.

As July approached, the year for which the men had volunteered was fast running out. The army needed men in California and steps were taken to encourage possible reenlistments. Those who were interested were told they could elect their officers and that they would receive a year's pay if they would reenlist for six months. Most of the men, however, were anxious to take their guns and go back to their families.

Company B from San Diego rejoined the other four companies of the battalion on July 15 for their last full day of service. The next day 317 men were dismissed following a final review. Each of the discharged men was paid $31.50 with no allowance for getting back to their families.

Fifteen men set out immediately to ride to Monterey where they were to join General Kearney and Colonel Cooke who were preparing to ride east to Fort Leavenworth. Of the 302 men who remained, 70 reenlisted, four decided to stay on in southern California, five chose to travel east by a southern route that hopefully would get them back to their families, and two chose to go by ship to the Mormon settlement Sam Brannon had started at Yerba Buena, on San Francisco Bay.

The discharged veterans who were left divided into two groups. A smaller group composed of 48 men followed a coastal route north to the Salinas valley. A larger group of 173 men, of which Jonathan and Sam were members, crossed the mountains to the Great Central Valley and worked their way northward along the foothills of the Sierras to Sutter's fort on the Sacramento river.

Daytime temperatures were high in July and August; the going was often slow over the rough terrain; several streams had to be crossed, and problems arose day after day because no one in the party had sound information on where they were going. Heading ever northward the men crossed King's river on August 11, the Stanislaus river on August 21, and arrived at Sutter's fort on August 25. Fruit had been available at scattered farms along the route, but many of the men felt half starved when they arrived at the fort.

Sutter's fort was located on the Sacramento river and stood midway between San Francisco Bay and the steep canyons of the High Sierras. John Augustus Sutter, the proprietor, was a German immigrant who had come to California in 1839. He had received a large grant of land from the Mexican government in 1841 and was later appointed governor of the area.

Sutter was an enterpriser and a man of imagination. At the time the battalion arrived, he owned several thousand acres, had a large herd of cattle, operated a store and some related businesses and had plans for constructing a flourmill and sawmill. He needed help in carrying out his plans and quickly offered the men wages ranging from $25 to $60 a month if they would join his work force.

A dozen men chose to stay. The others, however, were anxious to get to their families. They outfitted themselves for the journey and left Sutter's fort on August 27 for their rigorous climb through the mountains. On the way they marveled at the size of the huge redwoods they encountered on the western slope of the Sierras. Some were as much as 50 feet in diameter and upwards of 150 feet high. The nights became colder as they climbed to higher altitudes and they were surprised when a rain storm one night covered them with a light blanket of snow.

Near the crest of the mountain pass, they met Sam Brannan, the man who had brought a shipload of Mormons to Yerba Buena, which was now known as San Francisco. Brannan had gone east earlier in the summer and had met with Brigham Young west of Fort Laramie. He had tried to convince Young that the Mormon migrants should come to California. Brother Brigham had his reasons for rejecting Brannan's proposal and Brannan had headed back to California while Young's advance party went on to the Great Salt Lake.

Brannan tried to sell the men of the returning battalion on the idea of going to the San Francisco area where they could join his settlement. Some were tempted by his arguments, but no one chose to follow him. Brannan was hardly out of sight when a Captain Brown, who had led one of the cast off groups of the battalion to winter quarters at Pueblo in '46, met them. He was officially on his way to Monterey to collect the army wages due to the volunteers who had gone to Pueblo. He brought mail for some of the men and a message from Brother Brigham.

Brigham Young had instructed him to tell them to stay in California until next year if the season was short and if they had prospects there for employment. He knew the saints who would reach Salt Lake that summer would have problems enough in producing sufficient food to care for the parties that were coming from the east without having to care for additional arrivals from the west.

Brother Brigham's advice called for a reevaluation of individual plans. It was already September. The men had little hope of getting to Salt Lake until long after the end of the growing season and they knew their presence could only add to the need for food. Yet most of them wanted to get back to their families. Many had no information about the whereabouts of their loved ones. Were they in one of the groups that crossed the plains this year or might they still be at Council Bluffs waiting to come next year?

Jonathan and Sam were far from sure what they should do. Sam saw it as his duty to stay until next year if that was what President Young wanted. Jonathan wanted to get back to his family. He had had no mail from them and didn't know whether Charity was in Salt Lake or still at Council Bluffs. Seeking certainty he went to Captain Brown and asked if Brown knew anything of her. The captain thought for a moment, then shook his head as he said: "I traveled with Brother Brigham's party for several days after we connected with him at Fort Laramie. During that time I think I met everyone in the company. There weren't any women traveling alone or with children and I don't recall meeting any Campbells so I would say that your wife must still be in Iowa."

Half of the men were determined to go on to Salt Lake. Jonathan planned at first to go with them but decided at the last minute that Charity would want him to wait until spring. Before the two groups parted some scouts came back to camp with a report that they had stumbled onto the remains of the ill fated Bonner party that had perished in the mountains the previous winter while trying to make its way to California. Caught in a blizzard that buried them in several feet of snow, everyone in the party had died from freezing or starvation.

Jonathan went with the other curious men to view the remains of the tragedy. He was appalled at the ghastly sight of bleached skeletons of men, women and children, scattered bits of clothing, some battered cooking utensils, and the ruins of wagons and a temporary camp. Many of the bones were scattered about in a manner that indicated that the site had been visited by wolves. It was a devastating sight that left the men wondering what might have happened to them had they been caught in a blizzard near the mountain pass.

* * * * *

Twenty of the men who returned to Sutter's fort chose to go on to San Francisco where they expected to work until the next spring. Sutter was sorry to see them go as he had jobs for the entire group. He hired the men who stayed and assigned them to such varied tasks as shoe making, carpentry, blacksmithing, digging mill races, and caring for his cattle. When he learned that Jonathan and Sam had worked with logging crews and at a sawmill, he eagerly assigned them to a crew he had sent to Coloma, 45 miles up the American river to build and operate a sawmill.

After the year he had spent soldiering, Jonathan really enjoyed the fall and winter he spent at the lumber camp. He liked working with the big trees, hauling the cut timber to the mill where it was converted into lumber. Sutter kept the camp well supplied with food and drink; and the men had little need or occasion to go to the fort. All of the workers were Mormons; they had their church services much as if they lived in a town; and they had leisure time, much of which was spent fishing in the nearby streams.

Heavy rains slowed their logging operations in January and brought a flood on the American river. On January 24 after the floodwaters had subsided, James Marshall, one of the crew, went to the river to do some fishing. He was surprised while baiting his hook to find flecks of gold in the sand washed up by the flood. Further examination showed that small gold nuggets were scattered throughout the sand.

Marshall's colleagues were excited by the discovery but decided they should keep it secret. News of their discovery spread rapidly, however, once they took nuggets to Sutter's fort to have them assayed. Would be miners soon came swarming to the American river in numbers, and with their arrival the men who had continued working at their logging operation shifted to spending most of their time panning for gold.

By early April more than 200 men, some from Sutter's work force and some from as far away as San Francisco, were roaming the area, selecting and claiming choice spots for mining. Some were equipped with pans, some with Indian baskets, with which they scooped up sand and gravel, which they swirled back and forth with water until only the heavier stones and hoped for gold nuggets remained.

Placer mining was hard, backbreaking work and the returns were uncertain. Some lucky miners found nuggets worth $1,000 or more in a single day. Most, however, had to be content with meager returns; and many found too little gold to justify the time and effort they spent looking for it. But the prospect of making a killing was always there in the thinking of most miners.

With the arrival of a horde of gold hungry prospectors, old rules for protecting private property were ignored. Newcomers appropriated Sutter's holdings along the river, killed his cattle, and helped themselves to items from his farms without regard for his ownership rights.

Jonathan's experience was typical of that of his fellow loggers when he came to the sandbar where he had been placer mining during his spare time to find the site occupied by a burly miner who cursed him and threatened to use his knife on him if he did not leave.

April saw fights aplenty between miners who claimed the same mining spots. There was a breakdown of law and order with no policing at first to protect anyone's rights. As more miners came to the area, men and women with other mercenary interests also appeared. Merchants saw an opportunity to sell their goods, drovers came to haul people and goods over the rough country roads; assayers arrived to weigh and count the gold. Prominent among the businesses that sprang up almost over night were numerous saloons and bawdy houses. Con men and swindlers also saw opportunities to tap the new source of wealth.

Sam Brannan came in April. He had no interest in soiling his hands as a miner. He came instead with a grandiose plan. He assured his fellow Mormons that he could acquire the property rights to the mining area and offered to rent mining sites to them. His terms called for paying 30 percent of their take to him, 10 percent to go as rent, 10 percent to be counted as tithing to the church, and 10 percent to be set aside to finance the building of a temple. It was a grand scheme but the men would have nothing of it. As several of them agreed, Brother Brannan was out to make his fortune by mining the miners.

The near chaos that prevailed at first was short lived. Responsible individuals among the miners saw that action was needed to restore law and order. Their solutions did not extend to recognition of Sutter's property rights. By common consent they decided that the area along the river was unappropriated public land on which individual miners could establish legal claims to pan for gold on tracts that were five yards square.

Living conditions improved in the mining camps after order was restored. The general environment, however, was not to the liking of Jonathan and most of his fellow Mormons. Sure, there was always the prospect they could make a big strike, but most of them did not value their small earnings that highly. They were disturbed by the churlish antiMormon comments they heard, disgusted with the abundance of foul language, and depressed by the drunkenness, debauchery, and low moral standards that abounded. They wondered why men sought gold when so many of those who found it during the day lost it in the saloons and bawdy houses at night. More than anything they wanted to get back to their families.

Groups of battalion veterans started meeting in April to make plans for their travel to Salt Lake. Most decided to start in June once the passes were open. Until then, they continued their work, some with Sutter and some in the gold fields, hoping they could put aside money to buy horses, mules, wagons and other supplies for their journey.

No attempt was made to send all the returnees back in a single company. One group started out in early June but found the high mountain passes so blocked with snow that it returned to Sutter's fort. A second group composed of 45 men, one woman and one child, known as the Lytle company, left Coloma on June 17. It had the task of cutting a new wagon route south of Lake Tahoe across the mountains, a route that would hopefully prove easier to follow than the older route along the Truckee river.

The Lytle company made slow progress as it worked its way through the mountains. At times they found themselves going up blind canyons. The route they chose to follow was hardly wide enough for wagons to pass; and at one point they found themselves going down an incline so steep they had to lower their wagons with ropes.

As the company approached the summit on July 3, three scouts were sent ahead to select the best route. Concern was felt when they did not return. Two weeks later their brutalized bodies were found in a shallow grave some miles up the trail. The scouts had been murdered by Indians that continued to steal their horses and cattle and shoot arrows at them until they worked their way out of the area.

The Lytle company had not much more than passed the summit when it was overtaken on August 4 by a party of 14 returnees who were riding to Salt Lake with horses and mules. This party, of which Jonathan and Sam were members, had left the gold camps only five days earlier. Traveling without wagons or heavy luggage, they were able to make far better time than the slow moving wagon train.

The horsemen stayed with the Lytle company for a day and then hurried on ahead to the Humboldt river. They followed the river north and east until they reached a cutoff point at which they turned east past the Great Salt Lake until they reached the western slopes of the Wasatch mountains.

Once they saw the mountains they knew they were in Mormon country. Salt Lake City would be only a day or two ride away at the south end of the lake. Jonathan had not been impressed with the arid country he had ridden through. Even along the Humboldt river there had been hardly enough grass to feed his horse. This new country was something else. As the men rode south with the mountains to their left and the glistening waters of the lake to their right, he decided Brother Brigham had been right in bringing the saints to this area. Put some water on this land and the desert could be made to bloom like a garden.

Tired after what had been a long days ride, the party camped for the night along the shore of the lake about two miles from a cluster of houses at Ogden. Jonathan was curious about the area and determined to see more of it. Taking Sam with him, he rode eastward into a benchland area that lay between two imposing mountain peaks.

As they rode, both men marveled at the impressive view of the two peaks that rose up into the eastern sky and the glistening waters of the Great Salt Lake behind them. About them was an abundance of what looked like good land that could be irrigated by water that flowed from several springs. About a mile from the camp, they encountered an old man with a flowing red beard who was carrying some traps. Jonathan hailed him and they were soon engaged in conversation.

"What do you call this place?" Jonathan asked.

"Tain't got no name yet," the trapper replied. "That new settlement down there is called Ogden. Named after Pete Ogden who used to do some trapping here with me. He's gone now."

"Are settlers moving in?"

"Naw. Not here yet. This here is still Injun country. They'll be here soon enough though. And then it will be no good for trappers like me."

"This is mighty pretty country with the mountains, the big lake, and streams."

"Yeah. Old Pete and me decided it looked a lot like the highlands in Scotland. That's why we called that mountain Ben Lomond. The other one is named for old Pete."

* * * * *

The men were up and ready at dawn to start riding the last leg of their journey. When they arrived at the settlement at the southern end of Salt Lake in mid-afternoon, they were frankly amazed at what they saw. Less than 14 months had passed since Brigham Young's advance party had come to this spot in the desert and already a thriving town was taking form. Unlike the hodgepodge scattering of structures found in most new towns, the settlement showed signs of careful planning. Wide streets had been laid out, trees planted, and several houses were in various stages of construction. City creek had been damned and water was being diverted through canals and ditches to numerous gardens and farming plots.

The men rode as a party to a church office where they reported their arrival from California. They then split up, each man going his own way as they sought friends and relatives. Sam was informed at the church office that his father Benoni lived with his family on an edge of the settlement. Jonathan was stunned when his inquiries about Charity yielded no information. No one at the office seemed to know her or know where she might be. After several agonizing moments during which he tried to find if she might still be at Council Bluffs, he went with Sam to his brother's makeshift house.

Ben beamed as he greeted his son and brother with manly hugs. His manner became solemn and somber when Jonathan asked for news of Charity. "We should have written to you about her," he half apologized, "but we did not know how to get a letter to you. Charity had her baby about two months after you and Sam marched away. Your baby girl lived for only a day or two. Char never did get well after that. She died from a winter fever a few weeks later."

Jonathan's dream of a sweet reunion with his lovely Charity suddenly crashed about him. For two years he had longed to hold her in his arms again and now she was gone, gone for the rest of this life. Strong man though he was, Jonathan broke down in tears. His voice cracked with emotion as he cried: "Char, you can't be dead. You promised we would be together."

Ben and Sam did their best to console him and Ben promised: "You will be together on the first day of the resurrection."

It was some minutes before Jonathan had himself under full control. It was not until then that he thought of his children. When he asked about them, Ben said: "We have them with us, brother. Abial and Neph are off doing some chores and Emma is helping at the house."

It was a joyous but somewhat restrained reunion when Jonathan met with his three children during the next hour. Emma, who was eight, had memories of a beardless father, and was reluctant at first to cuddle up to this bearded stranger who claimed he was her father. Abial, who would be 12 in January, and Nephi who was nine and a half, ran to meet him and throw their arms around him. Both, however, were disappointed when he showed more interest in asking them about their mother than in inquiring about their activities.

There was no shortage of work for willing hands at the desert settlement. During the weeks that followed, Jonathan worked at several callings as he helped friends and neighbors put together sorely needed housing for the flood of saints that were arriving after their long trek from Council Bluffs. Some of the more prosperous saints arrived with wagons loaded with farm and household goods. Many others were poor, almost destitute, converts who arrived exhausted and worn after pushing handcarts loaded with their meager belongings for the more than a thousand miles from Council Bluffs.

Several companies of saints that had left Council Bluffs during the summer of 1848 arrived at Salt Lake during the months immediately following Jonathan's arrival from California. His brothers William and Benajiah came with a company that arrived in early November. Jonathan and Ben were happy to greet them and their families. They were saddened though with William's report that their father had died. William had tried to persuade Jonny, who was 87 that he should stay in Illinois. But the old gentleman had insisted on going west with his son and had died as much as anything from exhaustion when he reached Mount Pisgah.

Throughout the rest of 1848 and the first months of the next year Jonathan worked and practiced his religion by going to church but avoided participating in the dances and social events that brought cheer to Mormon lives. His undying love for his lost Charity preyed on his thinking and demeanor. His reluctance to spend time socializing with others bothered his brothers.

Ben took matters into his own hands by asking the bishop of their ward to counsel with Brother Jonathan. The bishop understood Jonathan's depression and explained: "Your love for your wife is natural, Jonathan: but you must let that part of your life go. There will be no breaking of your commitment to her if you find contentment and satisfaction

with others. In your best interests and the best interests of
the church, you must start living a normal life. The church
has many single women and young widows who need
husbands. It is your sacred duty to find love and marry
again."

Jonathan harkened to this advice. With the encouragement of his brothers and their wives, he began attending
the social gatherings and dances the saints loved so much.
He met several attractive women who seemed well disposed
toward him. It was not until March though that he met a
charming young lady who really intrigued him. At 27,
Lucinda Shipman Callahan was ten years his junior. She
had two children, a son Andrew who was five and a
daughter Agnes Ann who was almost three.

One of the first questions she asked as they danced
together was: "Did you know Thomas Callahan while you
were in the Battalion?"

"Thomas Callahan? No, I do not recall him. What
company was he in?"

"He joined up in Company B."

"That explains it. I was in E and we did not mix much
with men from the other companies while we were on the
march. Once we got to California, I got to meet most of
those who were stationed at Los Angeles; but the boys in B
were at San Diego."

"Well, in case you are wondering, he has never
come back. No letters, no nothing. I'm a wife with two kids
and don't know whether I am a widow or not."

"I'm sure he did not die. We would have heard about
that. Sounds to me like he was one of the guys who
reenlisted or maybe one of the slackers who found the life
out there easy and decided not to come home."

Jonathan was soon sure he liked Lucinda. She was
good company and being with her made him feel alive
again. His feelings for her weren't like those he had had for
Charity; but after seeing her and escorting her to parties for
several weeks, he thought he loved her. At any rate, he
wanted to be with her. When he finally spoke of their
possible marriage, she agreed but insisted that she must
first have her situation clarified. "The church says you men

can have more than one wife but it doesn't say a wife can have two husbands."

Jonathan went with her to see their bishop and then to counsel with John Ritchie, a higher church authority. After hearing her story and checking to see if the church had any reports as to Callahan's whereabouts, Ritchie reported: "As near as I can see you are as free a woman as if you were a widow. When a man forsakes his wife and children and doesn't communicate with them for as long as he has, he has deserted them and you are divorced." Accepting this conclusion as being legal, Jonathan proposed marriage and the couple were wed in the late spring of 1849.

Jonathan continued to work at various jobs at the Salt Lake settlement during the summer months. Meanwhile he acquired a wagon and team of his own together with some farming equipment. Sam was still his closest friend and companion. The two men spent considerable time working and visiting with each other and both agreed that next year would be the time for them to take up farming again.

Near the end of summer Sam announced that he too was getting married. He and Kate were looking forward to a wedding on her birthday in November. Two weeks before the wedding, Jonathan disappeared. When he returned after three days of absence Sam demanded: "Where have you been? We've been looking all over for you."

"I decided it was time I do some checking." Jonathan explained. "I found that area we saw up north of Ogden has been opened up for settlement so I went up there and put a down payment on enough land for two farms."

"Two? What do you need the other one for?"

"That my friend is my wedding present for you and Kate."

"A present! Golly, gee! That's great of you. Thank you, thank you. That old trapper said the place looked liked Scotland. Maybe we should get some pipers and have them play 'The Campbells Are Coming'".

"No Sam, once we get squared away on our farms, we will be through coming. With us it will be Campbells came."

ABOUT THE BOOK

The telling of history always involves elements of fiction. Even when an abundance of source material is available, personal judgments affect how one interprets questions of how, what, when, and why events took place. What one reports reflects the viewpoint of the observer; and when one does not have access to a full array of facts, as is usually the case, even the most impartial and unbiased recorder has to fall back on his or her imagination.

The tale told in _Campbells Came_ is history. It also contains a healthy measure of fiction. How much truth is there in the tale? All of the leading characters were real people, their names and dates are those recorded in family bibles, the battles and major events reported are a matter of history, and they lived at the places and amid the societies described.

There is much in the history of this family that was never recorded. It is known though that Sir Duncan Campbell commanded Argyll's army at Inverlochy. His grandson William fought in the Earl of Argyll's ill-fated invasion of Scotland and later served as a colonel in the defense of Londonderry. William Campbell and his sons James and Samuel migrated to New Hampshire and the two sons later moved to Cherry Valley. Family records indicate that James' son, Colonel Samuel Campbell, commanded the patriot force at the end of the battle of Oriskany, that Joel and his sons moved to Ridgebury, Pennsylvania, where the family lost land it had cleared to holders of expired warrants and that Jonathan went on to harvest timber in western New York while his son Jonathan marched with the Mormon battalion to California and was there when gold was discovered along the American river.

These details from recorded history provide the bare bones skeletons that are fleshed out here with details from the author's imagination. Like ornaments on a scrawny Christmas tree, these fabrications may provide more glitter than an honest assessment of what happened might justify. But then again, their lives could have been filled with far more drama than here described.

The author realizes that he has sometimes over-glamorized and in other cases perhaps defamed the roles played by individual characters. Apologies are extended where appropriate for examples of mischaracterization. At the same time, credit is due to them for providing the framework for a fictional account which hopefully honors their contributions to the family's history.

The telling of this seven part saga reflects months of extensive examination of a considerable trove of historical materials. A short list of the more significant source materials for Parts 1, 2, and 3 includes: Jon Buchan, <u>The Marquis of Montrose</u> (1913); "Genealogy of the Family in Auchinbreck", written in 1784 and reprinted in <u>Highland Papers</u> (1934); Tony Gray, <u>No Surrender: The Siege of Londonderry</u> (1975); Ronald Hutton, <u>Charles the Second</u> (1989); Nesca A. Robb, <u>William of Orange</u>, vol. II (1966); Tom Steele, <u>Scotland's Story</u> (1984); David Stevenson, <u>The Scottish Revolution 1637-1649: The Triumph of the Covenanters</u> (1973) and <u>Revolution and Counter Revolution in Scotland</u> 1644-1651 (1977); F.C. Turner, <u>James II</u> (1948); John Willcock, <u>A Scots Earl in Covenantry Times</u> (1907); and William R. Young, <u>Fighters of Derry</u> (1932).

Comparable sources of background value for Parts 4 and 5 include: Brian Richard Boylan, <u>Benedict Arnold, the Dark Eagle</u> (1973); A.G. Bradley, <u>The Fight With France for North America</u> (1905): Martha Byrd, <u>Saratoga</u> (1973); John R. Cuneo, <u>The Battle of Saratoga: The Turning of the Tide</u> (1967); <u>Early Records of Londonderry, New Hampshire: History of Otsego County, New York</u> (1878); James G. Layburn, <u>The Scotch-Irish</u> (1962); Angelo Campbell Pickett, "The First James Campbell of Cherry Valley, New York"; Arthur Pound, <u>Johnson of the Mohawks</u> (1930); John Sawyer, <u>History of Cherry Valley</u>; and John Albert Scott, <u>Fort Stanwix and Oriskany</u> (1927).

Significant sources of background information for Parts 6 and 7 are provided by Alphonse Button, <u>Genealogical Sketch of Early Descendants of Mattheus Button</u> (1903); Gladys Burhans, The <u>Ridgebury Story</u> (1962); Edwin G. Gudde, <u>Bigler's Chronicle of the West</u> (1962); D. F. Heverly, <u>Pioneer and Patriot Families of Bradford County, Pennsylvania</u>; Benjamin H. Hibbard, <u>History of the Public</u>

Land Policies (1930); Donna Hill, Joseph Smith the First Mormon (1977); History of Bradford County, Pennsylvania (1878); Norma Baldwin Ricketts, The Mormon Battalion (1996), and Samuel W. Taylor, Nightfall at Nauvoo (1971).

* * * * *

349